SEEKER

THE UNWOVEN TAPESTRY
BOOK ONE

MORGAN CHALUT

Cover design copyright © 2021 by April Klein
apridian.de

Published by Water Dragon Publishing
waterdragonpublishing.com

ISBN 978-1-953469-72-4 (Hardcover)

10 9 8 7 6 5 4 3 2 1

FIRST EDITION

To Michelle,
for your unending and unwavering support,
and the (probably) thousands of hours you put into reading my drafts.
Anyway, here's book 1 again.

SEEKER

1

A MAP OF LIGHTS, THE EARTH AGLOW. *The sensation of spreading thin, like a tapestry coming unwoven as he disbursed himself, his mind, through unseen paths. Each tree and blade of grass he passed lit his map as he floated on the currents of life, outward in every direction. People burned so brightly, he could pinpoint every one as he searched, Seeking. Their magic glowed inside them, but none as blinding as that which he hoped to find.*

The constant, gentle throb of the earth's life beneath him was background now when once it was captivating. Light in motion, a river nearby, moving so quickly, each drop of water spinning in an endless dance. Focus on the town ... he stretched further, the tapestry unweaving, but not yet undone; he had more to See. Ah ... the lights of people were sharp in his vision, but this one burned so brightly it cast those around it into shadow. He wanted to get closer, but knew his time was short. Too short; he'd only just found what he was looking for! If he got closer ... no. It was time.

Donovan returned to himself, overstimulated and with sensation overwhelming his senses. A headache throbbed in the front of his skull and he groaned, curled into a fetal position as his hearing swelled in and out, louder and then softer. His sense of smell did the same, telling him things he had no care to know about his surroundings, before fading to almost nothing and back. A familiar mental exercise helped him relax at least enough to think more clearly and slowly, slowly the sensations faded and his senses calmed.

He took several deep breaths of relief and managed to sit up on his second try, propped on a tender elbow. Everything ached. Or was it numb? No, it ached. He put out a shaking hand and felt a waterskin quickly supplied. He uncorked it with his teeth and took a long pull of the water, bitter with herbs. They burned his still-sensitive tongue and he grimaced until they worked, dulling some of his headache and settling his nausea. When he finally opened his eyes he was squinting, even with the curtains drawn; it was always so when he went out Seeking.

His partner crouched at the foot of the bed, patient, worried. He did not speak or make any sound, until Donovan waved his lethargic permission.

"Did you find him?" Lucas asked. His voice was low and soft, lambskin on tender ears.

Donovan took another deep draught of the herb-laden water and croaked, "He's here all right."

"Blue glories …" Lucas said. His eyes were alight with excitement, but he kept his head and did not raise his voice, for which Donovan was grateful. Lucas put out a hand to help him, but Donovan returned the waterskin instead.

The younger man took it grudgingly, but Donovan said, "I'm fine. Nothing sleep can't fix, so save your strength for tomorrow."

"Any Hunters?"

"Not that I Saw …" Donovan hesitated. "… but they're easy to miss. How long was I gone?"

"Nearly four minutes. I was getting nervous." Lucas unfolded Donovan's blanket and draped it over the older man. "Don't want you catching cold, eh granther?"

"You mind yourself, boy," Donovan teased in return, forcing a weak smile. He felt awful. Lucas knew, and there was no use hiding it, but succumbing just felt wrong.

"Go to sleep," Lucas said softly. "I'll stay up a bit longer."

Donovan didn't need any more urging. Sleep came swiftly to his exhausted mind, but before it claimed him, he saw that burning light and wondered, *Who are you?*

*   *   *

Donovan woke with the dawn, a moment before Lucas's breathing changed, indicating his rise into wakefulness as well. Habit was hard to break. The younger man groaned, yawned hugely and rolled to his feet. He washed his face with water from the basin provided while Donovan slid out from under the blanket, feeling much better than the night before. It would be hard to feel worse.

He dressed quickly, the sights from his Seeking still vivid in his mind. If he and Lucas hadn't arrived so late last night, they'd have the child already, and be on their way to the Order by now. Still, haste bred mistakes. It had taken them a few days of riding to get here; Hunters could already be close.

Lucas was better with a blade — and any kind of combat — but both sheathed a regulation foot-long knife into their high boots. Lucas wore a short sword as well. Any time the two ran into trouble, Donovan's job was to run with their charges, while Lucas faced down the problem. Together for nearly six years now, they were a good team, Retrieving children with magic and bringing them to the Order for training. When word had come that there might be a magus in Philipa, they were the obvious choice — or so they'd been told. Donovan didn't want to get his hopes up: magi were beings from legend these days.

"Ready?" Lucas asked, running a hand through his shaggy hair. He'd lamented the need to get it cut, but they hadn't had time. Safe within the walls of the Order after their last Retrieval, they'd had about half a day to prepare before being sent out once more.

"Ready," Donovan confirmed. He opened the door to the hall.

Their room was reserved for Retrievers, but a call and response were required for it to be supplied. It wasn't safe for innkeepers to be so obvious in their support of the Order these days. When Hunters came through, they weren't generally picky about who got in the way.

Still, he and Lucas had been to Philipa before — twice now — and Hanover was nearly a friend. He and his daughters made good money in the horse-town, housing merchant-visitors in their three-story building. They each nodded to him while he took inventory behind the bar, and made their way into the chilly, fresh air.

A woman lay asleep by the porch, a bottle in her hand showing her penchant for celebration. Despite the early hour, the town was not entirely still. The smells were the same as when they'd arrived: the almost-overpowering scent of horse overlaid with iron, smoke, leather, oil, grain, and dung — but it was dampened now with last night's dew laying over everything. It would snow any day now, and the overcast sky was heavy with promise.

Donovan shivered, rubbing his chest and arms with futile effort through his coat. Lucas gave him a sympathetic look. He loved winter like Donovan loved summer, but he didn't have aching joints to worry about yet.

The entrance-gate wasn't far, and they could see the seven-foot stone wall that encircled the town. Not that it was much of a circle anymore. Through the generations, as the town had expanded, it had been knocked down in places to allow for the growth, and rebuilt as needed. A determined person wouldn't struggle to gain entrance, but anyone trying to steal one of the town's famous horses would have a difficult time of it.

They passed soldiers in red uniforms doing their rounds. One stopped by the unconscious woman to nudge her awake and send her home. This town had plenty of guards; merchants were always willing to pay their taxes if it meant more security for their wares.

Shops were coming to life as the owners or apprentices hung brightly colored flags to catch the eye and encourage buyers to visit. The brothel across the street from the inn was asleep, most of its business done by now. The balcony was bare, and the musicians quiet. A few men and women stumbled out, yawning, heading home or to work.

Lucas looked relaxed as they walked, but Donovan knew he was keeping a clear eye on everything. Despite his youth, he'd proven time and again to be far more capable than almost anyone else Donovan had worked with during the last sixteen years Retrieving.

They made their way past the shops toward the guardhouse, twisting and turning down the streets until the squat building revealed itself. Soldiers coming off duty were leaving in small packs — none looked especially friendly — but Donovan put out a hand to catch their attention.

One young man stopped, his friends carrying on without pause. He frowned after them but asked, "Help you, sir?"

"Who is the commanding office on duty, please?"

"Gallagher."

Lucas grunted involuntarily and the soldier smirked. "Aye, that's our love of him as well. Might have better luck with whatever you need if you wait a few hours for Vandò to come on duty."

Donovan smiled. "We'll take our chances. Thank you."

The guard carried on, jogging to catch up with his friends, while Donovan and Lucas continued the opposite way. The guardhouse door stood open, with benches available for waiting. The inside smelled strongly of honey, cedar, and sweaty feet. The main room had several desks: some with tired bodies bent over them, soldiers finishing reports of the night's work. Others were home to a dozen fresh-faced soldiers, starting their day with mugs of steaming beverages and hand-held food. Donovan heard shouts from the back of the building: recruits were being put through their paces.

Lucas grinned wickedly at the sound. He'd briefly joined the military as his mother and siblings had done, but found Retrieving more to his preference. With his magic and skills, he could have climbed the ranks easily, but Lucas had confessed to Donovan early on that he didn't do well under that kind of strict authority. Besides, he loved children and planned to be a father. What better use of his abilities than Retrieving?

They took the familiar path to the office of the on-duty officer and Donovan gave the open door a gentle tap-tap with his knuckle.

"Yes?" came an impatient growl. Commander Gallagher wore his uniform sharply and his beard and mustache were both barely flecked with gray on his weathered face. His desk was crowded, but neat. The wall behind him held a map of the surrounding area, cleanly drawn with notes written here and there. A filing cabinet stood against the wall by the window, covered in small nicks as if regularly used for target practice. Two chairs sat before his desk, but they looked rarely used, the guards left standing, and the civilians taken care of in the front room.

"Who're you?" Gallagher demanded.

Lucas gave a charming smile. "We received notice that a mage was in need of Retrieval." He twisted his heel out slightly to show the knife sheathed there. The blades had plain grips and pommels, but if you knew what you were looking for …

"You're Retrievers?" Gallagher asked, a touch of fear pushing his tone from irritated to angry.

Donovan nodded. "We'd like to know where our charge is, and we'll be out of your way within the hour."

Gallagher grunted and pushed his chair back from the desk to open a drawer and finger through the crowded files within. Donovan contained his irritation. This man's counterpart usually had the information immediately at hand, ready for their arrival. Bad timing.

"So what are you, then?" Gallagher asked, picking through the pages.

Lucas's eyebrows rose and he looked at Donovan in disbelief.

"I'm a Seeker," Donovan answered calmly.

It wasn't exactly rude to ask, but it was generally accepted that it was the mage's place to offer information about their magic first, if they chose.

"And you?"

Lucas flashed another winning smile. "I'm a Healer. Always happy to assist." His tone was too bright, and Donovan hid his amusement. Lucas had no time for petty people, but was always the consummate professional.

Gallagher held out a file, but neither of them moved for it. "Well?" he demanded, shaking the stiff paper.

"Generally a phrase is offered up, which we reply to appropriately," Donovan said carefully as he took the file. He flipped it open to confirm what little they'd been told.

"Who has the time?" Gallagher rolled his eyes. "All you need should be there. Have a good day." He sat back down behind his desk.

"The reason for the code, Commander, is to make sure that we're the appropriate people to Retrieve the children. Otherwise, you could be handing them over to anyone claiming to be what they're not."

Lucas's tone was patient, but Donovan could hear the anger seething underneath. This was a matter of life and death.

"Anyone like Hunters?" Gallagher asked in the same tone.

"Exactly like."

"People like them only come here because of people like you. Take all the mages you want, but do us the favor of not bringing them back."

"You —" Lucas started.

Donovan put a hand on his arm, "Thank you. We'll dispose of the record ourselves once we've cleared the boy's contract."

"Fine." Gallagher had already dismissed them in his mind and had gone back to what he was doing when they had arrived.

Out front, Lucas let out a great puff of air, steaming in the cold. "That piece of trash is going to get people killed."

"We'll report him when we get back. There's no doubt he isn't following protocol and he'll be dismissed, with someone responsible put in his place. We can't do anything about it now."

"By stone, I can. I can rip his elbows off and make him juggle! UGH." Lucas kicked at a stone and shook his hands violently. After a moment he closed his eyes and took a deep breath, visibly calming himself. "You said we needed to clear the boy's contract. He's indentured?"

Donovan smiled at how quickly his partner came back to business. "He's working as a hostler's apprentice, so that makes things easier."

"Much," Lucas agreed.

Instead of taking the child from his family and standing by through the tearful goodbyes, or being offered more than they could fairly take, or having to fight angry relatives who didn't agree with the decision to send the child away, they only needed to use Order funds to buy the boy's contract.

They set off at a fast pace both to complete their task, and to keep warm.

"I want to Seek again before we go," Donovan said.

Lucas looked at him in surprise. "Oh?"

"If the Order knew that the boy was a magus, as the report suggests, then someone else would know, send it off to the Hunters, especially if that Gallagher didn't keep it to himself. You know how rumors can fly around a place like this. I don't like that I didn't See any last night."

"Better the enemy you know than the one you don't, right?" Lucas said thoughtfully. "If they have a seat at the shop, you might be able to do it there with little disruption."

"That'd be the preference."

"All right, we'll ask. The boy can pack while you Seek and we'll collect our horses after."

"We shouldn't have left our gear in the room."

"You're very nervous all a'sudden."

"I have the bad feeling we might need to run."

Lucas put a hand to his sword. "It won't be the first time."

They passed a dozen shops as they returned toward the front of town, all of them with invitingly warm glows. The noise increased as they got closer, stamping and whinnying from the probably hundred stalls inside. This was the larger of the two stables, but the second was across the street, adding its own sounds and smells to the cacophony.

A large sign, made of very thick and colorful glass in red, blue, green, and yellow swung gently out front. A couple of horses peeked out into the fresh air from open stall windows, whickering at passerby.

It was already busy, even at this time of the morning, though Donovan knew from experience in this town that the population of buyers would only grow. He couldn't imagine what it took to run this place as he looked for the owner through the crowds.

"Help you, sirs?" a young boy asked. He might have been twelve — or a scrawny fourteen — with shaggy blond hair and a bright grin.

"We're looking for the owner," Donovan told him above the sound.

"Looking to buy? I can show you the beasts if you like — I know all about them. I'm in my sixth year apprenticed."

Donovan smiled at him. "No, we're not looking to buy. We just need to speak to the owner."

"Sure." He turned around and darted through the crowd.

Donovan and Lucas did their best to follow until they breached the press of humanity, away from the horse stalls, and into a back room of the building. It was much quieter here, but there was a regular stream of boys and girls running messages — offers, no doubt — on bits of paper.

When Lucas and Donovan arrived in the doorway, their little guide gestured to them with aplomb.

"Yes, yes, all right Ruben, go on. Gentlemen, I'm Garth Ward."

"Ruben?" Lucas asked for confirmation.

The boy looked at him.

"Is that Ruben Smith?"

"Why?" the boy asked suspiciously.

"Can you wait outside the door for just a couple of minutes while we speak to Master Ward, please?" Lucas asked him.

The boy looked at the stable owner, who nodded, and stepped out to close the door, eyeing them as he did so.

"Help you, sirs?" Garth asked.

"We understand you hold the contract for Ruben Smith," Donovan told him.

"I do. You're Retrievers?"

Donovan blinked. "Yes." He held up the file. "Gave it away?"

The stable master nodded. "My third apprentice taken in four years. I'd swear it's the shop. The last one swore he'd return, but I don't see that likely. He was an Empath, you know — very good with the customers."

Donovan flipped to a page of the file. "If you don't mind ..."

Garth sighed hugely. "I'll miss him around here — practically one of my own brood, he's been here long enough."

"Six years, he said," Lucas mentioned.

"Mother sold him to me when he was just barely eight. She'd found some beau and decided to pay off her debts and leave town. Still, he's one of my best I can easily say; got a real knack for the beasts." He signed the form and Lucas countersigned, handed it to Donovan, who tucked it into a pocket.

"Just his contract, then, and you'll be settled."

"Ruben!" Garth called. The boy came inside again.

"Aye?" he asked, arms crossed. "Did you sell me?"

"In a sort. These men are the Retrievers and they've come to claim you for the Order learning. You're getting proper schooling."

Ruben eyed them. "I thought you'd be bigger."

"Don't be a loaf, Ben. Go and get your things. They're in a hurry."

The boy ran off.

"Do you mind if I take a seat and do a bit of Seeking?" Donovan asked.

The stable master's eyebrows rose. "I can't promise it'll be comfortable. My wife's a Seeker, and says it's an unpleasant experience."

"She's right. Unfortunately, it's needed." Donovan smiled through his trepidation.

"I'll head to fetch the boy's contract for a few minutes, and set the boy to gathering his things. Should be ready by the time you are."

"Thanks very much."

Donovan went to the chair the stable master vacated. Lucas posted outside the door to stop anyone from knocking or interrupting. Donovan wished it was much darker — easier on his soon-to-be-sensitive eyes — but the barred window didn't have a shutter that he could see. He leaned back, rested his hands on his lap, and closed his eyes. He slowed his breathing and pulled all of his attention to himself, away from sounds in the front of the building.

He mentally prepared in his usual way: deep breaths and slow exhales, relaxed the tension out of his shoulders, back, chest, neck, and jaw. Slowly, ever so slowly, he strode into the room of his mind and opened that window that led to the outside.

It took great effort of will not to slam it shut again: pain flared through his skull; flashing lights bounced behind his closed eyes. Sound became an unbearable pressure, almost physically pushing him deeper into his chair. His mouth erupted with the flavors of his last meal, old and stale, and his clothes snagged and pulled and tore at his skin, now so sensitive.

He forced himself to take steady, even breaths, letting the flood of senses pass over and through him as he pushed his consciousness through the window in his mind, and out of the room.

Separated now, the assault dimmed; though as always, his time was limited. His consciousness shot outward, far across the earth along those unseen paths in every direction. He could See the entire town, barely contained within the stone wall, the outlying farms and houses all within his Sight. From here, he could See the life-lines of the world, all of them glowing and sparkling through him to form the great map in his mind.

The earth's low, thrumming glow; the trees and rivers all keeping beat with it. He'd learned long ago how to ignore those. People were much faster; you almost couldn't see their life-beats, the patterns were so fast. He looked for the dimmest glows, searching methodically, but quickly.

He could See Lucas's glow in the shop and that bright, bright shine from the magus almost in hand. Dozens and dozens of other lights throughout the town, but he ignored them, searching for what was harder to spot.

As he suspected, two faded glows moved through the town. He placed them on the map of his mind and felt panic build. Quick as lightning, Donovan flew back to his body, through the window in the back of his mind, swaying as the flood of senses struck him again.

He groaned, and croaked, "Lucas, water?"

Lucas opened the door and hurried to his side, offering up his waterskin again, the mixture of herbs familiar. They were less potent when they weren't fresh, but they helped anyway.

"They're here," Donovan said through his throbbing headache.

"How many?" Lucas asked softly.

Donovan held up two fingers.

"Where?"

"Tavern." He took another large swallow, feeling nauseous despite the herbs. "Don't need the packs," he said.

"We do need the horses," Lucas argued. "We won't stay ahead of them on foot."

The door opened and Master Ward poked his head through, saw them talking. "All set?"

Lucas nodded. "Working out logistics."

"Here's the contract, if you want to go ahead and sign. Ruben'll be out in a moment."

Lucas went to the counter and put down his signature. It didn't do the contract-holder any good now, but when the taxes were collected, they'd settle with him then, if he showed the signed contract.

Garth blew on the ink to dry it. "Have a safe journey." He smiled, nervously glancing at the sweating and shaking Donovan, but disappeared into the front again.

Lucas turned back to his friend. "Don, just relax." Lucas put a hand on Donovan's shoulder.

Immediately, like sinking into a bath, cold clarity rushed through his body and removed all of his aches and pains. His head cleared, his muscles relaxed, and his heartbeat slowed. He felt the tension leach from his shoulders.

Lucas gritted his jaw in pain, but he didn't stop until Donovan was able to take a deep, clear breath and answer calmly.

"We can buy new horses while we're here, we'll leave the packs and forage. I know there's a soldier's waystop nearby, and they'll hold us as long as they can, until we can get a larger force."

Lucas shook his head. It was clear he was trying to ignore the pain he'd Taken on from Donovan's Seeking. "Don't have money for three new horses; if we wait for friends, they'll do the same." He took a tight breath, tension stiff through his jaw. "Take the boy to the gate and start down the road, stay hidden. I'll bring the horses."

"Lucas ..."

"I'll be fine. I won't take unnecessary risk. Besides," he grimaced cheekily, "I have a surprise for them if we meet."

Donovan agreed reluctantly.

"I'm to go with you?"

They both looked to the doorway where Ruben lounged, a mostly empty pack hanging off his shoulder.

Donovan stood and put out a hand to shake. "Donovan Rudd, Retriever."

The boy shook firmly. A dark horse-bite on his arm, mostly healed, flexed when he gripped. "Ruben."

Lucas waved tensely, pain lines clear around his eyes. "Lucas Fain."

"How old are you, Ruben?" Donovan asked.

The boy shrugged. "Probably fourteen."

"Do you have family in town?"

"Nah. My bond-master should be able to sign anything you need," he shrugged again, gesturing toward the front.

"No, we took care of your contract," Donovan said. "Usually goodbyes are in order."

"That's all right. They told me they would send for someone, so I made my waves then."

Lucas came forward. "Don, I'm going. I'll find you at our last camp. Do you mind?"

He put out a hand and Donovan hesitated for only a second before shaking it firmly. A buzz ran through his body, tingling in his extremities. Everything seemed to speed up very slightly, and he felt light-headed for a moment, like he was tired, dazed, or had been recently.

The moment passed and Lucas released his grip. "Thanks."

Lucas exited the shop and started for the inn. Donovan watched him go, nerves gnawing at his stomach.

"Ruben, do you know what Hunters are?"

The boy nodded, his lips pressed tightly together. He was short for his age, but lanky, with shaggy blond hair hanging almost into his eyes. Freckles scattered his cheeks, and it was clear in his eyes that he wasn't a fool.

"Some came to town and killed a bunch of folks, what, four years back? They tore up a whole family; I knew them. They were nice, but they had magic. Guards tried to break it up, but they got killed, too. Brought down three Hunters and lost ... fifteen people? That old cooper up the street ran out and chased down one of them with fire, and a couple of others helped, but the town was a mess for a while after."

Donovan rubbed the back of his neck. He'd heard about that, but had forgotten. After a while, Hunter tragedies blended together. "I need you to trust me."

"How many are here?"

"Two."

"And they want me?"

Donovan nodded. "It's my job to keep you safe."

"Your partner went after them, then?"

"Yes."

"And we expect to see him again?"

Donovan gritted his teeth for a moment. "Absolutely." He led them out of the shop and into the crowd.

"I'm quick on my feet, if you were going to ask," Ruben said.

"I was." Donovan managed a smile. "We've been in tighter spots than this, and I've never lost a charge."

"Oh? Were any of them a magus?" Ruben asked bluntly. "They want me bad, right?"

"When someone's trying to kill you, there isn't much concern about how much they're trying to kill you," Donovan pointed out, scanning the faces around them. He cursed his magic, wishing it had more purpose. It made him nearly useless for barely a glance at the danger. He couldn't even see the Hunters' faces, which would at least be something.

"Do you want to go through the wall?" Ruben asked. "Might be quicker."

Donovan looked down at him. "You have a way through the wall?"

The boy jerked his head. "This way. Years of the town's 'need' made a 'have'."

They walked off the main streets, past some of the poorest housing; clotheslines and sickly gardens marred their path, but Ruben walked confidently. He followed the wall for a short distance, then gestured victoriously. Donovan stared at it, uncomprehendingly.

"Good, right?"

"It must be," Donovan answered, unsure of what to look at. This piece of wall looked like any other.

"Mostly smugglers use it, but suits us, too, as long as we close it."

He tugged at a piece of the stone wall and it swung forward on greased hinges. Donovan's eyes grew wide. Someone had carefully cut through the stone, all the way through, and affixed a thin layer of it onto a gate of boards, lined up to be indistinguishable from the rest. It hid a narrow space in the middle, enough for a few friendly people to pass through, and another gate on the other side.

Ruben made sure the gates latched, and they set off through a field, headed for the main road on a more direct route.

"The guards don't notice?" Donovan asked, glancing about.

He stumbled, tripped before he could catch himself and landed on his chest and hands, groaning. Ruben was wide-eyed as he helped him up. He was also clearly trying not to laugh. Donovan dusted off his clothes, more embarrassed than bruised.

"The guards?" Donovan prompted.

The boy fought down his grin. "They're not spaced right," he said. "They figure you're coming from one direction or the other, but can't quite see the spot. Someone's cousin figured it out when they were on duty and passed it along, and my friend Suresh told me because his ma's a smuggler and they use it all the time, and it's been passed down for generations or something like that. Anyway, they don't mind I use it, so long as I follow the rules and stay careful. Wish I could have been bought by them, but Suresh said smugglers don't buy contracts. And I like horses." He shrugged.

Donovan kept an eye out, but the road wasn't especially busy. They passed a few travelers heading for the town, and a few heading away — most bearing strings of horses — but none gave them more than a passing glance.

When they reached the tree line, Donovan headed straight in, while Ruben followed nervously behind.

"Aren't you worried about getting lost?" he asked, trying to keep close.

The older man smiled. "One thing I'm never worried about is getting lost. You know what I did at the Order, all my years?"

"What?"

"I studied maps."

"Why maps?"

"I'm a Seeker. When I use my magic, I can See all these little spots of light. I don't See buildings, though — or not clearly. Land, rivers, mountains, trees, those I See — anything living. We study maps, to always know what we're looking at and, even though I stopped practicing for a long while after leaving, that's something that doesn't leave your head quickly."

They walked a bit farther.

"The report said you'd made fire and spoken into someone's thoughts?" Donovan prompted.

Ruben nodded, and ducked under a bit of plant life. "It was all an accident, but everyone got nervous when they heard me, but said I didn't move my mouth. I'd only made the fire earlier that morning, and they were already sending for a Retriever, but then they got scared. Master Ward was nice enough. He's used to his 'prentices showing magic, but the others acted like I was sick with something, or different than I was before."

"Magi are rare," Donovan agreed. "It's been a long, long while since there's been another."

"Sure, and they all have legends and stories about them. If I've got magic, I'll learn to use it, but I don't want to be heroic. I just want to raise horses and have a farm, have children." He shrugged again. "Normal things."

Donovan smiled sadly. "That's all I wanted, too. I wish you luck of it."

*   *   *

The building was livelier than it had been when they left that morning. Scores of people moved in and out, enjoying music, gambling, food and plenty of drink, even this early.

Lucas's joints ached, his head throbbed; he was tense in every muscle, weary and nauseous, but he put the feelings aside. They were only Borrowed, and not his to keep.

He went inside the inn. Hanover caught his eye and Lucas saw that the man was sweating, not just from his work; there was terror beneath his smiling façade. His eyes grew wide when he saw Lucas; the rag in his hands was nearly torn into pieces.

Hunters, he mouthed. *In your room.*

Lucas swallowed hard, nodded, and headed for the steps. He stood at the base of the stairs and let his face crumple in pain for a moment. Everything he'd Taken from Donovan was hitting him hard, plus a little of his own for using his Talent. He was almost grateful the Hunters were waiting for him; they'd see what he could do.

He let the moment pass and composed himself once more.

'*Pain is temporary — given time it will fade into distant memory. Time is motivation and movement. Busy yourself with work, time will pass, and so will pain.*'

The repeated mantra gave him strength as he climbed the stairs with quick, but cautious steps.

The hall was empty, quiet. One set of dishes sat out to be claimed, but otherwise it was very neat; all of the doors were closed and lanterns in their places. Lucas walked at a measured pace to the very end of the hall, to room fourteen, and stopped. Adrenaline pushed Donovan's pain to the back of his mind. He knew, academically, what was waiting for him, but you never knew for sure with Hunters. Their variance was their strength.

Well, he had variance now, too.

Lucas pulled his knife from his boot. The blade was about a foot in length with enough grip for one hand, and a striking pommel for a base. Double-edged, and kept wickedly sharp, with three inches of serration on its base. It fitted his palm securely, and Lucas was glad to realize that his hands were neither sweaty nor shaking. If he died here, Donovan would be able to take care of the boy — which was all that really mattered. Their trip would be hard without supplies, but it would be possible. Leaving these Hunters alive, however, without at least making an effort to remove them — that was impossible.

Lucas opened the door and immediately dropped into a crouch. Two crossbow bolts flew over his head: one stuck in the wall across the hallway, and the other embedded in the doorframe to his right. He rolled forward into the room, gained his feet, and took in his surroundings inhumanly fast. The Hunter now behind him was attempting to reload his crossbow. Lucas threw his weight backward to crush the Hunter against the dresser against which he leaned. The Hunter dropped the crossbow bolts and grunted with irritation. The basin of water splashed and shattered to the floor.

The Hunter pushed Lucas away, and Lucas gladly used the momentum to launch himself at the second Hunter. This one had a very noticeable scar across his mouth; Lucas aimed to give him another. He cried out in pain as Lip-Scar smashed down on his wrist with the empty crossbow. Lucas managed to hold onto his blade, but barely. He punched Lip-Scar with his free hand, and turned his palm over to slap the Hunter on the opposite cheek, pushing all of Donovan's pain from his body into his enemy.

The Hunter roared, clutched his head, and fell to his knees. It was a manageable pain once you'd adjusted, though Lucas had included as much of his own hurts as he could. He couldn't count on that one staying down for long, but it helped in the moment.

Before he could finish off Lip-Scar, the first Hunter crashed into him from behind, grabbed him around the middle and pinned his arms to his sides to squeeze the breath from him. Lucas wheezed as his feet were lifted from the ground. He ignored his empty lungs and waited for the Hunter to slam him back to earth. When the man obliged, Lucas made sure his knees were bent, causing the Hunter to crouch unexpectedly, now off-balance. Lucas forced his elbows out as hard as he could, breaking the Hunter's hold around him.

Lightning fast, he flipped his knife in his palm and speared the blade down into the Hunter's foot to pin him to the floor. Screaming, the man reached for his mutilated appendage, and Lucas rose fast, his right fist punching up into the man's nose and sending him reeling. Pinned as he was, the only direction he could move was down. He hit the floor hard and lay unmoving.

Hearing mumbling from behind, Lucas spun in a panic and kicked at Lip-Scar without proper aim. The Hunter leaned easily out of the way and stood from where he'd been crouched in pain.

Lucas took a defensive stance to face him. The Hunter smiled, wiped a bit of blood from his nose and licked it off of his finger.

"Thank you," he said.

Lucas bared his teeth in reply.

The Hunter slammed his palms toward Lucas, but even the additional reflexes he'd Borrowed from Donovan could not get Lucas out of the way in time. He jumped to hopefully save himself, but still tripped into the legs of the fallen Hunter behind him. Trying to keep his balance, he thumped into the opposite wall, but his flailing and unpredictable stumbling saved him from the second burst of air Lip-Scar launched with a hiss.

Lucas lunged for the prone Hunter's discarded crossbow, throwing it haphazardly at Lip-Scar for a distraction, and wrenched his knife out of the floor, and foot, as he charged forward once more.

Lip-Scar batted the crossbow out of the air and it crashed into the floor. He moved barely in time to swat Lucas's knife away. They engaged, each trying to stab or punch or bludgeon the other, and each managing to counter the other's attacks in some way. As their speed increased, Lucas felt the reflexes he'd Borrowed straining to keep up and keep focused, but the Hunter, too, was flagging. He was too distracted to mutter forth any more of his blood magic.

Lucas stabbed with his knife in his right hand, releasing it into momentum's grip. He pulled his fist back, and then forward to smash into his adversary's left jaw. Lip-Scar moved to deflect the knife but realized too late that it should not have been his target.

Lucas's strike pushed blood and spittle from the Hunter's mouth, and he did not wait for the man to recover.

Grabbing the back of the Hunter's head, he pulled the creature's face down into his rising knee, and felt more than heard the crunch of cartilage as they connected. He released the Hunter, who reeled back and staggered into the wall behind him as Lucas buried two punches into his torso. The Hunter's lips were moving to speak, so the Retriever slammed callused knuckles into his throat to make the Hunter choke and wheeze, clutching at his crushed larynx.

Lucas spotted his knife where it had been cast aside on the bed, and threw himself beside it, grasping tightly at the hilt. Regaining his feet, he threw all of his weight behind the point of the blade and buried it in the Hunter's temple with a wet cracking sound, and a sensation he would remember forever.

The life drained from the Hunter's face as he fell bonelessly to the ground.

Lucas allowed himself time to pant and gasp for air. He felt nauseous, like bile was bubbling in his throat. He turned away to deal with the first Hunter and finish the job.

AGONY.

Lucas screamed, choking and retching, and looked down at the three feet of steel punched through his belly. The first Hunter had drawn his sword and was driving it through Lucas's body; blood and bits of intestine shoved toward his spine.

Lucas grabbed the blade to pull it out, to save himself, but his strength was departing with his innards, puddling on the floor beneath him. He fell to his knees, eyes pooling and overflowing with tears, his mind buzzing with terror and panic and pain.

The Hunter released the blade and dragged himself backward across the floor, his boot a bloody mess from where Lucas had earlier pinned him.

"Idiot," he snarled. "Did you really think you could win?"

Lucas reached toward him with a shaky, bleeding hand.

"I can't even help a wound like that. Good luck."

Lucas's fumbling hand landed on the Hunter's leg, down his shin to his ruined boot. The Hunter, his reflexes dull from the thought of victory, didn't move in time, and Lucas's scrabbling fingers found the hole he'd created.

"Stop — *argh!*" the Hunter shrieked, reaching for his wounded foot, but Lucas dug through the leather to the flesh underneath, burying his fingers to the bone and gripping, for his life depended on it.

The Hunter screamed louder, his leg flailing futilely, but it wasn't long before a red stain oozed across his shirt, and his voice trailed off to howling and whimpering and gasping as he writhed on the ground. He held his stomach as the wound appeared beneath his undamaged shirt, bloody and fresh.

Lucas wrenched the sword from his gut, coughing and gasping, crying, his hand a death-grip on the Hunter's foot. He refused to let go for a moment, even as the Hunter died. He dropped the sword with a heavy metal *thunk* and sat staring at the body before him. Sweat poured down his face, stinging his lips and eyes.

When he finally allowed himself to let go and pulled his bloody fingers out of the Hunter's knife wound, he fell to his side and lay on the floor, hands convulsively pressed to his stomach while his heart raced and his bowels trembled. He had pissed himself, but it was hardly the most important thing on his mind.

He didn't know how long it was — although it couldn't have been more than a couple of minutes — before steps sounded outside the room and the door was pushed tentatively open. His eyelids fluttered up, and he managed to focus on the person in the doorway, despite a pounding migraine. Hanover stood there, his smile nowhere to be seen. His youngest daughter stared over his shoulder. They both gaped at the room with fear and confusion.

Hanover looked surprised to see Lucas still breathing and said, "Wound like that, sir, I don't know if I should fetch the Healer. Do you want last rites?"

Lucas held up his hands to see the blood that had stained them, the gore beneath his nails, and said hoarsely, "No, I'm all right. I need a headache cure, please, quick as you can, and Hanover, give me a hand to my feet."

The daughter ran off back the way she'd come. Hanover stepped gingerly into the room, trying to avoid the bodies and bloodstains. There was less mess than there should have been, most of the blood having been sacrificed for the dark magic. Hanover stopped at Lucas's feet and put a hand out to help him.

"Gently now, please," Lucas said, gripping his hand weakly.

The innkeeper pulled him forward into a sitting position, where Lucas sat for a moment, wincing and holding his stomach as the muscles there clenched and tightened. He managed a deep breath. Then he got to his feet, where he swayed until he could catch his balance. He looked at the damage around him with a blank, drained expression.

He was soaked through with sweat and blood and piss, his muscles all shaking with strain. He'd fought before, so many times, but it was never easy to kill. The sensation of crunching his blade through Lip-Scar's skull echoed through his hand again, and he could still feel his nails scraping and squirming through the other's foot. He shuddered.

"I don't have the funds with me to pay for this; I'll write to the Order on your behalf. They can take the cost out of the taxes you would owe by the end of the year — will that be acceptable?"

Hanover nodded jerkily, "Anything you need, sir. It'll be no trouble."

Lucas could see the fear written plainly on the man's face, but didn't try to fix it with one of his charming smiles. He didn't have the strength. The daughter returned with a mug of water which she handed to Lucas after stepping carefully over the legs of a dead Hunter. He could see the bits of familiar plants still dissolving into it, but didn't wait.

He downed the bitter water in a couple of huge gulps, handing Hanover the empty mug, and then stumbled to the bed.

"I'm so sorry," he said to the innkeeper.

He needed to keep his hands busy, so he started shoving supplies back into the packs, not particularly caring where they ended up. As he did, Lucas thought about how unimportant each item really was.

"We could have just left," he said softly, thinking aloud.

"You did a great service here," Hanover answered, clutching his daughter, his voice tight.

"If anyone follows, tell them everything you know. Don't make them think you're holding back — they'll find us without your help, but we'll outrun them. We always do." He attempted a brave smile, and wondered if it looked as awful as it felt.

Lucas looked down at his ruined shirt and stripped it off, throwing it aside with a sodden *thwap* and smearing at the blood on his stomach, shuddering at how close he'd come. He pulled a fresher shirt from his pack, already bloodied from his hands, and gestured at the bodies.

"If you call the local Healer, he'll take the bodies, with the Order's compliments. The supplies you should be able to sell. I'm so sorry, but I do have to leave."

Hanover nodded vigorously. "Of course. T-thank you."

Lucas nodded heavily and took the packs.

He made his way to the inn's attached stable, saddled the horses and secured their things. His fingers slipped several times at the familiar tasks, fatigue in every inch of him. As he buckled and tied, all he could see was the stain of blood on his hands, despite the thorough scrubbing he'd managed in a nearby water bucket. He'd killed before, but this was the closest he'd ever come to death himself. His hands tripped over the equipment again, and the stable hand took pity on him, finishing up the rest with professional quickness.

He rode out of town, bringing the little herd of horses on long lead ropes, and made his way toward the previous night's campsite. Donovan would travel through the woods, but on horseback Lucas might reach it before them, despite their head start. That was good. It would give him more time to get rid of the blood.

*   *   *

"You were killed?" Donovan asked after the long silence had been allowed to grow and mature.

Night blanketed them. The winter air was cold, but their coats were warm. A gentle breeze stirred up the smoke from their small fire, which crackled and popped as it ate its wooden fare. The stars shone with a constant brilliance that could take the mind and hold it until the sun rose, if given the opportunity. Trees rustled their leaves fitfully, their branches swaying and creaking. Owls hooted and bats squeaked, while hedgehogs and other rodents moved the deadfall in loud paths across the forest floor. Small game ruled these woods.

"Almost." Lucas hunched on the ground in his blanket, arms around his knees like a small child. Ruben was asleep in the spare bedroll they'd brought for him, dead to the world, child-like snores his only sound.

"You're going to tell the Order about this, right?"

"Of course I am, it'll be in my report. I just didn't want the boy to know."

"I'm glad you were able to do what you did, Lucas."

He nodded compulsively. "I could have lived without it happening at all, though. Now it's stuck in my head forever." He picked under his nails with shaky hands.

Donovan chewed on the inside of his lip. "They're going to send more."

"I warned Hanover not to lie for us."

"Let's hope that saves him."

"We can't outrun Hunters for long. Not if they know we have a magus." Lucas looked at the sleeping form. "Is he a magus? Really?"

Donovan nodded and Lucas's eyes seemed to light from within. "The report showed him to be a Mentalist and an Elementalist both. Two magics. That means he'll learn to master them all."

"Blue glories," Lucas whispered reverently, staring at the sleeping boy.

"We won't need to outrun them for long," Donovan said, bringing them back to the previous topic. "We're a few days yet from the Order, and we'll stay mounted as long as we can. If needed, we'll lash each other to the saddles and sleep in shifts, as before."

Lucas nodded pensively. "How far behind us are they, do you think?"

Donovan stirred the fire with a long, thin branch, throwing sparks into the air. "I can Seek if you want, find out how many and where."

Lucas shook his head. "We're going to need our strength to get as far as we can. Tomorrow night, perhaps."

Donovan agreed, silently relieved. He hated the feeling after using his magic — so weak and drained and sick. Training had been bad enough, and he'd left the Order swearing he'd never use it again. He'd succeeded for nearly forty years, too. He stabbed the fire again, emotions long suppressed climbing to the surface of his mind. He let out a sigh, pushing the thoughts down where they belonged.

"You should get some sleep," Lucas finally said, staring into the flames. His shoulders were hunched, his expression dark.

"You're one to talk. How's the headache?"

Lucas shrugged one shoulder. "Manageable."

Donovan stood, shaking his bedroll open, and loosened his boots, but didn't remove them. He looked at Lucas, who hadn't moved. "Go to sleep, Lucas."

"I'm not going to be able to sleep tonight, Don. I'll keep watch."

"If you're sure ..."

"I'll wear myself out tomorrow and sleep then."

Donovan climbed under his covers. He could fall asleep anywhere, but imagined it would be hard for Lucas to fall asleep for a while, with his own death on his mind.

2

"HOW FAR OFF IS THIS PLACE?
Ruben rode alongside Donovan, and did better in his seat
by far. Horse riding was a skill Donovan had developed through
miles and miles of practice, but he possessed no natural talent.
Ruben looked as though he had been born in a saddle, in
comparison.

"Less than five days from here," Donovan answered, speaking
loudly over the sounds of hooves. He led the pack horse behind
him, its lead tied to his saddle. Lucas rode ahead to check their
path. The wind had picked up and they all shivered in their coats.
Donovan's rear felt like solid ice.

Ruben grinned. "Do you want to see a trick?" he asked.

Before Donovan could answer, the boy had nudged his beast
into a canter, wheeling through the field. In a blink, he was
kneeling on the saddle, arms outstretched for balance. A moment
later, he was back in the seat until he let his legs fall to one side,
bouncing from the ground back atop the beast and over the other
side to do the same.

Laughing, he came back to where Donovan anxiously waited, warm now as the worry coursed through his veins.

"This is a good horse!" Ruben huffed, flush with excitement.

"How did you learn to do that?" Donovan managed to ask above his pounding heart.

"Being bound to the stables," the boy answered. "I learned tricks so I could ride about and advertise the beasts for purchase. I love horses. When I'm out of my contract, I'm going to own my own stable."

"You're free now, remember? The Order paid your contract."

"Aye? I thought I was to apprentice there instead — learn magic like any other trade, but this one I start with a knack for, right?"

"You're not bound there," Donovan explained, as he had done for countless other children. "It's to get your education and learn to control your Talent so no one gets hurt."

The boy digested the explanation. "So I can leave at any time?"

Donovan hesitated and Ruben laughed.

"'s what I thought."

Donovan opened his mouth to explain, but thought better of it. The idea of a magus was still a fantasy in his mind; how did you explain unlimited power to a fourteen-year-old? How did you explain the needs of a kingdom and the duty you should feel toward your country, your people? Donovan scoffed at himself, *"Prime example I am, leaving as soon as I could and never looking back until I had to."*

Ruben looked around. "I haven't been much farther from town than this." He waved at the side of the hill they rode next to. "In spring, that's all over little yellow and blue flowers. Beautiful."

Donovan smiled. He'd seen that before, Retrieving here nearly a decade ago.

After a moment, Ruben asked, "Those two Hunters from yesterday ..."

"Yes?"

"Lucas killed them?"

Donovan nodded.

"He's a Healer, then? I saw him Take your pain in the shop."

"He also took my reflexes," Donovan added. "We needed to get you away, and he needed every advantage."

Ruben's face split into a grin. "Is that why you fell outside the walls?"

Donovan smiled ruefully. "He's done it before. I should know better how to behave so that doesn't happen as much."

"I'll learn to do that, right? Healing? Taking reflexes and fighting Hunters?"

"You will absolutely learn to Heal," Donovan said thoughtfully. "I'm sure your Talents will give you some ability to fight Hunters. It's not all magic, though," he explained. "Retrievers are taught to fight, to subdue, and we're taught when it's best to run away. If you can't end a fight quickly, you should always run. If you bleed where they can use it —"

Ruben interrupted, "That's what I remember most about when they came — no blood, really. It was over quick: all those folks dead, and almost no blood."

"It fuels their magic."

He frowned. "Will I learn *that* magic?"

"Absolutely not," Donovan said firmly. "It's illegal and, besides which, it's evil. The Order has sworn to eliminate all the blood mages, though they've been growing bold of late."

Hard lines formed in Ruben's face for a moment and Donovan imagined he was remembering the images he'd described in his town.

"I'll help," the boy said firmly.

They took a break for lunch, and Lucas rode back toward them with nearly as much skill as Ruben had shown. The boy quickly brushed the beasts down, helping fill their feedbags while Lucas started a small fire, warming his hands and setting slightly squished rolls to toasting.

Around a mouthful of cheese and sausage, Ruben asked, "Do you think they'll send more Hunters after us?"

Lucas's eyes darted to Donovan's before he said, "I'm sure they'll try, but we gained some distance today, and the Order isn't too much farther."

"Donovan said it was a few days, but we're on the main road. I'd just set some of my people along this way, in case we got lucky, you know?"

Lucas looked at Donovan again. "That's ... a good assessment."

Donovan chewed solidly through his lunch. "We've seen that before," he answered carefully, looking back at Lucas. "I wouldn't dwell on it, though."

The boy shrugged, his attention on the food, like any normal fourteen-year-old not blessed with untold, unending quantities of world-changing magic. He burped, blushed, muttered an apology, and continued on.

Donovan finished his lunch and wandered to his horse, checking her hooves. Lucas came up a moment later, petting the beast's nose.

Donovan said quietly, "He's made the same point I did when we started. We should carry on through the woods now; I have that path mapped already. You said the road would be quicker. I didn't want to argue, but I have to disagree now, circumstances as they are."

Lucas chewed the inside of his lip. "Where would we cross the gorge? The bridge is the best option."

"Not if it has Hunters waiting."

"Every bridge we build, they manage to tear down within a year — except that one. They won't destroy it — they need it as much as we do, and now it's the only place to cross." He ran a hand down his face. "The Order needs to post guards."

"We'll suggest it in our report. Until then, how many Hunters do you think will be guarding it? We can rappel down, wind our way up?"

Lucas shook his head. "Through the woods and up and down the gorge will lose us time; we decided that a week ago."

"What's time compared to security? We could take an extra week, but if they don't find us, what's the worry? I'd rather they can't find us than depend on our chances of outrunning them."

Lucas let out a frustrated huff. "Let's carry on the road another day to make some speed and we'll head through the woods when we can."

"All right," Donovan agreed half-heartedly.

"We won't regret it."

After lunch, they rode several more hours, keeping the horses to a walk-trot-canter-trot-walk to gain time and save their strength. Donovan checked their back trail compulsively until he saw three shapes mounting the distant hill, faint, but visible.

"Lucas," he called.

The young man turned to see where Donovan was gesturing and swore.

"Off the road?" Donovan suggested wryly, worry coloring his tone.

Lucas led the way, a carefully blank expression hiding his fear.

Ruben glanced between them and said meekly, "We have to rest the horses soon; they need to drink."

"There's a river just another mile off," Lucas assured him. "We need to rest, too."

"The Hunters?"

"We don't know they're Hunters. And they'll probably miss us ..."

*   *   *

They rested the horses, alternating between riding and walking beside them while Donovan led the way through the woods. It would gain them some advantage: if the Hunters came looking for them off-road, they could lose time in the search. The first ones to the gorge had the lead, but knowing they might be there already was itself a benefit, even if there was no way around.

By the time night had fully fallen, the horses were stumbling with fatigue. Exhaustion weighed heavy on Donovan when he finally reined in and dismounted at an acceptable camping spot. The other two followed suit without question, pulling off tack, and brushing down the tired horses, making sure they were staked down within reach of grazing.

Lucas had bags under his eyes, not having slept the night before, but he went about his tasks without hesitation. No fire tonight, but he gave Ruben a handful of jerked pork and a small pouch of assorted fresh vegetables with two bread rolls and his own waterskin, half-full.

"Head up that tree; I'll give you a boost."

Ruben looked at the tree in question and accepted the lift, given that the first branch was far overhead. He tied the waterskin to his belt, put the food in his shirt, then stepped into Lucas's cupped hands and hauled himself upward. He went up a few more branches to a comfortable fork and waved, barely visible in the darkness.

Lucas waved back with a grin and said, "Get comfortable — I'll be right up."

The boy fished his cold dinner from his shirt while Lucas went to find Donovan.

Lucas found him drawing a map on one of the blank pieces of paper all Retrievers had to carry for this sort of situation. Lucas was always impressed with Donovan's mapping abilities, but the older man never seemed to think it was anything to brag about.

In a few minutes, he had a very clear diagram with landmarks and written instructions, including a scale with a rough calculation of Ruben's stride. "Good enough?"

"Perfect." Lucas folded it neatly, then walked back to Ruben's tree.

He aimed and jumped in a powerful burst, catching hold of the branch and swinging his legs over it to work his way to the top. He dusted off his hands, found Ruben, and situated himself in a fork nearby.

"How's dinner?"

Ruben grinned. "I've had worse."

Lucas grinned back and handed him the map.

Ruben looked it over before seeking Lucas's eyes with his own. "I'm to carry on alone?" His voice wavered.

Lucas shook his head. "Not at all. However, our job is getting you to the Order by any means necessary. That means making sure you have the means to carry on without us, just in case, aye?"

Ruben fidgeted with his shirt sleeve. "Do you think they'll attack in the night?"

"We're hoping they'll pass us by. That's all guessing those folks behind us were Hunters at all. Could be we're overly cautious."

"'Better overcautious than underground'," Ruben quoted. "Garth always said."

Lucas laughed. "I'll remember that one. Does the map make sense?"

Ruben squinted. "I think so. It's hard to make out in this light."

"Fair. He has water marked. Remember, too, that if we aren't back to the Order when we're expected, they'll send folks out to look for us, so it's all right to take our time."

"Sure."

"Try to get some rest. I'll throw up a bedroll. You might get a bit chilly, but if you start to freeze, you give a whistle and I'll help you out."

"Where will you be?"

Lucas pointed into the darkness. "I'll be across the way in the next tree. Don will be on the ground amongst the horses. Anything happens at all, you stay in this tree." His voice turned hard. "Like I said, our job is to get you there by any means." He clapped Ruben on the shoulder and gave it a squeeze. "We've been in tighter spots and never lost anyone. You remember that."

The boy managed a smile. Lucas made his way down, then tossed up Ruben's bedroll as promised.

Donovan handed him a cold dinner and made a small spot of mud with some of their water. Lucas smeared it on his face, neck, hands and arms to hide his pale skin; Donovan's was naturally like midnight.

"Anything we're missing?" the young man asked.

Donovan listed on his fingers, "Weapons, the charge is safely away, map, precautions taken."

"Where?"

"Everywhere." Donovan pointed to specific trees, making connecting lines as he said, "Trip lines there and there and there. All the sharp stones I could find tossed about there and there. The horses are in the center, and I'll be at the base of Ruben's tree amongst them."

"Don't get stepped on."

"I'll try," he agreed, rolling his eyes. "Be thankful you have properly working knees, youth."

"Thanks, granther. I'll try not to fall to my death."

Lucas scrambled up into his tree, staying low in the branches and effectively disappearing once he was settled and quiet with his bedroll unfolded and about his shoulders like a blanket. Donovan carved out some dirt to make it more even amongst the tree roots and pulled his cover over, becoming effectively invisible. Only the horses made any sound now, with the occasional shifting or snorting, but soon they too were asleep.

Lucas drank in the silence of the night, keeping his muscles rotating between tense and relaxed to move his blood and stay warm and ready. It wasn't the first time he'd been in a tree, switching from moment to moment between wanting a fight and dreading one.

He blinked calmly, scanning the surrounding area. Donovan had offered to Seek for the pursuers, but Lucas was relieved when the older man had changed his mind. He didn't want to spend the night holding Donovan's pain, or even Pushing it into the surrounding trees; he needed his strength for the eventual fight he knew was coming.

Seekers were an interesting bunch; Lucas pitied them. When he used his magic, it didn't hurt him nearly as badly as it did them — even though it was arguably more powerful and much more useful. Every magic had a cost, usually headache and nausea, but Seekers paid more than most, and no one knew why.

Donovan was invisible amongst the horses. Even knowing where he was, Lucas couldn't spot him. He was probably dozing, half asleep and half alert, waiting for any sound out of place to jar him to his senses.

He hoped Ruben was getting some rest, but doubted it. He likely understood what was at stake; children they took from contracts seemed older than those they brought from their homes, and tended to keep their minds to themselves. But Lucas had been Retrieving for five years and knew how to read them: Ruben was scared, but not hysterical; he'd be all right.

Magus. The word was known in legend and spoken of the same way one mentioned the gods. Limitless power with no cost — it had been generations since one had been born, though there were always rumors, and this one was in his charge. Lucas swallowed hard, heart thudding in his chest. If the boy was trained, there'd be no need for hiding; he'd crush their enemies with a thought. Or so the stories said. He smiled at himself, wondering if he'd be mentioned in the tales of Ruben's eventual great deeds and future legends of his own.

The stories of Hunters were as wild as those of the magi. Lucas remembered the strength of the force that had shoved him the day before and felt a shiver go down his spine. *Blood magic.* They'd mentioned it in classes at the Order, but very little solid information was available. He knew it took a cost more than just the blood-price: once you used blood magic, it was addictive, but further details about the cost or method were few and far between. He knew that's what they were facing now. There would be no reason for the Hunters *not* to prepare their magic before initiating the fight, however it was they did that.

Lucas gripped the blanket tighter around his shoulders, memories of his last battle flitting through his mind. He'd always been afraid of death, even with his Healing magic to help ward it off. His recent visit to the black gates did nothing to dispel that fear in him. He thought of his mother, her iron strength and inability to fail, imagined her comforting embrace and familiar words whenever he was nervous:

"All things in their time, Luc. And when you do go, you take them with you and finish the fight properly in the gods' arena."

He grinned.

*   *   *

Donovan's eyes snapped open. The horses stood like sleeping statues around him. He strained his ears, ignored his pounding heartbeat, and listened to the forest to hear what had awakened him. Although he knew he was well hidden from view, he still felt very exposed.

The wind shifted some leaves behind him, but it was otherwise quiet. The bugs had gone silent, and the rodents had returned to their burrows. Someone was nearby.

He didn't move, but let his adrenaline lend him wakefulness. If he'd had Lucas's magic, he could have stolen some measure of alertness from the first person to attack him, much as Lucas had borrowed Donovan's reflexes to augment his own in town. Who wouldn't be a bit reckless when you had a magic like Healing?

If he had been a Mentalist, they could speak mind-to-mind, which was a power Donovan would happily trade for. Their magic had little cost compared to his own, which was only particularly useful during war campaigns, to see troop movements. Mentalists were highly coveted by the Order, used as spies to hunt out blood mages, or high-ranking couriers for the royal family. He knew of several who lived outside the employ of the Order and the Palace and made plenty of money doing odd-jobs with their Talents.

There it was: Donovan heard the very deliberate, very careful footstep of someone sneaking into camp. His hand tightened on the grip of the sword Lucas had given him, and he wished he was better with it. One of the horses rumbled, stomping. Donovan silently rolled his head to see that there were feet within his view. Lucas was waiting for his move, he knew.

So he waited.

There was no need to rush just yet. There were at least three Hunters after them and, if they'd sent this one ahead, the others would be watching and waiting to spring a trap of their own. Let them grow nervous, waiting for their prey to appear.

Donovan kept calm and demanded patience for himself. The sneaking visitor had passed the first horse and was moving around to the next, touching here and there. He'd not yet bent to look below them — he'd likely see Donovan if he did, and then they would be forced to act. He hoped desperately that Lucas would keep still. Their time together had built much trust for one another, but trust only took one so far. Fear was a powerful motivator.

The invader moved past the second horse, looking it over. He was beside Lucas's mare, bending to untie the beast. Trying to take her? Surely the Hunters had mounts of their own. Why take the horse?

Suspicion roused Donovan into action. He clutched his sword and rolled to a crouch as quickly as he could without making much noise. The intruder was only a couple of feet away, still trying to be silent, tugging the horse's stake from the ground. Donovan circled to the first horse, a hand on her rump, and then stopped behind a tree. He waved at Lucas's hiding place, and saw a twig drop in answer.

The man Donovan could see wore a heavy pack and led the mare by the lead rope, glancing over his shoulder to check for followers. He looked quite pleased with himself and, judging by the symbol stitched onto his jacket and the instrument with his bag, he was no blood mage.

Donovan rolled his eyes and stepped out from behind the tree to draw the visitor's attention. The man saw him and blanched, gasping with surprise. The mare responded to the sudden tension in her lead by whinnying and trying to rear up. The stranger quickly gained control of the creature, pulling her back to the ground, but by then, the other horses had responded with whinnies of their own, probably waking half the forest.

"Gods and kings, where did you *come* from?" the man asked, staring back at Donovan in disbelief.

Donovan glared and waved to Lucas again. His partner jumped down from the tree a moment later, looking thoroughly surprised to see the newcomer. He walked up to the would-be thief and took the reins from his unresisting hands to stake his mare back down.

"Hello," Lucas said.

The man looked up and said, "Trees. That's new."

"You're interrupting something potentially dangerous, friend," Donovan told him, irritated and tired. "And you just tried to steal our horses. This is about the time you either explain yourself or move on."

"I would much rather explain, honestly," he said, shrugging off his massive pack with difficulty. "The night is young, and I have been walking since dawn."

"The night is almost over, and we've no interest in your stories."

"Noticed that, did you?" the newcomer asked with a dimpled grin. He nodded at the bard's symbol stitched on his vest. "You would not happen to have anything with which a weary traveler could satisfy an abused and empty stomach, would you?"

Donovan walked up to him to glare from closer. "Look, bard. If you know stories, you know Hunters, and if you know Hunters, you know fear, so when I tell you that we're waiting to encounter three of them that were on our trail, understand that I'm not lying when I say we don't have time for amusements."

The bard grew serious. "Three Hunters, you say? They rode by me hours ago. They must have missed your traps. Which were very clever, by the way." He held up two lengths of sturdy twine, and handed them to a frowning Donovan, who bundled and pocketed them.

Lucas walked up to the conversation. "Hours ago?" He looked at Donovan and swallowed hard. "They were riding for the gorge."

"As we thought," Donovan soothed him. "We'll know to expect them."

"Can I come down now?" Ruben asked.

The bard spun in time to see the boy jump down with his blanket around his shoulders like a cape. Ruben looked at the bard with curiosity, but said nothing.

"There are more of you, I wonder?" the bard asked the boy, scanning overhead.

Ruben didn't answer.

"They were definitely Hunters?" Donovan asked, drawing the distracted bard back to the topic.

The man nodded. "Aye, three of them, riding like the law was behind and salvation ahead. You can tell by the stink of them — I know every story, and if a bard cannot recognize a Hunter, no one can."

Lucas appeared to be calculating. "They're definitely at the bridge by now."

"We'll go another way."

"We don't have the rations for an extended change of course."

"There is a very small town a day from here," the bard told them. "It has an orphanage that could help; I came from there. I know the owner and she could keep us undiscovered for a time."

"Those are west of here," Donovan agreed. "But we have to go east if we have any hope of getting around. We can take the ferry at High Waters, and pass through Kanan ..."

"West would give us that town, and we could get supplies onto the horses, to continue down to the mountain pass." Lucas countered.

Donovan shook his head, "That'd take twice as long for half the gain. Kanan's our better bet; easier to go unnoticed in a larger town. The mountain pass will be snowed in this time of year; and if it's not, it will be soon. Snow is coming, I know it."

"What about engaging them directly?"

All of them looked at the bard, who had made the suggestion.

He shrugged at their expressions and continued, "If we know where they are, at least we come prepared, and I would wager they are expecting us, you, to try and go around. Besides which, if I knew we could get ahead, I would send more riders, further away, to come up behind and trap them. Us. If we were them."

Lucas put a hand under his cheek and gritted his teeth with frustration. "More than three Hunters, all rested and prepared; I don't like our odds."

"You killed two of them in town, though," Ruben pointed out, looking up at him.

The bard's eyes widened and he looked at Lucas for explanation.

"I had surprise and a healthy dose of luck. They didn't start their casting until the fight had begun. It's completely different."

Ruben shook his head, "Maybe not. You don't want me to fight, so why not Take my reflexes like you Took Donovan's, *share* them with Donovan, and both of you are healthier, except for some headaches, right? You could Take my wits, my health, my hearing, just about anything, and keep me a'horse with ropes, or safe in a tree without any trouble while you deal with them, right?"

Lucas glanced at the bard, then at Donovan and grimaced.

Donovan took over, "We're not getting anywhere right now, and, if our pursuers have passed us, we have time to recuperate. Let's eat and discuss this on full stomachs."

He started to pick up sticks for a fire. The bard joined him quite readily, and Lucas and Ruben followed more reluctantly.

Donovan built up the fire while Lucas dug rations out of his pack, the two of them making a meal of eggs from a well-wrapped glass jar and toasted rolls stuffed with salted ham.

"That smells delectable, gentlemen," the bard said, rubbing his hands together with anticipation.

The sun was starting to come up now, lighting the horizon, and providing to each of them a much better view of their little clearing. Ruben moved the horses to better grazing while the men cooked, and he cleared up Donovan's blanket so it didn't get stepped on. Now, he was back with them, accepting the first ham-roll heaped with eggs.

"You never gave us your name," Donovan said, handing the bard his breakfast.

The man had already taken a healthy bite, but he jumped to his feet and bowed with a flourish, chewing as fast as he could. He held out an urgent finger to keep their attention, and they watched him for a few long, very awkward, moments until his mouth was clear enough to say, "Of course! I am the mightily eloquent Whitman Acres, at your righteous service. Any story you may request, any tune you have a fancy for, any game you see fit to speak of, I am well-versed in them all. Whom do I have the humble honor of addressing in your good selves?"

He looked at them eagerly. Ruben snorted and took another bite of his breakfast while Donovan made quick introductions.

"Wonderful names!" the bard continued. "I have tales of heroes with those titles when you would like to hear them. Fraught with dangers overcome, charming companions I have detailed descriptions of, and incomparable adventures that will keep you so excellently balanced on your toes, the dancing schools will wish to recruit you. You will, of course, be unable to attend their sessions until the stories are completed and your fears and humors assuaged."

"I think we're fine for now, Whitman Acres, thank you," Lucas said wryly.

"'Whit' is perfectly acceptable for regular conversation, my friend Lucas," the man grinned.

He had an easy smile in a doughy face. At first glance, he looked overweight and, indeed, the way he inhaled his breakfast suggested heavily to that possibility, but they could tell from this short distance that his girth was more muscle than fat. He had a barrel chest and shoulders like an ox. He stood just below six feet tall, managing somehow to make himself less physically imposing than one might expect, without intimidation or apology.

His sandy-blond hair formed tight curls. Green eyes sat in a freckled face. Ears that were just a bit too big, slightly stuck out to the sides of his head. His clothes were plain — a faded blue shirt that laced from the middle of the chest to his neck — but he left it loose, the collar lying as though forgotten on his shoulders. He wore a faded red vest upon which were three curved lines on the left breast — the sign of his profession. His faded black trousers, worn at the knees and crotch, seemed a bit short for his height. He looked like any other bard they'd run across in their travels.

"Unfortunately we can't accept your company on our trip, bard," Donovan told him once he'd settled back into his seat.

"Not at all? I am a friendly fellow, but I can be quiet as a mouse if you so desire, so quiet you will forget I am here. You have those lovely horses, and one such as myself is heavy on his feet ..."

"Yes, well, there's also the issue with you having tried to steal one of our beasts," Lucas pointed out.

"Don't encourage him," Donovan muttered to Lucas.

Ruben failed to hide a giggle behind his hand.

"My good sir!" Whitman cried, looking offended. "I saw the tracks of four creatures and thought I might find some good company, nothing more! Your camp proved empty, however, and I did not want the poor creatures to grow hungry, or lonely. Nothing is worse, and horses know it as well as men."

Lucas shook his head again, clearly taken in, and amused at the bard's charm.

"Where are you going, Whit?" Donovan asked, trying to bring the conversation to a more reasonable topic.

"Why, to the Order of Magic and Learning!" he exclaimed proudly.

"It's just called 'the Order'," Donovan muttered.

"Surely you are heading that direction as well, gentlemen? Retrievers such as yourselves, I wonder …?"

Donovan and Lucas grew tense, glancing at Ruben, who took their cue and looked nervous.

The bard held up his hands apologetically. "I meant nothing by it; merely took in the look of you and made the best guess. You must be excited!" he said to Ruben.

Ruben looked at Donovan and swallowed. "Um, yes."

"It is a fantastic place! You won't be disappointed." He smiled encouragingly.

"We can't afford to be held back, as you can imagine," Donovan explained. "You've already heard that there are Hunters on our trail, and you're a liability."

"Not so!" Whit exclaimed, putting up his fists. "I am an excellent fighter, one of the best! I have two dozen fights under my belt and plenty more won without such garments. Bare fists, sticks, staff, sword, or bow — I am as competent as they come. I would be an excellent addition to your adventuring crew!"

"We're not adventuring," Lucas scoffed. He rolled his eyes at Donovan.

"Of course you are! Look at you!" Whitman shot back. "Two men in fighting figure, swords belted about their waists with a young boy, their protégé, in tow. One, a Healer of some excellent and otherworldly skill, the other, more mysterious in his age and experience, pursued by Hunters from all sides! What for? Theft from the blood mages? Some passing insult? A murder of their comrades? They race to reinforcements across the countryside, a mount apiece keeping them to quick pace. You say you're not on an adventure? I say you have no idea what an adventure is! Along their journey they encounter a well-traveled bard, Whit-ful and strong, ready to aid them however necessary!"

"How old are you, son?" Donovan interrupted, staring at him.

"Thirty-five, sir. Just turned. My mother would be proud and surprised I've lived to manhood, and my father would exclaim to the entire bar, 'I have a son? When did that happen?' It is a wonderful time to be alive, sir."

"Whit—" Lucas started, but he was interrupted.

"I swear I will not slow you down, not a Whit —" The Retrievers groaned. "But I have a true need to reach the Order. I cannot put information into a letter as those can be read by nearly anyone with the learning of it and I really can be quite useful to Retrievers such as yourselves, as unimpressive as I may seem, which is on purpose, I assure you, and the why for which I have managed to avoid discovery thus far. If nothing else, I am really quite entertaining and if you engage in battle earning you a gruesome facial wound or a leg chopped off, you will be glad I am along to lighten the mood."

He held up his hand, swearing to his words as he spoke at high speeds.

For a long moment, the only sound in their clearing was the stomping of the horses and the occasional bird or bug.

"Facial wound?" Ruben finally grinned.

Whitman turned his attention to him. "Indeed, young sir, the most devastating of injuries to a man, *unless* it heals into a dashing scar — which all the lovers will find very brave. I, myself, am one day hoping for an excellent shoulder scar with which to prove my daring. So far, I have been unsuccessful — usually I finish the fighting before the ruffians can aid me in that regard." He winked. "Truthfully, I will follow even if you try to leave me behind. You will feel bad eventually, especially with no one riding that spare pack beast, and me afoot and jogging behind."

"We could just kill you here," Lucas said, crossing his arms.

The bard didn't look phased. "True, true, but I will put up a fight and it will only tire you."

Lucas laughed at that. He and Donovan shared a long look before Lucas nodded and Donovan shrugged.

"All right," Donovan said. "You're welcome along, but do bear in mind that it's because of our pursuit, and we need all the help we can get."

"Worry not! I have the aid of three people about me — four, counting myself — and all of them are in your service. Shall we be away, then, as we are fed and watered and being Hunted?"

"One question," Lucas said as they all started to stand.

Whitman looked at him.

"Why make yourself a target? They know we're coming, but not you."

"A mind after my own studies, I will declare," Whitman grinned. "Because the pace will be faster, but I was not lying about loneliness being one of the worst experiences. The mind says terrible things to a man when his companions do not speak over it. Satisfied, sir?"

Lucas nodded slowly.

Ruben jumped up excitedly and started to saddle the horses. Donovan wondered how excited he would be when the fighting began. If only he could keep them all so innocent and carefree ...

"My sister was claimed by your people when we were small children," the bard said, watching Ruben, his thoughts far away.

"You'll be able to visit her at the Order, then, I expect," Donovan said, packing away their supplies with practiced motion.

"Unlikely," Whitman answered, pitching in. "She and her Retriever were murdered and hung in pieces around the village when the Hunters caught them."

*   *   *

Whitman proved to be a surprisingly good rider. They had to put his pack on Ruben's horse to keep the creature from being weighed down, but the packhorse was sturdy, and they seemed to get along. He kept his lute with him, and would guide the horse with his knees while he played various pieces. Half the time, he seemed to be making up the music as he went along, humming to himself for harmony.

Lucas acted as their scout again. He stayed far enough ahead to give them proper warning, and returned periodically with little news. With the lead that the Hunters had, they would be well settled at the gorge, and better rested, waiting.

About midday, Lucas came back, waving them down. There was no clearing here, and it was tight within the woods with little space to maneuver their horses. A pine-spice pervaded the air; needles covered the ground, softening their steps. Lucas wiped his sweaty hair off his forehead, despite the chill of winter, and came to a halt beside his partner.

"We're about three miles from the bridge. I saw their trail, fresh. They've been scouting this way, looking for us, most like."

Donovan nodded pensively and pictured the area ahead. "Did you see any of them?"

Lucas drank deeply from his waterskin. "No, but I figured I'd get us some warning."

"I do not mean to interrupt," Whitman said as he rode up alongside them. "Well, I do, seeing as I am, and I knew that I was, which was why I said that I did not mean to, since I wanted to be polite, but there are riders coming up behind us, and they, too, do not appear particularly friendly."

Ruben joined them, and agreed with the bard's words. "Four riders, aye, about a mile back from us; I saw them coming over the rise a ways back."

"This is just wonderful, isn't it?" Lucas cursed, spitting grit from his mouth.

"Backtracking and going around is sounding better and better." Donovan calculated quickly. "They'll be on us soon, likely before we make the bridge, unless we hurry."

"So let us hurry," Whitman said, hands out entreatingly. "A fight at this distance will be heard by either group, so there is no point in risking reinforcements from either party when we know that we will fight them all in the end, and indeed, the world will be fewer at least one Hunter, yes?"

Lucas spoke, "I agree with Whitman, no matter how he looks with those big ears."

"You are a scholar, my dearest friend," Whitman answered solemnly, a hand on his heart.

Donovan chewed on his lip, mind racing. His horse paced nervously beneath him. "Whitman, you'll go ahead with Lucas; I really hope you weren't jesting when you said you could fight. I'll keep Ruben with me here — we daren't leave him alone, but I don't want the two of you to be completely overwhelmed. Call for me and I'll come riding." Lucas nodded sharply and held his partner's gaze for a long moment.

"Where there are four, there are more," Whit said absently, digging through his pack.

"We'll ride hard for the bridge and engage them there," Lucas said as he dug into his pack. "Hopefully we'll have the first batch down before the second arrives. I'll leave a trip rope to catch at least one of them."

Lucas shrugged on a leather vest riveted with metal. Donovan handed him the twine from last night and then put on his own vest — a Retriever's friend in times of danger. Lighter than chainmail, and much cheaper, it was scant protection, but good enough to turn most of the power of a blade, most of the time. The Healer then secured his pack next to Donovan's to free up his own beast, and put out a hand for Donovan to shake. The older man took it.

"Take care, Lucas. Don't do anything reckless."

"Who, me?" Lucas teased with a levity his face didn't show. "Can I?"

Donovan nodded and felt a cool wash of magic flow through him, taking hurts and aches he hadn't even realized he felt. Lucas didn't bother to hide his grimace, but he nodded thankfully and rode for the trail.

Ruben watched him go, wide-eyed and eager.

"We'll stay out of the way," Donovan told the boy. "We need to keep you out of their hands." Ruben looked hurt, and Donovan continued, "Until you're trained up, Ruben. Give the Order a few years, and you'll be more than a match for a group of Hunters."

"I like that idea," the boy nodded seriously and received the bag Whitman handed up to him.

In the short time they'd been stopped, the bard had donned a thick quilted shirt and leather vest much like their own, leather gloves with chainmail links on the backs, and a belt with thick leather strips that hung over the legs. He held two short sticks in his hands.

"I was not jesting about what I can do." He winked. "I hate to leave my instrument in hands other than my own, but it will do us no good to frighten the ruffians away with my incredible skill upon its strings. They will only cry for the beauty of it, and our victory will be nothing impressive." He sniffed, wheeling his mount and riding after Lucas.

*   *   *

The two of them rode at a canter down the trail, laying low down the horses' necks, finding the rhythm in the hoof beats. Lucas slowed and dismounted next to a pair of likely trees to quickly tie a tripwire to catch someone unaware. He mounted once more and joined Whitman on the road to the fight.

The trees ended unexpectedly, and they burst into the light and onto an open hillside, sloping down toward a deep gorge, spanned by a bridge that three riders could cross abreast. The gorge fell about three hundred feet to churning water and rock, and was half that far across. Two riders, plain-looking men, stood guarding the bridge. A third wheeled his mount around just ahead of them, the beast prancing in place, eager and agitated. The scout must have just seen them and ridden back to inform his fellows. Too late for that. Lucas streaked ahead; Whitman close behind him.

"Plans change the moment battle engages," Lucas muttered, eyes fixed on the scout.

Loosening his feet in his stirrups, he leaned forward. The scout turned to face him, glaring over a thick beard and grinning with confidence. Lucas drew the short sword from his belt and the scout did the same. The man's eyes grew wider now, and confidence drained from his face as Lucas continued barreling toward him at speed.

At the last moment, Lucas stood in his saddle and veered his mount off course and away. He jumped into the air and threw himself at his opponent with a terrible scream.

The scout answered with a bellow of his own and thrust his sword up to skewer the leaping madman, but the yell startled the man's horse, and he had to swivel to keep balance, turning his blade out of Lucas' path. Lucas landed on him a moment later, knocking them both to the ground. The horse whinnied in pain and fear and bolted away.

The landing was hard, but not as hard as for the scout under him. They rolled apart, losing each other, but Lucas reversed his momentum with a quick jab of his heels into the dirt. The scout was still trying to breathe, his sword loose in his hand. Lucas jumped up and fell across his torso, hammering a fist into the man's diaphragm, making him wheeze in pain, unable to take another breath.

Lucas hesitated, then jabbed a fist into the scout's throat twice in quick succession, effectively crushing his wind-pipe and dooming him to suffocation. No blood, no power. With luck, the others would fall as quickly.

He rolled to his feet, wincing at the new bruises, and picked up the scout's discarded short sword. He swung his own to remind his muscles how to fight with two weapons. His eyebrows rose when he saw that Whitman had engaged one of the other two Hunters. The bard had effectively blocked the second from the fight by keeping the first between them, trading blows with sticks versus sword. He kept his horse moving to block the second Hunter's advance and seemed to be doing well enough, but it would only take them a moment to overtake him. Already, the second Hunter was muttering, bringing up his magic.

Lucas ran for him. The Hunter saw, but did not stop muttering, instead turning to engage him. Lucas prepared to dodge, but continued his sprint, arms pumping for speed, while his hands gripped the two swords tightly.

He was very close before a burst of invisible force streaked toward him — the only tell was the breath of wind it sent before, and a slight shimmer in the air. Lucas dove to the ground, rolling tightly, the swords tucked so that he didn't injure himself as he went. He remembered his mother's teaching voice saying, *"Just so, boy. Exactly."*

Lucas felt the force pass by and he rolled to his feet, still running. The Hunter blanched with surprise, preparing another attack. Lucas eyed the distance and threw himself to the ground again, rolling directly under the Hunter's horse and standing to turn in one fluid motion. The Hunter twisted around to see where Lucas was.

This one has good reflexes. Lucas's sword swipe missed him as he swung his leg out of the saddle and over Lucas's head, realizing that, with Lucas so close, being mounted was not his best option.

Sword in hand, he muttered to make his magic and stall. Lucas stepped into the saddle stirrup, and lunged over the top, again barely missing the very surprised Hunter with his blade.

Cursing, Lucas mounted fully, tucked one sword under his arm, and hauled on the reins. He kicked savagely. The poor creature screamed in protest, but reared onto its hind legs, kicking the Hunter to the ground. Lucas patted the creature's neck in apology, riding forward in a quick trot.

The horse didn't want to step on the downed man, but Lucas urged it. They followed the Hunter as he rolled about, trying to gain his feet. He stopped muttering, concentrating more on staying alive and avoiding the sharp hooves. Suddenly, he clapped his hands with a loud "Feh!" of magic and the horse's eyes went wide with fear. It screamed and bucked, throwing Lucas into the air.

He released the swords immediately and forced himself to relax. He tried to aim his legs toward the ground, but knew he would miss. Sure enough, he landed hard on his shoulder while the horse ran away, still screaming and bucking, into the woods. Lucas rolled swiftly to the side. He couldn't stay still for long.

A hail of magicked pebbles struck his bare neck and arms. He shielded his head with his arms and rolled defensively toward his closest blade. The pebbles stopped pecking him and he gained his feet, panting for breath. The Hunter he was facing had started muttering again, glaring cold hatred at Lucas. The Retriever answered the stare with one of his own and started forward, his attacks ruthless. High, low, low, middle, low, high, he drove the Hunter back with the force and speed of his blows. A small cut on the back of his ear was smarting — a prize from the hail of pebbles, and several more made themselves known on his hands. Sweat was beginning to run down Lucas's forehead as the sun crept toward its full height. He'd need to finish this quickly, or risk the Hunter using his own blood against him.

In his years of fighting, Lucas had found that many Hunters relied too much on their magic, which he appreciated, given his weapons practice from childhood and onward. Unfortunately, this Hunter didn't appear to be among that number. The Hunter had stopped giving ground and was attacking with his own flurries. They traded back and forth, hesitating and feinting, darting for attacks, follow through, and retreats. Lucas stayed light on his toes and concentrated on his opponent's weapon and chest to see where he'd move next, what target he would reveal.

THERE!

Lucas lunged. His blade drove deeply into his opponent's thigh muscle. The man screamed and fell to the ground as his leg gave out beneath him. A crossbow quarrel materialized in his head an instant later, silencing him before Lucas had a chance. Lucas spun and crouched low to the ground to make a smaller target. He saw Whitman, still mounted, reloading the crossbow with the stock against his hip.

The bard nodded to him, a black eye forming on his doughy face, and called, "Nasty weapon. Can you believe his friend leveled it at me? Damned indecent! Rude, using a crossbow to kill someone. At least have the decency to learn the proper bow, or run me through with a spear. Need a lift?"

Lucas shook his head and grinned in relief and awe. His face fell a moment later as three more Hunters rode onto the plateau before the bridge. The first was standing in his stirrups, pointing threatening at Lucas as he came.

"Excellent timing!" Whitman yelled, aiming and loosing in one fluid motion. The quarrel struck the second rider in the neck. Lucas couldn't hold back an amazed *whoop* at the incredible shot. The rider clutched at the wound, reeling, making her horse spin until she fell off, her legs kicking in agony. The two others immediately wheeled their horses and started for the young bard. Whitman dropped the crossbow, the time required to load it making it useless now in close combat.

"I was aiming for her chest," he said conversationally. His eyes were bright with excitement. He drew his two sticks, notched from the earlier fight, and swung them above his head. He yelled, "The bard-warrior faced down six worthy foes, terror filling his marrow as he charged courageously forward, yelling his battle cries!"

Lucas would have laughed if he wasn't so worried, but instead picked up his second sword and ran after Whitman. Adrenaline filled his veins with strength and energy; he hated how much he loved this. The Hunter on the ground was still kicking; Lucas ran toward her, intending to finish her swiftly.

Instead, he jumped backward just as a large tree speared into the ground where he had been standing. A Hunter bared his teeth with anger at having missed his target. *Hunter magic.* Lucas snarled. He threw one of his swords like a spear and then darted after it, low to the ground.

The Hunter knocked the blade away without moving, burying it point-first in the ground with the power of his magic. Lucas was already sprinting to ram his second sword into the belly of the Hunter's horse. The poor creature screamed, rearing and flailing before it collapsed and trumpeted its final shuddering breaths. Lucas thought a quick prayer for forgiveness — slaughter of innocents was always a crime.

The Hunter managed to jump free, to run to his fallen comrade. Lucas swore violently and hurdled the dying horse to pursue his prey. The Hunter had thrown himself to his knees, one hand on his companion's face, the other in the pool of her blood. Lucas yelled in fury, demanding more speed as he sprinted, intending to take off the man's head.

Too late.

The Hunter dodged with inhuman speed, ducking and coming to stand before Lucas could even stop his momentum and turn around. By then, the Hunter was prepared, muttering and throwing his bloody hands forward in an attack. Lucas again dove to the ground as a burst of force caught his legs instead of his torso. It spun him violently backward and he lost his sword again, bouncing across the ground. He heard a pop in his shoulder and gritted his teeth behind thin lips. If he could get close enough ...

He leapt to his feet, refusing to stay down. The Hunter sauntered toward him, his back to the fight between his partner and Whitman. Lucas saw Donovan engaged in a battle of his own with the fourth Hunter they'd seen on the hillside — he must have hit the tripwire and lost his horse, continuing on foot, and Donovan had come to back them up. *Where was Ruben?*

No time for that. Lucas wrenched his attention back and took a comfortable fighting stance. "Too afraid to face me without magic, then?" he yelled.

The Hunter laughed humorlessly. "You can't goad me, Order brat. I'll finish this quickly and claim the boy." He was grinning.

The hand that had rested in his friend's blood came up and drew down his face to leave smears of reddish brown down his nose and cheeks. It disappeared even as the blood around him spilled and evaporated. "Don't worry. We'll take good care of him."

Lucas's lip turned up in distaste, nauseous at the thought. He started forward to close the distance, light on his toes, ready to dodge however necessary. The Hunter drew back a fist as though to punch, despite their distance. Lucas ran toward him, dove into a roll and came up much closer than he would have managed by walking. The ground shook behind him as a divot appeared in the earth where he'd been. Lucas shot forward on his knees, hands outstretched, hoping to catch the Hunter's legs.

The Hunter leapt into an incredibly high and showy flip before landing with a confident grin. Lucas rolled sideways out of the way, and then backward over his shoulder onto a knee again. The Hunter took a moment to catch his balance, and Lucas darted in, fast as lightning. He planted his shoulder in the Hunter's crotch, his other hand gripping the man's collar. Standing, he threw the Hunter to the ground with a roar of strength, catching hold of his leg and twisting it violently.

The Hunter yelled with surprise and then again in pain. Lucas brought his leg up to kick-break the one he held, but it jerked out of his grip. He stumbled forward, and then back as his legs were kicked out from under him. The air whooshed out of him and he let it, trying not to wheeze until his lungs could recover.

The Hunter's heel swung down at his head. Lucas caught it, barely, his weakened shoulder protesting the mistreatment. He twisted the Hunter's leg violently; its owner was forced to spin to relieve the pressure. Lucas tried to maintain his hold for just a moment longer; enough to deliver his pain and Donovan's fatigue. It was really wearing on him, especially with the new pain in his shoulder.

The Hunter spun from his grasp, but was still prone, now perpendicular to him. Lucas rolled backward over his aching shoulder again. He rose to his knees and drew his knife from his boot. Diving forward, he nevertheless hit the dirt as the Hunter, reflexes magically improved, rolled away. A boot slammed into his face. Lucas grunted with pain, tasted blood. His heart fluttered with fear. He stayed on one knee, hands in a guarded position, the knife gripped tightly in his palm. The Hunter faced him.

"I thought you were going to kill me quickly," Lucas said, smirking with a sense of ease he didn't feel.

The Hunter gave a relaxed smile and answered, "I was waiting for the right opportunity."

Lucas felt a gentle prickling on his face and realized that the blood from his nose was disappearing as quickly as it fell.

The Hunter bared his teeth in a feral grin. He kicked with his right boot. Lucas blocked with his left arm, swung his knife wide, and jerked it quickly out of the way as the Hunter leaned forward to strike at him. Lucas returned with an attempted left-handed punch of his own, but missed. He edged forward, just slightly, closing the distance between them.

The Hunter noticed and backed away two paces. Lucas rose to his feet as his advantage was lost, and started to close the distance between them again. Over the Hunter's shoulder, Lucas saw Whitman running toward them. He was far, his fight having carried him several yards away, but if Lucas could just distract this one long enough ...

The Hunter lunged with impossible quickness. Lucas gasped and crouched, hoping to thwart the Hunter's advantage. Instead, the man raised his knee into Lucas's jaw and sent him stumbling back two steps. His teeth slammed together with a loud clack that made his ears ring. The knife was wrenched from Lucas's hand and the Hunter swiped it in wide arcs while Lucas danced and dodged, giving ground as he tried to figure the timing catch the man's wrist.

NOW!

Lucas threw his left hand forward, earning a sliced forearm, but ignored it. He managed to grasp the Hunter's wrist tightly and, in a burst, released his pain and injury into his enemy. The fresh cut on his arm disappeared and so did the rest of his hurt and fatigue. He glowed with victory.

The Hunter winced, surprised for a brief moment. Lucas's hand warmed. The Hunter took a tight grip of his own and the pain slowly returned. The cut reopened. Lucas held tightly, confused and aching anew.

The burning started then, as though his skin was starting to singe. Lucas redoubled his grip, trying doggedly to force his magic to overpower whatever this Hunter was doing. Surely the tainted mage couldn't keep this up ...

The man leaned forward, grinning again, and said, "You've never faced another Healer, have you? I don't even need your blood. But I'll take it anyway."

The blood mage thrust Lucas's knife into his own chest. Lucas' stomach dropped. *Pain.*

"I die. Or you die."

Lucas looked down and saw a rapidly growing bloodstain on his shirt. It grew as the pain in his chest increased ten-fold, aching, burning, stealing his breath.

Blood dripped onto his shoulder. Blood ran down his top lip and, even as it flowed and dropped, it disappeared, sacrificed for more power, more magic. His eyes wouldn't focus. A sound was coming from his throat; he couldn't stop it, couldn't control himself.

His legs started to shake. His arm felt as though on fire, his chest bloomed with agony, but still the Hunter held his grip. His hand felt melted to the skin of the other. His magic poured out of him, and then back in; the pain compounded itself, blossoming larger, like some kind of ever-expanding field of agony. He knew that as soon as his blood started to flow, he had lost. But he'd had to try. It was only a matter of time now. He wheezed and panted for breath as his lungs constricted. He wanted to speak; his mouth twitched, moved.

The Hunter, visibly feeling his part of the pain, but somehow still smiling, leaned forward to hear Lucas's dying words, his surrender, admission of failure. Through the haze of agony, Lucas focused on only one thing. He reached up with the last energy left to him and grabbed the knife, still sticking from the mage's chest, and with a quick jerk, pulled it free. The Hunter released Lucas's arm in surprise, peeling his fingers and palm away, but Lucas managed a desperate jab with his knife, up and into the soft flesh of the Hunter's jaw and pinned his chin to his brain.

The Hunter looked surprised as he fell, dead, onto his back. Lucas felt the tension in him lessen. But as he hit the ground, shuddering and shaking, he realized that the agony was not fading from his body. Whitman skidded to a panicked halt a mere moment later, looking down at the two men in horror. He let fall his sticks and dropped to his knees beside Lucas.

"Oh no ... Wh-what can I do?" he plead. "It wasn't supposed to happen this way, Lucas, I'm so sorry."

"J-just got ov-ov-over c-c-c-onfident. Is all. P-please — Don—," he choked, lungs heaving as they filled with blood.

"DONOVAN!" Whitman screamed as he propped Lucas's head on his knees.

It made new pain flourish in the garden of his death, but Lucas didn't mind. Familiar words came to him, *"Pain is temporary — given time it will fade into distant memory. Time is motivation and movement. Busy yourself with work, time will pass, and so will pain."*

Donovan came at a sprint; Ruben at his heels looking stricken. *Poor thing.* Lucas had been looking forward to seeing the boy's face when they entered the Order's wall, saw his first class schedule, or the library ...

The pain seemed to have reached its apex; it wasn't getting any worse. *How much worse could it get?* His legs spasmed and he couldn't breathe, could only cough, sputter on his own blood. He saw it spray from his mouth and his instinct was to cover it, spare his friends the sight of it, but his arms, limp and useless, wouldn't move from the cold ground.

Donovan fell to his knees beside him, tears already pouring down his cheeks. Lucas regretted that he was their cause; his partner had suffered too much already.

"F-fo-" Lucas tried to say.

He swallowed convulsively, choked on the blood in his stomach and lungs. He closed his eyes, his face a mass of tears and blood as he coughed and finally, died.

*   *   *

Lucas looked terrible. Blood leaked from his ears and nose and mouth; a large dark patch discolored his chest. The burn of a hand marked his left wrist, and most of the skin on his same hand was gone. His chest was still, his eyes painfully squinted shut, while his mouth gaped open, slack.

"I am so sorry," Whitman said softly, his face a mask of disbelief.

Lucas's head rested on the bard's knees, and Whitman looked down at the face he supported with sorrow greater than Donovan would have expected from one they'd known for so short a time.

"I thought Healers couldn't die," Ruben said softly from behind.

"Everyone dies." Donovan stared unblinking at the ruined body of his friend.

"What were his rites?" Whitman asked as he stroked Lucas's face with a tender hand.

"The Elements," Donovan answered mechanically. He felt sick.

Whitman closed his eyes, head bowed in prayer. After a few moments he said, "We should take him with us, to be burned and thrown into the wind."

Donovan rose to his feet. He felt decades older. In the years he had known Lucas, he had come to love him. He'd trusted him with his life more than a few times, and the lives of all the children they'd Retrieved together. Now ... he felt a familiar hole in his spirit that he knew nothing would fill. He was sure it would fade with time, and he'd feel, perhaps, less broken, less shattered. But for now ...

Donovan looked from his partner's body to the Hunter that Lucas had killed even as he was dying, not quite managing to cheat death this time. The Hunter looked surprised to have the long knife run up through his head. The bodies of others were strewn about but, despite the battle, other than what was left on Lucas, Donovan saw no blood on the battlefield.

Afternoon had come, although snow-heavy clouds obscured the sun's piercing eye. The trees behind them rustled fitfully in a light breeze; Donovan could hear the river in the gorge pouring past. His mind was clearer than it had been since the pursuit had begun and, through his rage and sadness, he felt a kind of serenity — one he both appreciated and despised in himself.

He let out a slow breath and said, "Collect their horses and kit. All of it. Bring it to the bridge, as quick as you can. If I do not answer when you come close: *Do not touch me.* Do not speak; do not make noise; stand downwind. Understand?"

Whitman opened his mouth to ask questions, but Ruben, wiping tears, ran off to obey and Whitman quickly followed. When they were out of sight, Donovan left Lucas and went to sit in the shade of a tree, clearing a spot in the dirt to sit. He didn't lean on the trunk, but isolated himself from his surroundings. Deep breaths followed as he prepared. His stomach clenched with anticipation, but he relaxed, carefully reaching to open the window in the back of his mind.

Again he was assailed on all sides by sensation. His clothing felt constricting and rough, tearing at his skin. The air that brushed past him flayed the skin from his cheeks. His ears surely bled from the sound of the leaves above him; the chittering of the squirrels and chirps of birds yards away sounded like screams in his ears. The taste of his own mouth made him want to retch; the expansion of his lungs was a bruising force.

He threw himself away from his body and into the earth, blessed numbness cooling the fever of his blood. He Looked as far as he could, Saw the trees back the way they'd come; the bright flashes of light showed him Ruben's progress and, more dully, Whitman's. He turned his attention to the path they intended to take and felt fear start to overwhelm him. Shadows were everywhere, racing toward the road they followed. For miles around, here and there, dozens and dozens of shadowed spots among the lights of ordinary folk waited for any word of the magus; of Ruben's coming.

He scanned as long as he dared, spread thinner and thinner before he finally returned to his body and slammed shut his mind's window in a flash of pain. He fell onto his back and closed his eyes. His head pounded and his stomach rolled with fear and not a little doubt.

He must have slept for a short time. Hoofbeats woke him with a start as Ruben led the small herd of horses to the bridge. Whitman walked toward him while Ruben maintained the creatures, all of which were skittish near the scent of so much death.

Donovan forced himself upright, holding his head in his hands as it tried to split open down the seams of his skull.

"You can speak, but softly, please," Donovan told the young bard.

Whitman held out a waterskin and Donovan took it gratefully. He gulped down the bitter contents and sighed with relief as it started to ease his headache and nausea.

"I see Lucas and Ruben are not the only mages among you," the bard said in a low voice. He crouched on his heels; his massive size somehow compacted into an unassuming presence. Donovan's eyes flicked toward his fallen friend and he felt a sob well in his chest.

"You are a Seeker," Whitman stated with certainty. "What did you See?"

Donovan cleared his throat roughly. "Trouble. We need to go."

"I will get Lucas cleaned up for travel." Whitman stood.

"Whit," Donovan stopped him. He stared into the distance, but saw nothing at all. "Fetch some heavy rocks and rope. We'll give him to the water."

Whitman frowned. "You said he followed the Elements. Their rites are specific. We shou—"

"Get the rocks, Whitman." Donovan climbed painfully to his feet, swaying. "We can't take him with us."

"We are going to the Order! It is the safest place in the world, and not three days from here! What do you mean we cannot take him? We have nearly half a dozen unmanned horses and plenty of daylight. Those clouds say it will snow soon, so he will keep unrotten if wrapped properly, and I know how." The bard looked angry.

Donovan squinted in pain; his head throbbed and his stomach rolled. It would only get worse without rest. And without Lucas.

His eyes watered and threatened to overflow when he looked again at his partner's prone form. "If we take him with us, we'll have to give him to the first village we come to. Even if we found someone willing to take him on the straight path to the Order, the Hunters would surely find him and desecrate his body, using his blood, even dead, for their magic. And we aren't taking a straight route to the Order. The way is blocked by more Hunters than we could manage, and all of them are looking for us."

"How can you know that? I do not believe Seeking allows you to read intentions."

"I can read a map, Whitman," Donovan snapped. "There's nothing of importance ahead except the Order, which is unassailable. The Hunters know we're coming, and they know we have the boy." He gestured angrily, "One of this mess must have been a Mentalist and sent information before they died. The Hunters are sure to know that we weren't killed here. I won't put Lucas into their hands any more than I will Ruben. We can sell their horses to buy the food we can't gather."

"You just left the last town that would give you anything resembling a good price. None of these villages will give you half of their cost when you are so obviously desperate!"

"I don't care!" Donovan shouted as his ears rang. "It doesn't matter! You don't have to come with us. I'll remind you that I've known you less than a single day. I'm not particularly keen on this path, but we have to move quickly, and that means getting rid of this herd and traveling beneath the notice of anyone we pass. They have eyes everywhere — *everywhere* — and if you think we can just kill them all, I'll also remind you that fighting on an open field is very different from fighting in a town with innocents around every corner — especially when you don't know the good from the bad. A crossbow or hammer or poison will kill just the same."

"You can See them, then, Look for them in every town we come to."

Donovan barked a laugh. He felt like he was going to vomit, practically blind with his headache even after the herbs he'd swallowed. "You don't know anything about my magic. I assure you, it's practically worthless at this point." He pushed on his jaw as though it would relieve the pressure in his head. "Get the rocks. We need to move on." The bard glared at him. "Or pay me for the horses and be on your way with them. We'll carry on without you."

Whitman's nostrils flared but he turned away. Ruben, still mounted by the bridge, was watching their conversion, obviously wondering what was going on.

Donovan went to his friend and knelt beside him. "I'm sorry, Lucas. I'm so sorry. I'd take you if I could, but there's just no way. Please, please forgive me." He closed his watering eyes and held a rough breath until its shaky release. "What were they thinking only sending us? They should have sent an army. I swear I'll get Ruben to the Order, Lucas. I'll get him there myself or die trying."

Whitman returned after a few minutes, red-faced and sweating with several large rocks in his arms. Ruben trailed after him with a length of coiled rope. Whitman made halters for the weights while Ruben stood beside him and stared down at Lucas's form. His young face was unreadable.

Donovan took another drink from his waterskin and then squeezed a little onto his dead friend's face, using the cuff of his sleeve to gently wipe away the blood. Lucas was handsome, and so, so young; only twenty-five. Ruben came to kneel on Lucas's other side. He reached out hesitantly to help clean his face. The boy looked sick, but determined.

Whitman paused in his work, and then continued when he realized what Donovan was doing. His expression softened a bit. Donovan did his best, wiping at the man's mouth and nose and ears, straightening his shirt.

Ruben stood and wrenched the knife from the Hunter's chin, cleaning it on the dead man's trousers, and then handing it to Donovan. He looked at it for a long moment and then gave it back to Ruben.

"The sheath is in his boot — take it. He wouldn't mind; it's a good thing for you to have."

"Done," Whitman said kindly. The ropes were secure around Lucas's ankles and the rocks were bound tightly.

They lifted him together: Whitman at the feet, Donovan at the shoulders. The effort made his head throb even worse. Donovan could not help but wonder if he had fought as hard as he should have. Maybe they should have left Ruben as the boy suggested, using his attributes to increase their own. Then Donovan could have joined the fight sooner. But he had known — *known* — that Lucas would be just as fine as he always was— perhaps a little bruised, but fine — returning with a terrifying story, but just a story. But no one was invincible; not even Lucas.

Ruben went ahead and waited at the edge of the cliff with Whitman's lute in his hands and the knife and sheath sticking out too high from his low shoe. The two men stood at the cliff's edge and looked down into the water below. The current was swift, with rocks kicking it into whitecaps and shimmering spray.

"Are you sure?" Whitman asked.

Donovan looked down at the body he held, its face wiped clean. Lucas looked asleep, resting to regain the energy he had lost, spent, borrowed. They could take him, couldn't they?

"On three," he said instead.

They launched him as far away from the wall of the gorge as they could and watched as he fell and fell and hit with an enormous splash, instantly claimed by the current and swept off downstream.

Ruben gave the lute to Whitman, who strummed it as he watched the body disappear, humming without words. It was a tune Donovan didn't know, but he liked it. They stood, listened to Whitman's chords, and watched the water churn.

"I was going to compose a song about his heroics, just to annoy him," Whit said, still strumming lightly.

"He'd have loved that," Donovan told him.

"I saw a future with a long friendship." The bard raised his arms into the air and said in a loud voice, "Take this friend, swift water, all the way to the sea! Carry him in your thousand strong arms to the place he might find peace and rest. His name was Lucas Fain and he was a fighter! He was a brother, a comrade, a gentle, friendly man, and though I did not know him long, I knew his soul, and a better man I could not find.

"We all have troubles, wide world, embracing world. We all make mistakes; we all seek forgiveness. Use this life passed to create another, just as good, that we might learn from his example, to grow wise in the world and harm only those who would cause injustices. Teach us to forgive, teach us to be strong, teach us to trust and to love and to laugh and to cry, because that is life! Life is hard, life is short, life is wonderful and full of fear, but with one good man on this earth, we triumph. Make our journey hard, so that the end is all the more victorious. Send us the lessons we need to become better people, and always let us remember the loss of Lucas, this good man."

Whitman nodded decisively and walked away, swinging his lute onto his back to gather his things and prepare to leave. Donovan felt the tears that fell down his cheeks, but didn't bother to stop them. It was a cheap price to pay for the loss of his best friend, his brother.

He turned away and put an arm around Ruben's shoulders. "None of this was supposed to happen," he said.

Ruben looked up at him and nodded. "I know. I-I've seen death before. I just … I knew him," he said simply.

Donovan squeezed his shoulders tightly. "You're going to get to the Order. You'll learn your magic, I promise."

"Like Lucas wanted."

"Just like that."

"I trust you," Ruben said simply.

"Yeah?" Donovan asked, wiping his eyes and nose.

Ruben nodded. He trotted ahead and mounted his mare, gathering the lead reins and urging the herd across the bridge. Whitman watched from the rear.

Donovan mounted. "Whit!" he called. The bard looked back at him. "Thank you."

He nodded. "Let us not make it a habit. Your eulogy will be terrible — I have only so much brilliance to use."

"I'd best stay alive, then."

"So should we all. Work to do."

3

RUBEN LOOKED TINY IN THE BORROWED CLOAK; it belonged to Whitman, who was three times his size. His introductory claim to have the assistance of multiple people about his person had proven true in the collection of clothing and supplies in his pack. He'd avoided answering Donovan's questions about the differences in styles, but they appreciated his having them.

Four days into their travel now, a storm had blown up the day before and brought the chill of true winter. They weren't looking forward to the night rising, when stars seemed to bleed ice instead of fire.

Whitman performed in the corner of the inn they occupied, cowering from the wind any time the door opened. He played his lute and sang with a wooden bowl on the floor in front of him. It held a few coins, half a loaf of bread, and a baked potato, still steaming, which wasn't a terrible take. He looked in good cheer, at least. Donovan warmed his hands around a mug of hot tea, recently returned from selling the horses they'd taken from the Hunters. He was sure he had done a good job of bargaining — he'd grown up haggling for his father's farm — but knew they were absolutely losing out. Everyone seemed surprised that he wasn't traveling the other way, back to Ruben's hometown of Philipa. But they still jumped at the chance to swindle him out of his beasts. Ruben had admitted he couldn't stand going along, knowing that the poor creatures were going for less than half their worth. He'd grown attached.

Whitman returned to the little table that Ruben and Donovan held and set down his bowl, propping his lute beside him.

"Ungrateful wretches would not know good music if it made a merry home amongst their overgrown nose hairs, plucking dulcet tones to every sneeze."

"Why not their ear hairs?" Ruben asked, shivering and burrowing into the cloak.

"Ear hairs are too good for the likes of them," the bard answered, perusing his bowl. "Ooh, a turnip! Gods bless and keep you, fine gentles!"

The door opened to admit someone; with it came a solid wall of icy wind. Donovan adjusted his brimmed hat, courtesy of Whitman's pack, and drew his wool coat tighter around his shoulders and hips. The sword he'd kept was belted around his waist; he wasn't confident in his use of it, but hoped the sight would give others pause.

"How went the sales, Don?" Whitman asked seriously.

"As well as could be expected. I paid the stable for keeping our horses while we're here, and I managed to buy another couple of days of feed, but we'll need to provision at the next town we come to. Our money should hold us a little ways longer, but not far."

"Should it come to starvation, gentlemen, I will serenade us into dreams of plenty so that we might die painlessly, dancing amongst images of pies and potatoes. And turnips, of course." Whitman took a healthy bite from the root vegetable and held it out to Ruben, who rolled his eyes and remained bundled inside the large cloak.

"Should it come to starvation, Whit, we'd eat you first," Donovan told him, rubbing frozen hands together.

"Nonsense! The boy would go first; we could eat him in a few hearty meals, whereas the majority of my cuts would go to rot before you finished. It would be a very sad demise, to be so thoroughly wasted."

"At least we can all agree that I'd be last," Donovan said, now rubbing his arms inside his coat to warm up. Old age brought experience and poor circulation.

"You are much too tough and stringy, good man," Whitman agreed. "It would definitely be the boy."

"I just hope to give you a terrible case of indigestion, and that you fart in front of everyone you meet," Ruben answered tartly.

Whitman looked askance. "How could you? After all I have done for you? I would even make it a clean and painless death, and then roast you above a perfectly laid fire and seasoned with lemon and sage and pepper! You would be *fantastic*." Whitman jokingly wiped drool from the corner of his mouth, eyeing the boy hungrily.

"Where are we going from here?" Ruben asked.

At the change of subject, the young bard grinned and bit into his turnip once more. He handed the potato to Ruben. It was soft, and still lukewarm, so he took a healthy bite, skin and all.

Donovan pulled the hand-drawn map out of his inside pocket and unfolded it on the table. He traced a finger along the creased page. "We'll continue along this road here until it turns. Then we'll keep off the road to cut across country until we catch this stream, which will lead us down to this town here. We'll provision and then race to the base of this mountain village; they do good trading with the Order and will be able to hide us. We'll send someone from there to bring a few soldiers for protection, and go with them to the Order."

"You know this area impressively well," Whitman mused. "Have you come this way before?"

"A few times, yes, but as I said, I can read a map." Donovan folded the drawing and tucked it away. "Now that the little herd is gone, we'll draw less attention."

"Assuming we can keep ours fed and watered," Ruben added. "They eat more than Whitman does, and I've never seen a man eat a whole pie before."

"It was raspberry!" the bard exclaimed, licking his lips and remembering fondly. "And that server only charged me for a slice — a skilled tongue attracts all the lovers, boy. Remember that for your future."

"Anyway!" Donovan sighed, exasperated. "We'll stay the night here. There's no reason to carry on while it's threatening a storm, and we'll leave at dawn."

Whitman exclaimed, "A plan! They steeled themselves against the troubles that would surely meet their path, planning and plotting their future, knowing full well that reassessment lay in their way for no strategy lasts through the first bite of battle."

"Now you make it sound like we're going to fail before we've even started!" Ruben whined.

"I am only making it more dramatic," the bard explained patiently. "This way, when we succeed and get you all trained up, I will be able to compose my epic and win fame and fortune across the lands! King Braun will reward me with more gold than I can count and the courtiers will throw themselves down at my feet."

"Oh yes? They'll be trying to get away from the shadow of your giant head, then."

Whitman clutched his chest. "A barb! So cruel the poisoned tip; so heartbreaking, to be betrayed by a friend. Avenge me, dear Donovan! With your last breath, avenge me!" Whitman slid under the table.

Donovan reached over and flicked Ruben's ear. The boy grabbed the smarting appendage and glared at the older man. Whitman came out from under the table at impressive speed, and plopped himself down beside the boy to take a bite from his potato.

"Hey!" Ruben snarled, wrenching his arm, and meal, away.

"You caused my death; the least you can do is give me a bite!" the young man replied, unashamed.

"You ate your turnip!"

"I offered you some!"

"All right, you two. Don't attract attention."

"I cannot help it, dear Donovan. I attract all sorts with my glib tongue, sultry voice, and excellent sense of hygiene. It is who I am."

"Yes, well, I'd rather the two of *us* stayed unnoticed."

"Until my epic is written, so when we get to the Order, you had best study hard, understand? I refuse to write a story and song about some mediocre mage who fails to even magic his own shoes tied."

"Hush!" Donovan snapped. "Don't speak so easily about our destination. The walls have ears, and I'd rather not risk a tail."

"Mm, no, that wouldn't look at all impressive," Whitman agreed. "Unless it were a cat's tail."

Donovan glared at him.

"Where are we sleeping?" Ruben asked. "I'm exhausted."

"We'll have to wait until the inn closes so we can kip down on the floor. I don't want to spend our coin on a room," Donovan told him.

"There is no reason not to," Whit said, looking into his bowl of earnings. "This will pay for one and it will be safer than being in the common area."

Donovan hesitated, and then nodded. "All right. Thank you, Whit. You're very generous."

Whitman grinned and exclaimed, "Of course I am! Heroes are always generous and kind and handsome. I would be a fool not to live up to my destiny now, as traveling in the company of heroes, after all, makes one a hero."

"You really need to stop saying that," Ruben said wearily. "You're making me want to run away to work on a pig farm."

"I wish you would!" Whitman told him seriously. "All heroes come from humble upbringings and, frankly, tending horses in a town that specialized their breeding and sale is a bit bold. You will probably end up being a mediocre hero and drag me down with you. Pig tending would be much more appropriate."

"Why don't you go purchase our room, Whit?" Donovan interjected, saving himself from the insults that were sure to follow.

The two bickered fairly constantly, but at least it was a sort of sibling rivalry — all of it biting, but with filed-down teeth. Whitman trotted off to talk to the barkeeper, haggling for a reasonable price on the room.

"How are you doing, lad?" Donovan asked Ruben.

Ruben shrugged within the folds of Whitman's large cloak. "Fine."

"Having doubts?"

Ruben shrugged again.

Donovan nodded slowly, thinking of the day to follow.

"I wish I could earn us something," Ruben said. "If I could get my magic to work, I could do something grand."

"Not all magic needs to be grand to be impressive, son," Donovan pointed out.

"Lucas was grand," Ruben said quietly.

A band tightened around Donovan's chest and stomach and made all of his muscles tense and sore. He managed a nod and swallowed the welling emotion in his throat. "He was, absolutely. You had a lot in common. I'm sure you'll learn to be grand in your own time."

Ruben nodded to himself.

"Look," Donovan said quietly, glancing around them. "I don't know as much about magic as any of the instructors in the Order — I'm not supposed to. I learned to Seek when I was younger than you, and then went back to my life, pretty much figuring that I'd never use it again. I can't tell you a whole lot about your talents, but I do know that the small things you've done are extraordinary — and rarer even than Healers — and that you're going to learn fantastic things when we get there, all right?"

"*If* we get there."

"Well, with that attitude," Donovan answered with a half-smile, hiding his own feelings on their chances.

Ruben returned a more genuine smile and then stood, seeing that Whitman was waving them over. They joined him and went through a doorway to the back of the inn. A set of stairs led down into a basement, but they avoided those, instead finding passage through a hallway lined with doors. It was darker than Hanover's inn in Philipa, and more poorly made. Some of the doors were dented or misaligned to their doorways; one had a string instead of a knob. Cheap cloth covered the holes in two others in a temporary repair.

Whitman led them to a door midway down the hall, and pulled it open without a key to let the other two inside.

'Cramped' was the first word that came to mind. The bed was made for one, but might fit two if they were friendly or small. A chair sat propped against the back wall, missing one leg, along with a board to slide across the door to lock it. Donovan didn't feel like it would help much, as there was a not-so-thin gap between the door and the wall, which would be easy enough to slip a blade through to lift the latch. Still, they put it down for the relative peace of mind, if nothing else, and stacked their bags in the corner.

Whitman laid out his sleeping roll and nodded at the bed. "The two of you can share that — I will risk the floor. It is sure to have fewer fleas."

"Ever the gentleman," Donovan said, eyeing the 'mattress' with trepidation.

A thin blanket lay stretched across it; it might have once been a light blue or green, but was now a suspicious gray from either too much washing or not enough — the latter being far more likely. A single, flat pillow rested at the top; a greasy stain on its middle showed where most renters put their head. The canvas outer-layer was more patch than original casing, with moldy-looking straw poking out of a few of the newer holes, or older patches. The frame was pine wood, old enough to look as though it needed a strong drink. It had ropes to hold the mattress and the knots looked firm, if frayed, but worn to nearly nothing where they met the wood. A stain, hopefully blood, showed at the foot of the mattress, a bit of the blanket, and onto the frame.

"I think it's moving," Ruben said nervously. "I want to sleep on the floor with Whit."

"You are being silly, Ben, it is not moving," Whitman told him. "The rustling sounds you hear are its excitement at finally having a companion to share the lonely nights with — it gets hungry in here all alone. Besides, you kick in your sleep."

"Come on, lads, we've been sleeping on the ground the last few nights, this is sure to be an improvement," Donovan said, giving the bed a few healthy pats.

After they killed the roaches and fleas that he'd disturbed, they made themselves as comfortable as they could on the floor, with two bedrolls below them to soften the floor; the other two atop for warmth. Ruben insisted on sleeping in the middle. They didn't bother changing clothes, and all three loosened their boots, but kept them on. Whitman was quietly snoring in moments; Ruben followed suit shortly thereafter. Donovan's eyelids were too heavy to keep open, but his mind was too busy to slow down.

Lucas's face kept flashing into view on the backs of his eyelids — his features faded and hard to remember precisely, growing fainter already. It made Donovan sad to know he'd eventually forget his friend's face without a portrait on hand. Lucas's burial still didn't sit well, but he knew they'd had no other option. You needed a very hot fire to burn a body to ash, and they hadn't the time or ability for that.

After passing through these towns, he knew they'd never have managed to send him to the Order and, in the end, they'd have buried him in some graveyard of a town he'd never known or enjoyed amongst bodies he'd never met.

The thought didn't comfort Donovan as much as he'd hoped. As far as Ruben's misgivings about himself: those would change, and quickly. Still, he worried that they'd face a threat he couldn't control, or the boy would grow impatient and try something on his own — it was dangerous performing magic without proper instruction, but he didn't know how to help. Any encouragement not to do anything would surely prompt him to opposition; children were like that at this age. With luck and good winds, they'd be able to follow the plan and arrive within the next three or four days. Otherwise, he didn't know what they'd do. There were too many Hunters, and no guaranteed way to tell the Order of their plight.

They were past arrival time already. Vale would wonder where they were and send out a search party — but even that thought caused a pang in Donovan's chest, knowing that the searchers would likely be captured or killed by the Hunters on the roads.

He sighed, shifting to a more comfortable position. Ruben curled sleepily into the line of his body and Donovan pulled the boy against him; the lad didn't wake for a moment, his breathing even and small. Parental feelings that he'd managed to subdue years ago started to waken, and now more heartbreaking memories threatened to overwhelm him.

He forced his mind aside from those thoughts and instead pictured walking down the halls of the Order, in and out of doors, through courtyards and into buildings, until that was all he saw. He continued this mental meandering until he felt himself floating away and falling into it, his conscious mind understanding that he was going to sleep at last while his subconscious was just longing for the rest that the images would bring.

$$* \qquad * \qquad *$$

It didn't last.

Donovan's eyes flickered open and he glanced down to see Ruben holding a finger to his lips, warning him to be quiet. Whitman was still quietly snoring. Donovan lay patiently, wondering what sound had caused him to stir, when it happened again. Someone was trying to open the door. Ruben looked at him expectantly, eyes wide and worried, waiting to be told what to do.

"Hunters wouldn't pick the lock," he whispered in the boy's ear.

Ruben looked calmer at that logic.

Donovan decided quickly. They would need to ensure that they were undisturbed for the rest of the night; there were still several hours before dawn.

He rose quietly to his feet and threw off the bedding in a large motion. The board across the door was being shifted bit by bit by a long, dull, pitted and rusty dagger. Donovan took a moment to compose himself. In a swift movement, he threw the board up and pushed the door open, hard, into the face and body of the intruder in the hall.

The man grunted and gasped with surprise and pain, stumbling and falling against the opposite wall, the knife flying down the hall as he flailed, before reaching to grab his smarting face. Donovan stepped into the hall and pushed a hard kick into the man's hip bone. The intruder yelped as he fell, sliding down the wall to his backside. Donovan put his hands out to brace against the wall as he brought his left knee up and forward into the man's face, slamming the man's head back into the boards.

The intruder's nose hadn't been bleeding, but now it was. He howled again, clutching at his face with gnarled and scarred fingers. Donovan stepped back and crossed his arms. He looked down at the cringing mass of unfortunate humanity who whimpered and grasped at his damaged face and bad situation.

"You knocked?" Donovan asked in a calm tone.

The man looked thoroughly confused as he glanced up and down the empty hall to see if anyone was going to help him. His mouth gaped open in surprise and pain.

"Thieving from travelers will get you nothing but a jail cell — if they have those in this miserable place." Donovan grimaced with distaste, weariness suddenly laying heavily on him. "Just go away," he finally said, turning around.

"You broke by dose!" the man exclaimed, seeming only then to grasp the situation.

Donovan looked over his shoulder with one eyebrow raised. "Be grateful. If you come back, I'll break your legs."

He continued into the room and closed the door. He laid the board down again, for all the good it would do.

Whitman was still snoring gently, a frown on his round face, but Ruben sat against the wall behind the door. Donovan looked at him curiously and Ruben shrugged.

"In case there was more than one."

"You're a good lad, you know that?"

Ruben nodded good-naturedly and laid back down, curling up on his side, knees tucked to his chest and hands under his chin. Donovan lay down beside him and pulled the bedrolls back over to cover them, concealing Ruben's entire body. Donovan shivered until his body warmed. He wished he'd thought to pack another coat. Why would he, though? He'd never planned to be out more than a few days.

He closed his eyes again. Just a few more days — maybe he'd finally retire. He was getting on in years, after all, and travel was a young man's game. They had plenty of Retrievers trained. He wasn't needed. He was just one more old mage in a world of young ones.

*   *   *

"I *cannot* believe you would be so cruel as to not wake me," Whitman complained.

They were on the road again, their horses frisky in the morning chill, displaced snow marking their path through the untouched fields.

"I sleep and dream of uninteresting dribble, while feet from me, a foul plot was afoot and thwarted by our very own Donovan Second-Sight the Merciful and Unforgiving!" He had a fist thrust out in front of him, looking very dramatic.

"I swear by all that is holy, Whitman, if you call me that ever again ..." Donovan shook his head while Ruben cackled.

Whitman shrugged, "It was one of the better ones I came up with. I am willing to reconsider, however. I do maintain that all of my work is mine alone and any suggestions made will be taken under due consideration, but no promises given as to whether or not they are accepted as final decisions."

"Spoken like a barrister." Ruben rolled his eyes.

"How *dare* you, sir!"

"Come on you two, it's early and we've a long day ahead," Donovan interrupted, pleading.

"This time ..." Whitman hissed, trotting past and making threatening hand gestures at Ruben.

Clouds floated thick overhead. The trees were still; the air without a breeze to stir them. A few winter birds chirped and rustled in the branches. They spied a doe in the bushes, staring at them with liquid brown eyes before she bounded away.

They passed the hours mostly in quiet. Whitman rode ahead while Ruben stayed beside Donovan, occasionally adjusting the packhorse's lead around his saddlehorn.

The boy asked, "What's it like at the Order?"

"What do you mean?" Donovan asked, scanning their surroundings with practiced caution.

"I mean," Ruben considered his thoughts. "I know people go there to learn magic, and lots of them stay to work. I know there's a wall — a *giant* wall around the place — but not much else.

"Well," Donovan said, "you're right about the wall — it's nearly sixty feet high with walkways for lookouts. There are several floors to the wall in case of attack to give archers plenty of position to aim from and mages space to work. Plenty of defenses in place in case of attack, but they haven't been used since I can remember. Lots of entrances and exits, too. It's a small town unto itself." Donovan smiled at him. "There is housing for those mages who stay there — some of them have families, so they're given more privacy. The students live in dormitories near the classes in shared rooms. The kitchen is heated all day and all night to make the food that everyone eats, and the surrounding towns and farms all have heavy trade in and out.

"The king removes taxes in percentages for those who aid the Order, so it's really good to do trade there. Inside is all polished stone and wood and it's beautiful. Artisans from all over the kingdom want their work displayed in the palace and in the Order, so there's quite a lot of that. There are special classrooms to keep the students and instructors safe. The infirmary is very good, obviously — it's bigger than the one at the palace — and some students without magic are there to learn surgeries and whatnot.

"They keep all kinds of animals that the students and aides care for — chickens, goats, pigs, all kinds — and there's an underground river that keeps them in fresh water. They have gardens, too. Not enough to feed the entire town forever, but on rations, they could survive a lengthy siege. And they have scholars there that don't use magic, because it has the most extensive library in the world — books on anything you can imagine."

"You talk about siege and armies a lot — are they often attacked?" Ruben asked, looking nervous.

"They used to be," Donovan answered. "Before and right after the Cataclysm when the Hunters were stronger."

"Do you know what caused the Cataclysm?" Ruben asked.

Donovan shook his head. "No one does. It destroyed the original Order and half of the palace; most of the records with it. Very little of substance remains from then — three hundred years and we still don't know much of anything about it — though there are scholars who have devoted their lives to learning what they can."

The boy's eyes were wide. "What about the people there? Are they all mages? Except the scholars, I mean."

"Most of them have magic because of being the descendants of others there, or being brought like you are. A large number of people brought to be trained end up staying to teach, or research new technologies and knowledges, or just live their lives in the community there. Their children go to classes, like you will. You're a couple of years older than the children usually are, but I think you'll fit in just fine."

"You left," Ruben pointed out.

Donovan nodded, "Yes, well, I had plans at home, and didn't think much of my magic."

"You still don't, though, right?"

"Right." He hesitated. "I can't use it often, and the information gleaned from what I can See is only helpful in situations like this, so a lot of times the effort involved doesn't justify the gain. I received my training, my family got a tax break while I was away learning since I was still a boy, and then I went back home and lived my life there."

"But how did you come back to work for the Order if you went back home?" Ruben asked curiously.

Donovan clenched his jaw for a moment before saying, "That's a more complicated story for another time, all right?"

Ruben nodded, looking chastised. They continued on in a somewhat awkward silence for a few minutes until Whitman trotted back to them.

"How goes it?" he asked.

"Fine," Ruben answered. "Did you see anything up ahead?"

Whitman glanced at Donovan after Ruben's quick answer and said, "I did not see any tracks. It opens up a bit before closing back down to tree cover. I think we should stop for dinner soon, rest the beasts, maybe walk a few miles, and then carry on. Donovan?"

Donovan nodded. "Yes, that sounds fine. Scout us a good place to stop, then."

The bard gave a half-hearted salute and wheeled back around.

Ruben looked eager at the prospect of food, but he was still quiet.

"I didn't mean to stop your questions," Donovan said gently.

"Oh," the boy started. "I just— you didn't seem like you wanted to talk anymore."

"I don't like talking about my past much, is all. But if you're curious about the Order, I'm happy to tell you more. The class structure, how mean the teachers are — things like that." He smiled encouragingly.

Ruben managed a small smile of his own and he said, "All right, then, how mean are the teachers?"

"So incredibly very mean; makes me seem like a gentle angel."

Ruben laughed. "You're not mean; you're just stony. Nothing wrong with being stony, so long as you don't wear edges — is what my da used to tell me."

"Did you know your father well?"

Ruben shrugged. "For a few years. I told you he got into a brawl and someone broke a bottle over his head and he got carried away, ma said. He went to prison in some other town. She couldn't afford me after that, and sold me to the stables. Garth said she left town after. 's all right. They'd be pleased, I think, that I was going to the Order and all — I mean, magic, right?"

"Right."

"So the teachers are mean, and they have animals, and it's hard to get in and out of," Ruben said pensively. "Sounds like a terrible place to go — I think we should turn back."

Donovan laughed and said, "Nope, you agreed to go, and you wouldn't want to break your word, right? Looks like you're stuck with me, all the way to the end."

"Figures. Does Whitman have to come along?"

"No, but he doesn't look like he's planning on leaving any time soon. You should ask him to show you how to use those sticks of his — they're probably safer than blades and easier to find on the road."

"I don't know about safer. Did you see that man's elbow explode when he hit it so hard?"

"True ..."

"I wonder where he learned to fight like that."

"I guess none of us really know much about each other, huh?"

"I guess so. It's all right though; I like you anyway."

"What about Whitman?"

Ruben chewed on his lip for a moment and said, "I guess he can stay. He's a good bloke. Don't tell him I said that."

"I wouldn't dare."

4

"A WORD IN YOUR EAR?" Whitman asked.

"Is everything all right?" Donovan stepped away from where Ruben was stacking branches for a small fire.

Whitman told him, "There is a town half a day ahead. I thought you might consider Seeking; it might be the kind of place they would post Hunters, going by the size and location."

Donovan nodded slowly.

"I would not ask it; I know it is painful, but I believe they will soon be able to anticipate our arrival. Should we find someone, we can select a new route."

"It's sound logic, Whit. You don't need to keep selling me. What's actually on your mind?"

Whitman gave him a long look. "The town is called Weston."

Donovan felt a shiver go down his spine, but kept his face blank. "Yes, I know. I plotted the course."

Whitman took a half-pace closer. "I have good ears for accents, and I read body language like it is a book about my own history, so forgive me for pointing out that your concern is very obvious when you keep still like that."

"Make your point."

"You are from here, are you not — this area, possibly even this town up ahead?"

Donovan blinked, but didn't answer.

"Look, if they recognize you—"

"I haven't been here in sixteen years."

"That is not long in places like this," the young man argued earnestly. "We can pass by, but we will need to hunt for provisions, which will slow us down, and buying grain for the horses would not be a bad idea since it will snow again soon, maybe today or tomorrow."

"We'll be at the Order in two days, Whit. We can last until then."

"Assuming we find no further delays, yes. I merely suggest we tread carefully. I do not know about your past, but I know something tragic happened. You do not need to tell me anything, but understand that *I* understand. That said, such a happening might inspire memories. Consider if people are still sitting down in the pub saying 'remember that bloke Donovan with the recognizable face? I wonder what he has gotten up to since the such-and-such happened' and they spot you ... If there are any Hunters, they will be on us like bears on berries — and even if there are not, they move quickly. They might catch up on the road. At the very least, we should sleep outside tonight."

Donovan weighed the words. "That's fine. After last night, beds aren't exactly appealing. If we want grain for the horses, we'll have to go into town."

"Then I will go — I will earn a few coins and make our purchases and we will pass by. If we are this close to the Order, I say we ride through the night."

"What happens if we meet a Hunter, then, exhausted and unable to run away with tired horses?"

Whitman conceded with a nod. "So Look ahead. I will make the meal and have a headache cure ready. Do you need to eat first?"

"No, gods, no. And I won't be able to eat immediately after, but I'll need more than my share before I sleep."

Whitman clapped him on the shoulder and walked away, making some joke to Ruben. He set to cooking while the boy brushed down the horses, taking off their saddles and packs.

Donovan inhaled deeply and took stock of himself. No injuries; nothing too sore or stiff. His back and rear would be impressively painful since they were still tense from riding, but there was no helping that. He found a shady spot and started to sit when Whitman trotted back over, bedroll in hand.

"I am sure it will not help much, but surely it is an improvement over sitting on the ground."

Donovan took it gratefully. "That's very thoughtful of you."

Whitman strolled away again while Donovan folded the bedroll and put it like a cushion beneath him. Sitting as comfortably as he could, he began his ritual once more, breathing, calming himself, patiently waiting until his mind was clear and his body was still.

When he opened the window in his mind, it let forth a burst of agony, and then he was away — spreading out, ever outward through the earth, viewing it from an impossible vantage, all the lines of life touching his as he passed through them like dots of light, twinkling here and there.

He scanned the area, seeing shadows where Hunters tread — their markings obvious for those who knew what to See. The village ahead, Weston, *home*, bore no such signs of shadow, but there was something bright ...

He looked closer, although he knew he needed to return to his body very soon. That spot there — was that a group, or —

PAIN!

Donovan roared with distress, racing back — he couldn't. He was stuck, stuck outside of his body while the torture continued. *What was happening?* Terrifying realization hit him like a shovel to the face. Instead of staring down at the world, he turned his vision up.

He Saw another form, a Seeker as himself. This had never happened before, but he had no time to hesitate. He drove forward aggressively and turned his attention to simultaneously building a wall to shield his mind from assault, and to forming his own attack. Time was the most important factor: if he didn't get back to his body soon, he never would. His senses would become overwhelmed and he would die, his mind turned to mush. Yet, his opponent would be facing the same problem.

With all of his being, he threw thorns of agony at his opponent's mind. The barrage on his own mind stopped for a moment before starting anew, but this time he was better prepared. He continued to attack his opponent, trembling with the effort. He tried to back away, toward his body, but as long as this other person occupied even a small part of his mind, he could not escape.

He struggled, imagining arrows, spears, ballista instead of thorns. The attacker hesitated, and he changed his tactic; keep changing, keep them off their guard. He switched to the bludgeoning force of a club, the shock and burn of lightning, the mind-numbing boom of thunder reverberating out of control.

The last one gained him a moment, but a moment was all he needed. His mind felt clear of intruders in that short second, and he fled to his shell, faster than he ever had, unable even to prepare himself for the physical pain of his return, which would surely be severe.

He opened his eyes and flinched — but there was nothing.

That was even more terrifying — had his absence flooded his mind with enough stimuli that he'd lost his senses? No ... A hand was touching his shoulder. If he hadn't been so confused by his gentle return, that would have terrified him more than it did; contact was harmful while he was Seeking.

He turned at the waist and saw Ruben, one small hand on his shoulder, the other on the trunk of the tree Donovan was seated under. The boy was frowning in concentration, tense through his entire person.

The tree was dead.

It had been alive.

Ruben opened his eyes, blinking and wavering for a moment. He saw that Donovan was looking and gave a small, sheepish smile. "Are you all right?"

Donovan stared at him, and then at the tree. Moments ago, there had been a healthy, living thing there. Now it was brittle, gray and old, and looked as though it could collapse at any moment.

"What did you do?" Donovan whispered.

Ruben shrank from his tone.

"Likely saved you," Whitman answered from beside him. The bard had never sounded so grave.

"What happened?" Donovan pleaded.

"I could ask the same question. You just went ... berserk."

"I what?" Donovan asked.

He looked back at Ruben, who nodded in agreement. Donovan put out an apologetic hand to him and the boy took it warmly.

"It was scary," Ruben said.

"First moment, you were sitting, a bit pale, but unmoving, seemingly lost in thought and far away, but in the blink of an eye you were screaming and holding your head as though some demon was clawing from your skull. Your eyes went bloodshot and your skin grayed. You were shaking and screaming, howling like an animal."

"The horses spooked," Ruben added.

"You'd warned us not to touch you, but before I could stop him, the boy ran over and grabbed your shoulder."

"You were really warm, like you had a fever, but much worse." Ruben rubbed his hands together. "I knew you were hurting, so I just ... did like Lucas." He blushed and poked the toe of his boot through the damp leaves. He still wore Lucas's dagger in his boot.

"He took pain into himself, Ruben. That's incredibly dangerous!" Donovan shook at the idea of the boy putting himself at such risk.

Whitman nodded, brows furrowed and eyes wide. "Ben there was panting like he had no breath, and the next thing I knew, he was *glowing* as bright as day and a chorus of angels was singing about his head, clothed only in—"

"For all that is holy, Whit, this is serious — what *happened?*" Donovan cut him off, trying to keep his calm.

He took a deep breath and looked back at Ruben. The boy stared back at him, and chewed the inside of his lip. He didn't look surprised by Whitman's words, but he was clearly listening very hard to them.

Whitman cleared his throat. "My apologies. There were no angels, but the boy *was* glowing, and the air around shimmered, like a mirage. He slapped a hand onto that tree and before my eyes it aged and bent, withered and dying. Even as that occurred, you stopped screaming and your skin colored healthy again. After a moment, Ben's glow faded, but he froze still as a statue. The tree kept decaying; one of the branches back there fell to the ground. I was worried they would rain onto you both, but you blinked a few times and shuddered like a dog in the rain, and here we are. It cannot have been more than two minutes."

Donovan didn't know what to say. Ruben was quiet behind him and Whitman was breaking up twigs.

After the silence had stretched thin, Whitman asked, "Do not hold back on my account, oh Seeker. What happened to you?"

Donovan rubbed his eyes with the heels of his hands as he remembered the sensation of entrapment, like a rabbit in a snare. A shiver ran down his spine.

"I was attacked," he answered.

Whitman's eyebrows rose and Donovan heard Ruben shift behind him.

"Someone, another Seeker, must have been Looking at the same time and they noticed me first."

"I have heard rumors of the possibility of such a thing, but rumors only," the bard said, intrigued.

"It's not something widely known. I usually don't even check, since my time is limited and the chance is very slim."

"And so you fought. Detail, please." Whitman's fingers were twitching, as though already composing for an epic mêlée.

"It was explained to me as a battle of wills, of imagination. I only tried once, as a boy in the Order with a classmate, and I hated it then. This was worse." He turned at the hips to look at Ruben. "Thank you. You saved my life."

Ruben looked surprised and confused. "Y-you're welcome?" he answered.

He came around to sit beside Whitman, fiddling with the discarded twigs on the ground and ducking his head shyly.

"You succeeded, I take it, so they are dead?" Whitman asked. His tone was somber.

Donovan stretched his neck. "I don't think so. I just managed to get back to my body, which was my goal. If they'd kept me out too much longer, without Ruben, I'd have likely died anyway."

"I imagine they are still out there, and now they know where we are heading."

"I'd say so. They might try again when they've had a rest, unless they have a Healer on hand. But the odds of running into them again are incredibly unlikely."

Whitman touched his forehead. "Forgive my assumptions: was it a Hunter?"

Donovan considered his answer. "I would think so. But I honestly don't know."

Whitman frowned in thought. "Do many Seekers know of this kind of fighting?"

"Probably," Donovan shrugged. "They didn't spend much time on it, but it's taught in your final year, as a warning more than anything else."

"Could it be that someone laid a kind of trap for you? Who knows that you're a Seeker?"

Donovan scoffed. "Anyone who might have wondered enough to ask; it's not a secret."

"What about from Weston?" Donovan looked at the young man, who returned the look pointedly. "Did you see any Hunters up ahead before the attack?"

"None that I noticed."

"I see ..."

Ruben was looking back and forth between the two of them. "Am I missing something?"

"Let's get back to the road," Donovan replied. "We can make a few more miles before we stop again."

"Are we staying in a town tonight?" the boy asked hopefully, as he helped Donovan to his feet.

"I think it's wiser if we don't."

"Only there's a big storm coming, and the snow will be pretty thick, so if we don't, we should at least get oats for the horses; they'll be hungry trying to stay warm."

Donovan turned to stare at him.

Ruben stared back, blinked, and then said, "Um, when I was Healing you, it was like I could see all over, like staring down at an anthill, but the ants had torches, like. And when I looked upward, I saw some big, heavy clouds coming this way, slow, but fast like when a horse is at gallop and far away and they're just in front of you all a sudden? They, the clouds, felt really cold, icy, and it was like a mare about to drop a foal — that feeling you get, you know? A sort of pressure?"

Whitman looked expectantly at Donovan.

He struggled to find the words, "I- that's not what I See when I'm Seeking. But I believe you."

"Am I in trouble?" the boy asked softly. "I'm really sorry — I know you said not to touch you, but you were screaming and I just knew I could do something ..."

"What you did was right, Ruben, you're not in trouble. I'm just at a loss of what to tell you, is all." Donovan sighed and ran a hand over his tight curls. "I was going to suggest that we press on past this town, but if Ruben's right, which he surely is, then we'll have to stop inside."

"We can keep to ourselves," Whitman suggested. "Do you know how long the storm will last? Will we be able to move on in the morning?" he asked Ruben.

The boy tilted his head in thought and said, "There will be snow, but it shouldn't be too deep for the horses, and we'll be able to leave by morning. Or afternoon. It depends on the wind."

"Sound advice," Whitman replied, coming to his feet with a bound. "Let us be going, friends. It is yet a couple of hours to shelter." He strode away to pack up their things and ready the horses.

"Ruben," Donovan said before the boy could run off to help. "What you did was right, and it was good. I am immensely grateful. But please try not to do any more magic until we get to the Order, all right? Without training, if something distracts you, or you get scared, it can go out of control. I don't want you to worry; I just want you to be cautious, and safe."

"Sure," the boy conceded easily. "I am sorry, though. I- I think I saw a bit of your mind?" He looked sheepish again.

Donovan felt his stomach flip. "You saw a bit of my mind? What part?"

"Well, two parts ... one was you very young, and you were running down a corridor, all white stone around. You were, um, you were crying."

Donovan vividly remembered his first time Seeking. He hadn't handled it well.

"And the other?"

"You were an adult, but I don't know how long ago. Before you had gray in your hair. You were holding a baby and there was a woman with black hair like yours and a big man behind her — he didn't look very friendly."

Of course he would see that. "Anything else?"

Ruben shook his head tightly. "Not that I remember. I'm sorry."

"It's all right; you didn't know. No harm done."

The boy nodded furiously. "I just didn't want you to think I was keeping secrets."

"Why don't you go help Whitman?"

"Sure." He trotted off, head down.

Of all the things to see. Donovan rubbed his forehead, still surprised at how good he felt. A glance back at the dead tree reminded him why.

If Ruben was already demonstrating his abilities in this way, the Order would need to get him trained quickly. Fire, Healing, Metalizing, even seeing weather patterns ... Donovan felt a sudden surge of urgency about his already-essential task. The town ahead would cause enough trouble as it was, if he was recognized. No, he'd keep his head down, and they'd pass through easily enough. His mind flashed back to the second image Ruben had shared. His hands clenched involuntarily. They'd have to go unnoticed. Things could get bad if they were noticed.

*   *   *

The storm landed when they were just an hour outside of the town. The temperature dropped rapidly, bringing a biting wind and blanket of snow. Ruben was still bundled in Whitman's cloak, which left Whitman in a summer-weight from his bag, shivering as the wind cut through the lighter cloth. Donovan had his wool coat, but it didn't do much against the icy breeze; it left his legs feeling like blocks of ice, burning with every movement.

When the town appeared in front of them, lanterns lit above its gates, their sense of relief was palpable. Even Donovan, who still knew this area like he knew his favorite meal, was worried they might get turned around with the snow coming down so heavily around them.

The stable wasn't hard to find — first thing through the gates and attached to the back of the small inn. Donovan led the way with his collar turned up and his hat brim down. The warmth inside the stable was a sudden relief, but they were slow to thaw.

The hostler put their mounts away. Ruben eyed the man with disdain, judging his abilities with a skeptical eye. Donovan nudged the boy along inside to find a table.

Whitman took care of paying the owner of the inn and stables — a slight man, short, but wiry. His name floated to Donovan's mind: Campbell. He didn't appear to recognize Donovan, who kept his hat brim between them.

The fires in two large, opposite fireplaces crackled merrily. Within one a large pot of stew hung boiling, with an arrangement of mugs lining the stone hearths. An older man playing the pipes in front of the second fireplace glanced up when they entered, spotted Whitman's lute, and narrowed his eyes without missing a note.

The inn seemed to be about half-full. A game of cards was in play in the corner; it looked like a business proposition of some kind underway in another. The middle of the room was primarily claimed by people drinking alone, others with friends, and one man with ledgers spread all over his table and a harried expression on his face. They chose a table near the center, as far from the other patrons as possible.

Donovan checked his pockets and said, "We'll each have a bowl of soup, but if we want to get grain and afford a room tonight both, Whitman will have to earn us something."

"I'll speak with the innkeeper, then," the bard said, standing and going to the bar.

Ruben took off the voluminous cloak, and draped it over the back of his chair. "Do you have any cards?"

Donovan looked at him with surprise, and said, "No, I don't. You want to play?"

"I could win us some money from those men there." He nodded in the direction of the gamblers in the corner.

Donovan frowned. "When did you learn to gamble?"

Ruben hesitated. That was answer enough.

Donovan leaned forward to whisper, "Boy, are you suggesting that you use magic to cheat at cards?"

"It wouldn't be much ..."

Donovan leaned back in his chair, and looked down at Ruben with his most impressive expression of disappointment etched across his features. The silence stretched horribly. Ruben grew more and more timid, shrinking in his seat and trying to look around to distract himself from his shame, but ultimately his eyes returned to the top of the table.

"What's going on?" Whitman asked with a smile. His eyes ran over the shrunken Ruben to the disapproving Donovan. He sat heavily and waited.

"Go on and tell the man, Ruben."

The boy swallowed hard, "I suggested that we cheat at cards. With magic. To get money."

Whitman nodded slowly, and looked sideways at Donovan. "That is pretty serious, Ben. You could be jailed for improper use of magic."

"I won't, though, I promise."

"Look, throw this penny into the bard's bowl, all right?" He handed Ruben a copper coin and the lad took off obediently.

Whitman ran a hand through his curls and said, "When this bard is done with his set, I am allowed to play until the inn closes, and that will afford us a room, but no coin. After we buy grain, we will be poorer than a church-mouse. If the boy can cheat at cards, then I say let him and damn the consequences. If anyone finds out, they'll let him off with a warning in these extenuating circumstances."

"It's not even the cheating that concerns me, Whit. It's the fact that he's already considered using his magic for devious deeds. And I just told him hours ago not to use his damn magic at all. If the Order finds out, he could be tried, fined, imprisoned — I want him to think about that idea with nothing but disgrace."

"That is all well and fine, but unless you can think of a better way— Did he say anything?" Whitman switched tone and volume mid-sentence, looking at Ruben with interest.

Ruben looked at the two of them sheepishly, unable to meet Donovan's eye. "He just nodded and kept playing."

"Hm. Well, maybe I can ease his mood. I will claim my meal in a little while. Time to lighten some spirits!"

Whitman strode off, lute in hand, smiling cheerfully at any patron who met his eye.

Donovan looked at Ruben and said, "I think you've learned that using magic dishonestly, taking advantage of those with or without is more disgraceful than I can express to you."

Ruben nodded again, close to tears now.

"Why don't you find out where we can purchase however much grain you think we'll need for the rest of our route? That would be very helpful."

Ruben swallowed hard, and hopped out of his chair to trot over to the innkeeper.

Donovan looked down at the table, his hat brim shading his eyes from the gentle light of the room. Normally he would have taken it off, but he'd already spotted several people here that he recognized; a few others were still wearing their hats, so he didn't stand out. No one had yet given him a second glance, but keeping his face low and his voice lower was the better plan.

He was tired. Incredibly tired. For being his age, he was in excellent shape physically and mentally, but this game of cat-and-mouse had him exhausted beyond what he'd believed possible. Dozens of Hunters, a magus-child in need of training, and a headstrong bard with more depth than he'd have expected, plus this round-about trip leading him back home, and surfacing memories he'd long ago fought to bury.

He missed Lucas. That man had a way with words and silences that kept his mind on the right track. He remembered the man's advice, *'Don't overthink it, Don, just put one foot in front of the other until the job's done.'*

Donovan waved down a serving woman and signaled for three bowls of soup. By the time she returned with them, Whitman was coming back from the other musician with a thoughtful look on his face. The piper was still playing, slower tunes than before, letting the quiet mood linger.

The young bard took his seat and dug into his soup with mechanical speed and precision, wasting not a drop, and barely stopping to chew. Donovan watched him with amusement, eating his own at a more leisurely pace. He wished he had some pepper to add a bit of seasoning.

When Whitman started to slow down, Donovan asked him, "Learn anything?"

Ruben arrived and hopped into his seat, not bothering with a spoon, but drinking down his broth as quick as he could.

Whitman answered, "Well, this bard considers this town to be his own and did not appreciate my reminding him that all bards are legally considered nomads and without specific claims unless given a letter of permission from the king. He does not have one, so he said he would finish this song and then let me play until midnight. It is the longest song he knows, of course, but I should get my turn soon enough."

Ruben reported, "The grain merchant is at the end of the street, but he's closed his doors and won't open until an hour after dawn tomorrow. The keeper says that if it's snowing hard, he's likely to open later — lazy man."

Donovan ate another spoonful as he deliberated. "That should suit us just fine. We won't be able to leave until the snow stops falling anyway, and it won't take us long to make our transaction."

Whitman looked up and opened his mouth to speak just as a stranger unexpectedly sat at their table. He spoke softly as he shuffled a deck of playing cards, "This isn't the sort of place a stranger wanders through 'less they're looking for something in particular." He looked up at Donovan and blanched, his hands stumbling on their shuffle. He recovered barely a second later, closing his mouth and clearing his throat. "Care for a hand?"

"Perhaps you can teach the boy to play," Donovan said carefully. His stomach was doing flips.

Marcus Sauls was an excellent gambler, ran a prodigious business in lumber rights, and knew Donovan like he knew his own mother. It was obvious he recognized Donovan, too, from that brief look on his face.

"What brings you to these parts?" Marcus asked, dealing the cards with practiced speed. Ruben watched him with bright interest; Whitman with subtle suspicion. He finished dealing and set the deck on the table, fanning his cards and sorting them.

"We're taking a round-about route toward ... well." Donovan suddenly wondered if he could trust this man he'd known since he was a boy. They hadn't spoken in nearly twenty years, after all.

"Don't want to share, aye?" Marcus supplied softly. "Your draw, boy." Ruben jumped to be addressed so suddenly. "Discard what you don't want, or lose points to force your left or right opponent to keep it."

"Something like that," Donovan agreed, drumming his fingers on the backs of his cards nervously. *What did Marcus want? They'd parted on decent enough terms, right?*

"Anywhere can be round-about depending on where you're coming from ... If you're thinking this hard in the first round, bard, the game will take all of your payment away — Feel free to fold. Your musician friend is leaving."

Whitman looked over his shoulder and grimaced. He laid down his cards and left with a guilty look at Donovan, who waved him away forgivingly and played his own move, his mind racing.

Marcus continued teaching Ruben, "First round done. So boy, draw two cards and lay them face up above the deck, then another below. You want to play your cards as though you have those two in your hand, aligning your cards with them. Draw and discard — you can draw from the face-up pile, but then we'll know what you have. Trade out entire hands and you gain back any negative points you've earned, but it's a hefty risk." He looked Donovan in the eyes for the first time since sitting. "But then, everyone likes a risk now and then, right?"

Donovan blinked. "What do you know, Marcus?"

"Give us a few minutes to lose the room's interest and we'll go back to my place," Marcus said softly.

They played a few more times around. Ruben seemed to get the hang of the game, but Donovan knew when they started that Marcus would win. Which he did. Easily.

He dealt again. Ruben looked at Donovan, who winked reassuringly. He hoped he wasn't wrong about Marcus's intentions because they could really use his help.

Marcus spoke in a low tone, "A gentleman came through town yesterday asking about you. Good timing that you came today. He didn't look particularly pleasant, despite all his smiling and handing out coins. Half the people here think that you're dead— which isn't surprising, considering the manner in which you left."

"We can agree to that."

"He's still here, your friend, but I haven't seen him tonight. Got the whitest teeth you've ever seen."

"Name?"

"None that I heard twice. So why aren't you dead?"

"I've wondered that myself more than a few times," Donovan answered, giving Marcus a mandatory card that he grimaced at.

"Your son doesn't look much like you."

Ruben glowered at the man, but kept his mouth shut.

"I found him in a sack labeled for north of here and figured I could use the reward."

"North is tricky business since the roads got busy."

"We've been taking the scenic route."

"I imagine that's the only thing that blew you this direction."

"Practically a Mentalist, you are."

"What do you need? Besides the red plow you're looking for."

Donovan gave them man a sour look and discarded a green tower. "Just a head start."

"I can give you that. When are you leaving?"

"When the snow stops tomorrow."

"You can't know when that is."

"Before the afternoon, after the morning," Ruben said, trading out his whole hand for the face-up cards and organizing them in his hand. He discarded those that took him over his holding limit.

"Mage, are you?" Marcus asked.

Ruben didn't answer, but glanced nervously at Donovan, then back at his cards while a blush colored his cheeks.

Donovan said to Marcus, "We've grain to buy. The horses won't be quick on frozen twigs and dead leaves."

"They might be light enough to carry, though. Two days won't kill them."

"It might kill us."

"Disgruntled the new neighbors that much, aye?"

"That much and more than plenty."

"Falling back into the speech fast, friend, aren't you? Why don't you trade bards again and come back to my shop now? I'll put you up and fetch your grain and you can leave with my wagons in the morning to hide your trail. It'll take you off course two leagues, which you can win back if you jump the river."

"It's chilly for river-jumping."

"A little death-by-freezing never harmed anyone."

"Ruben, tell Whit that we won't need that room. Be quiet about it."

Ruben laid down his cards with a look of disappointment; clearly he wanted to keep playing. He joined Whitman on the hearth, hands in his pockets. Marcus lifted the boy's cards with the corner of his own. His eyebrow disappeared into his shaggy bangs. "I see why you're taking him north; he's a good bluff."

"Sauls, are you thieving from the travelers again?" a loud, drunk voice came from behind them. A man fell heavily into Whitman's empty chair and banged a meaty fist on the table. "You owe me two drinks since I saw you last."

"I think you've claimed them from someone else, so it's them I owe now. Go away, Tim, I'm talking business."

"Cards ain't business, and business ain't cards — give us a hand and I'll leave your slate clean."

"Tomorrow when you're sober. Taking money from drunks is almost sinful."

"I'm hardly drunk, Sauls. Who's your friend, anyway?"

Donovan was studying his cards, hat brim low. He and Tim Mullin had never been close, but they'd been on speaking terms. It was hard to know if he'd be recognized —

"That's never Donovan Rudd!" the man said, alcohol and surprise carrying his voice and idiocy through the room.

"That man's dead and strangers don't like being bothered at their tables," Marcus snapped, raising his own voice.

"Stranger my left ass — give us a handful, Donny!" The man laughed and slapped Donovan on the shoulder.

No other plan coming to mind, Donovan stood and punched Tim hard in the cheek, sending him out of the chair to land on the floor looking dumbfounded.

"Don't touch me," he said, pitching his voice lower. "I don't know who you're talking about. Marcus, our deal is off if this is the company you keep."

"He's barely company, Blake. At least let's talk prices before you leave?" Marcus was giving wide eyes, which Donovan acknowledged.

"In your shop, then."

Donovan waved to Ruben and Whitman, turning on his heel and walking out the door. He didn't slow down until he was out of sight of the windows, then he waited for the two to catch up, already desperately missing the warmth of the inn.

"That was exciting," Whitman said, pulling the thin cloak tight and rubbing his arms.

Ruben snuggled into the thicker cloak again, mostly disappearing into its folds.

"At least he was drunk," Donovan said as he shook the pain out of his hand. He was almost grateful for the cold, numbing his knuckles.

"He cannot have been the only one to recognize you, though."

"Marcus will take care of it. Let's go."

They continued down a side street, the turns all coming back to Donovan's mind as he took in the familiar landmarks. Plenty had changed in the time he'd been gone, but so much was still the same. Too much.

They were half-frozen by the time they reached Marcus's shop, which was, naturally, locked. The spare key was gone, too, which was more than disappointing. They huddled together in the doorway, trying to block the wind. Whitman wasn't complaining; despite being the biggest, he was also wearing the least, and paying for it. His lips were turning blue in the wind chill while his jaw wracked with shivering spasms. Ruben bounced from foot to foot, trying to keep his cloak closed with both hands.

Marcus scurried up the street a few minutes later, key already in hand. They moved and he unlocked the door to let them hurry inside. Out of the wind, they felt significantly better, but Donovan immediately set to building a fire in the metal pit in the center of the room. It was already laid with tinder and logs and didn't take long to catch. He and Ruben warmed their hands while Whitman shed his cloak, taking Ruben's and hanging them both by the door.

Marcus locked the door and took their packs and Donovan's sword belt, grimacing at the weight of Whitman's bag as he set them out of the way in a distant corner.

The shop was spacious, but busy with small stacks of lumber laid in neat piles along the wall, labeled and priced. A map dominated the far wall with copious notes written in a neat hand all over it. Donovan remembered summers spent cutting down trees and hauling and splitting wood for Marcus's father to sell.

The interior was mostly a single floor, with a small loft on one side. The fire pit stood in its middle with a metal pipe that carried the smoke through the ceiling. There was a front and back door. A couple of windows lined the walls; they were all expensive glass, and the one Donovan had broken as an adolescent with a mishandled board had finally been replaced. They were currently shuttered against the chill.

A flat ladder was mounted against the wall where the loft jutted out, showing extra room upstairs. Marcus glanced up at the loft space and then pulled three chairs from his front desk area and arranged them around the fire. He rolled an empty barrel over to be Ruben's seat. The boy hopped up cheerfully, and drummed his heels on the outside of the wooden container.

"Can we play cards again?" he asked.

Marcus smiled and looked at Donovan. "I don't think I've ever had someone ask me that so happily."

"Yes, well, he hasn't lost his money to you yet."

"What do you do here?" Ruben asked, looking around curiously.

"I sell lumber," Marcus answered, leaning forward on his elbows to warm his face.

"You don't keep much stock."

Marcus laughed. "Smart boy — I sell lumber rights, then. Does that suit you?" Ruben didn't look convinced. "I own most of the surrounding acreage and when people want to get the lumber from the land, I sell it to them, offering the services of my crews and tools for a reasonable fee."

"What's to stop them from just coming along and cutting down the trees that they want while you're here and the crews are sleeping?"

"Well, I have several small houses built along my properties and the foremen sleep in those buildings to keep an eye on things. There are dogs, too, which I've had specially trained, and there's a lovely copse of yew that is just perfect for making longbows, which is a hobby of mine. I've gotten rather good at it, I think."

Ruben nodded slowly. "I like that."

"Glad to have your approval, then."

"Are we staying the night here?" Whitman asked tightly, his shivering finally starting to abate.

Donovan glanced at Marcus, who nodded. "That's the plan."

Marcus continued, "I'll buy your grain and you can follow my wagons to the work site in the morning to hide your trail," Marcus explained.

Whitman looked at Donovan. "Why the change of plans?"

Donovan shifted in his seat. "It gives us a safer place to stay and an easier escape in the morning. It'd be hard to leave without a tail in fresh snow, especially if someone other than Tim recognized us ... me."

"Other than Tim and Marcus, you mean."

"I daresay your friend doesn't trust me, Donovan," Marcus said, leaning back in his chair and regarding Whitman with interest.

"I mean no offense, of course, but we have never met and, while it appears that the two of you have been good friends in the past, nearly twenty years have come and gone and Donovan never mentioned you as an ally, which means he doubted that friendship at least to some degree. I worry about the ease with which you encouraged us to join you in this secluded place, and your perfect plan for our leaving in the morning. I assume you will be kind enough to gather our horses from the stable as well when you are out fetching our grain? It is an awful lot from a man expecting nothing in return, who will surely be in some place of hardship should he be discovered. Which you will be, of course. Everyone saw Marcus take the 'strangers' to his home, and it will be the work of a moment for the Hunters to find you. Their questions are usually rather pointed."

Donovan's lips pursed with displeasure, but he didn't say anything. He was running all of Whitman's good points through his mind, not wanting to believe any of them.

Marcus put his hands out to the sides. "You make an excellent argument, bard. I take it you're this suspicious naturally?"

"My mind enjoys finding holes in any arrangement."

"You would make an excellent barrister."

Ruben giggled nervously and Whitman looked at him sideways, saying, "Yes, that has been said before. I *have* been wondering if there is any proof you could offer, but I really believe that there is not. You have made a ready friend of our lad here, and you have already befriended Donovan, which leaves me to play the part of the watchdog."

"I see. Then why would you speak your suspicions so early?" Marcus asked. "If you really thought I was your villain, why not wait until I believed you were asleep and then check my actions?"

"Because I do not believe you are working alone."

There was a loud, merry laugh from the loft. They all jumped and twisted to see. A man was standing on the edge, only the front of him lit by their fire, the rest shrouded in darkness. He had a wide smile, his teeth glinting in the uneven light; the corners of his mouth twisted up at angles that made him look too charismatic; threateningly cheerful.

He held a long yew bow in one hand, strung, with several arrows twined through his fingers. His other hand was empty, but the fingers were splayed, as though he was stretching them, readying them. He had prominent cheekbones and his face was long, ending in a pointed chin.

"While this conversation is fascinating, I must say, I've been waiting for it to move along to something a bit more interesting." His flashing eyes found Donovan. "You'd be the Retriever?"

Donovan's mind was racing. *Should he answer? Was this man a Hunter? He had to be. Who was he to Marcus? Was Whitman right? Had Marcus betrayed them?*

The smiling man raised a thin, blond eyebrow. "We'll take your silence for assent, then." He plucked the string of the bow and it made a low *thrum*. "I enjoyed our battle of wills. We must do it again. Did the boy help you? You know that's cheating." He grinned. "Dangerous job, Retrieving. You run into all sorts on these roads." He winked and turned his attention toward Whitman, who slowly came to his full height.

"You've encountered many Retrievers, then?" Whitman asked, hands out to his sides to show he was unarmed. The bowman smiled widely and directed his attention back to Donovan, who also stood.

"Don't worry," the smiling man said cheerily. "I don't have to kill you so long as you give me the magus."

"That isn't going to happen," Donovan answered with a stillness he didn't feel. His heart raced.

Ruben hopped off the barrel and pressed his back into Donovan, who put his hands on the boy's shoulders protectively.

He dared a glance over his shoulder to see that Marcus hadn't moved, but watched Donovan and not the smiling bowman.

"I hate to make you a liar, sir." The smiling man *tutted* his tongue with a pouty, false frown. "One professional to another, I have never failed my duty to Retrieve."

"You've never Retrieved for the Order," Donovan said flatly, certain.

"Not for the Order, no," the bowman agreed.

"You'll fail this one," Donovan told him.

"Again, the *lies*, Donovan ... Please, don't try anything; I can put an arrow through two men at this range."

"Personally, I take pride in my ability to lie, but my skills are significantly dampened when there is a longbow involved," Whitman said with false cheer.

Donovan took the hint not to rile their challenger's temper.

"I've always loved bards." The smiling man's grin was back in place.

"As have I," Whitman agreed. "Care to hear a tune?"

The bowman laughed. "Normally by now people are asking *who I am* and *what I want*, but here you are, bold as brass, looking for a copper penny. *Bards.* Excellent creatures. Have you yet made master?"

"You know, that is always the first question people ask, but alas, no. However, I am sure to after I write up the music to this particular instance."

"Ah, yes, *The Stranger's Bow* I expect you'll call it?"

"I was more taken by *The Madman's Smile*, but I am willing to reconsider."

The man's smile dipped, but was soon back in place, this time with a complement of narrowed eyes. He didn't answer, and they waited, tense.

'*Say something else; tell us what you want*' Donovan thought furiously.

He glanced down at Ruben, his heart racing. The boy looked nervous, but not yet scared.

Donovan took a steadying breath and said, "Since you mentioned it, who are you and what do you want?"

The smiling man took in a lungful, letting it out slowly from his nose as though considering the question with all the time in the world. He winked at Whitman and then turned his attention to Ruben, baring his teeth in a feral grin. "I can tell you that I have been instructed to obtain a certain someone with as little fuss as possible."

Donovan turned the boy away protectively.

The smiling man waggled the arrows between his fingers as a reminder. "Please. I try *very* hard not to leave trails of bodies behind me these days."

"You know, me too," Whitman said, his voice light.

"You must know what the boy is, Whitman," the smiling man said, just as lightly. "A magus, after all this time; I can't imagine you're not giddy at the prospect."

Whitman's expression had changed from one of amusement to suspicion. "Do you know me?"

The smiling man grinned and turned back to Ruben. "How about you, boy? Do you know what you are? What it *means* to be a magus? Of course you don't. How could you? How could anyone?"

Ruben didn't answer.

"Leave him alone," Donovan threatened. He felt a vague hint of pressure in his mind, like a burgeoning headache.

"A bit of jest never hurt anyone," the smiling man sneered. "Feeling paternal, are we, Donovan?" The smiling man's eyes had grown unfocused, but they snapped back to Donovan's face. "History certainly repeats itself, my, my. This *is* a twist of fate."

The smiling man leapt from the loft, landing with a loud *thud.* He straightened quickly, apparently uninjured, despite the distance. They all jumped in surprise, except for Marcus, who had been all but forgotten, but who now scurried to stand behind Donovan to keep them from going anywhere. Donovan glanced back at him, his expression more sad than surprised now.

"Your knees will age for triple if you keep that up," the bard said nonchalantly.

Whitman stood opposite the fire from Donovan and Ruben, his posture relaxed, but his eyes were darting this way and that. Donovan wondered what plan he was preparing and wished they had some way to communicate. If only he wasn't a Seeker, but any other kind of mage. He tried to relax his jaw, hearing his teeth creak with tension.

"Ah, well, what's a few years?" the smiling man said. He paced to the center of the room and again *thrummed* the string of his longbow like an instrument.

"Two against two," Whitman suggested. "Though I expect I could make short work of your man Marcus there."

Donovan saw that his old friend had drawn a short knife, but wielded it without much enthusiasm; his heart didn't seem to be in it. Donovan regretted handing over his sword belt, but wasn't sure if he would have been able to use the weapon anyway.

"You never said it'd be *him*," Marcus complained through gritted teeth.

The smiling man shrugged. "I didn't know it would be. Happy coincidence, it seems."

"Marcus, put the knife away," Whitman said calmly. "Whatever this man has offered you, you know the Order can do better."

Marcus shook his head firmly. "They wouldn't. They'd make promises and then put me on trial for dealings with blood mages, they would."

Donovan's eyes narrowed at the smiling man. "Blood mage?"

Their opponent waggled his hand, head bobbing back and forth. "It's a bit more complicated than that," he explained with a cheeky smirk.

"Let's get this over with," Marcus snapped, taking a sharp step forward, but rocked to a stop at the smiling man's sudden gesture.

"Ah, ah," the smiling man stalled him. "Gently now. We don't want any accidents, do we?" He directed his words towards Ruben with an almost tender look on his sinister face. "Come away from Donovan now, Ruben, and everything will be fine."

"Over my dead body," Donovan snapped, clutching the boy closer.

"That is, more or less, the ultimate plan should things escalate from here." The smiling man's expression hadn't changed, but it had taken on a more haunted look.

"Donovan," Whitman said urgently. "We need to consider the options."

"What options?" Donovan snarled. "They're not taking Ruben."

"Ah, thinking you might pursue and kill us after we have the boy in our possession, Whitman? It's a shame you can't communicate your plan to Donovan."

The bard didn't answer, but watched Donovan with a worried expression.

"Come now, the more we talk, the less inclined I am to kill you on a whim before I go." He released a tittering giggle.

Donovan backed away a pace and pulled Ruben carefully with him. The smiling man nodded to Marcus over Donovan's shoulder, but as soon as he came close enough, Donovan jabbed a hard elbow into his old friend's face, sending him stumbling back, blood leaking from between his fingers. Donovan angled toward the wall and backed them toward it.

"What are you expecting to do?" the smiling man asked, amusement flashing in the glint of his eye.

"Whatever I have to," Donovan snapped back. *What would Lucas do?*

"You are a strong-willed one," the smiling man said, fists with bow and arrows perched on his hips. He looked over his shoulder at Whitman, who had started to stalk closer. "Much like your sister, eh, Whit?"

"W-what?" Whitman stuttered, seeming to shrink. Surprise, confusion, and worry marred his previously confident features. "What-what do you know about my sister?"

"Oh, enough, I'd say. Beastly little creature. Stay where you are or I'll pin you there." He put an arrow on the string, but did not draw.

Whitman didn't move, and the smiling man turned his attention back to Donovan and Ruben.

"The boy, Donovan."

"He's mine."

"He isn't, and you know it. I won't hurt him." The smiling man almost sounded sincere. "There are things you need to know," he told Ruben earnestly.

The boy stood wide-eyed and stared between the lithe, smiling bowman and the bloody-faced Marcus.

"Things like what?" Ruben asked, sounding more apprehensive than afraid.

Donovan squeezed him. *Don't engage, Ruben, don't let him get into your head.*

The smiling man grinned. "That would be telling. Come away from the Retriever, now. Don't mind the bow; it's merely insurance against the irrational."

"Don't listen to him, Ruben. We're going now." Donovan started moving them toward the door.

"Don't do that, Donovan," the smiling man ordered, drawing back his bowstring with an almost hungry expression.

Donovan stopped. Whitman again inched closer to the smiling man, but Marcus pointed him out with bloody fingers.

"I said I'd pin you, Whitman. I'm not one to make idle threats. Place your hand on that wall."

Whitman put his hands up to his shoulders furiously, backing away a few steps.

"On the wall," the smiling man repeated. "Hand on the wall or I'll shoulder the risk of shooting Donovan *through* the boy."

Whitman slammed his right hand against the wall. The arrow flew. In the same instant, Whitman withdrew his hand and roared with fear and rage. The arrow hit the boards and stuck, quivering.

Seeing their opponent distracted, Donovan launched himself and Ruben toward the door. The smiling man spun away from Whitman and nocked another arrow in the same movement, loosing it to *crack*, shaking, into the door. Donovan and Ruben skidded to a halt.

The bowman nocked his third arrow and pointed it steadily at Ruben. "Don't think I won't," he snarled. His smile had been replaced with childish irritation. "For the good of everything, I would. Don't test me, *I would*."

Donovan froze, clutching Ruben to him while his mind spun for options.

The boards creaked as Whitman hurtled across the room, his meaty fist raised.

The smiling man lowered his bow and side-stepped the punch as though he could anticipate its trajectory. "You're no hero, *Whit*," he laughed. "What good does your death do this story?"

Donovan moved toward the door again while Whitman had the villain once again distracted, but Marcus ran forward to intercept, waving his knife warningly. "I don't want to," he said thickly through his swollen nose. "I don't, but I will."

"*Why?*" Donovan snapped as he kept Ruben protected from the blade.

"I've lost *everything*," Marcus lamented. "This is all I have left."

Behind him, Whitman looked to be running out of steam, swinging again and again and connecting with only air, despite his skill.

"Don't you even want to know who I am?" the smiling man asked, dancing around him.

"You —" Whit began.

The smiling man struck him with a kick so fast that it was almost unseen, straight up above his head and into Whitman's face. Whitman howled and staggered backward, blinking blood out of his eyes from a split eyebrow and bloodied nose. He crumpled to the ground in the next instant as a loud *CRACK* rippled through the air and his scream filled the space above all other sound.

His knee now bent the wrong way.

He took his hands from his face to clutch at his ruined leg even as blood poured from his flattened nose. His eyes wide and scared and unbelieving.

The smiling man, with barely any sign of exertion, turned to check on Donovan, but Donovan wasn't moving. Instead, he stared at Whitman lying prone and injured. He couldn't think of what to do; his mind was a complete blank.

"You're a little boy still, Whit," the smiling man said. He closed his eyes as if to savor the moment and gather his thoughts.

"I wish your master had – more faith in you," Whitman panted from the ground.

The smiling man's eyes opened slowly. "What's that?"

"Clearly you're – limited – in your options. You can't – kill – the boy – or the Retriever. I'm – the – the demonstration. All you – can do – is kill me – in the hopes – that Don will – give up. But he won't."

Everyone's eyes were on Whitman now.

"Are you trying to *goad* me?" the smiling man asked incredulously. He put his head back and laughed boisterously, but it sounded forced nonetheless. "I think I'll have to take your thumbs before I finally let you die."

"I understand. It's all – you have. I pity you."

"Do you, now?" A tinge of anger had entered his voice.

"You've clearly risen – high – but you'll never- have what you want. It'll go always – to those more powerful – saner – than you. Always running – and never quite – making it. I feel your pain."

"You feel — you feel *my pain?*" The smiling man laughed again, this time through clenched teeth, looking down at the broken man.

Whitman still bled from his face, the mess pooling in his ears and dripping to the floor. "All you have – is your cleverness – but how long – before someone – really *tests* you?"

WHAM!

The smiling man flew past Whitman, and hit the ground hard, losing his bow and arrows to clatter across the floor. He staggered upright like a disjointed puppet with a hand to his back as he tried to regain his balance. He stared in disbelief at Donovan, who slowly placed his foot back on the ground.

"Thanks, Whit," he said.

"My pleasure," the bard groaned, letting his head drop to the ground.

Marcus backed away from Ruben, who held Lucas's long knife to his belly. Donovan eyed the smiling man warily, but he didn't move as Marcus and Ruben pulled Whitman to the wall to sit him upright. They tried not to jar his damaged leg, but he whimpered nonetheless. Ruben quickly returned the point of his knife to Marcus's side, encouraging good behavior.

The smiling man stood casually with his back to the fire pit, which had all but burned itself out. It was now mostly a pile of gray ash with black flakes crusting it, which allowed the frigid air to advance through the room, and sent massive shadows to hunt through the dying light.

He held up his hands appealingly and said, "Come now, Donovan. Are you the kind to kill an unarmed man?"

Without bothering to answer, Donovan threw his heel toward the center of the man's chest, fully expecting to be blocked. He was prepared to use the momentum to his advantage, but instead found empty air and had to hop to regain his balance.

The smiling man had jumped at the last moment and now perched on the chair that Marcus had previously occupied. He looked amused. "You can't hurt me, you know."

"Fine, then. You stand there, and we'll carry on our way."

"Ruben, you won't learn anything hiding behind the walls of the Order. I and my *friends* can teach you so much more."

"More than the Order?" Ruben asked skeptically.

"Much, *much* more," the smiling man assured him. "Or you can go with these men and learn from a bunch of stuffy teachers in stuffy classrooms, the same nonsense they teach *everyone* else, giving you no chance to really learn *your* magic."

"Your manipulations are hardly subtle," Donovan said, mostly for Ruben's benefit.

"However, still working," the smiling man answered casually.

Ruben shifted his weight from foot to foot. "I don't even know you," he pointed out. "Why would I trust you?"

"You trusted Donovan, and you know him as well as you know me," the smiling man countered, still balanced on his chair.

Donovan hesitated. He knew the smiling man was trying to get Ruben onto his side, but he also knew that it would only sow more doubt in the boy's mind if he tried to silence the smiling man now.

"Ruben, do as Donovan says," Marcus said softly.

Ruben glared at him.

"Not helping, Marcus," Whitman groaned from the floor.

Marcus seemed to have lost the will to fight, but Ruben kept his knife pointed where it would be useful.

"Out of curiosity, Donovan, what was your plan to leave?" the smiling man asked. He stood with his hands clasped behind him, looking like any scholar Donovan had seen wandering the halls of the Order. "It's two feet of snow out there by now."

"What was *your* plan?" Ruben retorted in Donovan's silence.

"Ruben ..." Whitman warned.

The smiling man chuckled. "Cheeky little mite, aren't you?"

"He's waiting on friends. Friends with sleds," Whitman suggested.

"We could use fire to melt the snow," Ruben suggested in turn.

"No, we can't," Donovan said shortly.

The smiling man's eyes had lost focus again, as though the conversation bored him. Before Donovan could even think about taking a small step toward him, however, his focus was back and his eyes now bored holes in Donovan's.

A slow smirk crawled across his lips. "I think the boy could do just fine with fire."

"It can be hard to control, Ruben." Donovan tried to explain as shortly as possible. He had to keep the boy from doing anything reckless, while he kept his attention on this odd adversary.

"But why would I need much control, right? There's snow everywhere and as long as the heat stays forward ..."

"That's the point, Ben," Whitman rumbled, his voice thick with clotted blood. "More than anything else, if we are experimenting with magics we do not understand, I would prefer we did more Healing."

"I don't have a tree to transfer to ..."

"You can use Marcus."

"That's not very nice," Marcus said indignantly.

"Neither is betrayal," Whitman pointed out.

"I-I didn't ..." his voice trailed off and he looked away, ashamed.

"I could move the snow, then," Ruben said to Donovan.

"Displacing. Another incredibly dangerous and difficult skill to learn, but yes, Ruben; you will master that within the Order," Donovan answered.

"Nothing is gained without risk," the smiling man shrugged.

"We can't just stand around *waiting*!" Ruben huffed, torn between logics.

"We were planning on doing that anyway," Whitman pointed out. "Would you like to go to sleep? That is where we would be if Marcus had not shown up so conveniently. I did say so. Did I not say how convenient it was? Someone make note that I was right."

"There are voices outside," Marcus said suddenly.

The smiling man grinned wider. "Marcus, be a dear and throw me that bow, would you?"

Marcus hesitated. He glanced at Donovan and shoved Ruben suddenly. The boy lost his knife and tripped over Whitman. He hit the ground as Marcus stooped to retrieve the bow, throwing it like an unwieldy spear. Donovan caught it and turned to face the smiling man again. Before he could blink, the smiling man threw himself at Donovan feet first, one heel taking him in the cheek bone, the other in the chest. Donovan grunted with pain as he fell hard to the ground. The smiling man scooped up the bow and sprinted for the loft ladder. Donovan jumped to his feet, raced after him, but the man was up the ladder like a squirrel, and they heard him rummaging for arrows.

Donovan skidded to a halt and ran back to Whitman, Ruben, and Marcus. He barreled straight for Marcus, who realized too late that Donovan wasn't slowing down. He used his momentum to jump up and snap a foot straight into Marcus's chest.

Marcus bounced off the wall, wheezing, waving the dagger he'd claimed in a weak defense. Donovan kicked it aside with disgust and grabbed Marcus's collar. He wheeled him around and held him like a shield in front of himself and the others.

When the smiling man's grin appeared again at the edge of the loft, he had a handful of arrows, one already nocked and ready on the string. Marcus was too busy trying to stop his shirt from strangling him to provide much resistance. Donovan kept him at elbow's length and crouched behind him to peek around his head.

"Whit, I really wish you were mobile," Donovan muttered.

"That makes two," the bard replied with pained frustration.

A gentle knock came to the back door a moment before another sounded at the front. No one spoke, but the smiling man's grin had faltered. The knocks came again louder.

"Donovan, do you remember what I said about a longbow at this height and range?"

"What?" Donovan asked, distracted.

"I said it could go through two men."

He loosed the arrow at Marcus, who shuddered in Donovan's grip as a high-pitched scream came from his tightened windpipe.

Donovan's grip faltered and he let Marcus collapse in front of him. He felt a deep ripping inside as his old friend slid off the arrow shaft to die, shuddering on the floor. Donovan looked down at the bloody, feathered shaft sticking out of his ribs. It was only buried an inch or two, but that was plenty when you were particular about the holes in your body.

Donovan stumbled back as agony bloomed, unrelenting, in his chest. He put a hand out to catch the wall, but missed. He tripped over Whitman's damaged leg, but barely heard as the bard yelled in pain. He hit the ground on his shoulder, hard enough to knock out his remaining wind, and flopped bonelessly to his back. Ruben screamed. Whitman yelled his name. His only answer was tight, quick breaths. He watched the arrow bob and shift as he did so. It stuck out of him like a flag pointing the way to his lung.

The doors at either end of the room burst open simultaneously in an explosion of frigid air. Three people rushed inside, white cloaks and boots making them momentarily indistinguishable from the flurry of snow that accompanied them. The fire, nearly dead, burst to life again.

Whitman yelled something to the three newcomers — one of whom was breaking off an arrow sticking out of his own shoulder and running toward the ladder into the loft. Snow from the ceiling showed that the smiling man had found the roof access and was running away.

Donovan saw all of this as though on the periphery of his vision, most of his attention drifting to small things around him — the gleam of a buckle on his boot, a melting snowflake from the door, and the matted feathers of the arrow, bloodied and torn from their trip through Marcus's body. Everything moved too slowly.

Ruben's face filled his vision. His mouth was moving. Donovan tried to bring his attention to what the boy was saying, but it was a struggle. *Poor boy.* He was alone, with no parents, and now Donovan was dying. He wanted to apologize for taking him from home — surely he would have been happier living in obscurity. Tears filled Donovan's vision. He didn't want to leave Ruben. He'd tried hard to think of the boy as a stranger's son and not his own, but the void in his soul wanted filling, and the child was just the right size.

"Argh!" Donovan yelled, snapping back to reality as new painful sensations brought his attention back in full force.

"Are you with me?" one of the newcomers asked. With a neatly trimmed beard, he stared through piercing blue eyes with concern at Donovan. Under his white cloak, he wore thick woolen trousers and several layers of shirt covered with molded leather armor, professionally made. It bore the interlocking rings of the Order tooled into the front.

"I—" Donovan wheezed and then stopped, wincing as the arrow bobbed again.

"We don't have a Healer, but Kath is a surgeon," the man said in a deep voice.

"It's in his lung," Whitman told the man. "He's going to drown if you don't move fast."

"I know my job," another newcomer said icily. She slung the full pack from her shoulders beside Donovan with a heavy *thunk*.

"Ark, hold him down. Boy, sit on his legs. Ready?"

A calming presence bloomed through him and Donovan felt his panic fade, and his body relax.

The bearded man came around and put his hands heavily on Donovan's shoulders to pin him to the ground and incited new pain to blossom through Donovan's chest. Ruben made himself uncomfortably heavy on Donovan's shins.

Then none of that mattered. Kath pulled the arrow out and Donovan passed into blissful unconsciousness.

* * *

"I want to see him."

"There's nothing to see. He's resting. If you wake him, he'll just be in pain."

"You gave him something for that, right?"

"It doesn't last long; it's best if he sleeps."

"Leave her alone, son. We'll be there soon and then you can see him all you want."

"Go on, Ben. He is still sleeping anyway."

* * *

Donovan opened his eyes, blinked at the harshness of the light and decided to leave them closed. He listened instead. He heard hoofbeats very nearby on either side, and the creaking of canvas and leather. He wiggled his toes and fingers experimentally, finding them warm and comfortable. He was wrapped in blankets, judging by the soft weight around him. His face was cold, but not frigid, although his nose felt frozen. His head felt like it was full of quilt batting, and his chest as though it was holding all of the pins.

He took an experimental inhale, stopping when his chest tightened and the pins multiplied, but got a whiff of snow, and horse, and wool, and lemon.

He decided to try his eyes again, and managed a very thin line of sight. He saw a rider on either side of him, both of them wearing white cloaks and face-cloths that hid their features. He appeared to be on a canvas stretcher, secured between the two horses. The sun was high and, aside from the crunch of the horses' hooves through snow, there wasn't much else to hear.

One of the riders looked down at him and said, "Kath."

The other looked and told him firmly, "Don't move about and keep your breaths small. Don't talk."

Donovan's brow furrowed, but he obeyed. The woman's voice was low and commanding, used to giving orders. He wanted to ask questions, but the warmth of his cocoon and the fuzz in his head quickly reclaimed him.

5

"— REASON HERE?"

"Returning from business."

"Who's with you?"

"One badly injured Seeker, an injured bard, and a boy to be trained."

"Anyone after you?"

"Possible, but ..."

*   *   *

"Whitman Acres, it's been a while since we've seen you."

Whitman turned his head, and felt as though he was floating; his mind was full of cotton. While the absence of pain was cause for celebration, he did not otherwise enjoy medicine of this type. Lady Pennison, a surgeon speeding toward the position of Head of Surgery, despite her youth and lack of magic, strode into the room already in her operating uniform.

"You are a vision of wonder, my lady, as usual," Whitman croaked. They'd given him a drink of foul-tasting medicine, and it had started numbing his body almost immediately, apparently starting with his brain. Still, it did nothing for the tension and fear coursing through him, shaking him to the core. *Had to keep a brave face, though; work to be done.* "Is Parel available to assist you?"

"He was on duty this morning; I expect he's sleeping."

He tried to force through the fuzz and found the words coming to him slowly. "We have been partners for years, in terms of medical aid. I am sure he would not mind being woken to help an old friend." His lips and tongue felt too thick for his mouth.

"Elliott has insisted that you be cared for immediately. He's always been keen on bards. I'm sure Parel will forgive me." She smiled kindly.

Whitman managed to fake one in return, his stomach flopping.

Unable to think of another excuse with the fatigue in his mind, he asked, "Is Oslan outside?"

"He has been in meetings all day, but I've sent someone for him. He'll be here when you wake."

He closed his eyes, trembling.

"Now, Whitman, I will do everything that I can to repair your injuries, and then a Healer will follow after me to correct what they can. You'll be unconscious for several hours."

A couple of surgeon nurses entered with a tray of tools.

Whitman swallowed thickly. Being entirely under the control of another person ... a shudder ran through him. It was one of his greatest fears.

"When you wake, we'll need an explanation of how these injuries occurred, young man. Were you kicked by a horse?" Her tone was jovial, but keenly interested.

Whitman felt a vague pressure as she stuck him with a needle, pushing liquid into his leg.

"A man, actually. A madman."

"I see ..." She said something else, but the fuzz finally won, and he relented, sinking into unconsciousness.

*   *   *

"Are you Ruben?"

Ruben raised his head from the chair he was curled upon, the voice waking him from a doze. He blinked tiredly and a woman's face came into view. She looked nice. He didn't trust her.

"Aye."

"Why don't you come with me?"

He sat up and stretched his neck. The waiting room, large and painted white, was filled with chairs and little else. There were only a couple of other people waiting together, but with Donovan rushed into one room, and Whitman rushed into the other, Ruben hadn't had anywhere else to go, nor anyone else to sit with. The chairs were comfortable enough, and he could watch the counter where the students and Healers checked in.

"Where abouts?" he asked, not yet rising.

She seemed surprised at his questioning her, but answered, "The Dean wants to speak with you about enrolling in your classes."

"Dean? I dunno about that. I mean to wait here for Donovan."

"He's going to be in surgery for several more hours, Ruben."

"Aye."

She waited for more, which he did not provide.

"How about I bring the Dean to you?" She smiled again, this time with sympathy, and walked off.

Ruben curled up, but didn't close his eyes. Students and surgeons came in and out of the rooms, most of them in no hurry, checking on patients and filling out forms. Ruben was glad he'd never had his contract purchased by a surgeon; he wasn't sure if he'd have been able to put his hands in another person, even if it was to make them better.

It took about half an hour, but the woman returned, this time with a man at least as old as Donovan beside her. His hair was as curly as Donovan's, too, but longer, puffed out from his head like a storm cloud. Despite being under the storm cloud, the man looked as kind as the woman. She left them alone, and the man took a seat near Ruben.

He put out a hand. "Good afternoon, Ruben, I'm Dean Villery. How are you?"

Ruben sat up and shook the hand firmly, as he'd been taught. Merchants liked firm handshakes; it made them feel important.

Villery was waiting for an answer, though, so Ruben said testily, "I'm all right."

"Did Donovan explain much about this place when you were on the road?"

Ruben shrugged. "He told me a bit. Mostly I figure we're set for a siege."

The Dean smiled. "Donovan and I have been friends for several years — ever since he started fetching young mages like yourself. See, in normal circumstances, he would have brought you to me and helped you get settled with a schedule and dormitory and your supplies. You'd meet your classmates and learn the layout of the Order so you can find places without getting lost." He smiled gently. "Needless to say, this is not a normal circumstance."

Ruben glanced down the hallway again, where they'd taken Donovan. He didn't answer.

The Dean didn't appear to be in any hurry. He lowered his voice slightly to ask, "Did Donovan explain what you are?"

Ruben matched the dean's volume, "He said I'm a magus."

"Do you know what that is?"

Ruben nodded, grimaced, then shook his head. "Kind of. I know the stories."

Dean Villery smiled crookedly. "We're in the same boat, you and I. I've never had a magus student, and I've been Dean here for, oh, close to thirty years? I'll have to go through the old records to see what the usual process was for getting you educated."

"Do I have to stay here?" Ruben asked. He suddenly felt claustrophobic in the large room.

The Dean didn't seem surprised. "Nope." He shook his head. "Do you want to leave?"

Ruben looked down the hall again. "I'm not sure."

Villery gestured to the room. "I will say this is not the best place for a new student to wait. While it is a miracle of modern medicine and training, it isn't very welcoming. I'd say it shows off our skills to a person who cares about such things, but to someone far from home ... it isn't a very good replacement." He smiled again. He had very straight teeth.

Ruben nodded.

"Can I show you some of the rest of the Order? Before you make up your mind about staying? Donovan and Whitman will be in surgery — in very good hands, I'll add — for a while yet. I'm told they'll both be just fine, but healing takes time, even with magic. Have you done any Healing?"

Ruben nodded.

"Really?" The Dean looked genuinely surprised. "When was that?"

Ruben hesitated, unsure of what he was supposed to share. This man had said they were friends, though ...

"On the road," he answered finally. "Donovan was, um, Seeking and I helped Heal him."

"Did Donovan ask for your help?"

"No, he was being attacked."

Dean Villery's eyes were wide and curious, but he didn't push.

"You can show me the place," Ruben told him after the silence settled.

"Dining hall first," the Dean said firmly. "I never adventure on an empty stomach."

Ruben managed a smile and slid to his feet.

"Come on, lad. Let's see what we can see."

*   *   *

Donovan took a deep breath and exhaled slowly as he came out of sleep. He'd been dreaming, but about what he couldn't remember — something good. He smelled lemon grass and cotton and stone. Where was he?

Wait — Marcus! Ruben!

Pain!

He sat up with a yell and threw his legs out to gain his feet, arms blocking his body. He stared around wildly and tried to take in details, even as his head swam and bobbed.

Someone behind him was speaking. He turned and struck, missed, and was gently directed back to the bed. Something waved under his nose — a strong smell, *very* strong — and he gasped, blinking, staring at the person with him.

A woman was holding him still with a surprisingly strong grip on his shoulder; the other putting a vial away in her pocket. She smiled at him and asked, "Feeling better, I take it?"

Donovan blinked at her.

"What's the last thing you remember, please?" she asked, giving his shoulder a reassuring squeeze and taking a step back.

She was dressed in white cotton trousers and a long-sleeved cotton shirt. Her black hair was lined liberally with gray, and sat knotted in a bun at the base of her neck. Despite the wrinkles around her eyes and mouth, she stood confidently with no other sign of age.

Donovan cleared his throat and said, "I-I remember ..."

"Take your time. Things might still be jumbled."

Donovan looked around the room. It was white stone, about ten feet long and eight wide, with a sturdy wooden door. It had no windows, but a landscape painting hung above two cushioned chairs on the far wall, with a small dresser between them and a water pitcher with glasses on top. The bed was set away from its walls to leave it accessible from all sides. The linens were fresh and crisp, like the uniform the woman wore.

Realization came. "We made it. We're at the Order."

The nurse smiled. "That's promising. Who's 'we'?"

"Whitman, Ruben, those strangers ... Where is everyone?"

"Your friend Whitman is being taken care of in the room next door. Ruben won't leave his side since we wouldn't let him in here to see you but once. Quite stubborn, that one."

"Yeah, he is that." Donovan gave a wry smile, then he frowned again. "Who was it that brought us here?"

"Order soldiers. They've been insistent on hearing your story and your friends are very tight-lipped." She returned his wry smile. "Still, though, do you remember anything before arriving here?"

"I don't remember arriving here," Donovan answered slowly. "We were in Weston ... oh." His face fell.

"I'll take that as a yes, then?"

Donovan touched his chest and looked at himself for the first time. He'd lost weight. Not much, but with all the travel he did, he didn't have much to lose. He was wearing a short-sleeved shirt, crisp and white like the nurse's, and trousers that stopped at his shins, also white cotton. He lifted the shirt up to his collarbones to find a bright red scar, newly healing, jarring against the midnight black of his skin. It was about the size of half his palm and mostly round.

"How long was I unconscious?" he asked the nurse, looking at the injury.

"About one week," she answered. "Your friends have been livid, since we've not let them leave until they were healed up themselves, and then them refusing to leave because of you still not woken. It's been tense, to say the least." Her tone was dour, but her eyes had a twinkle, telling him the bard at least had charmed this motherly woman.

"Can I see them now?"

"Of course. Try not to overdo it, though. The magic took a lot of your strength, which will come back in time, but you need to be careful and kind to your body, yes? You might find yourself breathless, but that'll heal as well if you carefully exercise."

"Thank you. What was your name?" he asked as she was leaving.

"Julle. Let me know if you need anything." She left, closing the door gently behind her.

Donovan pulled his bare feet onto the bed and laid back, stared at the ceiling and let his mind wander until he was almost in a doze.

The door opened again a few minutes later and Ruben peeked around it.

"Donovan!" he burst in the rest of the way.

He stopped at the bedside and gently reached up for a hug. Donovan hugged him back as tightly as he could, and noticed immediately how weak he was. Still, relief coursed through him to see the boy looking well.

Whitman soon followed in a wheeled chair, turning the wheels with his hands. His right leg, wrapped in a plaster cast, was extended to keep it straight.

"How's the knee?" Donovan asked.

"Poor. I'll be allowed to walk on it in the next day or so, but it'll take weeks to heal up to where the Healers will Take it. Most of the higher-ranking ones are out on assignments, and students are not allowed to Take injuries of this caliber." He smiled ruefully. "A few weeks is not a lifetime, however. I will be the most patient patient they have ever … Healed. Damn. Simply could not find the word there. Anyway, how is the chest?" Whitman asked.

Donovan touched the scar through his shirt. "Good as new, more or less, as I understand."

"The Healer in charge was worried about you. Killed half a dozen saplings transferring the injury. Apparently that arrow left splinters." He winced.

"Oh." Donovan looked at his chest again and felt grateful to be alive. "I see they fixed your face as well."

"Gods bless them, yes!" Whitman said, relief lighting his unbruised face. He reached up to touch his nose, no longer broken. "I was terribly worried about that. Still, they said it was the worst break they had seen in a long while, so I have that in my favor."

"Well done." Donovan turned to Ruben, who rolled his eyes with amusement. "How about you, Ben? What have you been doing?"

"Mostly reading. Dean Villery gave me some books from the library, but he made me swear not to spill anything on them, or get them wet. They're about the Order. The ones about magic and the history of the Order are interesting, but the rest are boring." He grinned.

"You've met the Dean, good! Are you enrolled in classes?"

Ruben shook his head. "No, not yet."

"Why not?"

"Stop frowning. I didn't want to agree to anything without you, is all."

"He would not let me assist him, either," Whitman added. "Something about not having magic and not knowing what was what?" He raised an eyebrow in mock severity.

"I'm sorry I wasn't there to get you signed up," Donovan lamented. "I meant to get you settled in."

"How dare you fail in your duties, Donovan," Whitman interrupted before Ruben could answer. "An arrow to the lung certainly does not take precedence to class scheduling. Shame on you, man, *shame!*"

Ruben swatted Whitman's shoulder. "It's fine, Don, honest. I haven't gone to my room assignment yet — he showed me where it is, but there's a couch in Whit's room that's comfy."

Donovan shook his head. "I'll talk to Hector — Dean Villery, today if I can. We'll get you sorted."

Ruben shrugged, clearly not concerned.

"Anything else happen while I was unconscious?" Donovan asked.

"I met Elliott," Ruben said. "He's nice. Busy, though."

"Elliott should be busy," Whitman said. "The Head of the Order does not get much time away from the job; too much going on around here."

"You're definitely going to shake things up a bit, Ruben," Donovan said. "Don't worry, though. Your only concern is learning to use your magic."

A gentle knock sounded at the still-open door and the nurse, Julle, entered with a tray. She smiled at Whitman and Ruben and set the tray across Donovan's legs.

"Eat that, and then you can go. I'll have some clothes fetched for you. And remember what I said about going slowly. You'll do yourself no good if you end up back here tomorrow."

She left again.

All conversation was forgotten as the first whiff of food made its way into Donovan's nose. It was only soup with vegetables boiled down soft, but his stomach growled angrily and suddenly the soup was the most delicious thing he'd ever smelled, let alone tasted. There was bread to dip into the broth, which he devoured eagerly. Ruben brought him a cup of water, and ran to refill it twice before Donovan was finished.

Halfway through his meal, he felt he should apologize, "I'm suddenly starving."

"Think nothing of it, my good man," Whitman said. "I have never been unconscious for a week, but I have had my fair share of Healings, and they do tend to sap one's strength and energy, replenished only by the finest vittles the Order can provide. Or anything, honestly. I was once tempted to fight a chicken for a dropped heel of bread before being convinced otherwise. Chickens are very mean."

"What did you do for the week?" Donovan asked around a mouthful of bread. "Ruben's been reading and avoiding classes; have you been stuck abed like me?"

Ruben grinned sheepishly, but Whitman waved a hand airily, dismissing the question.

"Bards keep themselves entertained, the better to entertain others. My week has not been dull, but I doubt it would particularly interest you to hear about it."

Ruben looked like he was about to ask a question, but Whitman continued.

"I expect you will want to finish in peace, so I shall retire to my own room. I imagine we will see each other again, Master Rudd. It has been a pleasure making your acquaintance, and I am glad to have attempted to steal your horse."

Donovan chuckled and shook Whitman's proffered hand. "Same. Don't be a stranger."

"Never, sir! Whitman Acres, bard to the world, stranger to no one but those I have not yet met!" He wheeled himself away from the bed and through the door without a look back.

"Odd fellow," Donovan said, cleaning the bowl with the last bite of bread. "Glad to have met him, though."

"Aye," Ruben agreed. "He helped me with the larger words in my books." Ruben stared after the bard for a moment. "He had half a dozen people in and out of his room. I kept getting chased off so they could talk in private."

"Bards are often asked to carry news; they probably wanted to hear it, is all."

"Even Elliott, though? I was told to call him Elliott," Ruben reassured Donovan's sharp look. "He talked to me and welcomed me for a bit, and then I was chased off again. I think Whit's important."

"Could be," Donovan shrugged. He put the bowl aside, finally satisfied.

Julle entered again with a tap at the door, this time bearing a stack of clothes. She set the pile at the foot of his bed and came around to take the tray.

"Record time, I expect." She laughed. "If you can walk without dizziness, you're free to go. If you feel at all strange, come right back, yes?"

Donovan nodded. "Thank you, ma'am."

"Come on, boy. Let the man have his privacy."

Ruben trotted behind the nurse with a grin and closed the door behind him.

Donovan slid his legs out from under the thick comforter, wiggling his toes and stretching his feet. He stood slowly and stretched his arms and back, filling his lungs, but feeling a tightness in his chest that hadn't been there before. Still, he was alive to appreciate it. He bent to touch his toes for a few moments before dressing. He folded his discarded hospital uniform neatly. They'd brought him clothes from his own room, which briefly surprised him, but he appreciated it, nonetheless. He assumed it was standard practice for people who lived in the Order; he'd never been in the Healing Ward for an overnight stay.

The hallway was long and lined with doors. Rooms similar to his own were waiting for the next emergency, or filled with resting patients. Guiding signs led him into a waiting area filled with cushioned chairs and benches. The counter was occupied by surgeons and nurses and students reading over the logs for the day and engaging in various discussions. As he entered, several of them looked him up and down before going back to their business, clearly recognizing that he didn't need assistance. A few people sat waiting in the waiting room chairs: one couple cried quietly while a somber surgeon spoke with them. They were given a wide, sympathetic berth. Donovan respectfully gave them plenty of space as well as he made his way to where he spotted Ruben, hunched over with a book on his knees. Donovan nudged his shoulder and the boy looked up sharply. He shook hair out of his eyes with a grin.

They walked together, slower than Donovan was used to, but the pace was necessary; his muscles were still waking. Ruben led the way. The white stone halls were no less clean outside of the Healing Ward, but there was less smell of cleaning agents, and the lighting contained in glass around the ceiling, while clear, was not the blinding brightness of the surgery rooms.

"How do they do that?" Ruben asked, pointing at the glass tubes that lined the top of nearly every wall. Caged lightning ran back and forth in the tubes, making a constant stream of light. It flickered slightly, but it was hardly noticeable, and less than a torch's light would be.

Donovan had spent so many years at the Order now that he'd grown used to some of its miracles of magic. "I'm not sure how it's done," he admitted. "Elementalists have some way of filling the container, but I don't know how it's maintained. You can sometimes tell when a different Elementalist filled the container, though, look." Donovan pointed at two different walls. The lightning in one moved a bit faster than in the other, and the colors were very slightly different.

"How does the glass not break? I've seen a house struck by lightning, and all of its windows were shattered."

Donovan shook his head ruefully. "I've no idea."

"I wonder if I'll learn to do that," Ruben mused, a keen look in his eye.

"I'm sure you'll learn that and much more."

They continued through the broad hallways, past the offices and classrooms for surgical staff and students, then out of the Medical Wing entirely. The change in décor was slight, but fewer pictures of landscapes hung on the walls here, and more portraits of famous mages and Heads of the Order. Occasional murals of mage-battles took up entire walls.

They descended a wide set of stairs as they passed into busier areas. Scholars and students bustled past alone and in groups to each new destination. People dodged through the throng, narrowly avoiding collisions, and the loud murmur of sound hung like a cloud above the crowd.

Donovan took a deep breath and smiled. He'd missed the bustle of this place, the organized chaos. The silence and peace of the road was its own joy, but whenever he spent too long in one place, he missed the other.

When they reached the bottom of the stairs, Ruben again took the lead.

"You know where Dean Villery's office is?" Donovan asked.

Ruben nodded and pointed as he walked. "He took me there a couple of times so I could come find him if I needed."

Younger students and fewer scholars were in the halls now. Older students were using the corridors to reach various classrooms, and teachers without classes this period were monitoring the noise and cleanliness of the place. All of them recognized Donovan and nodded or smiled in greeting. A few quickly shook his hand and welcomed him back before letting him carry on his way.

He could tell the rumors were loose by the way a fair number of people saw him, and then looked at Ruben with renewed interest and awe.

Dean Villery's office was around the corner from the dormitories; most of the classrooms were across the wing.

Ruben pointed at one dormitory room, the door closed, and said, "That one's mine."

"Have you met the other two boys yet?"

"No. One of them's about to graduate to another room, though. I think the other is in his first year, but he's been here for months."

"I'm sure you'll get along. I made friends with my roommates when I was in classes. We're occasionally in touch even now."

They turned at the end of the hall and arrived at the dean's office door. It stood open. A page traded a stack of letters and notes from her satchel for another one of nearly equal size from the dean's desk, already crowded with correspondences and schedules, complaints and compliments, and all manner of other business.

He looked up and smiled brightly to see them, casting a younger glow on his harried face.

"Donovan! Ruben! Do come in! Thank you, Heather, I'm sure I'll see you again later."

The girl settled her satchel of letters and trotted out of the room, closing the door as she went.

"Good to see you up and about, Don," Hector said, leaning across the desk to shake his hand.

Donovan gripped his friend's hand warmly. "It's good to be up and about," he agreed, "though I wouldn't mind having a bit more breath in my lungs."

"Don't be greedy. Ruben! Have you been enjoying those books we found?"

"Yessir. They're mostly interesting."

"Mostly! You wound me! Those are my favorite texts!" He winked and turned back to Donovan. "We're a bit later than expected, but Ruben will be with us for some time. Besides which, he'll have plenty of private tutors to get him all trained up, so I can't imagine he'll struggle." He grinned at the boy, who beamed back.

"You've mocked up a schedule for him, then?" Donovan asked, sitting heavily. His knees were twinging with the work of walking after being so long abed, and his back ached both at the lack of movement, and its reintroduction. *Make up your mind!*

The Dean lifted a stack of papers and pulled one out, handing it across the table. Donovan scanned, angling the page so that

Ruben could see. A fairly straightforward schedule of the day had blocks of time inked in with classes scribbled onto it.

Donovan looked at Ruben, who already looked overwhelmed. He reached over and ruffled the boy's hair and then pointed out some of the blocks. "As well as magic, you'll be learning history and reading and math and such, so that's why there's so much going on. Hector, you've got him learning four magics this semester?"

"Yes, Elliott insisted." The dean leaned back in his chair, looking tired. "Healing, Mentalism, Displacing, Seeking — his roommate Frin is a new Displacer, so they'll be able to go to classes together. The other roommate, Arnold, is a Mentalist. But he's nearly graduated, so he should be able to help. You know how Elliott feels about Mentalists, of course, and Healers are always in high demand." He looked at Ruben again. "It's mostly rumors at this point, so I want to make sure — you don't get sick at all when you use your magic?"

Ruben shook his head and shrugged.

"No nausea, no headache, no numbness in your hands or feet, anything like that?"

"I don't think so," Ruben replied. He looked at Donovan. "Do you get that?"

Donovan smiled ruefully. "Unfortunately, yes. None of the numbness, though I might consider that a blessing, honestly. I get headaches and nausea, though. Sometimes I get dizzy. My whole body aches, really."

"That's awful! You did so much Seeking when we were coming here!" The boy looked aghast. "I knew you felt bad, but you didn't say it was *that* bad!"

Donovan reached over and hugged the boy awkwardly to his side. "It's the price of magic, son. You're sweet to feel that way. Just remember that all of your classmates will be suffering those kinds of things, so be sympathetic and patient toward them."

Ruben nodded, frowning thoughtfully.

"Hector, you don't have etiquette on here anywhere," Donovan said, returning to the schedule.

"Not for this semester, no," the dean agreed.

"You don't think they'll start in on him this soon? I wouldn't bet on it."

"Where would you want to put it?"

"I'd say halve this History period and put beginning etiquette in with it there. We can reassess next quarter."

"I can do that." The Dean grabbed a quill and made a note.

"And I'd think he should start with the Elementals, since he's already shown an affinity for that — fire was what brought us to him in the first place." Donovan looked at Ruben. "Any opinions on that, Ben?"

"I ... don't think so?"

"That's all right. It's a lot to take in. Let's start with Displacement, Elementals, Seeking and Mentalism with ... this period for time in the Surgery Wing, no practicum. Move the magic to the morning, the classwork to the afternoon."

"That's a good point. Normally all of the magic classes are in the afternoon and evening so that the students can retire to their rooms to sleep and rest instead of having to learn anything else," the Dean explained to Ruben. "I'd structured your schedule in the same way, though of course you won't need that kind of arrangement. We'll leave Displacement in the afternoon, though. It'll keep you awake through the second half of the day, and you'll still be able to go with Frin. I think you'll get along." He smiled again. "Jaynes should have time for Seeking in the afternoon as well ..." he muttered to himself, making another note.

Donovan nodded at Hector's notes and said to Ruben, "It's busy, but if you feel overwhelmed at all, you let Hector know. He'll be able to move things around so you're not drowning."

Ruben nodded. "When do I start?"

"You can start in the morning," the Dean answered, making more scribbles on the schedule.

Ruben looked at Donovan, who nodded in agreement.

"All right!" the boy exclaimed. He looked excited. It was quite a change from the wary suspicions he'd had on the road.

Hector smiled at the boy. "I need to talk with Donovan privately for a few minutes. Would you mind stepping outside?"

Ruben slid out of his seat and left, closing the door behind him.

"I'll have this ready soon," Hector waved the schedule. "I need to notify the instructors and have the tutors sorted out, but I've been conferring with them already, so that won't take any time." He put down his quill and leaned back in his seat with a deep exhale.

They sat in companionable silence for a moment before Hector said, "I was sorry to hear about Lucas, Don. He was a very good man, a good Healer. A great partner."

The now-familiar lump filled Donovan's throat as he nodded stiffly. His face was warm.

"How'd it happen?"

Donovan cleared his throat and answered, "We had to fight through Hunters. He brought down several on his own, but the last one ... the last one was a Healer himself. Looked like he turned the magic back on Lucas, and with the added edge of blood available ..." Donovan shook his head. "They went down together."

"Gods all ..." Hector ran a hand across his thick, stormy hair. "I'm so sorry."

"Me, too. I have to tell his mother, his siblings."

Hector was silent for a long, thoughtful moment. "That boy out there is going to change things."

"You're telling me. With how desperate the Hunters were to get their hands on him, I wouldn't be surprised if we were attacked here for the first time in a century. And soon." He gripped the arms of his chair. "Sending just two of us ..." he uttered through gritted teeth.

"Elliott wants him. You know how he can be. He won't like that you exchanged Healing for Elementalism, but I'll take the credit."

Donovan grimaced. "He said as much when we were sent out — I should have questioned Vale then. I had worries about being sent like a normal Retrieval, and I was right. They'll want my report, and I expect Elliott to send for me." He put his chin in his hands. Anger was making an appearance in his gut.

Hector scratched his face. "Tomorrow, most like. He's been swamped lately. I guess some new information came in recently and he's been after it like a hound on steak."

"Good news, hopefully."

"The king won't wait too long, either. His people have already been asking me questions and I've given them a healthy fear. They shouldn't be bothering the boy, but if Ruben's to learn anything without distraction, he'll need to get used to curious eyes."

"They'll get bored soon enough when he shows he's a normal boy like any other."

"He isn't, though."

"Any child is still a child. They're all capable of amazing things — sometimes very dangerous things. That's why you're here. Still children, though."

Hector smiled crookedly. "Mm. Thanks for that. Any word on when you'll be sent out again?"

Donovan spread his hands. "Not soon. I need to finish recovering." He touched his chest. "And I'll have to break in a new partner."

He closed his eyes, willing the tears away. He mostly succeeded. Hector didn't comment as he palmed his eyes tiredly.

"Have dinner with me and a few others tonight. We'll toast Lucas, and get some weight back on your bones."

Donovan chuckled. "All right, I will."

"Are you taking Ruben to the quartermaster?"

"I'd planned to. It's been a while since I've gone." He pursed his lips. "Lucas always did that part."

"I ask because you might want to pass it off to an older student instead. You were right about needing to see Elliott: he and Vale were on my back this week about getting that report like you said. That group of soldiers that found you is close-lipped, but rumors make their way around, and with no report filed after this long, people are bound to make things up worse than usual."

"Right. Thanks for that. I'll see you tonight."

They stood together and Hector came around the desk to grab Donovan in a tight hug.

"I'm really glad you're all right, Don."

"Thanks, Hector. I'm glad to be here."

Donovan left Hector to his work. He found Ruben down the hall staring at the glass tubes of lightning up at the ceiling with a thoughtful frown on his face, hands on his slender hips.

"You can ask your tutors about it tomorrow," Donovan said, coming up behind the boy.

Ruben nodded. "I will, too." As they started back the way they'd come, Ruben asked, "What now?"

"Now I need to find someone to take you to the quartermaster for your supplies. I have to make a report about the trip."

"Can't I come?"

Donovan smiled and shook his head. "No, you need to get ready for your first day tomorrow. You'll have some catching up to do, and I might be a while. It won't be interesting."

"I don't mind!"

Donovan looked at him with a raised eyebrow.

"All right, all right."

They threaded their way through the halls, then Donovan turned them down a new corridor.

"Dining hall?" Ruben asked, showing off his knowledge.

"Nearby."

This section of hallway wasn't nearly as busy, despite its proximity to food; most people had already eaten lunch, and dinner was several hours off. Even so, the Order was a big place, stuffed with people, and there were always those who kept odd hours to the rest of the bunch, if the noise ahead was any indication. Before reaching the dining hall, however, Donovan turned right and led them down an empty corridor. Several office-like rooms lined the hallway, but none of them appeared occupied until they reached one near the middle of the hall.

Donovan opened the door and light and sound spilled out. Students of every age were seated and sprawled across every surface of the large room. A medium-sized fireplace on the far wall with a hearth contained a pot of bubbling liquid that smelled like cider. Several chipped mugs and tankards sat crowded around the stone to stay warm. Couches and lounging chairs, most in various states of disrepair, lay all over the room; several long tables lined either wall, with a few single-person desks scattered around as well.

Plenty of the students had books and documents, seeking assistance from and giving it to their peers for various classes. A small group in a back corner held instruments, quietly practicing. Those who weren't studying or working lounged or played games. Nearly half of them recognized Donovan. They hailed him, waving and calling out greetings. The Retriever grinned and waved back, putting a hand on Ruben's shoulder.

"I need a favor, please."

The noise level lowered as those nearest the door paid attention.

"Ruben's new, first day tomorrow, and he needs to be kitted out. Came here with the shirt on his back, and a few odds and ends, but nothing substantial."

"Who's his roommate?" a boy asked.

Donovan looked down at Ruben to answer.

Ruben cleared his throat, "Um, Frin? And Arnold?"

The boy made a disgusted face at Arnold's name. "Yeah, I'll help. No stress. Hey, Molly!"

"Thanks, Joseph."

The noise level rose again as the two students stepped into the hall. The noise cut off immediately as the door closed.

Donovan turned to Ruben again. "I'll come track you down when I'm free again, all right? You'll be fine." He gave Ruben a warm smile.

Joseph came out with a young woman, both of them putting out their hands to shake. The boy was about seventeen, trying valiantly to will a beard into existence. He was nearly as tall as Donovan, and is hair, wavy and long, was kept pulled away from his face in a low horsetail.

The young woman was about the same age, thick-boned and broad-shouldered. A head taller than Joseph, she possessed muscles a blacksmith would envy.

"Ruben, yeah?" Joseph asked.

Ruben nodded.

"I'm Molly," the girl told him with a kind smile.

"What's your magic, then?" Joseph asked.

Ruben glanced at Donovan, who shrugged one shoulder, encouraging him with a nod.

"Um, I'm a magus."

The newcomers stared. "Say again?" Joseph asked.

"I ... I'm a magus?"

Molly looked at Donovan, disbelief on her features.

"Keep calm, children. He's just as new as you ever were, and he's got far more to learn."

"I'd think so!" Joseph said, running a hand up and down the side of his face, eyes still wide. "What- what can you do?"

"Nothing yet, really. I mean, I made fire. And I Healed Donovan once and spoke into someone's mind ... not much else?"

"Good gravy!" Joseph looked at Donovan again, who was unable to keep a wan smile from his face.

"Go easy, Joe. He needs paper and shirts and all the rest. Stop terrifying him."

Molly grinned in excitement. "That's brilliant! We've not had a magus in — in forever! I'm a Mentalist, me."

The older boy swallowed and took a deep breath, forcing himself to calm down. After a moment, he managed a small chuckle. "I'm a Healer, myself."

"Oh!" Ruben said. "I want to learn more about that, but my schedule had — what was it ... no practice?"

"No *practicum* this term," Donovan supplied.

"Yeah?" Joseph let out a toothy grin. "There's a lot to know about Healing someone."

"I killed a tree, I think ... when I was helping Donovan."

"That happens. Best option, really." He put an arm around Ruben's shoulders and led him away, Molly on Ruben's other side.

Donovan watched them go fondly. He'd brought both of them to the Order, years ago. Molly's farming family had sent for someone to come get her because they couldn't leave in the middle of harvest. They'd been terrified that Hunters would come if they knew. Donovan and Lucas had shown up and nearly been drowned in thankful hugs, taking more food and favors than they ever could have needed back with them on the road.

Joseph's father had tried to keep quiet about the boy's skills. Joseph had tried to run away more than once and, when the two partners showed up to take him, he'd been in tears with gratitude. Lucas had fought off the father, who refused to let him go, and filed the report with the city guard. A neighbor had reported Joseph's magic to them, and the father's attitude, so they'd been prepared. Joseph had never spoken of why he'd needed to run away, but after a couple of months in the safety of the Order, he'd thrived. Donovan wouldn't be surprised if he stayed on as an instructor in future years.

Donovan touched his new scar and thought about Lucas again. He'd practically grown up here; his education started long after Donovan had already left. They'd been nearly forty years apart in age, after all. The young man's family had been military through and through back generations. His mother lived in town, still.

With Ruben in good hands, Donovan set off with a determined stride. He wound through the halls and corridors and this time his legs ate the distance. Unexpectedly winded, he arrived in a section of the Order that shared a floor with the Medical Wing but on the opposite side of the enormous building. This was where the Retrievers lived.

He took a moment to catch his breath, then headed toward an office he knew well. He knocked at the open door and a woman looked up, squinting her heavily scarred face.

"I see you're not dead," she said. The greeting was never polite, but it was the one she used every time he came back from a job. Her voice was hoarse and low, scratchy, as though she'd eaten horseshoe nails for breakfast, and it had been for all the years he'd known her.

"Still breathing, thanks."

"Not Lucas, though."

He shook his head.

"Shame. He was good enough."

"I'll drink to that."

"You want another job? I hear your lung took an arrow. Or was that exaggeration?"

She leaned back in her chair, her right arm behind her head, the left only a stump at her shoulder with the sleeve of her jacket pinned up and out of the way. A look of boredom settled into its familiar place above the burn scars on her cheek. His eyes were momentarily drawn to her neck where a permanent mark showed a successful hanging, which had still failed to kill her.

"No, that was true."

"Got a scar?"

He nodded.

"Don't be shy, let's see it."

He rolled his eyes and pulled up his shirt.

She eyed the angry mark and let out a low whistle. "Impressive. Either he missed, or he was a sadist."

"I'd lean toward the latter," Donovan said, putting his clothes back in order.

"Punctured is no fun. Hanging's worse, 'course."

"Of course."

Any injury one of them returned with, Vale could top, and readily told the bare-bones story behind each of her scars. She hadn't been Retrieving in two decades, but still knew the kingdom like the back of her remaining hand.

She was in charge of the Retrievers, providing orders and overseeing their packing lists, handing out stipends, and all the rest. When he started, Donovan had hated the woman, but while she hadn't mellowed with time, he'd come to understand her gruff nature was not malicious; she just didn't have a care to speak gently. She was fiercely protective of her people, even so.

"And? I imagine those in Med-Wing say no marching 'til you've got your breath back, aye?"

"Basically."

"What're you doing here, then? Go wander, sleep, whatever; I've work." She gestured at her desk.

"I need to make my report."

"So write it out. I have to slot you for a new partner."

He clenched his jaw and took a step further inside, closing the door gently behind him.

"Oh?" she asked and sat forward. Her arm dropped to her desktop.

Donovan sat in the rarely-used chair before her desk and let a deep breath slide from between his teeth, feeling the heat rise through him again.

"Spit it out, old-timer," she said gruffly.

"What were you *thinking*?" he snarled suddenly. His breath was coming in short bursts now, his throat tight and his eyes stinging.

"I thought I was sending you on a job," Vale answered hoarsely. She didn't look surprised at his tone.

"Some job!" Donovan let out a half-crazed laugh. "Hunters on our backs from the moment we landed in Philipa and more chasing our tails across a dozen towns; Lucas *dead* — *murdered* at Merritt's Gorge because you sent *two* of us to fetch a *magus*?"

"Unconfirmed magus," Vale corrected softly.

"*Confirmed*," Donovan snapped. "You shouldn't have sent two Retrievers; you should have sent an army."

Vale leaned back in her chair with a gentle creak of leather and wood. "Is that what you think." Her raspy voice was low and emotionless.

Donovan continued, "We were outnumbered at every turn, Vale. Every step, they knew we were coming, where we were going, and it was by the skin of our damn teeth that I lived, and Lucas—" he stopped, throat too constricted to continue. He dropped his head into his hands, letting the tears pool against his palms as he tried to regain control.

"While you compose yourself," Vale coughed sharply and swallowed, wincing. "You think a dozen people would have moved better, faster, more decisively than two? You think a dozen would have attracted the notice of so few Hunters? Yes, *few* I say. They could have sent two hundred and they sent, what'd the bard say, two in town and half a dozen at the gorge? You think it was left to chance who I sent? My best fighter, Healer to boot, and most experienced Retriever next to myself? If he hadn't met his magic's match, Lucas would be alive today and you'd *both* be griping that I should have sent an army. But you're here, aren't you? You made it. You brought the magus, and now the Order can train him up and in half a decade we'll see what he can do about this little war we're facing." She coughed again, a snarl of irritation on her features, and reached for a blue and yellow glass mug on her desk, drinking deeply.

Donovan sat silently. It was the most he'd ever heard Vale say at one time.

She went on, "Don't snap at me like I don't know what I'm doing. I said it was a shame we lost Lucas, but *that's the job*. It's dangerous work and we die all the time; you know that. Best I can do is see you all get extra training and stay awake on your assignments, and in the *meantime*, I'll start training a new batch of fresh youngsters ready to die for the right to bring *children* all over across this kingdom in the name of an education in magic so they don't accidentally kill each other in their little backward towns and villages."

She smirked humorlessly. "What do you want from me, Don? You want me to say I chose wrong, that I made a mistake? You want me to say the decision I made was *incorrect*? Looks to me like it went about as well as we could have expected, worse than we hoped, but some days the luck just dies and takes you with it. Write your report and have it to me by morning. Let me know if I should question any of the decisions *you* made. Dismissed."

Donovan unfolded slowly and walked to the door. "What if he'd been captured, Vale? Killed?"

"The boy?" Vale shrugged. "I'd say I made the wrong choice in sending you two."

Donovan opened the door and stepped through.

"Hey," Vale croaked behind him.

Donovan turned around.

"It's this magus to blame for all these Hunters — more out there now than shit in a horse-field. I've requested soldiers to meet our folks on the roads and bring them in, and anyone who goes out now will have escort. Don't come see me until you're ready to go out again. Unless you're done with that, elder. What are you, sixty-five?"

Donovan managed a half-hearted smile. "You're one to talk."

"But never lie."

He closed the door and leaned on it, staring at the floor. He didn't know what he expected from his talk with Vale, but that certainly wasn't it. And now he didn't know how he felt. His rage still burned, but Vale had blanketed it with backward compliments and a twisted, but sound, logic.

"Oi, you're Donovan — I'm Landon."

Donovan blinked away his musing and looked up to see a smiling young man, about Lucas's age. His straight blond hair, cut short in a militaristic style, accentuated his square jaw.

"Is this a bad time?" Landon asked as his smile faded.

He looked familiar, but it took a moment for Donovan to place him. "You came to help us in Weston. You were struck in the arm. Are you all right?"

Landon grinned again. "A couple of stitches sorted me out. It stings, but I'll live. I didn't suffer a punctured lung," he pointed out.

Donovan shook his hand firmly. "I appreciate your help, really."

Landon waved off the praise. "Sure. We did our job, no trouble."

"Was there something I could help you with?" Donovan asked.

"Nah, I wanted to make sure you were all right, is all. I went to the Medical Wing, but they said you were discharged and I'd just missed you. Took me a bit to figure out where to look; I was about to give up."

"I had business to attend to; I'm behind on everything," Donovan said sheepishly.

"Makes sense," Landon bobbed his head. "Glad to see you're healing. If you need any soldiering, don't hesitate to find me."

"Thank you, Landon, I'll keep you in mind." Landon grinned again and left down the hall.

Donovan rubbed the back of his neck. He knew what his next duties would be, and wasn't looking forward to them in the slightest. Still, there was no point in putting it off.

6

THE WALL SURROUNDING THE ENORMOUS BUILDING of the Order was the height of fifteen men, a miracle of craftsmanship, and practically impenetrable. Hundreds of soldiers and mages of various sorts protected the walls, and all of its tricks were kept updated; a masterwork of architecture that anyone could be proud of. It had been built long before the Order inside was finished, but even so, it had room for the gardens, training grounds, and living quarters that it protected. Space had finally grown tight, so housing on the grounds was highly coveted. They'd started restricting the grounds to families of professors and long-term scholars, and those who maintained the building. Donovan had heard of waiting lists and didn't envy those on them — their children might see an opening before they did.

Exiting was less of a trial than entering. Soldiers and mages, mostly Mentalists and Empaths, scanned the crowds. He'd seen plenty of people stopped in his years here, but only a couple of times were they detained. No one today suffered that fate, and the line moved quickly. Few were in a talking mood, huddled down in their coats. Breath steamed in front of everyone's faces, and made a hazy mist above the entire line.

The dozen gates leading to various sides of the place didn't eliminate the traffic, but, through the years, the rules of the road had grown strict. Wagons and other large vehicles were kept to the inside of the road where ruts had to be regularly maintained. They stayed to the left of the road, single file per direction.

Pedestrians followed the same 'walk on the left' rule on the outside of the road. It wasn't a long walk to the city proper, but there were two small guard shacks on each side of the road to provide direction and aid when needed. Both had warm braziers burning within. A few temporary tents hawking drinks and snacks were allowed to sell, but were required to pack up by nightfall. Only a few were allowed along the road to keep from slowing traffic, and the rule was first-come, first-kept.

The metropolis was loud enough that Donovan could hear it from the Order's gates, which he appreciated, as it allowed his ears to get used to the level of sound. Officially named Thairnsdale, but usually referred simply as 'the city of the Order', it was a sight to make any visitor stand in awe. Home to tens of thousands of people, and temporary stop to thousands more, it assaulted the senses even from a distance.

The Order was stuffed full of people, but it was nothing to the press of humanity in Thairnsdale. Built in layers circling the Order's wall, the market was first, with regularly placed warehouses to keep the Order stocked with goods from the faraway fields. Permanent shops by the merchants stretched all the way around, covering three streets on both sides. If you couldn't find what you were looking for here, it didn't exist. Today, it was partially hidden by the steam of humankind, and Elementalists were out in force, offering to infuse small objects with heat to keep in your pockets, and going around to businesses to warm the floors or walls. Donovan waved them away politely, his coat warm enough for his walk.

He entered the first layer of the city and passed one of five large amphitheaters — this one was currently empty, or at least not drawing a crowd. Buskers reciting poetry and playing instruments with frozen fingers sang and drew along his path. He dropped a few coins for them and continued on his way amongst a crowd of school students. These did not attend the Order, but did attend instead the vocational schools here, where they learned sculpting, painting, singing, writing, dancing, acting. He shook his head and grinned at the conversations of the youth and separated from the crowd.

Temporary housing and some residential areas were next, small houses stacked on top of one another to save space. They reminded Donovan of the tenement buildings in towns he'd visited, but these had glass windows and were far less dreary. Unless you were a resident to Thairnsdale, there was little reason to venture beyond this layer, and there were plenty of indications of that, including a deep and wide circle of water fed from underground and maintained by Elementalist mages through the year. Littering into it was illegal. It was perfectly safe to swim in — people were swimming now, despite the freezing temperatures. It was rare for it to freeze over, but it had happened in the past, resulting in a roaring winter festival.

Boats were poled along, offering relaxing and romantic trips, or as ferries to cross if you didn't want to use a crowded bridge, as Donovan was used to doing. He didn't mind the crowds usually, although today they seemed to press particularly close. One could use any of twelve bridges to cross: one for every road and gate leading into the Order; on the other side of the bridges started the homes for permanent residents.

Most of the houses were small, but comfortable enough for the two or three children the families typically had. Once in a rare while, a spot of garden meticulously maintained could be seen. Neighborhoods lay side-by-side, but rarely touching, separated by more shops — smaller than those in the marker layer — providing food, clothing, and other necessities for daily life. Many of the neighborhoods had their own personalities, expressed with colors of stone, roofing tiles, or paving bricks. It was hard to get lost after a few visits.

Though he had rarely continued to the centermost layer, Donovan knew that there lay the grand manors of the nobility, with gates and guards patrolling. Guards patrolled in every layer, and each had guard houses with barracks to sleep in. They were rotated throughout the city to keep them honest and alert, and employed plenty of mages in their ranks. They were all trained to react quickly to put out fires, especially — the city's greatest fear besides plague.

The street he strode down now was a familiar one; he'd made this trip many, many times since gaining Lucas as a partner. Five years was a long time to know someone — although it seemed like hardly any time at all these days. The neighborhood was done mostly in red and orange shades of brick; the street could feel like walking through an oven in the summer, but it was comforting now. The paving stones, patterned in swirls until the edges of the outward sloping lane, gaped with drains to keep from flooding. Strings of pennants stretched between most of the homes, snapping in the wind. Many of them bore prayers to send the messages with the elements that touched them. A dog chased a feral cat across his path, causing his steps to stutter momentarily.

His feet turned and stopped without his attention, and he stared at the house he'd come to think of as a second home: two stories high, narrow in the front, with a covered entryway six feet long and garden the same depth, round stones etched with prayers lined it. Ivy climbed the face, revealing three sets of shuttered windows closed against the chill. A bronze globe rotated with the wind at the peak of the roof, squeaking gently, and signaling to the world their faith. Donovan had never found comfort in religion, but he didn't begrudge those who did.

He must have been spotted, because the door opened and a woman his age stepped out. Her short hair, spiky in the back, but not messy, looked as though she was constantly running very quickly. Her trousers and shirt were practical and comfortably warm for the season. Barefoot, she tapped one foot gently to an unheard beat. She held up a stone for him to see and tossed it to him. He caught it deftly. Carved into it was a simple prayer for health and security. He walked to the garden to find a spot that didn't disturb the growing vegetation and planted it halfway to its top. When he turned back to the entryway, the woman was gone, but the door was still open.

It took his eyes a moment to adjust to the dim lighting inside, but he could hear a chair pulled out from the table and so he walked to it. Before he could sit, though, Kail grabbed him in a tight hug, barely felt through his thick coat, but which he readily returned, sorrow welling up in his chest again.

They held each other, no words necessary, or possible, around their shared grief. When she released him, she said, "It sure is good to see you."

"I'm so sorry," he replied.

She nodded and sat at the kitchen table, motioning for him to do the same. Lucas had taken after his mother in clear ways. Their hair had been the same brown; their eyes the same blue. He'd taken his father's pointed nose, where his mother's was more rounded. Lucas had been taller, but had her slim frame. If she'd had a brother, Lucas might have been his twin.

She had a kind face, but anyone who'd raised five children mostly by herself had steel in her. Her comfortable clothes nonetheless held military-clean creases — one didn't stop practicing old habits without good reason.

The kitchen had a large chalkboard mounted low on the wall, covered in basic mathematics, and there was evidence of various hobbies on the table and counters: locks half picked, knives laid out for sharpening, candles hanging to dry by their wicks. A half-constructed barrel sat in the corner; one of the staves wore a jaunty hat, half-finished.

Being the same age, but working alongside her middle son, put Donovan in a strange role with the family. He was a friend-brother-father figure, but didn't mind. They always invited him for holidays and family dinners, never expecting more than his presence at the table.

Happy memories flooded his mind as Donovan sat at that table and he rubbed a rough palm over the polished surface. He smirked at the jeweler tools, and almost-completed cross stitch shoved out of the way. She had built the table, he recalled. From a piece of wall tossed aside after a house fire. The memories felt wrong, now, as he sat here in this home. Tainted, without the one who'd been with him for the telling of each. He took a deep breath and finally looked up. Kail had her hands clasped in front of her; infinite patience from a lifetime of practice coated her like a second skin. She didn't rush him, didn't speak at all, but waited until he was ready.

For the first time since waking, Donovan told the whole story of what had happened. It wasn't an explanation or excuse. It wasn't a description of the route he'd taken, the decisions they'd made, and reasoning behind it. He didn't tell her why they'd gone — she knew that much.

This time, he told the story of a son's death to his mother.

*   *   *

Finished, it felt as though a weight had been lifted from his shoulders. He still mourned the loss of his best friend, but the guilt was fading — not gone, not yet. It would never go away, he knew, but those family memories weren't wrong, spoiled, anymore. Now they were nostalgic, and sweetly sad, and only a little bit angry.

They both had dry eyes. Kail wasn't one for tears and never had been.

She'd listened without questions until he finished, and now asked, "I guess you succeeded, then?"

Donovan nodded. "Ruben's up getting kitted right now."

"He'd have appreciated that. No point in dying if the job isn't finished in the end."

He managed a soft chuckle. "That's the truth."

"They sent me the official letter and his gear a week ago. I'll send you back with half of it when you leave. I asked about you and they said you were healing, but not what got you."

"Oh, an arrow. I was unconscious the whole week, else I'd have come sooner."

"I figured. He'd have been miffed someone else was doing your Healing. Possessive of his patients, that one."

"He was." Donovan smiled, and Kail grinned crookedly. "I'm going to write to the others."

"Good luck. I hardly hear anything from them these days. Barely a letter escapes the General's lands, you know that. What's your plan now?" she asked.

Donovan sighed. "I really hadn't gotten that far."

"Best think quick or they'll give you assignments."

"I know, I know ..."

"Don." He looked at her. "Best figure it out. I don't imagine you'll be going Retrieving any time soon, so what needs doing now?"

"We need to find that bowman."

"The one who shot you. You think he's calling the orders now?"

"No, he was under his own orders, but I doubt he was low in their ranks. And he- he knew what he was doing."

"So find him," she said bluntly.

He nodded thoughtfully. It wouldn't be easy to find an unnamed bowman, and Marcus was dead. He would need help, that was for sure.

"What else?" she asked. "You've got skills, so find someone who needs them. If you can't find a job, make one that they didn't know they needed. Rise through. You're meeting with Elliott, you said, so make him know he needs you. Stay busy, or wither away."

"All right ..."

"I mean it."

"I know."

"Get going."

He managed to smile again. "Do you need anything?"

She shook her head. "Nah. I'm as I always am."

"You know where to find me."

"Come back for holidays and dinners, or I *will* come find you."

"Yes, ma'am."

They hugged again, tightly.

When they broke apart, she pulled a canvas backpack out from under the table. "Here. Take this all to the Order with you. It's either their gear, or things you might want, so sort it first, but I don't need any of it. I moved that portrait we got done last year to the hall; he'd have liked that."

"He would have."

"Be well, Don."

"I'll see you, Kail." He put his coat back on, took the bag and left, traveling back the way he'd come.

*   *   *

Going through Lucas's things was hard — emotional, but cathartic. He used his key to access Lucas's room, next to his own. The layouts were the same: bed against the wall, desk with stool underneath, closet, bookshelf. Retrievers weren't often in their rooms, and so didn't require much living space. Compared to his own meager belongings, Lucas lived in a gallery. Drawings of people framed on the walls — friends and family mostly. Donovan spent too long staring at those, remembering the events that had prompted the young man to have the work commissioned, and the time he'd spent sitting to have his face drawn at his friend's request.

Books of poetry and adventure and magic crowded the shelf, their spines worn and the pages bristling with markers. He had an oversized book with a collection of feathers and leaves and flowers pressed carefully between the pages; each one marked with a date and species and location of collection. Living plants cluttered the place; Healers often cultivated gardens to have easy access to things they could Push injuries and pain into.

A map on the wall with little paper flags marked each of the locations they'd traveled together, some with tallies if they'd gone more than once. Colored yarn connected the flags together to show their routes. Another book, this one on the desk below the map, held more carefully notated recordings. Instead of feathers and leaves, it was full of anecdotes of their time on the road, names of the children they'd Retrieved, jokes and stories they'd told, and trouble they'd encountered.

Donovan sank onto the mattress and flipped through the book for hours. He had nowhere else to be, and nostalgia was an addictive drug. He didn't feel nearly so guilty now; railing at Vale and telling Kail what had happened helped him with that. He'd lost people before and knew that the feelings of loss would fade to memory. Still, until then, the hurt remained fresh and, while it stung, the nostalgia also worked as a balm on his soul. He expected other Retrievers to come by, but none did; they were all on Retrievals. The hall was quiet, empty. He wasn't as close with any of them as he had been to Lucas. But having work in common, they could consider themselves friendly.

Someone cleared their throat, and Donovan looked up, blinking bleary eyes that had been staring at small handwriting for too long.

Vale leaned against the doorframe, staring at him. She had an air of infinite patience; he wondered how long she'd been waiting, watching him.

"Memories?" she asked in her rough voice.

Donovan nodded.

"You taking his things?"

"Some of them."

"Box it up. I need the room."

Irritation flared in Donovan's chest. Vale must have seen it on his face because, while she wasn't one for explanations, she told him, "I waited the week you were out. And you've had today. We need the space."

"I know."

"You want a new partner?"

"No."

"They need training, and experience."

Donovan ran a hand across his curls and scratched the back of his neck. "Not yet."

The woman nodded. "I'd considered you for my replacement, once."

Donovan blinked. "What?"

Vale had been in charge of the Retrievers the entire time Donovan had been employed with them. The idea of her retiring had somehow never occurred to him — considering the already broken and battered state of her when she had started the job. He figured only death would retire her.

"I'm not dead yet, you daft turtle. Anyway, you're too soft-hearted. Can't make the hard decisions. I was going to give it to Lucas, honest, but he had to go and get kilt." She eyed the room. "Nice map." She limped further inside the room to get a closer look. "Boy sure liked his records. Reports were always good, too, except his damned tiny writing."

"When are you retiring, then?" Donovan asked curiously.

Vale waved her hand at him. "When I feels like it! I get to bully you lot, so the work stays worth it for now. Get your box stowed away. I'm moving a new one here in the morning."

She limped away without a glance back.

Donovan closed the book, stood, and stretched with a groan. He stopped a page in the hallway and sent them to fetch him a container, then started dismantling Lucas's room at last. He mounted the map with its flags and yarn above his own desk and, of course, kept the journal of anecdotes.

The page returned with two wooden crates, carried by friends, and Donovan slowly filled them with the contents of Lucas's shelf and closet and desk. The bed had the Order's uniform sheets, but Donovan claimed the quilt Lucas had purchased on a visit up north. It was bright and covered with geometric shapes in different colors, and it matched the rug Donovan had on his own floor from the same place.

He was sweating by the time he finished shoving the two crates into his own room. They took up most of the floor space. Another page came by and knocked politely at his open door.

"Yes?" he asked wearily.

"You've been invited to dinner, sir. Dean Villery requested you come when you're ready."

He nodded and waved the page away, straightening from his aching slump. Seeing friends would do him good.

Donovan cleaned up as best he could and made his way down the familiar path to Hector's room. He'd been there plenty of times — possibly as much as he'd been to his own room, in terms of meaningful time spent. Hector had a larger space, given his position with the Order, and preferred having people around. The usual group would be there; the names and faces changed occasionally through the years, and Donovan was glad to be included.

The door was closed, but he let himself in without knocking; he'd known Hector too long, and he knew he was expected. When he entered and was noticed, a gentle cheer went around the room, and he grinned, warmth flooding through him.

He was ushered to a chair and ordered to remove his boots. A cup of hot tea was pushed into his hands and the conversation continued where it had left off. He listened with one ear, mostly soaking in the comfort of being with friends-turned-family after the past few days. Weeks.

Hector, usually impeccably dressed when working, wore a baggy cotton shirt and loose cotton trousers, his feet bare. He held a glass of whiskey in one hand and a thick book in the other, using each to gesture in making his argument.

He sat perched on the arm of a chair in which Tafaney Prenn was seated, looking half-asleep, curled up under a blanket. Taf was a year or two older than Donovan, but a hard life had added decades to her bones, and she didn't leave the Order much anymore. In her prime, she'd been a soldier, hunted blood mages and bandits on the outskirts of the kingdom. She rose to captain with haste and stayed there, refusing further promotions.

Andrea Browne was listening intently to Hector's argument from her seat on the floor, her arms propped on the coffee table, which was laden with various light foods. She chewed on some seeds from a bowl by her hand. Donovan didn't know her as well; only that she was a scholar from the palace, doing research on various agricultural techniques used in the surrounding countries, and their impact on the soil. For all that, she did manage to make interesting conversation, and was often quite witty when she wasn't so serious.

Kerik Dusek had been a scholar for the many years Donovan had known her. She studied various social experiments — a new one every time they spoke. He liked her a lot for the little time they spent together. She was usually soft-spoken, but had a way with language that meant that when her words were caught, they were never misunderstood. She knew at least four languages fluently, and collected ancient war chants whenever she translated a new one. He hadn't realized there were so many from across the world until she'd shown him her collection.

John Garendow stood, also listening to Hector's argument — which Donovan still hadn't determined the topic of. He was short, only an inch or so over five feet, and whip thin. Also a soldier, a sergeant, training the recruits in formation marching, and the more experienced in various acrobatics that could be used in combat. Donovan had watched some of his classes, participated in one or two, and thought they were very fun, if grueling. John and Lucas had been close friends.

Normally Lucas would have been in the thick of things. He had always been invited to these gatherings, too, and had ever been the youngest. Donovan sipped his tea, encouraging it to burn through the lump in his throat.

"Here now," John said beside him, giving his shoulder a squeeze. "None of that tonight, mate. Stuff yourself with food and get lost in the conversation."

Donovan wiped his eyes with a laugh and thanked him, grabbing a small ceramic plate and piling it high with vegetables, cooked and raw, along with thinly cut meat and slices of fruit.

He listened tiredly, lost in thought, as the arguments faded, the sides agreeing to disagree about … whatever it was, and then the topic switching to more mundane things.

"Donovan found him. Do you think he'll learn quick? We could use power like that."

He swallowed a grape painfully and said, "Ruben's bright. He'll be fine."

"You know Elliott will want him battle-ready before he's sixteen," Andrea said, rolling her eyes. She picked at a bread roll, putting small pieces in her mouth to dissolve.

"Elliott wants as many children trained and ready as soon as possible, and who can blame him? How many Hunters were after you this time, Don?" John asked.

He shrugged. "A lot. I never got a good count while Seeking; mostly I was checking our route."

John nodded. "Right. But 'a lot' is still telling."

"Elliott wants what's good for the Order, and a magus is good for the Order," Taf pointed out. "He's never been accused of wasting lives, and everyone in the country knows that he prefers spies to armies. Without information, you're fighting blind."

"But at least you're fighting," Andrea countered.

"What could you do with unlimited time Seeking?" Kerik asked Donovan curiously.

He sighed wistfully. "Quite a bit. I could be more methodical for one thing — really look for Hunters, maybe go up a few times a day to look for patterns of movement? I could definitely fill out better maps."

"You and your maps," Taf muttered playfully.

"What's he studying this semester, Hector?" Andrea asked.

"Elementalism, Mentalism, Displacement, Seeking, and surgery training."

"For Healing next semester, certainly," Andrea said, nodding. "Those sound like Elliott."

"And me," Donovan pointed out. "I suggested Elementalism since he's done fire already before."

"Elliott loves his Mentalists," Andrea said. "There's a few to watch in classes now, and you know he already has plans for them."

"He would," John rolled his eyes. "No childhood for thems with magic."

"We're losing this war, John," Taf said softly.

Donovan considered what he'd seen and heard in his years as a Retriever. Children were the targets, it was true. Whether they could be stolen away and trained, used as fighters on the side of the blood mages, or killed to deny their value to the Order's forces, it was a horrible thing, and it had only grown worse. The Order had no standing military of mages, but everyone knew the call might go out. They could be asked, drafted, to fight for their kingdom, and everyone had asked themselves the same question: whether or not they would. No one asked to be born with power, but wasn't it your duty as a member of a society to help however you could? Did that mean sacrificing your life to save someone else? It wasn't an easy conversation to have.

He looked around the room. Everyone was asking themselves that question. Several of these people had already answered it: yes, they would fight, but several others still hadn't.

Tafaney had continued speaking, "We can only train the ones we find already born to do magic. Whereas *they* just have to show anyone off the street how to do theirs. Both take years of practice, but if our sides were reversed, teaching brute force instead of finesse, I'd have won by now. Either their leader is an idiot, or they're playing a different game."

Someone knocked. Donovan twisted around, but Hector leapt up and ran to answer it. Donovan was surprised to see a plaster cast extending out from a wheeled chair.

"Whitman Acres, everyone," Hector announced. "I said I'd be bringing someone new. We've spoken several times, and I thought he'd fit in well with us."

Donovan waited for Whitman to get settled; John gave up his spot and moved to Donovan's other side. "Good to see you again, Whit," he said.

"You met on the road, yes?" Hector asked.

"He tried to steal our horses," Donovan agreed.

"*A* horse, *a* horse, I will thank you to remember," Whitman said above the laughter. He was grinning.

"What brings you to the Order, Whitman?" Andrea asked politely.

"I typically winter here when not feeling up to the trials of travel and, as you can see, I am rather less mobile than I once was."

"You're a bard. Master yet?" Taf asked.

"Alas, not yet! I have an epic yet to compose, in the works, of course, but it could take several years more to complete. It follows the life and adventures of someone I only recently met, and I would hate to be premature in my assumptions of where his future will lead." He winked at Donovan.

"Wha— *me*?" he asked incredulously.

"No, you bowl of porridge!" Whitman laughed. "Ruben! The young magus, whose power will dwarf those of a thousand mages, remember?"

Taf giggled into her blanket while John snorted. Kerik smiled into her hand while Hector put his head back and laughed with Andrea. Donovan gave an exaggerated show of relief.

"What's the topic, then?" Whitman asked, looking around. "My sense of time has been compromised and I apologize for being so late. I do not want to distract from the conversation, however."

"We were speaking of the theoreticals of this forever-war, and the likelihood that their general is terrible," Andrea answered, looking at Taf.

"Not terrible. I didn't say terrible. I just wonder why we haven't been overrun yet," the older woman countered.

"Because of the options they hold in terms of recruitment?" Whitman clarified.

"Mmm."

"Probably because of the reputation they hold," he opined. "Just about everywhere, people know that Hunters, blood mages, are bad news. In most major towns, and plenty of small ones, your neighbor is as likely to turn you in as soldiers are to find you. Recruiting would be difficult from that fact alone. You cannot keep an entire town in fear — you risk one person escaping and the entire might of the Order's military would descend. Even if you had enough people available to you, you cannot *force* a person to do magic."

"That's a straight point," John agreed, nodding. "So their recruitment would be nearly as slow as our own."

"Definitely faster," Taf argued.

"You believe we might be outnumbered, but perhaps not by so unmanageable an amount?" Hector asked above his glass.

"A few mages can turn the tide of a fight," John argued. "Put that into terms of a few thousand, by chance, and we'd be overrun in a pop." He snapped his fingers.

"A few thousand mages?" Donovan winced. "And each of them able to do at least as much as one of our more imaginative casters can, and more once the blood spills. That still puts them firmly on the winning side, in my estimate. I'm with Taf: Why haven't they decided to field an army yet?"

"Maybe they were waiting for a general," John shrugged. "You said they were awful keen to get their paws on our magus boy."

"I've seen first-hand what a person can do when they use both our magic, and blood-magic. I'm surprised they didn't try harder," Donovan said, sipping his tea. It was lukewarm now, but still tasty. He thought about his argument with Vale and felt his anger rising again.

"Maybe they wanted him to get here, worried and nervous. Saves them the effort of teaching him," Taf said. "And he'd be well-motivated to get trained up."

"You're a suspicious one," Whitman said. "I like you."

Taf grinned and wiggled further under her blanket.

"This fight has been ongoing for generations," Kelik pointed out. "Our factions have fought since our histories have been recorded."

Hector agreed, "But they've grown more aggressive in the last decade or so, I feel. Something *has* changed."

"Something like what?" Andrea asked around a mouthful of olives.

Hector waved a hand dramatically. "Any number of things. Perhaps they have a new leader."

"The general they've been waiting on?" John suggested.

"If there has been a change, we'll see it soon enough in their tactics, regardless," Taf said, yawning indiscreetly.

The conversation continued for another while. Most of them had mornings free, and no reason to wake early, but soon enough, the party dispersed. Donovan made the trek to his room automatically and fell into bed with barely another thought.

7

"**F**ANCY SEEING YOU HERE."

Donovan spun in his seat, startled, and grinned sheepishly. "I was waiting for you, actually."

"Why else would you be in the library?" Whitman teased.

His leg remained in a cast, but, instead of his wheeled chair, he was propped up with a crutch under one arm, a satchel slung across his chest and resting comfortably on the opposite hip. He had emerged from the depths of the library to find Donovan waiting at one of the first tables inside.

"I wanted to see if I could help with your research to find the bowman — the Smiling Man. I'm not much use elsewhere at present, but I do know how to read."

"A useful skill," Whitman replied, eyes thoughtful.

"I'm sorry about your knee," Donovan said suddenly, surprised to find himself mentioning it.

Whitman's eyebrows rose to his hairline. "It was not your fault. If I had maintained my temper, I would not be in this position, would I?"

"Still ..."

"... are the trees in the evening shade with nary a breeze to wave them."

"... what?"

"I assumed you were looking for the correct words to follow so uninteresting a word as 'still'. No action to it at all." He winked.

Donovan grinned.

Before he could speak again, Whitman continued, "I am actually on my way to a meeting at present. You should accompany me."

"Should I?" Donovan asked, rising.

"Yes, I think so. You might find it interesting."

Whitman began to limp away, out of the library, and Donovan hurried to catch up.

"Can I ask who the meeting is with?"

"You may!" came the chipper reply.

Donovan groaned inwardly. "All right, who is the meeting with?"

"Excellent delivery, Donovan. You said the sentence exactly as you first suggested you might."

"You're not going to tell me."

"No."

"Why not?"

"Because our lives are all brightened by a sense of curiosity. It makes us aware of the smaller things around us, encourages the mind to process more with less, and, when the information is finally gained, we are all the happier for knowing."

"You're odd."

"I have been told it is one of my sweeter features."

Whitman was slower with the crutch, but was still half a head taller than Donovan. He made good speed, except on stairs, which he had to take one at a time.

As they walked, Donovan tried to guess where they were going. They were staying in this wing, he decided, when they didn't cross the atrium, but here it was all offices and rooms for certain higher-ups who worked primarily as scholars, or for the king. He'd been here several times before through the years, but hadn't made it a habit.

The artwork was portraits mostly, with busts and the occasional statue lining the halls. No more students wandered around, but there were plenty of pages running past one direction or the other, and the occasional adult messenger or servant. The Order didn't have many servants; those who stayed within the walls worked for the visitors who could retain them.

"Wait," Donovan said as they didn't turn off toward a row of offices he knew.

Whitman didn't slow.

Donovan stopped.

The younger man pulled a few steps ahead before rocking to a halt and half-turning back. "It does help when I can build up momentum with this contraption, and now all of that has been wasted."

"We're going to see the Head of the Order?"

"Elliott, yes. You were supposed to meet with him soon in any case. You can share my time." When Donovan didn't start walking again, Whitman asked, "You are not intimidated, are you?"

Donovan thought about the last time he'd seen Elliott. The man could be intimidating in the right circumstances, but he'd been more elated than anything at the prospect of a magus, sending Donovan and Lucas to Retrieve the child with a personal requirement of excellence.

"We cannot fail in this endeavor. It could be a mistake, an accident, and the child is merely Talented, but if he is a magus ... this could be everything."

Retrievers didn't generally meet with the Head of the Order before the normal course of their duties, but Vale had brought them to him at his request. Lucas had been excited, already planning how he would tell his mother the news when they'd returned.

"No," Donovan said, releasing the tension from his fists. "I'm not intimidated. I just don't think it's ... polite. To come unrequested."

Whitman was watching him with another thoughtful look in his narrowed eyes. "He was going to ask for you eventually. He has been busy."

"I expect he's very busy," Donovan agreed readily.

Still, a week had passed since Ruben's arrival ...

"Come with me."

"What are you meeting with him about?"

"I want your input when you hear."

"I could give that to you now and leave you to share my insights as your own."

Whitman laughed merrily. "Stop fretting or I expect you will do yourself an injury."

Donovan looked down at his brown canvas trousers, gray cotton shirt, and leather jerkin. Whitman wasn't dressed much better in cotton slacks and a nicer shirt, but last time he'd had a chance to dress up a little and shave.

Technically, Elliott ran a school of young magicians. In reality, he was the head of a complex city-within-a-city with a military that functioned under his command, and he answered only to the king. He had no legal authority over the city outside of the walls, but the mayor of Thairnsdale made sure that Elliott's *requests* and *suggestions* were seriously considered on major decisions — he presided over a very large portion of the city's income, after all. On the occasions when Donovan had spoken with him, he'd been business-driven, and very kind, but they'd never spoken on a personal level. Who had time? Nerves gathered in his belly, but he didn't have much chance to dwell.

They had to navigate one last short set of stairs and Whitman waved for a rest, leaning on the railing with a look of frustration raging across his features.

"I sprinted these three at a time only months ago."

Donovan made a sympathetic expression. "You'll be able to walk mostly as normal when it heals, though, right?"

"'Mostly' being the operative term," Whitman answered, getting his breath back. "But I plan to become rich enough to hire a passing Healer to take care of it for me. Or get the boy to do it."

"I'm surprised the Healers didn't do it when you were in surgery," Donovan said as they moved on. "Transferred it into a tree and called it done."

"As I understand, it is a fairly difficult process across species, and much easier once the leg has done as much of the healing as it can. The chance of *keeping* some of the injury is higher the more there is to Heal. You should have seen Ruben pour your injury into the tree. It was truly remarkable. My adjectives are lacking in describing it, though I will certainly give my best attempt when I publish."

"As the tree died, would I have died if Ruben hadn't helped me?" Donovan wondered aloud. "Or did it just require more energy to Heal me than the tree had to offer?"

"We will have to wait a few months for his classes to start teaching him theoreticals, and then we can ask to find out. The teachers are usually too busy with their students to bother with us ordinary folk, I have discovered."

"Maybe they just don't like bards," Donovan suggested.

Whitman gave him an amused sideways glance. "Entirely possible, if extremely unlikely." With flair, he pulled open the large oak door to the Head's offices.

The door opened into a small entrance chamber. It held a large desk to the left of the door where a severe-looking older man, his face soft, but his eyes sharp, scribbled away at a stack of parchment, working his way through the day's forms and documents requiring permissions and grants from the Head's office. Besides several oil lamps, a leather couch, and two wooden chairs, the room felt empty and cold. A door to the next room was straight ahead, but firmly closed.

The man looked up from his work, and nodded sharply. "Master Acres, welcome. I'll alert him you've arrived."

He stood from behind the desk and went through the next door, pulling it open with no squeak or drag, and then closing it behind him. Whitman limped to a chair, adjusted the crutch beside him, and opened his portfolio to read his notes. A light sheen of sweat glistened on his round face. Donovan took the couch, grateful for the respite from their walk. He was still tiring far more quickly than he used to; it made him feel old.

The secretary returned a few moments later, sat behind the desk, and got back to work with his inkpen and books. Donovan looked up when the main door opened and a young boy ran in, his face flush. He had a leather satchel on his hip, which he gripped with determined ferocity.

"Notes, master?" he asked politely.

The secretary handed the boy a stack, which he tucked away, and then separately he added another. "This in person, please. If she's not to be found, I'll have it back."

"In person or returned, aye," the boy answered, tucking it into a different satchel pocket, quickly running off again.

The door into the Head's office opened and Elliott himself appeared. Of average height, he moved with proud shoulders and militaristic stride. His hair was gray, matching his mustache, both neatly trimmed. He handed a stack of papers to his secretary with a word of thanks and waved to Whitman, returning into his office and leaving them to follow.

Expansive and rich, the room was suitable for entertaining the wealthy and powerful when necessary. Off to the right was a recessed sitting area sunk into the ground with comfortable chairs and a couch around a low table; a large rug on the floor depicted the building of the Great Wall around the Order as seen from above. The town had been a small village then, and had expanded tenfold.

Ahead was another large desk similar to the one in the outside room. Floor-to-ceiling bookshelves lined the walls; a ladder on rollers accessed the higher ones. A balcony, accessible by a spiraling staircase of wrought iron behind the sitting area, lined half of the room and contained several more shelves and chairs. It looked to be a more private, intimate space.

Behind them, against the wall through which they had entered, stood a short row of counters with cabinets to provide libations and satisfy any hunger that might cause attentions to wander. The dark, polished wood of the floor matched the bookshelves. Lamps gave the place a soft, comfortable light; a bit more even than the bottled lightning did in a more muted space as this. Thick curtains covered the windows on the left, keeping the winter air from leaking through the glass.

Elliott was pouring a drink for himself at the counter and held up a glass. "Drink? For ... either of you?"

Whitman accepted, but Donovan took only a glass of water, carrying Whitman's drink for him as the bard led the way to the sunken seating area. Whitman navigated the step down and collapsed dexterously onto a couch, propping his crutch beside his seat. Donovan sat gently beside him and set the drinks on the table. He clasped his hands in his lap and waited to know why he was here.

Elliott eyed him with a flat curiosity as he sipped his drink, and Whitman said, "Elliott, this is Senior Retriever Donovan Rudd, I am sure you know."

"Yes, we've met. I was going to send for you later this afternoon," Elliott said, acknowledging him with a bob of his head.

"I thought he might be useful to me, and brought him along to kill two birds with one stone."

"All right then." Elliott smoothed his mustache with a practiced gesture. "What do you have for me, Acres?"

Whitman handed him the portfolio from his satchel and said, "All of the information that I possess about the infiltration is there, which I have been diligently confirming during my recovery, and since you granted me the Mentalists. It took longer than I had hoped to put together, but I appreciate your flexibility; it was deeper than we thought."

Donovan reminded himself to keep breathing. He couldn't decide if his mind was a snowstorm of thoughts, or just a ringing blankness of confusion.

The Head opened the folder and scanned the documents inside. His eyebrows rose and then fell. A look of concentration overtook his features.

"Did you learn when this trend began?" Elliott asked. His expression was difficult to read.

Donovan looked at Whitman. He wanted to know what the information was, but was yet unwilling to ask.

"Sir, it has been happening for generations," Whitman answered promptly. "There have been increases recently — within the last three to five years and more. I imagine it was a vague plan that they did not know how to push forward, but now their numbers have shifted dramatically, and recruiting is up. Someone new has taken over; someone with a plan. I would bet it happened around fifteen or so years ago, perhaps a bit more. They are crafty after this many centuries, which means we have a real problem. These people have been identified, but how many others could we miss?"

"The weak are caught and killed, leaving the strong to fight again," Elliott mused, flipping a page.

"A bit of good news, to complement," Whitman said, pulling another folder from his satchel and handing it over.

Elliott looked up at him, eyebrows raised.

"Information detailing the location of their training grounds."

"Finally! You're positive?"

Whitman nodded. "We have been unable to find them because they are underground, beneath a village. They gather in a series of caverns."

"No wonder ... The Seekers couldn't see the Poisoning because there was life above it ... That's brilliant!" Elliott looked stunned, impressed.

"Poisoning?" Whitman looked confused.

Donovan explained, pleased to be able to contribute, "When we, Seekers, see a person that looks like it's darker, or shadowed, it indicates blood mages, as opposed to the lines and spots of light and life that would otherwise be there."

"Ah, of course!" Whitman looked back at Elliott. "I used that to plot a series of routes they may have taken, and identified a few more people I might have missed based on the likelihood of their recruiting. Anyone from that town has been flagged."

The Head of the Order took a deep breath and let it out slowly. "We need to put someone in that city as quickly as possible. How far away is it?"

"Six days by horse — named Anturn, north of here. Main exports are wheat and corn. They have two mills running from the river nearby, their main source of income. The town has been growing, but not quickly, and I know why — the Hunters need a smaller location to keep hidden. I have not moved any of my people, waiting on your instruction. I do recommend discretion. If someone is found there ... our hand would be revealed and removed."

"I'm sorry to interrupt," Donovan said softly, "but what is happening, please?"

Elliott glanced at Whitman and answered, "The Order has been infiltrated by blood mages. I've spent the last two years identifying those people with the assistance of Whitman and the Order's core of Mentalist mages. Now the job is to contain them."

Donovan felt his heart racing in his throat. "Oh."

Whitman assured them, "I have been careful, making sure that the information does not go beyond anyone absolutely necessary. We have to keep their plan from moving forward too quickly — whatever it may be. Though we can guess," he said, turning to Elliott. "Wholesale destruction. They have never had this many inside the walls before. In modern memory."

"How many of them are children?"

"Not as many as I first feared, suspected. There is a column there with my figures. The harder ones to identify were those without magic. Who suspects the gardener, the cleaners, the cooks?"

"Why didn't our Mentalists catch them at the gates?" Elliott asked, a smoldering fury rising behind his eyes.

"Because they did not come here to destroy the place immediately," Whitman explained. "They came to build up their lives and possibly have children and jobs, and wait for the signal. It is harder to catch a plan such as that, unless they are quite fearful and an Empath wonders why, assuming they do not take it for casual nervousness. Many of them were positioned in the military. We have been training our enemy to attack us."

"Blood mages inside my walls, confirmed at last," Elliott said softly, hot rage burning in his voice and lowering its tone. "We're moving forward as I have suggested?"

"For the most part, yes, sir. All the details are there. We gather a large group of military personnel and have them double-checked by a group of Mentalists. Send them to detain all of the people on that list simultaneously. With luck, it will be bloodless. I do have my doubts, however."

"How likely is it that you missed someone?" Elliott asked, looking at the list of names in front of him.

"Extremely likely, sir," Whitman answered promptly.

Elliott looked up at him with a rough expression.

"Sir, this plan has been in motion for years. The odds that we missed someone are very high. The odds that we are detaining innocents is also very high. Some of those people might have defected. Some might be completely accidental. I erred on the side of caution."

"When can you be ready to implement this plan?"

"Within the week."

"We have to inform the king."

"I took the liberty of sending one of my people, sir. It saves us the risk of a letter or messenger being intercepted."

"If the Hunters have infiltrated the Order so thoroughly," Donovan said, "what's to say they haven't done the same within the palace?"

Elliott smoothed his mustache thoughtfully.

Whitman quirked a small smile. "Good, Don. I had another team working on that, and they did find a great number of persons — some nobility or people in positions of power, same as here. We would need to enact the same plan there, at the same time. It will be quite a feat, but I believe in our people."

"What about the city?" Donovan asked again.

Elliott lifted his chin. "What about it?"

Donovan looked to Whitman. "You said you've been going through the records of everyone here, but how many of the people who live in the city have records you can reference? They might be in on the plot as well."

Whitman looked to Elliot with a grimace. "We will have to inform the mayor, and send the military into the city in case of riots. We do not have enough people for that — they will have to come second, and more will escape."

"Do it," Elliott said. "I'll inform the mayor and get the Mentalists into the barracks. I've already recalled as many as I can to be checked and sent out, per your suggestion." Elliott nodded decisively. "I want regular reports. Master Rudd, before we end this meeting, I wanted to ask what you thought of the young magus's loyalty to the Order."

Donovan blinked at the rapid change of subject. "Loyalty? He's only been here a day, a week. I would say he's a smart boy who understands the evil that blood mages are willing to do."

"Will he fight to protect this place?"

"He doesn't know how to control his magic yet, sir," Donovan said carefully, keeping the rising irritation from his voice. *What could the Head of the Order expect from an untrained child?* "When he's been trained, we can expect him to do what he believes is right to protect our way of life. Until then, he's a fourteen-year-old boy."

Elliott nodded sharply. "Very well. Dismissed."

Donovan and Whitman stood, the latter collecting and planting his crutch.

They made their way out into the entrance room, and through to the corridor. The silence held as they made a slow stride toward busier halls.

"Who are you?" Donovan finally asked.

Whitman smirked. "Who do you think I might be?"

"You aren't just a bard."

"No bard is 'just' a bard," Whitman agreed. "Though some are arguably less employed than myself."

Despite the deserted corridor, Donovan lowered his voice, "Ruben thought you might be important. You're a spy? You're one of Elliott's spies?"

"Yes. And now, so are you."

"What?" Donovan stopped walking. "I can't do that."

"It is not all running about and hunting the Hunters, Don," Whitman said, rocking to a halt to face him. He spoke softly. "We need people with experience, who know what to look for, know when something is not as it should be. The ideas you had are exactly what I need. You see missing pieces."

"But- I'm just a Retriever! I've been thinking about retiring! Look, if I'm seen talking to Elliott every week, reporting, then I'll be found out, right?"

"Which is why you will report to me," Whitman explained gently.

Donovan stared at him for a moment. "You're not just a spy."

"I would argue that no spy is 'just' —" Whitman started.

"You're the *head* of the spies?!" Donovan demanded in a harsh whisper.

Whitman glanced up and down the hall and gave a faint nod. "Shall we press on? I have a lot of work to organize ... "

Donovan blinked, feeling dazed, and forced his legs to move forward. He didn't know what to think. He'd thought of Whitman as a bit mad in the best ways — very clever, as bards often were, and generally a good man. He still thought those things, but now he had to add Master of Spies somewhere in there, and it wasn't lining up with his previous impression of a somewhat silly, definitely young, man.

"What were you doing when you found us?" Donovan asked slowly.

Whitman didn't answer readily. "My purpose there was two-fold: I was tracking a contact that had stopped reporting. She was quite skilled, and I had her assigned to be recruited by Hunters I knew of in the area. She had been found and killed."

"You found her ... remains?"

"No, the killers felt it necessary to gloat to me. Four of them, but one as young as fifteen." Whitman shook his head. "They were not clever, and were new to their magic."

"You killed them?" Donovan asked, softly.

"Yes." The regret in Whitman's voice spoke volumes to his nature. "I came to find you a day later. It was luck that I happened upon your trail as readily as I did, but I was expecting you to be nearby." At Donovan's expression, he added, "I had a hand in sending you and Lucas to Retrieve Ruben."

"We wouldn't have made it without you, I think."

"Likely not," Whitman agreed without ego. "We decided it would be better for a small group to pass, hopefully unnoticed. I am sorry that plan failed you both."

Their conversation had to end as they crossed into crowded corridors, weaving their way back in the direction of the library. Whitman pulled a set of keys from his pocket to open a door and locked it behind them.

"You live here?" Donovan asked, surprised.

His idea of where Whitman the bard would live, and where Whitman the Spymaster lived did not align again. The floor was carpeted, the colors around the place were forest tones. Oil lamps sat mounted on several walls. The room bore a couch against the wall, and a desk on the opposite side of the room, with shelves and drawers covering every available bit of surface. All of them had locks.

"I do," Whitman said, hanging his satchel on a peg by the door which also held two coats.

"This is barely bigger than my room," Donovan said with a smile.

The room was larger than Donovan's, but not as large as Hector's, with the benefits that the Dean of Students was entitled to. Surely the Spymaster was entitled to at least as much as the Dean. *But then, he had to stay hidden, didn't he?* There were probably very few benefits to the job that he could visibly enjoy. "But it's much nicer."

"Yes, well, we never wanted much space, and it is near the library, which was no small feat. There is a bedroom through there," he pointed, "and a short hall to the sitting room. We do not use it much, working as much as we do."

"We?"

"My husband, Oslan. He will be along shortly, if I recall his schedule correctly."

"I didn't know you were married."

"Blissfully. Contain your jealousy," Whitman winked.

"Of course, I feel I should offer my condolences to your husband."

Whitman scoffed.

Donovan wanted to peruse the shelves, but sat on the couch instead. "I'm not sure what you want from me," he finally said as Whitman busied himself behind the desk.

"Neither am I," the younger man admitted. "Only this morning did I decide to bring you along. Imagine my surprise in learning that you were looking for me, as well." He pursed his lips. "I might hold you to that offer for research assistance when we solve this more immediate issue."

After a moment, Whitman looked up from the desk. "You can ask, if you want."

Donovan cleared his throat. "How did you come to this position? You're barely in your thirties!"

Whitman smiled thinly, and sat back in his chair. It looked sturdy, but still creaked under his weight. "I told you my sister was murdered."

"By Hunters, yes."

"She was eight years old; I was eleven, already two years into my bardic training. I was home visiting and we were all so *excited* that the timing was as it was, because how *amazing* that she was going to the Order as a mage and her big brother was here to see her off in the morning! Her escort arrived in the evening and we put him in my bedroom while I shared with Wren. We stayed up all night talking.

"We found she was murdered the next evening. Her heart was on the doorstep, her entrails a guide-trail leading from the house so that we could take in the view of the rest of the pieces hanging from the trees and buildings. It took eight years for any other children to willingly agree to go to the Order after that. Their parents refused to send them, and the littles cried to be told they had to."

"It's not mandatory to come to the Order ..." Donovan said slowly, horror tinging his voice.

"We had no teachers in our town; none willing to bear the brunt of the threat of Hunters. The thought of being sent to the Order became a torturous threat, and not until an Elementalist that hid her power got scared and almost blew down a house did the king order an outpost built less than a mile away, and the roads broadened, the brush and trees cleaned and cleared until they were more passable and available for travel. Then he sent three instructors to weed out those children, and adults, hiding their powers and ordered them, with escort, to come here for training.

"It is better there now, but just imagine how little eleven-year-old me felt that day, and ask yourself how I could stop at becoming just a bard." He shook his head. "My master worried about my mental state and after Empaths and Mentalists all failed to turn me from thoughts of revenge, he called another master to come train me. That one knew more than music and travel.

He held out his palms. "I was groomed for this role. Once I learned what I needed from my master of music, I was brought to train with my predecessor here. She taught me the rest of what I needed to know, which of course, I cannot divulge to any but the next Spymaster."

Donovan's eyebrows twitched and rolled with emotion. "When I was eleven, I was enrolled here. Four years later I went back to my family's land and didn't much think about the place."

Whitman smiled. "I like my life. It is terrifying, and incredibly busy, and very stressful, but I am good at what I do, and excellence is a drug to which I prefer to remain addicted."

The sound of a key turned their attention toward the door. A young man entered and locked the portal behind him with a practiced motion. He saw Donovan and smiled politely, stepping forward to shake his hand.

"I didn't know we had company," he said.

Whitman unfolded from behind his desk and said, "Oslan, Donovan. Donovan, Oslan."

"Ah, of course. Welcome," Oslan said.

He stood a few inches shorter than Donovan, with neat, short black hair, a carefully trimmed goatee, and the strongest grip Donovan had ever encountered. The handshake wasn't too tight, but even from that Donovan could tell how much power the young man was holding back.

"Oslan is a clerk. He sits in on all of the most interesting meetings," Whitman told Donovan. The last bit must have been teasing, because Oslan rolled his eyes good-naturedly and hung his bag on the hook.

He went around the desk and they embraced, shared a brief kiss, and Whitman passed a piece of paper to his husband.

"So you did."

"And he agreed."

"When?"

"Next few days."

Oslan nodded thoughtfully, drumming his fingers on the desk.

"I recruited Donovan an hour ago, my love. You can speak freely."

"There's going to be bloodshed."

"I know." Whitman pushed a slow fist into the top of the desk, his knuckles white.

"You can't join the fray."

The fist flattened. "I know that, too."

The tension broke when Oslan asked, "You're going back out?"

"No, but Donovan is," Whitman answered, sinking into his desk chair with another creak of wood and leather.

Donovan stood, hearing his dismissal. "Am I?"

"You have just learned a great deal; I expect you need time to process. I know I would."

"Yes, well ... I do have chores to catch up on."

"Chores are good."

Donovan didn't move.

Whitman smiled kindly. "Try not to dwell on it," he suggested. "There is nothing you can do at present to aid me in rooting out

165

these infiltrators, and it is not likely they would reveal themselves now. Go about your day as if nothing was different."

"But when you do come for the infiltrators ..." Donovan took a breath. "It will take the Order some time to recover."

"I expect so, yes," Whitman agreed. He looked sad at the prospect. "Still, it must be done."

"If there's anything I can do ..."

"I will inform you immediately. Thank you, Don."

Donovan rose and left the room. The lock clicked behind him.

He walked with a slow stride through the halls. The thought of any number of Hunter infiltrators passing him by was daunting, but he tried to take Whitman's words to heart: it wasn't likely that they would ruin their cover just to spite him here and now. Besides that, realizing that Whitman, a man he'd known for mere days, was the Spymaster was also intimidating. He had to know secrets not even the Head of the Order knew, and he would have dozens of contacts spread across the country to gather his information.

And now I'm one of them Donovan thought incredulously.

His feet took him down a few hallways and stairs and, when he eventually stopped and looked around, it took him a moment to realize where he was. He gave a weak smile and stared down the line of doorways that held the quarters for students. A few of them stood propped open.

Pensively, he meandered down the hall, counting the numbers and recalling names of those other students who had resided with him during his education here. When he came to his old room, the door open, he glanced in. Two boys lay on the floor, a book of maps in front of them. One noticed him and nudged his friend.

They stared, curious, until the first said, "Are you lost, master?"

Donovan smiled. "No, I just found myself walking past here and thought I'd visit my old room."

"Oh, aye?" the boy asked. "It's had a few owners since then, I'd expect." The second boy nudged the first, who blanched. "Meaning no disrespect, o'course. Sorry."

Donovan grinned at them. "None taken. What are you studying?"

"Maps," the second answered.

The first still blushed with shame.

"Maps of which areas?"

"All of them," the boy answered with exasperation. "I'm to learn them all as best I can so's to know what's what."

"Seeker, are you?" Donovan asked, leaning on the door frame.

The boy nodded. "Seeker and he's Empath, and our other mate's a Healer, so he's always away."

"I expect so. I'm a Seeker, too."

"Oh, aye?" The second boy sounded excited. He sat up from the floor and said, "Are you any good?"

"I do fine. I get a lot of practice these days, but I didn't used to."

"Nah, it's dangerous," the boy agreed, looking a bit low.

Donovan hesitated. "But the maps help. Or you could try standing on top of very tall buildings and looking straight down at night when all the lamps are lit, or looking up at the clouds and stars with nothing else in view."

"No one's said that — they just said 'maps'. What else?" He looked eager now.

Donovan considered for a moment and said, "Go sit somewhere public, out of the way, but in the thick of things. Sit somewhere and close your eyes and try to fall asleep like that."

The boys laughed.

The first one said, "Fall asleep sitting in town? I'd rather keep my pockets full, thanks."

Donovan grinned with them. "No, really, it relaxes your mind and body, and you learn to sort out the distractions and find a kind of calm. I had to figure that one out on my own. When my teachers learned I was doing it, they suggested more maps."

The boys laughed again.

"Does it stop hurting so much?" the young Seeker asked.

Donovan hesitated again. "I won't lie to you and say that it does, but you do get used to the idea that it won't last forever. Pain is fleeting, and if you think about how your senses are getting so strong as to take in that much information, it's a neat idea. But you should learn to pick your own herbs and make your own medicines, because otherwise you'll spend a lot of money on headache cures." He gave a rueful shrug.

The boy nodded pensively. "Pain is fleeting — I like that," he said. He looked at his friend. "I wish they taught all of this in classes."

"You should be an instructor!" the young Seeker agreed. "We don't even get told where the magic comes from, even."

"Oh, it just comes from everywhere," the Empath boy said dismissively. He paled and shook his head when they looked at him. "I mean, that's what my pa says. Makes as much sense as anything, right?" He laughed nervously.

Donovan smiled. "As much as anything," he agreed. "I'm glad I could help. I didn't do very well here, and I'm wishing I'd tried harder. Are you both going to stay with the Order or go home?"

"I'm going home," the young Empath said quickly. "I want to be a thatcher like my pa — he's the best there is, and he's been training me already."

"I don't know yet," the Seeker boy answered.

"Don't make hasty decisions," Donovan advised.

"What's your name, master?" the boy asked.

"Donovan Rudd. You?"

"Osten Vash."

"I'm James Thatcher," the other said proudly.

"Well it was good to meet you both." Donovan grinned. "Say, do you know where Ruben Smith is staying?"

"You know Ruben?" James asked.

"I was his Retriever." Donovan agreed.

They both stared at him, eyes wide, mouths gaping.

"What?" Donovan laughed, surprised by their responses.

"But you killed a dozen Hunters!" Osten said, awe written clearly across his features.

"I really didn't ..." Donovan answered.

"But you were *there*! All of it was true?" James demanded.

"I don't know what 'all' he told you, so I can't say ..."

"He's a magus, though — there hasn't been one of those in ages."

"As I understand it." Donovan couldn't hide his amusement. "Do you know which room is his?"

"I'll show you," Osten said, jumping to his feet and sprinting past Donovan with James on his heels.

They skidded to a stop in front of a door to the left, four spots down.

"He shares a room with that Mentalist, Arnold Coulter and Displacer Frin Halter. Do you want to knock?" Osten was standing back from the door, excitement in his eyes.

"Sure," Donovan said. He rapped his knuckles on the door. Rustling came from inside before it opened. A tall young man, probably seventeen, with red hair and a pale face, stood in the doorway.

"Here for Ruben?" he asked.

"Are you Arnold Coulter?"

The boy grinned. "Yes, but I was just listening to their excited squeaking — I didn't read your mind." He put out a hand. "Good to meet you, Master Rudd."

"And you," Donovan said, shaking it. There was something about Arnold that set him on edge immediately.

"Ruben's in Displacement classes with Frin at the moment. I can tell him you came to visit, however."

"Do you know when he'll be back?"

Arnold tilted his head thoughtfully. "Not likely for another quarter hour or so."

"You can stay and talk with us," Osten suggested.

Arnold smirked condescendingly. "Why don't you two go back to studying, and I'll entertain Master Rudd. If you'd prefer to wait?" Arnold asked him politely.

Donovan nodded. "Thank you, I think I will."

He winked at the younger boys, who grinned sheepishly and ran back to their room, waving.

Arnold's room looked like every other in the student corridors: a set of beds stacked one over the other on one wall and a loft bed across from it, allowing three students to a room. One long desk sat under the loft bed with stools stowed underneath; a lantern hung underneath the bed to illuminate the desks, each of which held stacks of parchment, ink and quills and drying sand, and a stack of books. A small closet contained hanging racks and a wardrobe to stow the boys' clothing; the bottom bed had three crates for storage underneath. There was no window, but the lightning around the ceiling kept the room bright. The addition of a comfortable-looking chair made the room feel crowded, but cozy.

Arnold gestured to the larger chair and said, "Please, have a seat. I'd offer you refreshment, but I'm afraid I haven't got any." He smiled contritely, pulling out a stool from under one of the desks and perching. "My mother always warned me that it would bring bad luck if I invited a stranger into my home without offering them food or drink, but hopefully that doesn't apply to dormitories." He shifted to a more comfortable position and asked, "What brings you to speak with young Ruben? Nothing serious, I hope."

Donovan hid an amused smile at Arnold's choice of words. Ruben was only a couple of years younger than this boy, but was apparently 'young' Ruben to him. "No, I just haven't been to see him."

Arnold nodded. "He speaks of you fairly often, so I was surprised by your absence, but I expected that you were busy with recovery and giving your reports."

Donovan blinked. "Excuse me?"

The youth smiled crookedly. "The gossip around this place ... I like to know what I can. I didn't mean to be rude, of course."

"No, that's all right ... "

An awkward silence stretched. "How long have you been enrolled?" Donovan asked.

"Coming on five years now, actually," Arnold answered breezily.

"You should be nearly done with lessons, I'd think. Or past done? I only studied for four years."

Arnold nodded. "Mentalists have a different curriculum, especially if we're determined to take advantage of all that we can. We're more likely to hurt someone else than ourselves, so our training is more intense — *ethics* and all that. I've received training in a number of fields to earn my certifications and permissions ahead of schedule. I plan to be an important person, if not here, then within the king's courts, and that requires that I learn all sorts of graces and politics and histories."

"Sounds like you've made a plan, then — that's good. My major strategy when I left was not using my gift any more than I had to."

"Do you think you succeeded at that?" Arnold asked, seeming genuinely interested.

"Not in the way I once thought," Donovan shrugged. "Tracking down youngsters and traveling through Hunter-infested territories doesn't lend itself to the quiet life, and I've had to use my Talent plenty of times."

"I expect so. Mine is not nearly so painful, though it can become that way if I'm not careful. Dominating willpower for entrance and supremacy is one most likely to end in a headache." Arnold grimaced. "The headaches are impressively awful, though. I can't imagine the strength Seekers must have, even to train their Talents."

"That's a kind thing to say." Donovan didn't like this boy. At all. He found himself imagining brick and stone barriers around his mind.

Arnold gave a curt nod. "If you don't mind my asking, when you'd planned never to use your gift, why did you join the Order?"

"I suffered a tragedy and offered my services shortly thereafter," Donovan explained quickly, practiced with his answer.

Arnold nodded again, slowly, thoughtfully. "I'm sorry for your loss, though I am glad to have met you."

"Oh yes?" Donovan asked, surprised.

"I think so, yes." Arnold had an odd look on his face before it broke into a grin. "What do you plan to do now that you're on suspension?"

"I'm not suspended."

"But you're not going into the field any time soon?"

"I'm recovering from an injury."

"I see ..."

The hair on Donovan's neck stood up.

"You didn't simply invite me in because you wanted to make polite conversation while we waited for Ruben, did you?"

Arnold didn't blink, silent for a moment. "You're one of very few born mages to come into such close contact with Hunters and escape without major injury. Or rather, with major injury that you survived."

Donovan didn't answer.

"I want to know how you did it, what happened. What are their methods, how did you best them?"

Donovan came to his feet. "I appreciate your hospitality, Arnold, but this is not something I'm willing to discuss with a student. I'll wait in the hall."

The door opened behind Arnold, but he didn't turn away.

"Donovan?" Ruben's voice asked. He sounded tired.

Donovan leaned to the side so that he could see both Arnold and Ruben. The boy's face lit up to see him, and he trotted forward for a hug, glaring at Arnold as he came. The other boy with him, likely Frin, looked completely strung out. He barely glanced at Donovan and Arnold, but climbed to the top of the bunk over the desks, pulled his blanket over his head and was unconscious moments later.

"What are you doing here?" Ruben asked.

"I came to see you. I've been remiss, and I'm sorry."

"That's all right! Was Arnold bothering you?"

Donovan looked at the older boy, who wore no expression.

"We were having a conversation."

"I try to avoid speaking to him at all," Ruben said rudely. He dropped his book bag at the base of the bed and crossed his arms, glaring at the older boy.

Arnold sneered, but said nothing.

"Ruben, why don't you come take a bite to eat with me," Donovan suggested.

"I can't," the boy lamented. "I have another class. You should come — it's Seeking; my first one, too."

Arnold let out a cough of laughter and gave Donovan a scathing look before turning away and gathering some papers.

"Something caught in your throat, Arnold?" Ruben asked darkly.

The boy glanced over his shoulder at them and said, "Of course not. Have a lovely class."

Ruben glowered.

They waited for him to finish gathering his papers, tuck them into a shoulder-satchel, and leave. He wiggled his fingers in a mocking wave as he left.

"I hate him," Ruben said bluntly. "He's always here, too, when he isn't at class. Frin says he used to always be out with friends or in town when he didn't have classes, but now he just stays in the room and I hate him."

"Forget about him," Donovan said, trying to take his own advice. "Or report him to the Dean if you think he's being inappropriate or immoral."

"I just might," Ruben said darkly.

Trying to lighten the mood, Donovan asked, "Are you enjoying classes?"

Ruben's face grew a wide smile. "You didn't lie."

"About what?"

"The teachers are mean."

Donovan matched his grin. He glanced at the sleeping Frin and said, "Should we leave him in peace?"

"Frin's the soundest sleeper I've ever met. I think you'd like him."

"Displacer, right?"

"Yep. He doesn't have any more classes today, so he'll sleep until dinner."

Donovan sank into the chair. "When I was here, we had a tutor and made our own schedules, but the place has grown since then."

Ruben perched on the foot of Arnold's bottom bunk. "I miss home," he admitted. "This place is nice, but there's a lot of work. I do like my classes, and they let me care for the horses for my scheduled chores, but then there's history and theory and mathematics and reading and practicals and herb lore." He let out a long-suffering sigh.

"Do you regret coming?" Donovan asked gently. He'd had this same conversation with his children before, but none had asked to return home yet.

Ruben shook his head. "No. I want to learn my magic. I just want to, I don't know, be home while I do it?"

Donovan reached over to tousle his hair and the boy scrunched up his face.

"That's normal, son. You'll get used to it, I promise. It's only been a few days. How are you liking etiquette?" Donovan asked, grinning.

Ruben made a face. "A bow is a bow. To have different kinds is just silly."

Donovan chuckled. "You'll appreciate knowing when you have to speak to barons and royalty."

Ruben glanced at the hourglass on the desk and said, "Walk with me? I don't want to be late. And it's Seeking! You should come!"

Donovan gained his feet and gestured for the boy to lead the way.

The stone hallways were empty; the day's classes on magic finished and all of the youths recovering in their own way. Their footsteps echoed faintly.

"I have one practicum every other day around all the non-magic classes, and on the *other* every-other-days I have two or three practicums. I have so many tutors because they can't keep going like I can. Sometimes I'll have three in one class."

"I'm not surprised."

"And it's supposed to take anyone wanting advanced training four or five years to finish their studies. My instructors say that if I want the same education, it'll take me eight or nine years on my current plan, because, while I don't get sick, I do get tired, and with as many classes as I have, there's only so much that I can keep in my head. And Frin says they won't even let me take the advanced training, because they'll want me working once I can do just about anything good enough."

"You know that you can tell them to fix your schedule if it's taking too much of a toll, right?"

Ruben looked at Donovan with confusion.

Donovan explained, "The reason they're pushing you so hard is because a magus is one of the most valuable resources in our world. You're very rare; extremely rare. Once in a century or more, rare, right?"

"Right ..."

"So the Order wants you fully trained as soon as possible, because there's so much you can do. Bridge collapsed? They have to send two dozen Displacers because they can only work for a short time before needing to recuperate, like your friend Frin. But with you trained, that bridge collapse can be solved by one person, in half the time. See what I mean?"

Ruben nodded slowly.

"If you don't want to hurry through and cram every detail about your numerous magics into your mind along with all of your other studies, then tell Hector it's too much. Find a schedule that works for you and propose it to him. I promise he'll accept. You just have to haggle. You're a valuable asset, Ben. Don't let them wear you out."

Ruben stopped at an open classroom and led them in. Donovan recognized it from his own time spent in this very room. Rather than glassed lightning, a single candle burned in front of a mirror on the wall. Thick, soft carpet padded the floor, replaced since his days. The walls were painted a dark blue to rest the eyes.

On a single shelf sat a box of herbs, a stack of cups, and a pitcher of water. The air smelled clean, but unscented, except for the faint sulfur of the candle wick. From a stack of pillows in the corner, two of them were already claimed by a man and woman Donovan assumed were Ruben's teachers for this class.

They smiled and beckoned him in, looking expectantly at Donovan.

Ruben explained, "This is my friend Donovan. He's a Seeker too, and I wanted him to come to my first class."

"Welcome, Donovan. Did you train here?" the man asked.

"I did, under Yulian, and I've been a Retriever for sixteen years."

The instructor's eyes brightened. "I know Yulian. He was still teaching when I became director, but has since retired. He gave a riveting lecture in my final year that I recreate for my students these days. Your presence is welcome. Feel free to offer your insights if you so choose. I'm Herman Jaynes, and this is my trainee, Van. She's in her final year, staying on as an instructor."

"Thank you. It's a pleasure."

"Ruben, set your bag against the wall with your shoes and stockings. Empty your pockets and remove any jewelry you might be wearing. You want as little touching your skin as possible."

"I have a question," Donovan said, as he pulled out pillows for himself and Ruben, kicking his shoes off in the corner.

"Yes?" Van answered.

"Do you know if Seeking will have the same effect on him as it does us, seeing as he doesn't suffer the consequences of other magics' tolls?"

They glanced at each other and Jaynes encouraged Van with a nod. Van answered, "We've never taught a magus before, so I'm not entirely sure. Our toll is sickness after we return to ourselves. The ... effects ... in the midst are very likely unavoidable."

"It's all right," Ruben said, bouncing over to plop onto his pillow. "I know it hurts. Don always looked terrible when he came back. And I did Heal him one time."

Donovan and the other two adults hid their smiles by turning away busily. Donovan secured the door. A large sign on the outside warned against excess noise and forbade knocking even in the most dire of circumstances. It was the quietest room in the building, its walls heavily fortified with internal padding; perfect for a nap if you could sneak away.

When Donovan rejoined the group, they were settling into their Seeking positions, seated with their legs loosely crossed.

"Let's begin. Van?"

The woman stood and trotted across the room to blow out the candle, returning to her seat more slowly in the pitch-darkness.

"It will be a little disorienting to return feeling blind, but you'll prefer it, I assure you." Jaynes's voice was low and calm. For that alone, Donovan felt that he was a good instructor.

"I want you to close your eyes and relax your breathing. Slow your heart, quiet your mind. Think of nothing but my voice."

Donovan heard Ruben slowly shift and relax beside him.

"Look inside your mind; picture its internal workings. Perhaps it is a home, a kitchen, a place you used to play. This is your mind, neat and orderly and calm."

Donovan always pictured his family's home. The polished wood of the floor that matched its walls, raised from the ground with a few steps to come inside. The doors and windows were always open, letting the breeze push in and out. There was bread on the hearth, and apples on the windowsill. A basket hung from the ceiling over the table with onions, radishes, peppers, mushrooms, tomatoes ...

He sank into the comfort of the room and focused again on what Jaynes was saying.

"... this window leads to the outside. It leads outside of your mind, of your body. Do you see the window?"

"Yes," Ruben murmured.

"Open the window, but do not go through. Is it open?"

"Yes."

"Open it as wide as you can and step away. Look through, feel the breeze, but stay inside the room. Memorize it, familiarize yourself with this place. It is a comfortable place, a calm place, one to which you are eager to return. The door is always open, you can come and go as you please."

After another few moments, Jaynes said, "Let's come out of the room now, Ruben. Come back slowly out of your mind. There's no rush, take your time. Feel your presence fill your body like a water pail, slowly working its way up until it is full."

"That was neat," Ruben said after a few minutes.

The darkness was still absolute, encouraging them to speak softly, slowly.

"I always enjoy establishing my room," Van said in the same low, soft, slow tones. "It's the most peaceful thing. I use it to fall asleep at night."

"My room is in the stables; I love it there." Ruben sounded as though he was smiling.

"Are you ready to go through the window?" Jaynes asked.

"Yes," Ruben answered, a hint of excitement bubbling into his voice.

"Lie down, then, and get as comfortable as you can. No clothing folded under you, nothing rubbing, your neck and back straight, your arms and legs unkinked. Donovan, will you be joining us?"

"I will listen and observe, thank you."

Donovan heard Jaynes move around and say, "I'm going to guide you, so I need to have contact. I'm just going to touch your shoulder a bit, there. Did Donovan explain what's going to happen?"

Donovan imagined Ruben giving him a sideways glance.

"Not exactly."

"You're going to push your mind out of that window that you've created. It'll be disorienting, like you're falling, but you need to go as fast as you can. In the time it takes you to get through the window and out of your body, you will be extremely sensitive to everything. Touch, taste, sound, sight, smell— it will all be multiplied by a thousand, and it will hurt."

"Does it hurt a lot?" Ruben asked nervously.

"It doesn't hurt for long. Pain is temporary. Just remember that and you'll be fine."

"Right ..."

"Once you are out of your body, you won't feel those things anymore, and you'll be spread thin, stretching outward around your center, and you will see flashes of light like a map of stars spread out around you. Take a quick look, and then come back through that window, as fast as you can. Do you understand?"

"Yes."

"Say it back, then."

"I go through the window, spread thin and see a map of lights, then back through the window."

"Good. We'll all be right here when you get back, and we'll talk about the experience then."

"Are you nervous?" Donovan asked.

"Yes," Ruben answered softly.

"We're still in no hurry, remember. Take your time. Find your breathing, build your room. Trust me, I've done this a hundred times and, while it isn't pleasant, the view is truly spectacular, and well worth it."

Ruben was silent, but Donovan felt the dread in the room lessen somewhat.

Jaynes led Ruben through the breathing exercise again, having him build his room slowly, thoroughly.

Donovan knew the moment Ruben went through the window. Jaynes didn't react, used to the process as he was, but the boy's body gave a mighty twitch and he gasped, then went completely still, as though dead.

His heart still beat, his lungs inhaled, but his mind was gone, and so was what defined him as alive. Donovan didn't move a muscle, keeping as silent as possible. Ruben's ears would pick up the sound of him breathing, ants walking across the floor, everything. The first time was always the worst, when you didn't truly know what to expect. After a longer time than Donovan expected, Ruben twitched again and gave a startled cry, then curled over onto his side.

Donovan reached out a steadying hand, wishing he could see the boy's face to judge his temperament.

"Ben?" he said softly. He didn't hear any sniffling. His first time, he'd bawled like a baby, but that probably also had somewhat to do with the aftereffects and illness.

"Are you all right, son?" He found Ruben's shoulder and laid a hand on him gently.

"That was beautiful," Ruben whispered.

Donovan's heart flip-flopped in relief. "I told you it would be."

"Why does my arm hurt?"

"Where?" Jaynes asked. "Your shoulder?"

"Yes."

"I was touching you so that I could follow. When you're out of your body, it makes you extremely sensitive. You never want to Seek in a place that is loud, or bright, or smelly, or where someone or something might touch you; it can damage you. Your shoulder is probably a little tender, like being in the sun too long."

"That's what it feels like."

"My hand feels the same. It'll fade soon, and now that you know what to do, I won't need to guide you next time."

"I could feel my clothes. I mean, more than I can now."

"Did you taste your mouth?" Donovan asked. "That's the worst part for me. Makes me keep my mouth fastidiously clean when I can."

"Now I know why you told me and Whitman not to touch you at the bridge."

"Seekers have it rough."

"Van, would you light the lamp, please?" Jaynes asked.

Van, nearly forgotten in her silence, stood and made her way to the wall to light the candle.

Donovan kept his eyes shut tight and waited for his pupils to adjust behind his closed lids. When he heard Van returning, he risked slitting his eyelids just a bit. The others were all shielding their eyes. The light wasn't bright, though, and, quickly enough, Donovan was smiling at Ruben's triumphant look.

Van looked like hammered death, but that was to be expected. It was worse when you were acting as a guide, but Jaynes looked mostly well. Usually the student's presence was an additional weight on your own mind, and you had to constantly monitor them without being able to do much to help, other than send vague feelings their way.

"Do you want a headache cure?" Donovan asked.

Van twitched her head in the affirmative. Jaynes man gave an appreciative nod and rotated his neck slowly. His muscles probably tightened when he went Seeking.

Donovan stood to accommodate them, listening as he debriefed Ruben's experience.

"I saw so many bright lights in here," Ruben said thoughtfully. "And some less-bright ones. They weren't dark, just not as shiny."

"You saw magic users and mundanes," Jaynes explained.

Donovan handed Van a cup and she gulped at it. Jaynes sipped, keeping his attention on his younger pupil.

"The brighter lights are the magic users," Jaynes continued, "though all life shines."

"Outside of the Order's walls there were a couple of dark points: are those Hunters?"

Van coughed with surprise, excusing herself when everyone looked.

"Probably. Anyone who uses blood-magic is tainted with unnatural death, and you can see the Poisoning. That's what it's called. You spread very far to see that," Jaynes smiled.

"What about when trees or animals die — do they show dark like that?" Ruben asked.

"Only unnatural deaths," Donovan explained, taking over momentarily. Jaynes had turned to monitor Van, who looked like she was going to be sick, even with her drink of cure. "Deaths caused by blood magic result in Poisoning, and that alters their life glow. What else did you see?" Donovan asked, giving the instructor and older student more time to recover.

"A river, and lots of trees and the city ..."

"You did go very far," Donovan said, impressed.

"It was beautiful — I wanted to see everything before I had to come back." He smiled sheepishly. Then he frowned with another question and asked, "To follow me, Jaynes had to touch my arm, but when you were attacked, the other Seeker was nowhere near you."

"Attacked?" Jaynes asked, his focus rapidly shifting. "Outside of your body?"

Donovan hesitated, and Ruben looked ashamed.

"I think I should have saved that question for later, huh?"

"That's all right," Donovan answered.

"But that doesn't make sense at all," Van said. "Without touch, another Seeker couldn't find you."

Jaynes cleared his throat gently and said, "We haven't covered that yet."

"Do you mind?" Donovan asked.

Jaynes hesitated, and then gestured at him to continue. He looked interested in the explanation.

Donovan ran a hand over his tight curls and asked, "How long have you spent Seeking at a time?"

"Just over two and a half minutes at the most," Van answered.

"In two minutes, do you think you could locate another Seeker?"

"I wouldn't know how to differentiate between the different magics ..."

"Right. You can't." Donovan agreed. "What about a specific person?"

"Again ..."

"What if you had a general idea of where someone was, based on their group number and general location in a secluded area?"

Van considered. "Well, sure, that wouldn't be too difficult, I think. If I was close by. And knew what to look for."

"Now, if you already know that one of them is a Seeker, how would you tell that he was using his magic?" Donovan looked between the two students and saw Jaynes was smiling slightly.

Ruben thought for a moment, and then shook his head, confused.

"You'd wait for the light to brighten? Or dim?" Van suggested.

Donovan pointed at her, pleased. "When you leave your body, you take your magic with you. If you were watching for it to happen, the light would dim."

"That still doesn't explain how you could attack another person's form. You're formless! You're a floating mind following paths of life across the earth."

"A floating consciousness with a beacon," Donovan gently corrected.

"I've never ..." Van and Ruben looked confused.

"Two minutes at a time, with Seekers not inclined to spend much time through the window, and everyone looking down and around as they spread thin, remember? To find another Seeker, you must look up."

Van's expression was serious as she processed the new information. Ruben's eyes were bonfires in his head, wide and bright with excitement. Donovan realized Jaynes was watching him with an inscrutable expression, but the teacher smiled and looked to the students when Donovan met his gaze.

"But what happens if the other person wins?" Van asked with a frown.

Donovan nodded seriously. "You die. You stay outside of your body too long and it overwhelms your mind and you die."

Van took and released a slow breath. "Looking up. I'll try that."

"Talk to your Mentalist friends about defending your mind and put those ideas to practice."

"Thank you, I will."

Jaynes stood easily and said, "I think that's enough Seeking for today, Ruben. We'll meet again next week. Until then, please see to it that you study topical maps of the area. We'll go over how to understand what you're seeing in your Seeking form. Van."

The young woman stood and they made their way out.

"That was a short class," Ruben said, disappointed..

"Seeking classes usually are. Mostly, they're about building your starting room, and getting used to the aftereffects — which you don't suffer."

"What happens if you don't go all the way? Through the window?" the boy asked.

"Well, I've never stopped to find out. It hurts too much on the way; I'd hate to spend any time there."

The boy rubbed his ears. "Everything is kind of tingly. Like you're louder and quieter and louder again."

"That'll wear off. I'm just jealous you can form coherent sentences. After my first class, we had half an hour just to calm down."

"I'm sorry."

Donovan waved away the apology. "Pah! For being born stronger? Should you apologize for having better eyesight than me, too?"

Ruben smiled. "I liked what you said, about looking up. I'm going to try that."

"You see stars, mostly. And clouds."

"I want to try it during a storm."

"Good luck." Donovan smiled. "What's next for you?"

"Self-work and study."

"Best get to it, then."

Ruben jumped to his feet with the elasticity of youth. Donovan did the same, much more slowly, knees protesting, clicking, the entire way.

In the hall, Ruben suddenly spun to grab Donovan in a hug.

"*Oof.*" Donovan hugged him back tightly. "Everything all right?"

"I'm glad you brought me here," Ruben answered. "Thank you."

Donovan ruffled his hair affectionately. "Good. I'm glad I did, too."

8

DESPITE— OR PERHAPS BECAUSE OF — the impending threat of infiltration, the next couple of days passed quickly. Donovan went about his usual business after a Retrieval with practiced motion. He sent his clothes to be laundered and repaired; he shined and oiled his boots; he returned his tools of travel to the Retrievers' supply room; and he put away the few personal items he'd taken with him. His room was only ten by twelve feet, plus a small closet, and he didn't own much, even with Lucas's belongings in their trunks on the floor of his space.

He spent most of the next day writing individual letters to Lucas's siblings, telling them what had happened. All of them were in the military in some capacity, and none were posted locally. He spent his afternoons with Kail. She let him help tend her home garden — a rare allowance — planting Lucas's Healing garden and nursing the vegetables, and then directed nearly every one of his movements until they got in a highly undignified and very short dirt-throwing war. It ended with him missing her completely, and then receiving a clod right in the mouth.

She made him stay and tell her stories of his time traveling with her son, and Donovan gladly did so, the anecdotes from Lucas's book fresh in his mind. They alternated between laughing and crying, the catharsis good for them both.

Several of Kail's students came to visit, and they tutored them with math and science and history, and then Donovan stayed for some dinners. Several neighbors joined, and they toasted Lucas's memory, and ate until they were stuffed. Kail was not a particularly skilled cook, but her neighbors happily contributed.

By the time Donovan made his way back to the Order each night, he was staggering with fatigue, but immensely and thoroughly cheered. He housed a ferocious yawn within his hands, widening his eyes in the hopes that they'd be more interested in staying open long enough to get him to his room. The stairs were mountains, and the hallways were all uphill, but he finally pushed open his little bedroom door and collapsed on his bed, barely staying conscious long enough to kick off his shoes.

*   *   *

"... the river of unconsciousness, but if you do not surface immediately, I will be forced to pour a bucket of water on your head."

Donovan's body felt like lead, but he forced his burning eyes to open, blinking in the dimness of his room, lit only by the single candle in Whitman's hand.

"Wassit'me ...?" he mumbled intelligibly.

"Four in the morning," Whitman answered briskly. The alertness of his voice was startling in Donovan's night-quiet ears.

"Whadeu'nt?" Donovan continued, pushing himself somewhat upright on his bed.

He'd managed to nestle down into the covers at some point, but far from covering him, they were mostly just twisted about his frame like a giant snake. He was cold.

"It is starting. Ruben is on his way here with a guard. I decided it was as safe as anywhere, considering the circumstances. The other children should be asleep, and there are guards in their hallway, but Elliott wanted extra protection for his magus. If all goes well, I will return, and the password will be me, very tired, because this cast is incredibly heavy, the crutch is a pain, my other leg is tired from all the extra work. And I didn't sleep at all. Questions?"

Whitman's speech was delivered at high speed, and had the sobering and waking ability as the bucket of water he'd threatened. Donovan's heart was racing; his stomach performed flips up in his chest.

"If you need to pee, I would suggest doing it now," Whitman said, turning away to look at Donovan's newly acquired map.

Donovan disentangled himself from the blanket and quickly used the chamber pot under his bed. It was rare that he used it, being that there was a water room at the end of the hall, but the urgency of the moment didn't leave him much chance to travel there and back.

"How long do you expect everything to take?" Donovan asked, putting the pot back under the bed.

"At least a few hours. Hopefully not more." Whitman turned around and balanced on his crutch as he surveyed the rest of the room. It didn't take him long.

"Why me? I mean, I'd expect you to have someone more capable to protect Ben, if anyone came after him."

Whitman nodded. "Oh, I do, but few so devoted." He smiled thinly. "Add to that Ben's trust of you, and you are a much better option than the others. And I need them."

He limped to the door and finagled it open around his handheld candle. He would need it in the main hallways, as they would be dimmed at this time of night. "Right on time."

A woman rounded the corner with Ruben at her side. Broad in the shoulders and chest; she was probably an archer, if Donovan was any judge. Her hair, thick and golden blond, lay carefully braided behind her head in a horsetail as thick as his arm. She stopped in the doorway, nodded at Whitman, and gave Donovan a faint smile of recognition, although he was sure he didn't know her.

"Hi, Don," Ruben said cheerfully, far too awake for this time of morning. "Hi, Whit."

He walked to Donovan's side and handed him a sheathed sword and belt.

"She let me carry it. They're heavier than I thought."

"They get heavier, I assure you," the woman told him. Her voice was low and clear. "Ready?" she asked Whitman. The two started away.

"Wait, you're not staying?" Donovan asked the woman. He looked at Whitman. "You said Ben was coming with a guard."

"And he did! But now Annette and I have to see to other things. You will be fine, Don. Lock the door and wait for the password. I will come for you in a few hours."

He limped away, and Annette closed the door behind them, giving Ruben a friendly wink.

Donovan locked the door and leaned against it. "Well," he said, thoroughly awake now.

Ruben looked around curiously. "What's in the boxes?"

"Lucas's things."

"Oh."

"He had a writing set you might like," Donovan told him quickly as the boy's face fell.

He opened a crate and retrieved a handsome wooden travel kit. The lid opened on a hinge and had a drawer to store paper so that it didn't blow away when out in the air, or get mussed when in the kit. Everything inside lay organized in little trays with small bottles of differently colored ink, a fancy quill knife, several quills, sand, and everything else he might need.

"Lucas liked to write and record things. You might find use of it for all of your schoolwork, if you'd like."

Ruben held up the bottles of ink, delighted in the options, and touched the knife and quills reverently. "Really?"

Seeing the awe in the boy's features, Donovan suddenly wondered if he'd ever had something this nice of his own. Growing up under contract didn't give people much chance for treasures.

Donovan smiled at the boy's excited face. "Of course! I won't use it, and it'd be a shame to sell. I think he had it made custom."

"Thank you!" Ruben perched on the desk stool and started going through the kit in earnest. "What do you want to do while we're stuck here?"

"I don't have any cards," Donovan lamented. "I wasn't expecting company."

"That's all right."

Donovan looked at the sword propped against the desk. It didn't make him feel much better. He'd never been particularly skilled with it; that had been Lucas's job.

"I had an Elementalist class today," Ruben said suddenly.

"Oh?" Donovan kept an interested look on his face as he surveyed his space, wishing he had a second door, or a crossbow, or useful magic. He couldn't help but wonder how likely it was that they would manage to stay out of the conflict.

"Mostly it was a lecture about how dangerous fire is, but she showed me how to warm things. No flames. It was still fun. I melted a candle in my hand; it didn't even hurt. And she said if I concentrate, I can be immune to most heat or cold without too much effort."

"That would have been nice to have a few weeks ago," Donovan teased.

The closet was deeper than it looked, and would do in a pinch if they needed to hide. At least for a short time. The sword drew his eyes again like a magnet.

Ruben grinned. "I offered, but you said no ..."

"I have no regrets about that decision. We all still have all of our fingers and toes." He wiggled his fingers for example and Ruben laughed.

The boy looked around. "I like your pictures."

"Thank you. I took most of them from Lucas's belongings; he was much more consistent about commissioning portraits of our friends. I like them a lot."

"Who's this?" the boy asked. He picked up the framed portrait on the desk. "They look nice — is this your wife?"

Donovan chewed on the inside of his lip for a moment. "My wife and daughter, yes. Cara and Kelsa."

"I didn't know you had a daughter," the boy said looking up at him, surprised. "I guess I didn't know you were married, either. Is this your ring?" He lifted the golden band from where it sat in front of the picture frame.

Donovan cleared his throat. "My daughter was killed."

A blush climbed Ruben's face. "I'm sorry," he said softly, carefully placing the frame back on the desk.

"That's all right, son," Donovan assured him, the ache in his chest a familiar friend.

"Was ... was she killed by Hunters?"

Donovan nodded. "She and her Retriever, both."

"Is that why you're a Retriever now?"

Donovan shrugged and bobbed his head side to side. "I'm sure it contributed. I hadn't exactly planned on this path for myself, but I do enjoy it."

"Where ..." Ruben hesitated.

"Go ahead."

"Where is your wife, then?"

"She left after Kelsa's death. I'm not sure exactly where she is now," Donovan admitted. "That's her father's ring — I mean to return it if she wants it back."

Ruben nodded thoughtfully. "Um, I like your map," he said haltingly, clearly trying to change the subject to something less personal.

Donovan smiled. "Thank you. It was Lucas's also. I scavenged a few of his things. My room was pretty bare before."

"Are these all the places you've been?"

Donovan nodded and moved closer. "I've been to more, but these are all the places we went together. I was Retrieving for a few years longer than Lucas; I was his first partner. Here's Philipa, where we found you," he pointed.

Ruben grinned.

They passed some time with Donovan once again telling the stories of his and Lucas's time Retrieving, and a few stories of his time before Lucas, with his previous partners.

"I'm not sure if you would like Nuncio. He takes some getting used to, but he was one of the best people I know. I haven't heard from him in years, though."

"You've been everywhere!"

"Just about, but not nearly as many places as I had once wished to visit."

The boy opened his mouth to ask a question, but stopped, eyes growing wide. "I-I think there's someone outside."

Donovan went to the door, but didn't open it. "Why do you think that?"

"I have ... a feeling?" Ruben looked confused and frustrated. "Maybe I was using my Mentalist magic? Sometimes it just happens, but my teacher said I just have to work on shielding my mind."

Donovan wished he had a window in his door to look out. He put a hand on the aged wood. All of the other Retrievers were out in the field. Maybe one of them had returned? Bad timing, if so. Vale had her office on this floor, but her quarters were two halls away. There wouldn't be much reason for anyone else to be here ... He glanced back at Ruben, who was frowning, probably trying to understand what his senses were telling him. Donovan decided he'd rather be cautious.

Unsheathed sword in hand, he put his back against the door and listened.

"I wish you could Seek to find out," Ruben said, frustrated.

"Me too." He could, but it would leave him defenseless, and then weakened. Not a good idea. "Don't," he told the boy sharply.

Ruben looked guilty. "I wasn't going to! But what if we could find out who's there?"

"You won't find that out. You'll only see how many, and which ones have magic — which won't be as helpful as you might think. And in the meantime, I'll be stuck here with a boy who can't help himself, in case we are attacked while he's out counting."

Ruben put up his hands, "All right, all right ..."

"We'll wait until- *oof.*"

Donovan bounced away from the door and then back as a force slammed into the other side.

"Knock, knock," came a man's mocking greeting.

Donovan felt the blood drain from his face. He turned around with one hand pressed against the wood as though to keep the way sealed. He recognized that voice. His chest ached.

He heard Ruben move behind him.

"Come out, come out, wherever you are ..." Another taunting call.

"I see three pairs of feet, but there might be more," Ruben whispered, standing from looking under the door.

"Do you think you can call for help? Using Mentalist magic?" Donovan whispered back.

Ruben looked worried. "I can try. I've only had one class."

"Now might be the time."

"What are you going to do?"

"Distract them."

It was the only plan he had. The people in the hall expected to break down the door, kill him, grab Ruben, and be on their way as quickly as possible. If he could slow them down, even a bit, help had a chance to reach them.

"Get in the closet," he told the boy.

Ruben jumped to obey and tucked himself away into the back of the small space. Donovan squared his shoulders and willed his hands to stop shaking. The sword was a small comfort.

I'm going to die here.

His eyes started to water, but he blinked hard and cleared his throat. Standing with his back against the door, taking deep breaths, he knew if he had to die, he'd die protecting the boy in this room.

Decided, he spun, threw open the door and smiled widely, the muscles in his face protesting the unnatural expression. "Gentlemen! Ladies! What can I do for you?"

The gathering hesitated, surprised at his tactic. One of them had his hands raised, fire building in his palms. Donovan had shared a table with him in the dining hall yesterday. He recognized another as having worked in the Healing Ward while he'd been recovering. A third he remembered vaguely from the library. He didn't recognize the other two of them. But he did recognize the final assailant. Donovan's blood turned to ice, while his bowels turned to jelly.

"How-how did you get in here?" His voice trembled.

The Smiling Man grinned. Donovan threw his sword at the Elementalist, forcing the man to dodge and lose the concentration that kept his flames alight. He didn't fall far, and now Donovan had no sword. Still, he kicked at the Smiling Man, who took a step out of reach uncannily fast and responded with a punch to Donovan's head. Donovan, however, was no longer there, having thrown himself to the ground to roll over his shoulder into the midst of the group.

From the ground, he kicked the Elementalist in the groin as hard as he could. The man coughed and choked, retching as he fell to his knees. Donovan stayed on the ground and swung his legs around to bring the woman beside him to his level. As she hit, and the air whooshed out of her lungs, Donovan rolled over to deliver two strong strikes directly into her windpipe and another into her face.

She choked and strong arms pulled him off of her; a blow to his stomach stopped his furious, panicked energy. His shoulders screamed under the pressure of his attackers pinning his arms behind his back.

"You should have let me have the boy in Weston," the Smiling Man said, strolling to the dormitory door. "It would have saved you the trouble."

The woman in front of Donovan struck him in the ribs again. He yelled, instinctively trying to curl into a ball, but the men didn't drop him. Then the woman shook her head and put a hand on his face. Donovan screamed as lightning coursed through his body, searing every nerve like a branding iron.

They dropped him to the ground. He landed hard, with no power to resist, twitching and writhing as the burning so slowly faded. The Elementalist stood over him, waiting for the shocks to dissipate. Someone kicked him in the spine and he cried out again. He felt like a heavy weight was on his chest; his heart raced, stuttered. Donovan forced his eyes open and saw the Smiling Man looking down at him with a thoughtful expression.

The Smiling Man went to open the dormitory door and hissed, wrenching his hand away from the now burning hot handle.

Donovan managed a weak chuckle, but was rewarded with another kick to his spine for the trouble. The first Elementalist had managed to gain his feet, but was limping, and clutching himself. He had murder in his eyes.

"Get this door open," the no-longer-smiling man demanded. Quietly he added, "I won't fail ..." A deep breath fixed his composure and he winked at Donovan. "I have rules," he explained.

Donovan had no idea what that meant.

The Elementalist touched the door handle and said, "I'll have to melt it off. It's blocked on the other side. Then she can Move it," he nodded at his bleeding companion on the floor.

She gained her feet after a moment, tears blocking her vision, hand still held to her face in a failed attempt to staunch the blood flow. "You broke my nose." The pain and damage in her voice took the venom from her snarl.

"Shock him again," the Smiling Man ordered.

The woman standing above Donovan obliged, touching his knee with a delicate finger. He screamed again, back arching as he shook uncontrollably, the branding iron returning in earnest. He imagined his skin burning and peeling away from his writhing muscles.

"Open the door, imbecile. We'll have the full weight of the Order on us in moments. We should have been finished ages ago."

The Elementalist was already melting through the door handle, scorching the wood around it. When it lay in a puddle at his feet, he stepped out of the way so that the Displacer woman could see through. As soon as her eye was level with the newly-made hole, she shrieked and threw herself backward, clutching her eye. She fell to the ground, howling and screaming, legs twitching. Donovan blearily recognized the handle of Lucas's quill knife sticking out of her face. Ruben was using what he had at hand, apparently.

The Smiling Man started to laugh. It was a horrible thing to hear mingled with the woman's screams and Donovan's own labored breathing. One of the men behind Donovan ran over to try and help, but he wasn't a Healer, and there was nothing he could do. Even if he had been a Healer, who would sacrifice his own eye?

"Ruben," the Smiling Man called in a sing-song voice. "I'm sure you can hear me, yes?" He looked down at Donovan's prone form. "I'm going to kill your friend if you don't open the door. Come out now and I will be merciful. If we have to come in after you, I'll be forced to make him suffer for the rest of his life. What do you say?"

He nodded at the Elementalist woman, and she shocked Donovan again. He felt his vocal chords rub raw as he screamed, twitching and flailing. When it stopped, his heart was racing so fast he couldn't breathe. He couldn't move.

Silence was Ruben's answer from the other side of the door. A treacherous and emotional part of Donovan wished the door would open, but the more logical side of him was glad. He wondered vaguely what Ruben had managed to block the door with, and how.

After another moment of silence, the Smiling Man strode over to Donovan and kicked him petulantly in the face. Donovan's nose broke with a burst of blood. His head cracked and bounced into the stone of the floor and he saw fireworks behind his eyes, suddenly dizzy and nauseous. Blood leaked into his mouth and he gagged and tried to cough, but he could only barely turn his head.

Sitting up was beyond his greatest efforts. Another kick to his stomach made him retch and wheeze and moan.

"Do you hear that, Ruben? Your precious Donovan is dying."

"We have to go. Someone is coming," one of the men said urgently.

Finally — where are the guards? Where is the alarm? Someone please help me. Help me …

Donovan imagined he was slowly drifting away. He found his family home with the hanging vegetables and the smooth wooden floors, the hearth fire and warm breeze, the scent of apples and baking bread. The doors and windows were open to let in the light and the air and the fresh scents of life and love.

Without conscious effort, Donovan followed the practiced pattern, striding to the window and passing through it.

The pain that struck brought him momentarily to his senses. He flailed mentally, trying to reestablish order in the jumbled mess of his mind. He wavered, not sure if he should go forward or back — which was which? He knew hesitation was a risk he couldn't take, but his thoughts were so slow. The pain was just more pain on top of the agony he already suffered. He felt himself sinking, finding the pain somehow less overwhelming than it ever had been. He sank lower, his faint consciousness exploring the sensations around him while the previous hurt that enveloped him somehow faded, taking with it his sight and hearing and …

Perhaps this is death.

He smiled, then, the faces of his wife and daughter hovering in his mind's eye, arms out to greet him.

"— possibility — head trauma."

"He — right mess."

"We — anything for — he wakes up."

"When will that be?"

"— being torn apart."

"It'll take — everyone down."

"A — people are leaving -."

"How could -?"

"— they all get in?"

"When did it all start?"

"You — here in days, you — take a rest."

"I — a rest, I need my friend — and functioning."

"The Head wants to see you."

"Tell him to come see me."

"— heard the King himself is traveling here."

"I can't imagine his guards like the idea."

"He's got quite the entourage with him, and his own users."

"I'm sure the Head loves that idea."

"They'll be tested like everyone else."

"The Mentalists aren't going to last too much longer at this rate."

"Everyone's being called in from the field."

"We need more Healers."

"We always need more Healers."

"— see that?"

"See what?"

"His hand moved. He's moving."

"I'm not sure ..."

"His foot, too!"

"Go get the surgeon. Come back, Donovan. Come back to us. Do not make me hunt you down in the dead-lands, because I *bloody* will, and when I write the legend of it, the people will weep for the beauty of my adventures, and they will throw old lettuce at your dented skull for driving me to such lengths, you will certainly see."

9

DONOVAN OPENED HIS EYES, and then immediately shut them again with a gasp of pain.

"What's wrong?" Ruben's voice asked softly. It echoed around Donovan's skull, banging about behind his eyes and jaw.

"Too bright," he croaked, his throat drier than a desert tomb.

He heard the boy move to extinguish the lamps and then return. Every footstep sounded like a parade drum in Donovan's ears. He tried to concentrate on his breathing, but even his lungs sounded like a bellows. The bed sheets under him chafed at his skin. He could smell his own body odor, and Ruben's. Whitman was softly snoring across the room, but Donovan knew he'd eaten lamb recently by his breath. The familiar and awful taste of his own mouth was offensive to him. It was as though he was stuck in a slightly-less-overwhelming variant of the in-between-place he endured right before and after Seeking.

"How do you feel?" Ruben asked gently.

The question roared at him and Donovan wished desperately his hearing would fade to keep the explosion of noise at bay.

Almost immediately, it did.

It took him a moment to realize that Ruben was speaking again, because now he could barely hear him. Donovan risked opening his eyes again, the dimness a relief against his headache, but he had trouble focusing his eyes. Everything was blurry. Concentration narrowed his vision, though, and, after a moment, he could see Ruben clearly. The boy was turned away, speaking to Whitman, who was coming over to claim the chair Ruben had vacated.

"What?" Donovan asked, straining to hear the younger man. Younger in years maybe, but Whitman's face had aged since last he saw it. New lines creased his features; a day or two of stubble garnished his cheeks. He looked haggard.

Whitman's voice swam into hearing range as though Donovan was rising through water. It equalized at last, and he heard, "— wrong? Are you in pain?"

He shook his head and instantly regretted it, as pain blossomed behind his eyes.

"Ugh." He put his hands to his head and pressed as though to squeeze everything out of his skull. "I have a headache. It's — I'll — I'm fine. It's fine. I just, my head feels strange."

"Strange how?" Whitman asked.

Donovan could hear him clearly, sharply, but it was no longer painful.

"You took quite a blow, and your unconsciousness had the surgeons worried. They said you have no lasting damage, but if you are in pain, maybe they should look again?"

Donovan waved Whitman's words away and held up a finger to wait. He put his hands back on his head. He felt jumbled and confused. The tastes and smells and textures around him had faded to a manageable level, but he felt overstimulated and overwhelmed. He took deep breaths, trying to calm down and piece together what he knew.

He was in the Healing Ward again.

Ruben was safe.

He was alive, somehow, despite encountering the Smiling Man again.

His headache was fading to a dull throb behind his jaw. He forced his neck and back and stomach to relax. There was no danger here.

"All right," he said at last. "I think I'm all right." He lowered his hands to his lap.

"Do you want anything for your head?" Whitman asked softly.

"Please."

Whitman nodded at Ruben, who ran out of the room, closing the door with exaggerated care.

"What happened?" Donovan asked.

The young Spymaster leaned back in his chair, causing it to creak ominously, and sighed. He ran a thoughtful finger down his nose a few times.

"The plan worked. Several fought, but were managed. We missed some, as expected, but we brought them under control when they fought back, or their friends gave them up. There was some pushback from those who did not understand why we were arresting the names on my list, but for the most part, it went smoothly. People have always known it was only a matter of time before the Hunters attacked here." He scratched at his incoming beard and sighed again. "Ten dead, thirty-seven wounded — about a third of them critical. Of theirs, eight dead, twenty wounded. Civilians: two dead, about fifteen wounded. It-it could have been much worse."

Donovan's stomach flipped at the thought. Twenty deaths in the halls of the Order. "They came right after you left. Couldn't have been an hour."

Whitman rubbed his face. "That boy Arnold Coulter, Ruben's roommate, was one that we had not counted on. Should have. He's slimy."

"I didn't like him."

"No one did, but he was clever enough not to push it further than basic dislike of his character. No reason to look into his background. Not that we would have found anything. He killed two guards on his own before they stopped him, and we're nearly positive he sent out a message to his friends when Ruben left the dormitory with Annette."

"Gods all ..."

"I know. And we still do not know how the Smiling Man got in."

"Why aren't I dead?" Donovan asked, grimacing as his headache flared again.

Ruben came in with a wooden mug, carefully watching to keep it from spilling. A nurse entered behind him: a young man who looked as tired as Whitman.

"Before you drink that, I want to check a few things," he said dully.

Donovan nodded and the man put a hand on his shoulder, closing his eyes. Donovan felt his shoulder grow a few degrees warmer, but otherwise, nothing.

After a few moments, the young man opened his eyes and lowered his hand. "Everything looks fine. Be easy for several days. Let us know if you have any dizziness or nausea or trouble. You're free to go when you feel well enough."

The young man left the way he'd come, and Donovan felt a profound sense of sympathy for him. He looked exhausted, and it was unlikely he would have a real rest soon. Ruben passed the mug and Donovan sipped, not wanting to flood his waking stomach. The flavors exploded on his tongue and he nearly gagged at the bitterness. He pushed the mug back at Ruben, who took it with a panicked expression. Donovan coughed hard, and groaned.

"What is wrong with me?" he moaned helplessly, sitting back against the pillows.

Ruben hesitantly offered the mug again and Donovan received it, eyeing the mix with distaste. Headache cures were never appealing, and they often left a gritty taste in your mouth, but they worked, and he'd had more than his share over the years.

He sniffed suspiciously, and sensed only herbs, faintly, like he had a stuffy nose. He risked another sip, and this time barely tasted anything. Heartened, he drank down the rest, unwilling to risk his mouth changing sensitivity again before he'd finished.

Quickly, the pain in his head started to fade, which was good, because Whitman hadn't answered his initial question. He gestured for the Spymaster to continue.

Whitman answered, "Ruben managed to send me something of a message. Mostly a panicked emotion, but when I realized from whom it came, I sent people your way. They were held up at a few points — those few we missed, like Coulter. The people attacking you did not seem to want to stay long. Especially when Vale joined the fray."

"*Retriever* Vale?"

"She heard the commotion; saved your life for certain. I have not seen water controlled like that in the entirety of my existence. It was ... it was most impressive."

Donovan agreed, "Another Retriever told me she had awards for service and combat in magic, but I've never seen them. She brags about scars, but not much else."

Whitman settled more comfortably in his seat and crossed his arms. "You missed quite the show." His expression darkened. "The Smiling Man escaped. He killed a guard and disappeared before anyone could stop him, but I saw him go. He dodges like he knows where people are going to be before they can even decide to move. It is incredible, and infuriating. Now that this nightmare is all but concluded, I can apply myself to discovering who he is. And I will."

"You arrested everyone else?"

"Nearly. An Elementalist of his escaped, too. I am hopeful we will get her."

Ruben had crossed the room to curl up on the couch and was watching them owlishly.

"They put classes on hold for everyone, but I still have tutors," he said as the conversation lulled.

"Oh?" Donovan wasn't entirely surprised. Except ... "Wait. How long has it been?"

"Two weeks."

"*Two weeks?*"

Whitman grimaced. "You do seem to withdraw from injuries, no? Other than the concussion, your wounds were fairly minor. Still, Elliott assigned a personal Healer to you. It has been decided: you are something of a hero."

Donovan frowned. "I was beat up in a hallway."

"You stalled six magic users so that the guard could arrive to help defend the only magus in residence."

"I was *beat up* in a *hallway.*"

Whitman rolled his eyes. "You have no theater in your soul, Donovan."

"No, but I'm pretty sure I had bone-shards in my abdomen."

Whitman barked a loud laugh, and Donovan winced as his hearing fluctuated again, seeming to deliberate between levels. He pushed his fingers into his ears and wiggled them.

"What's next?" he asked. "You've captured the infiltrators, so the Order is safe again?"

"For the time. As Ruben said, classes are on hold until all of the parents can be reassured, and we are approaching the winter break anyway. I expect Dean Villery might push through to that. Elliott has ordered everyone away to return to the Order, or risk being labeled a traitor." He nodded at Donovan's surprise and continued, "He wants to have his Mentalists check everyone again, now that we have the time. Might as well be thorough. Otherwise, the guard numbers in town and at the gates have been increased. No riots in town, but there were some small pockets of violence. A couple of burned buildings and injuries, but no casualties. There is too much military presence in Thairnsdale for those to build much speed. Yet." He winced.

"Ruben, will you find out where my clothes are?" Donovan asked. "I'd like to go ahead and clear this room for someone else."

Ruben slid off the couch and trotted away.

Whitman was wearing a wry smile. "And the other reason you wanted him out of the room?"

"The Smiling Man really did want to kidnap him," Donovan said quickly. "They didn't want him dead. They were willing to waste time torturing me to bring him out of the room willingly. I don't know who that man is, but I want to help you find him and kill him. He's dangerous. I haven't seen him demonstrate magic, but he's a killer, Whit."

"I agree."

"Ruben needs protection. He needs to learn to fight, and he needs to stay here. The Order has been cleared of Hunters and sympathizers, so now is the time to put him in the public eye. He's a student, and he isn't. We need the people to understand that he's more: he's a magus."

"You want to make him a figurehead."

Donovan shrugged, trying to understand what he wanted to express. "I want every worker and teacher and student and scholar to take it as a personal offense the next time someone tries something, anything, that might put him at risk."

Whitman nodded slowly. "I will see what I can do."

"I'll talk to Hector about getting him assigned to assist the soldiers. He can clean equipment and whatnot instead of the stables. They'll get protective when they see him as one of their own."

"You *are* a clever one."

"I'm not a fighter," Donovan explained. "I will fight, but Whitman, I'm an old man. You gambled, and you were lucky. Ruben saved himself; we had nothing to do with it. It was luck that the guard came in time, that Vale came to help, and it was luck that they took their time torturing me. You can't gamble again. He needs proper protection."

"We cannot have him tailed everywhere he goes, Donovan."

"No, but the next time something like this might happen, you stick him in a windowless room with a dozen armed guards and mages you can trust, not with an old Retriever whose best idea is a delaying tactic."

The Spymaster nodded. "I understand. Do you—" he stopped as the door opened, and Ruben returned with a stack of clothes.

Donovan clapped his hands together. "All right, both of you. I'm fine. Let me get dressed and put my head back together." He smiled reassuringly and they both left him alone.

When they were gone, he sighed, rubbing at his aching head. *Now what?*

*   *   *

Donovan sat upright, gasping for breath, legs thrashing. He was covered in sweat, and it burned in his pores. He groaned and put hands to his ears, the sound of his blood pulsing through his body louder than the sea in a storm. He gagged, feeling as though burning knives were digging into his skull, and threw the covers away, standing in the middle of his room, bare and shaking. His heart pounded, stomach swirled. *Deep breaths, calm down ...*

Heart still racing, he staggered to his door and checked the lock again. He leaned his forehead against the grain and pressed as though he could pass through it. As he ordered his body to relax, it was slow, but did respond. His senses faded to normal and then less. Now they had him feeling nearly numb. He shook with adrenaline and cold. He climbed back into his bed and lay on his stomach, pillow bunched beneath him. Something was so wrong.

*   *   *

"Good morning."

Donovan looked up, and saw a woman staring at him.

"What?" he asked languidly.

"I said, good morning," she repeated politely. "Didn't sleep well?"

"No." It took him a moment to recognize her as the guard who had brought Ruben to his room before ...

"Annette," she reminded him, matching his slow stride through the corridor. "You're Donovan Rudd."

"How are you?" he asked politely. He knew his tone failed to hide a lack of interest, but he was very tired, and very frustrated.

"I thought the surgeons gave you a clean bill of health," she said curiously as they walked out of the Medical Wing. "Did they miss something?"

"I don't ..." he rubbed his head. His hearing seemed to be coming in and out again. "I don't want to talk about it, if you don't mind. It's rather personal."

"I apologize. I'm incurably curious, and often rude. Can I treat you to breakfast?"

He looked at her blearily. Before, her blond hair had been braided out of her way, but now she had it braided in the front to keep it out of her face, but loose in the back. It hung nearly to her waist. She was dressed, he noticed, in a very expensive-looking set of riding clothes, high boots, thin trousers, and jacket.

"What were you doing in Medical?" he asked, wondering why she'd targeted him to speak to.

She shrugged. "I broke a finger while riding this morning. They were kind enough to see to it for me."

He blinked slowly.

"Breakfast?" she prompted.

"All right."

"It'll do you good."

He didn't try to make further conversation as they walked and she didn't push him, which he greatly appreciated. He assumed she had ulterior motives for starting the conversation with him, but couldn't guess what they were — other than perhaps talking about what had happened in the fight. She wouldn't be the first to ask, and he still didn't want to talk about it.

They found two clear seats at the end of a long table. She scooped food onto their plates without asking, but he was too tired to care. His stomach was entirely uninterested, but it did smell vaguely good, so he took a few small bites. Soon, his plate was empty, and she was serving him more casserole and eggs and ham.

"What are your days filled with, if you're not Retrieving?" she asked after their initial hunger had been satisfied.

Feeling a bit more human, he answered, "Catching up with friends and business. I was going to help Whitman in the library today, but might try for a nap instead."

"Nightmares?"

He glanced at her, but her gaze was unembarrassed, and non-judgmental.

"Yes."

"I always have nightmares after a fight. Especially when it results in recovery time. They'll pass."

"I know."

"Of course." She smiled.

"And what do you do?"

"I spend my days in leisure and want for nothing." She winked at his raised eyebrow. "*I* am here on loan from the king to assist in training the Order's military in ranged combat. I'm quite good at it, you see, though I do despise teaching."

"So you live at the palace?"

"Currently, I live here, though yes, I have spent considerable time at the palace in previous years."

He nodded. He'd run out of questions.

"We do have something else in common, other than our mutual charming bard friend," she said after a moment of silence passed.

"What's that?" He swallowed another forkful of casserole.

"I, too, am a Seeker."

Her tone suggested this to be more dramatic a reveal than he took it to be. "Oh."

She laughed. "I agree. It's not the most impressive of magics for all of its potential wonder. Those who have it don't want it; and those who don't have it want more than we can give them. Finding us unable to assist, they decide they don't need it after all, and send us away, educated and unwanted."

He smiled a bit at that. "I suppose you have something there."

"We make ourselves useful in other ways, though. You with your Retrieving, me with my, ugh, teaching. The darlings don't even know how to string their bows when they come to me, and I'm supposed to teach them to hit moving targets from dozens of yards away?" She flipped her hair dramatically and tore off a mouthful of bread roll with just her teeth.

"I wish you luck of it," he told her, amused, taking another bite from his plate.

"Interesting combination you've made there," she said casually, nodding to his concoction.

He glanced down and realized he'd accidentally pushed the fresh strawberries into his breakfast casserole, and the mustard from his sausage had mixed its way in. He couldn't taste anything at all.

The moment that he saw his plate, however, his taste started to return and he grimaced, reaching to pour himself a cup of milk to wash the taste away. Appetite thoroughly overwhelmed, he pushed his plate away and sighed.

"Interesting," Annette mused, twirling her fork on her plate.

"I—" he hesitated, not sure how to explain, or even if he wanted to.

"Bump on the head do more damage than you thought?" she asked, not unkindly.

"Probably," he admitted. "The surgeons and Healers say it's nothing, and that my brain is probably just still recovering. Then they remind me that I'm not young anymore. Again and again." He smiled grimly.

"So you can't taste things?" She clarified.

"No, it's ..." he closed his eyes for a moment and put out his hands as though answers would fall into them. "It's everything. Sometimes sound, or taste, or hearing. Everything comes in and out, comes and goes, like doors opened and closed by some unkind hand. I wake up in the night because I can hear everything in the hall around me, and it's so loud I want to scream, but then it fades away to nearly nothing and I can't hear myself speaking. Or my skin gets so sensitive it's like I've been burned in the sun for days, and then I'm numb a moment later. Or this happens," he gestured at his plate. "I'm probably going mad." He attempted a smile to reassure her, but now that he'd said it aloud, he knew he'd been wondering for days.

She didn't say anything.

"I'm sorry," he said, embarrassed. "I'm not even sure if I'm making it up at this point."

"You should see if you can bring on the increase or decrease on purpose. Some kind of controlled experiment," Annette said thoughtfully.

He looked up. She met his gaze squarely, intelligence ticking behind her eyes.

"I can't control it."

"I think it's possible you haven't explored all of your options," she argued. "There's always a chance that it won't go back to normal." She spoke frankly, but her tone was kind. Still, what she was implying ...

"You think it's a new kind of magic." If she wanted to be frank, he'd participate.

She nodded. "Why not?"

"Because magic doesn't change. I'm a Seeker, we know that. How could I have two kinds of magic?"

"You've heard of magi, I expect?" she teased.

"That's one type of person!" he said, exasperated. "They're so rare as to have myths written about them! They can do so many things, we have no way of telling what was and wasn't real!"

She nodded calmly. "I'm not disagreeing."

"But you still think it's magic."

"Yes."

"And you want me to experiment."

"Right."

He laughed, giggled until his stomach hurt, chortling and wiping a few errant tears from his eyes. He knew they were from stress, not true mirth, but he couldn't stop.

Annette still didn't look annoyed by the time he managed to get ahold of himself, but let the last few of his chuckles die away before she spoke again.

"Are you busy this afternoon?"

*   *   *

"Where have you been?" Whitman asked.

He was in a private study room in the library. The librarian who had been his silent guide left them alone, and Donovan sat at the table. Whitman had an assortment of snacks beside him, mostly raw vegetables. The entire table was covered in literature of various sorts: some in languages Donovan didn't know, one so faded and damaged he couldn't understand how Whitman could read it.

"I just had breakfast with Annette Kraemer."

Whitman raised an eyebrow and took a nibble from a turnip beside him. "I'm surprised you made it out unscathed."

"She was pleasant company," Donovan laughed. "Very ... intense. Very ... um, decisive."

Whitman grinned wickedly and exaggerated another crunching bite.

"I'm scheduled to meet her again this afternoon," Donovan said. "How do you know her?"

Whitman flopped a hand about dismissively. "Who can remember something like that — I barely remember meeting you."

"You tried to steal our horse."

"Clearly you do not suffer the same tenuous hold on memory."

"You'd make a lousy bard if you had a poor memory."

"But a brilliant exaggerator and liar! Which is all bards are, truly. Am I telling the truth? I do not know!"

"All right, then, you'd make a terrible spy."

Whitman winked at Donovan. "Truth in those words. However, no justice to be found. I still will not answer your question."

"She's one of yours then."

"No, she is much too intelligent and clever and witty and handsome to ever fall prey to my charms. Even I, as humble as I am, fail to breach the mountain of brilliance, skill, beauty, and talent that is Annette Kraemer."

"Dammit, Whit, you aren't going to tell me anything about her, are you?"

"Give the boy a biscuit, he is a clever lad!" Whitman cackled outrageously and crunched off another bite of his turnip.

Donovan rolled his eyes, too amused to be irate. "You're in a fine mood today."

"I took three steps without my crutch before collapsing to the ground in insurmountable agony."

"That's ... good?"

"It is wonderful! Three steps begin each story! Three steps multiplied complete every task. Three steps are the start to my future! Which, incidentally, looks quite something like my past — only older and more likely to ache during storms."

Donovan shook his head, amused. "I'm happy for you, Whit."

"You are a gracious gentleman," Whitman said serenely before shoving the rest of his turnip into his mouth like a large-jowled dog.

"Have you had any success in finding the Smiling Man?"

Whitman's eyebrows flew into his hairline and he held up an excited index finger, making eager grunting sounds that Donovan took to be an affirmative answer, but explained nothing. The bard flipped his hands about impatiently, pointing vigorously to his desk, strewn about with papers. Donovan waited awkwardly, unable to make any more conversation until Whitman had finished chewing. Still, he expected good news, judging by the reaction. Whitman rolled his eyes about in an amused manner, drummed his fingers on the desk and made pained faces as he swallowed overly large chunks of vegetable.

"No!" Whitman finally answered. His voice was strained and he coughed, as his eyes watered up. He rubbed his chest to help the turnip go down.

Donovan stared at him. "No? No, you've had no success?"

"No, I have had no success in my *specific topic* of the Smiling Man himself, but I have managed to find three articles with the same information regarding the subject of mental fighting for Seekers. Two of the writers are dead. But the third is our very own Director of Seeking, Professor Herman Jaynes. I believe you've met. He did leave the Order recently, but I have sent him a missive and am hoping he'll be responsive."

"Well, that's good, then, Whit. Well done."

"Your enthusiasm is overwhelming, dear Donovan."

Donovan smiled apologetically. "From your antics I was expecting a bit more than the possibility of a meeting with the

Director of Seeking; I did meet him — he's a nice man. I just don't know if he'll have the information you're looking for."

"One cannot pin all expectations so high. He might have more information, leads with which I can work. Research, research, research! In the meantime, I will continue my attempt to buff the gem of curiosity with the polishing cloth of discovery."

"You've an interesting way of turning a phrase, Whitman."

"Dear man, how long have you known me, now?"

"Are we including the time I've been unconscious? Because I think that almost doubles the outcome ..."

Whitman laughed. "Go see Annette. I have work to do."

10

DONOVAN WALKED DOWN the students' classroom hall. With classes resumed, most of the children were occupied, but he knew the way. Annette had suggested they meet in one of the Seeker classrooms, and had sent a page to tell him which of them was scheduled to be available.

The door was open, so he walked inside to see Annette was messing with a series of items on top of a desk that had not been there before. Two cushions rested near it, thrown in the same general direction from the stack in the corner.

"Take a seat!" she said eagerly. "Oh, and close the door. Take off your boots, if you like! I prefer Seeking without them."

"Are we going to be Seeking, then?"

"I don't intend to," she answered brightly. "But it might happen. We're experimenting! Prepare for anything!"

He walked to her side to see what the desk held: several bottles of perfumes, a bag of assorted candies, a few different hand-held percussion instruments and a military whistle, a writing set much like the one he'd given to Ruben (but not nearly as fine), and a small box of different types of fabric scraps.

"What do you want to start with?" she asked.

"You tell me."

"Which sense bothers you most?"

He felt foolish, but answered, "They all bother me." He hadn't experienced an episode since breakfast, and he was feeling silly again. She waited, though, and he decided, "Sound, I suppose. Hearing."

She grabbed up the various small instruments and sat gracefully on her cushion. Donovan dropped down with less fluidity and crossed his legs, which immediately prompted his knees to ache and crack in protest. They warned that he wouldn't be able to sit like that for long, but Annette, who couldn't have been more than ten years younger, probably less, seemed perfectly comfortable.

"Ready?" she asked.

Without waiting for an answer, she blew the whistle. Meant to carry for miles, the sound *shrieked* from the instrument and Donovan yelled, slamming his hands over his ears.

After the noise ceased, he dropped his hands and snarled, "You could have deafened us both!" He realized that he couldn't hear his own words, and threw his hands up in exasperation, yelling, "YOU *HAVE* DEAFENED US BOTH!"

He saw Annette's lips moving and tried to make out her words. His hearing came back just in time for her to ring a small silver bell. He winced, expecting his ears to be tender, but they were fine.

"You could hear that?" she asked.

He nodded. "What did you say before?"

"Oh. I said you were shouting at me before I stopped blowing the whistle. Your hearing must have gone away, but you thought I had stopped. Not the case. And I could hear you perfectly well. No need to shout."

He let out a deep breath through his teeth. She was trying to help.

She picked up the whistle again, but he stopped her. "How about a different sense?"

A cheeky smirk crossed her features. "All right then. I'm already building a theory. Hang on."

She rose without effort and put the instruments on the desk, only to return with the bag of candies and a box of perfumes.

"Smell or taste?" she asked.

He eyed the candies warily, wondering what she'd mixed into them. "Smell."

She pulled a bottle out from the perfumes and handed it to him. "Smell that." As he gingerly pulled the stopper she snapped, "Sniff it, Donovan! Don't be a baby!"

He took a whiff and immediately sneezed, coughing and gagging. It was the strongest smell he'd ever encountered, and that included having been sprayed by a skunk while on a Retrieval.

"What is that?" he retched, thrusting the bottle back at her.

"You don't sound stuffed up," she answered thoughtfully. "Here, smell this one."

"I can't smell anything after that last dose!"

"Are you sure?"

"I—" he shook his head, rubbing his nose. "No, nothing."

"No lingering smell of what I just gave you?"

"It's lingering ..."

"I can still smell it strongly, and I didn't even get the whiff you did. I probably shouldn't have started with it, but there you are."

"Ugh, there it is again," he said with distaste. "It's coming in and out."

"Interesting. Like you're rejecting it, trying to get away from it, and so your senses respond ... Smell this one." She handed him another vial and he took a nervous whiff.

"I don't ... peppermint?"

"Interesting ..."

"Why?"

"Because that's water from a five-gallon bucket that I put a drop of peppermint oil into."

"Are you serious?"

"Quite serious."

"Really, though, what was that first one?"

"A perfume my sister had commissioned. No idea what they put into it, but she fired them and never wore the stuff. It was supposed to make a statement. I kept it in case I needed to kill someone and hide my trail from dogs."

He smirked; she didn't.

"I can see why Whitman keeps you around. You're as odd as he is."

She chuckled. "Eat a candy."

"What's in the bag?"

"Candy."

"And?"

"You tell me."

"Is anything lethal?"

"If it is, I probably brought the antidote."

"... I can't tell if you're lying."

"Oh?"

"I can still smell that perfume."

"It does persist, doesn't it?" She waved a hand around ineffectively. "Can you smell the peppermint oil?"

He considered and took a deep inhale. Immediately, his nose was, again, assaulted. A moment before, it hadn't been much bothered, but now he could smell the horrible perfume very well, and the peppermint water faintly in the background.

"Ugh, yes." He pinched his nose, grimacing. "We should change rooms. And you should destroy that stuff."

She looked around thoughtfully. "You know, we probably should go outside."

"It's freezing!"

"We'll build a fire. It'll be fun." She unfolded to a standing position again and started to pack her things in a box from behind the desk.

Donovan climbed to his feet, joints snapping and popping in the attempt. "Now?"

"Are you doing anything else?"

He threw his hands up with exasperation again, having no answer.

"You'll probably want shoes."

*   *   *

Hours later, Donovan sat shivering, cocooned in a blanket in Annette's room with a warm cup of tea in his hands, the steam curling up to heat his face. Annette was similarly posed on a couch opposite his cushioned chair with her legs curled up beneath her.

Her room was nicer than his, nicer than Whitman's and about on par with Hector's. This front room was decorated in neat reds and whites; an expensive rug covered the floor, and delicate shelves lined the walls, showing figurines and bits of stone or coins, the occasional book and bottle of wine that she seemed particularly fond of. He felt out of place on her tasteful red couch-chair. A fancy bow and quiver of quality, red-fletched arrows sat in the corner by the door.

"I think we made excellent progress," she said again, mostly to herself.

Her tea had some kind of liquor added, and it gave off a delicious vanilla scent. Donovan tried to concentrate, to increase that sense, but his magic, if that's what it was, didn't cooperate.

He said, "I do have a headache, but it isn't the kind I'm used to. There's nausea, too, and a feeling like I have cotton in my sinuses. But compared to Seeking, I could get used to these aftereffects."

"So you agree that it's magic?"

He gave an exasperated sigh. "I don't know what else it could be. How can someone control their senses as I did? But I'm no magus."

"True," she said thoughtfully.

They'd spent hours outside, probing his limits. The fire hadn't defended them against much of the biting cold, but once they realized the trick of activating his increases and decreases, neither had wanted to return inside.

Every time he was overwhelmed by a sensation, he could withdraw from it, lower his senses to numbness. It didn't stop the sensation, and he could still suffer the effects when his sense came back, such as the smell or taste lingering. If he wanted to increase his senses, he couldn't be particular, so a pleasant smell across the room meant that he'd pick up any other smell in the area as well. Without a strong stimulus, he struggled to control it, and it was much easier to withdraw than increase.

"I'll keep practicing," he assured her. "I want to know if I can do this on my own terms."

"I wonder if there's any reference to this kind of magic in the library. Perhaps forgotten, or overlooked?"

"I can ask Whitman. He'd likely know."

"True. His memory approaches inhuman, and he keeps it honed. By which I mean, of course, that he loves to show off." She winked.

Donovan sipped his tea and tried to think of another topic of conversation. He was comfortable and didn't want to go yet.

"How long are you staying at the Order?" he asked. The room looked lived-in, and not a temporary abode.

"Another few months, likely. Until I get permission to abandon my attempts here."

"You don't think you're helping?"

"Oh, they can certainly arch better than they could before I arrived, but let me assure you, little of it is from my aid. I haven't the patience for true teaching, as I've said. Truthfully, I'm more a status piece. 'Our troops trained with Annette Kraemer. Beware.' That sort of thing."

"Are you so well known? In the military?" He hadn't heard of her, but he didn't often engage with those who might know her.

"In some places, perhaps." She took a demure sip. "I've certain awards that are hard to come by. Too, I've proven that while competition shooting and battle shooting are different, I have the skill to impress in both."

"How long have you been arching?"

"Since childhood. It was one of the few militaristic hobbies my father allowed me to pursue. Lest I risk damaging my pretty face," she explained, teasing, running a finger down her strong jawline.

He smiled. "I think my father would have preferred I join the military. I was never interested and, after coming back educated from the Order as a boy, I was certain then I didn't want to go. He served and came home to farm, so I couldn't imagine there was much to it I would like."

Annette waved an arm in a wide arc, "Travel, see the kingdom, be ordered about in everything you do ..."

She discarded her blanket, set her teacup on the low table between their seats, and went into the next room. A moment later, with the teapot in hand, she refreshed her own cup, and then his.

"Drink up, or you won't get big and strong," she mocked.

This was a new flavor, a hint of lemon, which he found bitter for the first few sips after the sweeter flavor from before. But it was good. He closed his eyes for a moment, and let the steam caress his cheeks. Annette returned a moment later, sans teapot again, and reclaimed her spot on the couch, bundling up and sipping.

Someone knocked a moment later.

"Oh, damn," she pouted.

"I'll take it," Donovan said, unfolding his covering and setting down his tea.

He padded to the door, barefoot while his shoes and socks dried. He expected a page, perhaps with a message to deliver. Instead, he found Whitman.

"Whit! What are you doing here?"

The bard looked up from the portfolio of documents he was scanning. His eyebrows rose. "Don! I didn't expect you two to still be meeting. How many hours has it been?"

Donovan gestured into the room, where Annette called, "Oh, come out of the hall, my lame little lamb."

Whitman grinned toothily and entered, looking for Donovan to answer his question.

"We were—"

"Darling, tell us what you know about magical enhancement of the senses," Annette interrupted. "Surely you have some myth or legend in that shaggy head of yours. Also, sit there so I can give you a trim. Honestly."

She rose from the couch and disappeared into another back room, leaving her blanket and half-finished tea abandoned like a rich woman's hobby. Whitman blinked, then shrugged and closed his portfolio. He crutched into the room and Donovan saw his knee was now in a straight brace, instead of the cast, but Whitman could move his ankle now. The brace was thin enough that his trousers could cover it if he wanted.

Donovan stepped aside as the larger man made his way to the seat Annette had indicated. Whitman set the portfolio on the low table, drained Annette's abandoned tea, and said, "Stories regarding enhancement of the senses, huh?" He frowned in thought. "Is this to do with your ... ailment?"

Donovan nodded. "She's been running me through experiments all afternoon."

"I see. The purpose of your meeting. Progress?"

"Masses," Annette replied as she swept into the room, tools in hand. "I've changed my mind, sit there."

She pulled a stool from the corner and patted the cushion encouragingly. It was lower than the couch and took Whitman a moment to perch. He looked comical with his towering frame seated on the tiny stool. Annette was still only a head taller.

"Shirt off."

Whitman unbuttoned his shirt and set it aside with his ever-present satchel. Annette draped a towel about his shoulders, clipped it at the back, and combed water through his curls until they were soaked. She started trimming while she filled him in on the day's activities. He listened with clear interest and asked the occasional clarifying question.

"There are certainly myths and legends and histories and theories discussing the truths and likelihood of abilities akin to those you describe," Whitman mused. "Plenty of magi claimed to have incredible precision with hearing, sight, smell. However, much of that was either considered exaggeration, or some kind of Mentalist ability that allowed them to identify the presence of people or animals nearby, giving people the sense, ah-ha ha, that they had improved their senses truly. But that is not what you have determined, Don, is it?"

Donovan shook his head.

"No, you are experiencing actual improvement of the sense itself ... fascinating ..." Whitman's presence started to fade from his eyes as he abandoned the conversation in favor of researching through his mind.

Annette snapped her scissors near his ear and he twitched back to them. "Apologies. Donovan, how much experimenting have the two of you done with your sense of touch?" He waggled his eyebrows.

Donovan blushed. "None."

"I suggested he strip down and tell his body not to feel the cold, but he refused," Annette added, winking.

"Probably for the best," Whitman said. "I imagine you might cease to feel the sensation of cold, but would still suffer its effects. I wondered for the purposes of injury." He paused and they all considered the implications.

"That'd be dangerous," Donovan said at last. "If I'd broken my arm and ceased to feel the pain of it, I wouldn't know how much worse I could make it with anything I did. I could ... gods all, I could destroy myself and never know ..."

"Best to shy away from that, I think," Annette said lightly.

"What measure of control do you have?" Whitman asked.

"Currently? None. We found a way to stimulate it into action. Loud noises that I shy away from or smells or bright lights. After that, it's easier to bring myself back to where I originated, or a bit more."

"I imagine it is akin to a new set of muscles. Keep practicing, and I have little doubt you will find the knack of it."

"That was our intention," Annette said, pushing his head down to attack the back of it with her scissors and comb.

Donovan had to ask, "When did you learn to cut hair?"

"Just the other day," she answered. "I needed a trim and chatted with the ladies and gentlemen in the profession. They gave me suggestions and examples, let me try a couple of choice snips, and I decided it was a skill worth adding to my hoard." She grinned toothily.

"As long as Oslan doesn't disagree with your very recent skill acquisition ..." Whitman said from the level of his chest.

Annette tossed her own hair. "Oslan adores me. And he's a forgiving soul."

"Don, have you considered when you will go to Elliott with your newly discovered magic?" Whitman asked.

"I hadn't, actually."

"He will need to know. This will affect a number of things, including abilities the enemy might possess." He glanced upward for a moment before Annette pushed his head back down. "Why are you pouting?"

Donovan crossed his arms and leaned back in his seat. "It just doesn't make sense: how can I have two magics? It breaks the rules."

"Perhaps not," the bard mused. "Seeking is the ability to see outside of yourself. It has always been a mystery why that particular magic is so much more debilitating than others. Perhaps the daily use of Seeking is not what we understand Seeking to be. Instead of leaving your body to perceive the life around you, you would be able to alter and adjust your senses to be of use more directly. From within, as it were."

Donovan considered. "If I dampened my senses before Seeking ... old Seeking, original — you understand. If I dampened my senses

217

before, I wouldn't have to worry about damaging myself by being away for too long ..."

"There's an idea," Annette said, eyes wide. "I wouldn't mind having a few minutes more for poking about and getting closer looks."

"You say minutes; I was thinking hours. How long could a person stay in trance?" Donovan wondered. "You could follow someone for miles, see where they stopped for the night ..."

"There, done," Annette said. She put down her tools and carefully pulled the towel from Whitman's neck. The floor and rug were covered with sandy-blond hair, but Annette didn't seem to mind as she returned to her place on the couch and under her blanket.

Whitman ran a hand through his newly sheared locks and asked, "I get no mirror?"

"Certainly not."

The bard rolled his eyes and asked Donovan, "Am I presentable?"

Donovan nodded. "Looks good. Much less shaggy."

"Excellent!" He donned his shirt once more and took up his satchel. "To continue, Donovan, I will see what I can do to locate a starting place for your research. However, consider speaking with Elliott soon, at the least to give him an idea of the possibilities."

"Perhaps when Donovan has control enough for a demonstration," Annette suggested. "And if this is a Seeker ability as we believe, I will start attempts of my own, as I do not appear as ... unlocked?"

"I don't recommend my method," Donovan said darkly.

*   *   *

The library of the Order was daunting.

Polished wood and stone, priceless carvings in the walls, statues, creations in glass, plush carpeting, and a penetrating silence were all coordinated to keep Donovan from ever fully relaxing in the enormous room. Lightning lined the ceiling to keep the place bright. No open flames were allowed, except in the hands of the librarians, who had special lamps with sand around the meticulously measured oil. The lamps would burn for only twenty minutes, and, if they overturned, the sand should extinguish the flame.

Donovan had used the library as a student many times, and visited occasionally as an adult, but had never found cause for the extended stay of the scholars. His research and studies had all concluded within days, or a few weeks at most, and he had never grown accustomed to the intimidatingly rich space.

Whitman, however, was right at home. He chatted with the librarians in a complicated sign language that had them all giggling silently, and had a study room reserved in the back hallway. Donovan had been invited to share the space, but wondered how long it would last. The table was only so large, and Whitman tended to spread as he referenced and cross-referenced through a dozen texts at once.

Donovan had only three books and a journal for notes. He was forced to dredge up memories on how to properly conduct his research but remembered enjoying the practice once upon a time. He was enjoying it again as he fell back into the practice.

One of his texts was a children's book; the other two were historical accounts of various magi written by people who had clearly heard of excitement and decided they weren't in favor. How someone could make battles or daring rescues so dull and boring was beyond his understanding. Still, it was interesting, even as he skimmed, pausing at likely looking paragraphs. With his most recent experience, which he still strove to accept, now he struggled to identify what might be exaggeration and might be lost magic.

Could a person sway an entire battlefield with Empathy? How far away was this person, to spy with Seeking? Did this magus really have the power to Heal themselves, without pushing the injury out into someone, or something, else? Could an Elementalist *breathe* water?

"When are you and Annette meeting to practice your magic next?" Whitman asked suddenly.

Donovan looked up from a passage about a mountain battle and blinked. "Um, tomorrow morning."

"It's nearly past dinner now."

He looked at the sand in the hourglass. "Damn. That passed quickly."

"I find the library often exhibits a time-altering field," Whitman said lightly, turning a page. He hadn't moved from his chair, still reading through a massive tome and speaking at the same time. "Do you translate *scheum* to mean *of* sky or *from* sky or *mountainous peaks*? If I were writing for a comedy, I know which I would choose ..."

"Generally I don't translate that at all," Donovan said, rising.

"Naturally."

"No luck, then?"

"I've only been looking for several weeks, Donovan, you cannot be hasty." Whitman looked up and blinked owlishly. "I have made considerable headway, but have yet to pin my prey."

"What are you *pinning* for, again?"

Whitman rolled his eyes. "A madman. Go, eat, go to bed, go learn your magic."

Donovan began to pick up his books, but Whitman stopped him. "This room is reserved for my research. I gift it to you, as well. Leave the books; the librarians will make sure no one disturbs anything."

"That's kind of them."

"Good night, Don."

Donovan passed a few late-night visitors on his way out, and wondered what they might be researching. Images of battlefields filled his mind. He remembered his father's stories and compared them to his own experiences with distaste. His father had been able to recall the bad food, poor equipment, terrible leaders, but had somehow left out the smell of death, the bowel-shaking terror. Granted, he was older now than his father had been then, and his father had been more thoroughly trained, but not against the odds Donovan had so far faced. Even in past Retrievals, they usually managed to outrun their foes, or had faced one or two that Lucas, or a previous partner, had been able to dispatch while Donovan hurried their charge to safety. He had now somehow fallen into a story of his own, and this one had more monsters.

Deciding against dinner, he turned instead toward his room. As he approached, he realized that more doors in his hall were open, and lights poured into the corridor. Retrievers had returned. He made a beeline to the open door across from his own and knocked on the frame.

Brett Schrick turned and gave a tired grin. "Heard you were already back."

"Been weeks," Donovan agreed with a grin. "How are you?"

Brett was about Donovan's height with brown skin, brown hair, and brown eyes. He was entirely nondescript, and often expressed his thankfulness for it. The only things that made him stand out were the missing tip of his left ear and first knuckle of his left ring finger, but he kept his hair long to hide the ear, and hardly anyone noticed the finger. His clothes were still dirty from the road, and Donovan spied a packed bag at his footboard.

"Just arrived?"

"I got in hours ago, but had to be sent through the Mentalists to make sure I'm not a Hunter spy. I'd be insulted with the accusation if I hadn't heard what happened a couple weeks back."

"It got hairy."

"Heard you about died watching the magus boy you brought back."

"I suppose."

"Hero."

Donovan rolled his eyes. "Get your mark?"

"And two extras," Brett replied, stretching his back with a creaking groan. "We went for a boy and came back with two girls as well. They started showing during our trip out."

"Good grief."

"Aye. Had to take in extra supplies for them while we was there, but the town was friendly, mostly, and we had chits enough. Worried about our group size, but one of the girls was good in the woods and kept our trail covered."

"That's a relief."

"Busier out there in the last month. I swear we heard about Hunters on every road. I kept us cross-country just in case. We should have been back days ago."

"Vale said she sent soldiers with anyone going out, and put everyone in bigger groups since I came back."

"Trying to scare them off, I suppose. We left before she did that; had no soldiers."

Donovan turned at a hand on his shoulder.

"'lo, Don. How's the day?" Gina Simonsen asked cheerfully. She, too, was still in her road clothes, but seemed more vibrant than Brett.

"Gina, how are you?" They embraced warmly. "Heard you had a herd to bring in."

"Three! Most I've ever found was two, honest. I expect we're not the first back, neither."

"I'm not sure; I've been away all day."

"Heard about Lucas," she said, sympathy clear in her expression. She squeezed his hand.

"Yeah." The grief was there, but not quite as overwhelming as before. This time.

"He was a good man," Brett agreed. "I'll miss him something fierce."

"You go see his ma?" Gina asked.

"A few times now," Donovan nodded.

"That's good. Brett, do you have my ration bag? I was doing my checklist and came up short."

"Might do. I haven't started yet."

"When you look ..."

"Right."

Gina leaned against the other side of the doorway and scratched at the stub of her other arm. She'd lost it halfway up the forearm two years ago, and complained that it was always itchy now.

"Who else is back?" Donovan asked, leaning to see down the hall.

"A new woman in Lucas's room. You met her yet?" Gina asked.

Donovan shook his head, feeling a little ashamed. "I've been busy."

"Looks like Shannon and Eljando are in, and ... is that Dell?"

"Gods all, he's been out three months, I swear," Brett groaned.

"*Noble* families take *persuading*," Gina mocked in an exaggeration of Dell's arrogant tone. "One cannot merely *swoop in* and *abscond* with their precious offspring. *Especially* when rival teachers and instructors *bar the way* to the *egress*."

Donovan shook his head with amusement and Brett barked out a laugh.

"Hey SHANNON!" Gina called. A long-necked woman stuck her mane of red hair out of the doorway of her room.

"What?"

"Wondering if you were back."

Shannon blinked owlishly large eyes. "I'm back."

"Run into any trouble?" Donovan asked before she disappeared.

"'Jano is with the Healers. Hunters did something to his leg when we were running to escape an ambush."

Brett swore violently, creatively.

"Is he going to be all right?" Gina asked with concern. She crossed toward Shannon's room.

Shannon thought for a moment. "They said he would probably live. They told me to come back to my room to wait."

Gina joined her and the two women disappeared inside. Shannon wasn't one for crying, but breaks in routine could fluster her. Eljando had been her partner for seven years and they performed well together.

"Poor thing," Brett said gruffly. "'Jando'll be fine, you'll see. Those Healers will get him set to right in no time."

Donovan nodded, but thought about Whitman's limp.

Dell came to join them in Brett's doorway and Brett made a small noise of irritation, but he was polite enough not to do more than that.

They all shook hands warmly. Donovan knew where everyone's irritation with Dell came from, but he had never had any specific issue with the man. Then again, they'd only spoken a handful of times, and never for long.

Dell leaned against the doorway that Gina had previously occupied. "Do you know if anyone else was injured?" he asked.

Brett and Donovan shook their heads.

"Sad business ... Eljando was a fine Retriever."

"Still is," Brett said pointedly.

"How's your charge, Dell?" Donovan asked quickly.

"Excellent! Parents and grandparents took some convincing. They were quite set to have him educated with tutors at home, but I pressed the issue of socializing with one's, ah, peers in magic, and the well-known resources our library contains. Eventually, they were won over." He smiled charmingly.

"Whereabouts was this?" Brett asked innocently.

"The Accardi Estate."

"That's, what, a week's travel by horse?"

"A week and a half in good weather and without having to keep off the road for all the damned blood mages and murderers," Dell agreed.

Brett shook his head. "What's his magic? Your boy?"

"Healer."

"I had a Displacer and two Empaths," Brett said. "Donovan got the magus."

"I heard! Congratulations!"

Donovan felt his face tighten. "It was a Retrieval like any other. We didn't know for certain he was a magus when we went anyway."

"Ah, your modesty fools no one, man!"

Dell was grinning. Donovan wasn't.

"Excuse me." Donovan walked toward Shannon's room and, as he passed, Lucas's door opened. A young woman stepped out shyly.

"I heard people talking, and thought I should say hello," she told him tentatively.

His mood softened in the face of her uncomfortable demeanor. "Welcome to our ranks. I'm Donovan."

They shook hands. "Olive." She glanced at Dell and Brett across the hall, and down toward Shannon's open door. "This isn't everyone, right?"

"No, no, no," Donovan assured her. "Everyone else is still in the field. Sometimes we align like this, but usually everyone comes and goes at any moment. It will probably get crowded in the next few days with the Order's recall going out, and there's a whole second hall of rooms. I imagine Vale has a plan to get schedules reorganized and distributed before too long. Do you have a partner assigned yet?"

She shook her head, and then corrected herself, "Well, yes, but I haven't met her yet. Still in the field, like you said." She smiled, her confidence growing as they spoke.

"Come meet Shannon and Gina," Donovan offered kindly.

She appeared to be a couple of years younger than Lucas; they might have shared some classes. He glanced through her open door to see what changes she'd made to the room. *Her room now,* he corrected himself firmly.

The two women were welcoming, despite the somber topic of their conversation. Gina could never stay sad for long, and Shannon wasn't one for strong emotions.

"Who'd Vale assign you to?" Gina asked.

"A woman named Silvana?"

"Oh, Silvy's great, you'll get along with her just fine!"

Gina patted Olive's shoulder warmly, and then sent a worried look in Donovan's direction. He agreed. The last that he'd heard, Silvana was assigned to Gregory, and their partnership was strong. He hoped that nothing had happened to Greg, and then realized the likelihood of that was extraordinarily low. Poor Gregory. Suddenly the empty corridor, which had once felt like progress, like Retrievers in action, was haunting. How many of their number would never return, like Lucas? Or, like Eljando, might return broken beyond repair?

Brett and Dell joined the group, Dell taking the desk stool while Shannon and Gina and Olive shared the bed. Donovan sat on a storage trunk, and Brett stretched his legs out on the floor and put his back to the closet wall. They exchanged news, swapped stories, shared fears of upcoming changes, and changes already in motion. Donovan felt easy in the presence of his fellows. He didn't consider any of them close friends, but they had an easy acquaintance that made conversation, at least for a while, simple.

"Someone else is coming," Gina said excitedly and trotted to the open door.

Olive looked surprised, but no one else did.

Donovan checked the hour mark on the candle and winced. It was late.

"Anthony, Faren, Meredith, and Kileen!" Gina said from the doorway. "Oh, and ... yeah, Silvana." She winced, but didn't leave the doorway, waiting eagerly for the group to show.

"Is she a Mentalist?" Olive asked the room.

"Empath," Brett answered. "Best I've seen, best on record, right?" He looked around and no one disagreed. "She said she gets something like a flavor for your emotions and can pick out who you are before you round the corner, clear as any Mentalist. But it's hard to turn off, too."

Gina waved her stump excitedly, welcoming unseen Retrievers toward their room. Shannon was clearly calculating the available space left in her quarters.

"I might go to bed," Donovan assured her. "It's late."

"Oh, keep your seat, granther," Brett urged. "The morning's going nowhere and you've naught to do to bring it."

"Looks like we're missing the party," a new voice said.

Donovan turned toward the doorway to see Anthony grinning down at them. He was missing a tooth, a molar just behind his canine, and sported a severe black eye and split eyebrow. He didn't seem bothered, though; much like Gina, his mood was hard to dampen.

Behind him, his partner Meredith looked grim. Perfectly pleasant company, but she was always more serious than you would expect of someone partnered with Anthony. She did have a streak of insanity about once a year, and started prank wars that would go on for months through the hallways, pushing adults to act far worse than the children they gathered. No one was safe. Vale had threatened her with violence and death more than once, but she could not be deterred.

Donovan saw Silvana walk toward her room with a casual wave. She looked exhausted, and Donovan didn't blame her.

Anthony and Meredith left their travel packs in the hallway and joined Brett against the wall. Meredith leaned her head on Brett's shoulder companionably and closed her eyes.

"Kileen and Faren are behind us," Anthony said. "They look rough."

"Speaking of ... your charge didn't want to leave home?" Brett asked him with a gesture toward his black eye.

Anthony grinned, showing that gap in his teeth again. "Nah, we got mixed up in a family squabble. Kid wanted to leave with big brother, but wasn't showing magic yet. You know me — if they want to come, I'll take them. Dad and uncle weren't having it, and ours got riled up. Mare had to calm down the kiddie and I put the adults in their place. Had to let them think they could take me, put them off their guard, you know. Still mad I couldn't find the tooth, though. Someone's going to step on it some night. Gross."

Brett and Dell laughed. Donovan grinned and shook his head at the youthful antics. He didn't often feel his age, but Anthony was the best fighter of their group, and somehow managed to get into more fights than the rest of them combined. Meredith had suggested more than once that his attitude combined with his face simply invite punching.

"Looks like they're inviting anyone, Fare'. We don't want to get mixed up in this crowd."

"Hey, Kileen," Anthony waved. "Middle of the floor's still free."

"Here, have the chest," Donovan said, rising.

Kileen pointed severely. "Sit. Stay. I don't take up much space, and you're not running away to solitude just yet." Donovan sat and put his hands up in surrender. A petite, birdlike woman with thin bones, Kileen had an elegance envied by many. She was quick, too, and not afraid to be heard.

Faren was a moment behind her. Gina had her arm around his waist, tutting in sympathy. His head was wrapped in a bandage that covered one eye. A spot of blood leaked through on the side of his head, too, over his ear.

He dropped his pack with a loud sigh of relief and said, "Where's Lucas?"

Donovan's stomach rolled over in sympathy and loss. "He's dead, Faren."

Faren swore violently enough that even Brett made a noise and Dell winced delicately.

"I'm *so* sorry, Don. What happened?"

Gina directed Faren to her vacated spot on the bed and helped him get comfortable while Donovan told the story. Kileen squeezed his hand sympathetically and Anthony kicked his boot in his way of showing respect.

"I'll miss him," Shannon said.

"Hang on," Kileen said, looking around. "'Jando's missing — he — oh, no ..."

"Healers have him," Brett said quickly. "Shannon said it was his leg."

The redhead nodded in agreement.

"What happened to your face?" Brett asked Faren, tapping his own for indication.

Faren gingerly touched the side of his head, near the spot of blood. "Stupid mistake. Sword came through the ear and I turned *toward* the damn thing. Lost the eye." He grimaced and Donovan saw him swallow hard to keep the emotions in check.

"Did you go to the surgeons already?" Donovan asked.

"Kileen stitched it, and I've never seen a better job done than one of hers. I'll go tomorrow; I'm too exhausted tonight."

"Hunters?" Anthony asked.

"Whole pack of them. If Kileen hadn't been there, I'd be dead four times over. Never seen her that mad."

The birdlike woman shrugged. "You know I hate stitching friends, and elements are plentiful when you know the magic of it."

"Have we ever come back this ragged?" Gina asked sadly, standing by the bed.

No one answered.

"Hey, who're you?" Anthony said suddenly, spotting Olive.

"Um, Olive," the woman answered.

"New, I guess?"

"Yes."

"Sorry you had to see us in this mess," Anthony said sincerely. "It's not usually like this."

"She's partnering Silvana," Shannon said.

"Oh. Yeah, I heard about Greg."

"I didn't," Donovan put in.

"They were ambushed on the road," Kileen explained. "Lost their charge, too. Silvy got a few of them, but had to run in the end. You know she hates running."

"Everyone else's charges make it?" Donovan asked. His heart broke for the dead child.

Everyone in the room nodded tiredly.

"Gods all, this is a mess," Donovan said. He leaned his head against the wall. He knew it was irrational, but some part of his mind blamed himself for bringing all the Hunters out in force.

"When will Vale send us back out?" Shannon asked.

"Not soon," Faren answered with certainty. "Our town got word from an outpost messenger not to send request letters; too much chance of interception. They're ordering soldiers to send Retrieval parties every couple weeks and, when we *do* go out, we'll have *escorts*."

"Harder to hide that way," Dell mused.

"But less like to be attacked," Brett countered.

"Unless they're not looking to survive, and just make as much damage as they can," Anthony pointed out.

"We'll have to wait for Vale's official say on it all. I don't imagine Elliott himself will be coming to tell us anything anytime soon," Brett said.

"I can't imagine he'll be doing anything outside of that office for the next few months. Clearing house was only the beginning of the trouble," Dell said seriously.

"Yeah, I heard about that — did they get everyone?" Kileen asked with concern.

"Hopefully," Donovan answered. "No real way to know for sure."

"Scary it went so deep. We passed prisoners on the road heading for Justice about a day out. Wouldn't want to be on that job." She made a face.

They fell into a mournful, contemplative silence until Shannon said, "I'm tired."

"We're all tired," Meredith agreed from Brett's shoulder. She hadn't yet opened her eyes, but he had a comfortable arm tight around her.

"Am I allowed to suggest we get some sleep before the sun completes its journey to morning?" Donovan asked, standing. "Or will you all gripe at me again?"

Kileen poked him in the ribs and he winced away with a playful whimper. Everyone else made their slow way to standing, grumbling and moaning, collecting baggage and disappearing into various rooms.

Donovan's own space felt large after packing into Shannon's quarters, and he suddenly wished he had company again. *Never satisfied.* Undressed, the lights off, he tried to get comfortable, but Dell's words echoed through his mind again and again.

What would the Hunters do next?

11

DONOVAN SPENT THE ENTIRE NEXT DAY in the Seeker training room with Annette, building a mild headache as he strove to control his newfound magical abilities. More than ever, he felt his age as he tried and failed to hear her whispering from across the room, read tiny script, smell a watered-down perfume, identify an herb she'd added to his water, and more. Annette didn't seem put off in the least when he failed every test, claiming that failure was key to good training. Her claimed impatience didn't show itself as she switched from trial to trial. When he was exhausted, they traded, and he did the same for her. She worked to engage her own magical abilities and despite the early failures, he was hopeful. He wanted desperately for her to succeed — if nothing else, it would show that these new abilities were a true part of Seeking, and not some extraordinary onset of late-developed new magic.

When they were both exhausted and went their separate ways, Donovan forced himself to the library with Whitman again. He read through texts and histories and tall tales, making copious notes about abilities and talents mages had claimed over the centuries.

Whitman muttered to himself, but not always in an identifiable dialect. His notes were in code and he often wrote with numbers. Some of the texts he was referencing were written in languages Donovan didn't know. Occasionally, Whitman's excitement got the better of him and he would flip through his books in a flurry of pages before settling quietly to visit some corner of his memory. He regularly disappeared into some kind of scholar's trance.

The evening after practice and research, Donovan eagerly assisted his peers with the various requirements Retrievers had: repairing equipment, returning tools, and debating schedules for their charges with Hector. Most of them had slept through their first day back, which did not surprise him in the least. Retrieval took plenty of energy, and everyone was beyond exhausted. Their charges were taken in and given tours by older students. It was a change from the normal, but these days, that was, itself, normal.

Donovan visited Silvana to offer his condolences. She didn't cry, just thanked him with a detached numbness he recognized from his own losses. He'd been tempted to sink into the numbness many times since Lucas's death. Silvy ate a little while he urged her, and he managed most of her tasks without prompting. Gina took over caring for Silvy's emotional comfort and Donovan left them alone. Gina was far better suited to the task.

Another very full day gone, Donovan collapsed into bed, ready for the excitement to end.

Several days passed with similar routine and he grew much closer to the other Retrievers. They bonded with the unprecedented amount of time spent together, sharing meals in the evenings, begging news from their returning fellows. With time to debate information and the future, the rest and lack of duties allowed anger to build as years of fatigue could finally fade.

Donovan hadn't yet shared with anyone the experiments he was running with Annette. He wanted to be sure she could do what he could before he opened that bag of angry cats — it would change so much, and so quickly. What if he didn't have the answers everyone would surely want? Whitman had again urged him to go to Elliott, but Donovan still didn't feel like there was enough to say. He had at least gained some measure of control over his hearing — which he practiced enough to make himself dizzy.

Another dozen Retrievers returned before the week ended. Vale gathered them all in the hallway to bark out what she considered sufficient information and then left them alone again. Faren had been correct: they were to stay, no Retrievals, while groups of soldiers did their jobs. Two more of their number were dead, three maimed, and none of the rest without injury, however small. Gina was dancing without pause throughout their number to use her Empathy and keep spirits from falling too low. Donovan sometimes heard Brett's gentle comforts above her sobs in the evenings.

Most Retrievers decided to engage in extra training for weapons, grappling, and magic, and they were not turned away. The older students were surprised to have adults in their classes, but the novelty quickly wore off. A few other Retrievers took shifts with the soldiers when they were allowed — either escorting prisoners to the palace, or manning the wall — wondering if today would be the day that the Hunters attacked in force.

*   *   *

The loud, clanging din of the emergency bells sounded throughout the Order. Donovan was startled awake and rolled out of his bed and under it in a matter of seconds. His mind buzzed and spun in an effort to understand what was happening. When one bell started, all of the others were immediately engaged, used in case of fire or plague or anything that needed immediate attention from everyone inside and around the Order's buildings, so the sound only grew as he adjusted.

Finally comprehending the situation, if not the specifics, Donovan rolled back out from under the bed, groaning as his joints protested the sudden mistreatment. He dressed quickly and indiscriminately and jogged into the hall to join the bustling bunch of Retrievers and others, some less dressed than he, but all with matching expressions of worry and concern.

"Do we know anything?" Milek asked, his deep voice easily heard through the continuous high-pitched clanging.

Vera shook her head. "They'll make announcements soon; we jes' need to get to a central place fer' the news. No use frettin'."

The stairs were cramped and crowded; the press of bodies had Donovan wishing he'd taken the time to lace his boots. The air was palpable with fear. What if it was the Hunters, come at last with their army?

When the crowd reached the ground floor and gained a bit more room, the noise grew as people caught sight of friends and family all asking the same questions. No one could smell fire, and the bells had finally stopped. Plague hadn't been a concern in the Order in seventy years, and, even then, it hadn't lasted long. Donovan scanned the crowd for Ruben and Whitman. *I hope Ruben is keeping calm, first alarms and all.*

The Retrievers and off-duty soldiers gathered and bunched as they came downstairs, claiming a spot in a corner and growing outward, repeating their guesses and grumbles. Donovan saw Annette across the wide room and turned toward her direction, leaving his fellows behind. She spotted him coming, and changed her course to intersect his. The crowd was only growing as more people descended the stairs, eager for information, and he grew frustrated with the lack of organization.

When Donovan managed to reach Annette, he asked, "Any ideas?"

"Some, and none of them pleasant."

"Have you seen Whitman?"

"Heading for Elliott's office."

"Is that good or bad?"

"It depends on whether or not the Head of the Order needs a bard at a time like this." Her penetrating look told Donovan in no uncertain terms that she knew exactly what Whitman's true occupation was, and what that might mean.

"This kind of emergency, though ..."

"Either war, or possibly something slightly less worse with a greenstick recruit on the bells. We won't know for another little while. Shall we join your friends?"

She took his hand and they wove their way back through the ever-expanding crowd. Donovan could never fully comprehend the number of people housed in the Order. Seeing so many together at once threatened to overwhelm. Groups were forming, butting into one another, merging, sharing rumors. Some were laughing; others were sobbing. Most were merely talking, wondering, debating, speculating. Donovan's bunch of Retrievers had split into smaller conversations, most debating the likelihood of an attack, and what their roles would be.

"— attack, they wouldn't have pulled us all down together, would they?"

"Why not? They'd have to rouse the army, and there's quite a few on reserves who would need to get to work."

"The clerks will know; they'll have to draw up schedules."

"I hope no one's hurt ..."

"I've always hated crowds," Annette told Donovan, eyes darting. "You never know how they'll turn, but they always do."

"Some people thrive in crowds."

"Certainly, but they tend to be half-mad, and in love with chaos. Public orators hate and love them — say the right thing and the crowd will make you fly. Say the wrong thing ..." She gave Donovan a look.

Just then, Donovan spotted a young boy in a hastily donned messenger's tunic climbing nimbly along the outside of the staircase banister. He managed to get about halfway up before he began to shout for attention.

"The emergency has been recalled!" he piped, projecting impressively across the room. "There is no fire, no plague, no prisoner escape. You are all urged back to your rooms. Classes and activities will continue as normal."

"Why was the bell rung, then?" one man angrily demanded.

Dozens more grumbled in agreement.

The boy waited for the noise to die back down before hollering back, "I gave the official word, mate, or do you want me to hang about this banister the rest of the night?"

There were curses and chuckles at that, and the boy made his way back down the banister. People swarmed him for more information, but he was too quick and managed to go about his business without being caught.

Donovan looked at Annette. "Shall I escort you to your rooms, m'lady?"

"Only if you plan to stay until breakfast."

Donovan gaped at her, his trickster's grin replaced with boyish embarrassment.

Annette squeezed his arm and laughed, not unkindly. "Oh, Donovan, you *are* an easy mark. Go back to bed and I'll see you in a few hours."

Donovan blushed and made a hasty goodbye.

The crowd that had hurriedly rushed downstairs was much slower to return. By the time he made it to his rooms, Donovan was impatient and irritated and tired, and his jaw cracked every time he yawned.

When he opened his door, he found a note waiting on his floor. He frowned and stooped to claim it. The parchment was sealed, but bore no mark; the wax was smeared, not given enough time to dry. He broke the seal and read:

Come to my rooms at once
– W

*   *   *

As Donovan approached Whitman's door, Oslan stuck his head into the hall. His hair stuck up at all angles and he wore only a pair of cotton breeches, his ribs showing down each side of his torso. A large purple-red birthmark colored quite a large portion of his left side.

He waved Donovan over and closed the door behind him. "Whitman hasn't yet returned. I don't know how long he'll be, but you're welcome to nap on the couch if you'd like."

"Thank you, I'll be all right. Do we know what's happened?"

Oslan shook his head and put out his hands. "I'm as blind as you, unfortunately. Half of the guards on watch are being held in offices on the Medical Ward."

"Are they injured?" Donovan asked, flabbergasted.

"Not as I'm aware — I can only assume they saw something and are facing questions. I imagine they'll be held until Elliott is satisfied."

"Why the Medical Ward?"

Again, Oslan shook his head. "I'm so sorry. I wasn't called to the meeting; I can only extrapolate from the limited information, just like everyone else."

Oslan ran a hand through his wild hair, encouraging it to lay down after he mussed it, but was not successful. He crossed his arms, and swayed from one foot to the other.

Donovan crossed the room to Whitman's couch and sat. He pushed his face into his hands and let out a mighty sigh. A headache was forming behind his left eye.

Oslan sat beside him.

After a few minutes of silence, the young scribe suggested, "Cards?"

*   *   *

"I'm not cheating, you're just bad at cards."

"The two are not mutually exclusive!"

The door opened roughly and a very exhausted Whitman entered. He leaned heavily on his crutch and held several pages of indecipherable scribble in his other hand. Two hours had passed since Donovan and Oslan had started their game, and dawn was not far away. The bard eyed their cards and let out a snort of exhausted amusement before he collapsed on the couch. He dropped his crutch carelessly, landed with a grunt, and lay for a moment.

He thrust out the papers and Oslan jumped to his feet. He laid a tender hand on Whitman's shoulder and listened carefully to the muffled noises that emitted from the cushions.

Oslan took the documents. "Of course I can transcribe, my love — I need only a moment." Oslan went to the desk and lit several candles, smoothing the pages and dipping his quill with practiced motions.

Donovan cleaned up the game and asked, "Well?"

Whitman bellowed out a sigh and pushed himself to sitting, shifting his bad leg with his hands to minimalize the strain. Settled, he looked Donovan in the eye.

"It is not good."

"No?"

Whitman rubbed his eyes. "A group of people were spotted approaching the Order. They were moving slowly, and the Wall Officer determined that they all sported injuries. She sent riders out to meet them with a medical supply wagon to follow, as is standard. In short order, she sent for the Watch Commander."

Whitman closed his eyes. He looked restless and miserable. "The first to arrive was a Mentalist. He is still in the Healing Ward. The people were all badly beaten, but ... the worst of it was their minds." He looked sick. "Donovan, someone destroyed their minds. They were left with barely enough function to breathe and walk at the same time. The single unbroken thought their minds held was to come to the Order. Our Mentalist went near to mad when he saw."

Donovan's stomach roiled. He couldn't hide the horror from his face. "Who are they?"

Whitman shook his head and wiped watering eyes. "Don, they're ours: our spies — every single one that infiltrated the training grounds and village of the Hunters. Elliott sent people as soon as he could gather them and *this* is the retaliation for our cleaning house."

"We knew they'd do something ..."

"Never this." Tears overflowed from Whitman's eyes.

Donovan stared at his hands, uncomprehending of this new horror.

"This constitutes official war," Whitman finally said. "The king is having his people examine the ... them. I have withdrawn all of my people from the surrounding areas for their safety, and I pray it is not too late. The draft will begin in two weeks."

Donovan considered the implications of that: classes would be accelerated, but the student population would increase. The option to train with family or neighbors will be revoked; Order attendance required. Everyone with a Talent would be trained combatively, and every village and town would be required to send a percentage of their men and women and all of their trained magic users as young as fourteen.

"There's never been a war in my lifetime," Donovan said softly.

"The Hunters have never been this strong. They have flourished, and we have only ourselves to blame." Whitman buried his head in his hands.

12

DONOVAN CROUCHED LOW TO THE GROUND. His breathing came in hard bursts, and he fought to bring it under control. He'd never liked running, and had come to positively detest it, which was unfortunate, as it seemed to be how he spent half of his time now. He put out a hand to stop the young Mentalist next to him from moving; she was counting on him to get her close enough to their prey without detection. Once they were within touching distance, she assured him she would be able to perform her duties safely.

"Be absolutely silent," he whispered to her.

He increased his hearing slowly, cautiously, listening to the sounds farther and farther away. The trees twitched and creaked in the gentle breeze, passing through their leaves like tiny applause. Insects burrowed through the dirt below; he heard far away birds as though they were circling his head. The breathing of his partner sounded like a forge bellows; he could hear his own blood pumping through his veins.

Hearing nothing of consequence, he stomped twice into the packed dirt off the roadside. To him, the magnified sound was achingly loud, certainly heard miles down the road. After a moment, he heard two finger-snaps, carried from a distance away, but it sounded loud enough to be right beside him.

He lowered his hearing back down to slightly over normal and ignored the faint headache he'd gained. "They're about two miles from us."

The young Mentalist nodded seriously.

Donovan eyed her and asked kindly, "Have you done anything like this before?"

She answered, "I'll be fine," and managed a nervous smile.

Kina was barely over fifteen. She had muscular arms and legs, long-fingered hands, and thick brown hair cut up above her ears.

Donovan felt suddenly protective and said, "You don't have to go through with anything. If you feel at all unsafe, just run. We will find you."

Kina's expression hardened. "No. This is important, and I'm here to do the work." She took a deep breath at her words and seemed to be comforted by them.

It had been four months since the Return of the Spies, their minds destroyed by the Hunters' rage. In that time, he and Annette had both succeeded in controlling their Seeking magic — the New Seeking. Once Elliott had seen their demonstration, he immediately ordered them to train as many students as they could handle. Four months was hardly any time at all to learn a new magic, but the adults had experience with traditional Seeking, and neither he nor Annette wanted a break. They pushed themselves as hard as they dared, and learned as they went. When the details of what they could do began circulating, Elliott ordered Donovan on missions as well. Donovan couldn't argue. He wanted to help, wanted to work. The Retrievers had all been sent back to their duties, now with escorts, but he and Annette made a good team, and he knew he didn't want another partner.

Bringing his attention back to the mission at hand, Donovan pulled off his backpack and set it in the dirt beside him. It was designed for camouflage with patched-together fabrics in various shades of dark green, gray, brown, and faded black, the better to help him blend into the woods. His clothes were similarly fashioned, but were less obviously camouflage. He'd requested the clothing specially made for himself and his trainee Seekers, so the pockets held a variety of useful items — several of which were experimental and self-made. The material was made of incredibly fine wool, gentle on the skin. One of his trainees referred to the outfit as 'tailored clouds'.

Donovan sat beside his bag and he and Kina waited in silence while he slowly increased his sense of touch. He grimaced as even the soft cloth he wore seemed to scratch and mar his skin. It took incredible mental fortitude not to be distracted and he urged his students, and himself, to be patient with themselves. He took slow breaths, focused on the ground below him. He fancied he could feel the tree roots below sucking moisture from the earth. Sweat dotted his face and body and made his pores burn, as though with acid. A mosquito bit his neck and Donovan stifled a yell, managing to only whimper. He dropped his sense of touch back to normal, and only then did he slap the damnable insect off his neck, rubbing at the spot angrily.

"What happened?" Kina asked anxiously.

Donovan shook his head. "Just a mosquito."

"You were concentrating like mad; were you listening?"

"Feeling — touch. *Usually*, it's less jarring, but has its own consequences." He scratched the bite again, and decided that he wouldn't try that for another long while. At least while they were in the woods.

"I think that's him." Kina gestured with her chin.

Donovan placed a pair of tinted spectacles over his eyes and increased his vision. The man on the road matched the description they had.

"You've good eyes," he praised.

Their prey appeared to be alone. Donovan scanned the surrounding trees on the other side of the road and found who he was looking for.

Annette. He grinned.

He gave a wave, invisible to the target walking down the road, but easily noticed by a Seeker with the eyes of a falcon. Annette raised her hand in greeting, then started through the woods.

"Get ready," Donovan whispered to Kina. The young Mentalist nodded and steeled herself.

When the target reached the prearranged place in the road, Annette sprinted toward him, not bothering to keep quiet; she was meant to be a distraction. The man hesitated in his stride, now almost directly in front of Donovan's hiding place. Donovan quickly lowered his vision to normal and stowed his spectacles in their protective box, shoving them into a pocket.

The Hunter looked warily around, a knife appearing in his hand. He held it readily, but was not yet muttering and mumbling to indicate his use of blood magic.

Just as Annette burst from the trees, Donovan darted out. His knees popped in protest. Donovan shouted a distraction as he ran.

The Hunter spun to face him and swung the knife in a wide arc. Donovan ducked under the outstretched arm, and grabbed over the top in a tight hold, gripping the back of the Hunter's shirt to secure him. Annette kicked the cursing man's feet out from under him before he could strike, and dropped him to the ground with the help from Donovan's hold.

Kina joined them quickly as Donovan wrenched the Hunter's knife away and pinned his wrists to the stony earth. Annette similarly secured his legs. Kina touched the Hunter's thrashing head. His shouting and cursing immediately stopped. His eyes rolled up and his lids closed as he was knocked into a deep sleep.

The girl sat on the road, hands on either side of the unconscious Hunter's head, her own eyes closed, and a look of fierce concentration prematurely lining her young features. Annette rose and dusted herself off. Donovan retrieved the Hunter's knife, admiring the forge of it. He dug into the unconscious Hunter's sleeve to claim the arm sheath, which he buckled on and tucked under his sleeve.

Annette watched with an amused expression. "We're making a pirate out of you, Don."

Donovan nodded. "The loot is a happy byproduct of my quest for honor. I'm on my way to becoming a romantic highwayman."

"Mmm," Annette answered, an eyebrow raised. "When Kina finishes, we'll want to make speed from here. The last Hunter didn't stay asleep as long as she'd planned, and this one was behind schedule. The caravan will leave at first light and, if we miss it, we'll regret being alone out here."

Donovan nodded. "Off road, then. I'll lead, and you can cover our tracks."

Plan decided, they had nothing to do but wait and hope that no one else came along the road. Minutes passed like hours. Donovan was sure his heart would burst from its panicked speed, but that was normal these days. He focused on controlling his breathing, and consequently his heart rate.

Kina stirred at last. She looked up and blinked rapidly. Annette handed the girl a waterskin, already full of the herbs they all used to fend off the headaches and nausea that were inevitable with their magic.

Kina took it gratefully and gulped a mouthful, looking slightly ill. "His mind ..." she said quietly. "I might be sick ..."

Donovan helped her stand and led her toward the woods, reclaiming his backpack from where he'd left it. "Have another sip and don't think about it. Look about, focus on something else. Hear the trees, smell the air. Breathe."

Annette followed, adjusting her pack on her shoulders, and watching their surroundings warily.

They gave Kina a moment to collect herself before Annette asked, "Did you get what we came for?"

Kina nodded again, returning the waterskin. "Yes. I'm amazed they let him travel around alone with that kind of information in his head, but it's good news for us. I mean, considering ..." She frowned and pursed her lips. "I hate keeping secrets."

"Desperate times, love." Annette patted her on the back. "We should go."

"Are we late?"

"Not yet."

Donovan led the way through the trees and away from the road. Though he rarely did any traditional Seeking now, his education with maps was a great benefit, now working for Whitman and Elliott as a spy. These days, he considered himself a glorified babysitter — rarely the one doing any real spying, and never by himself, but he figured that was for the best. His experience was what they needed. The youthful vigor was something he was happy to leave to younger stock.

He glanced back at Kina. Unfortunately, war meant that the stock was getting younger and younger.

They made good time through the woods, traveling long after the sun went down. Donovan was in favor of a quick rest, but knew the longer they carried on, the better off they'd be. All three of them knew that sleep was unlikely, and it hadn't even come up. He kept his vision slightly increased, which let him see better through the darkness and foliage, but had a tendency to make him dizzy if he moved his eyes too quickly. It took practice. His hearing he left only slightly improved; he didn't want to risk a migraine. He heard Annette jogging to catch up with him, but did not slow his pace. She would have told him to stop if needed.

"We're being followed," she said quietly when she caught up. "Any idea who it is?"

"Yes. If I'm right, it's very bad news."

Donovan nodded slowly, running through their options. "Any chance it's a friendly bard coming to steal our horses, only to turn into a good friend?"

Annette smiled. "We haven't any horses."

"What do you want to do?"

"I can wait while you two carry on, draw him past." She shrugged. "Getting behind him worked last time."

"Assuming it is our Hunter friend, he'll be prepared this time."

"Do you have an alternative?"

"Let's both stay behind, send Kina ahead to draw attention — she knows the way to the caravan in case anything happens."

"You're very optimistic, Donovan," Annette said sarcastically.

"Do I have to remind you how many times I've been unconscious since meeting you people?"

Annette grinned. "Come on then, we'll play your way."

They waved Kina to join them and explained the plan in soft tones while they walked. The girl looked nervous, but determined, patting the pocket with her map.

"If you miss the caravan, find a room to hole up in," Annette finished. "When the caravan arrives without you, they'll send someone looking."

"Are you not expecting to rejoin me?" she asked. Her tone was strong, but her eyes were wide, scared.

Donovan shook his head. "Of course not. We plan for the worst, is all." He gave her a paternal smile and squeezed her shoulder to his chest. "Don't worry about making noise; you're supposed to be three people."

She managed a pained smile and started walking again while Donovan and Annette stepped off their path, confident in the shadows and trees to hide them. Donovan raised his hearing very, very slowly, until he could make out their pursuers' slow progress after them. His stomach started to flip-flop in anticipation, as usual. He hoped one day it would stop doing that, because now was not a good time to feel like stepping away to use the bushes. Annette tapped his arm and held up two fingers. Donovan concentrated for a long moment, shook his head and raised three. They looked at each other in the darkness, worry mirrored on both of their faces.

They didn't have to wait long before several dark shapes appeared, moving slowly up the path. One, ahead of the others, occasionally dipped down to touch a broken branch here, a boot-print there.

Annette grimaced, but Donovan didn't blame her. Trails were hard to disguise from someone who knew what to look for.

He pointed at the scout, and then to himself. Annette nodded and squeezed his shoulder as he prepared, quietly tightening the straps on his backpack, waiting for his moment ...

The scout drew even with their hiding spot and Donovan burst from cover. He heard Annette do the same behind him, running toward the enemy. He launched his left fist at the scout's raised head, missed, and followed up with an elbow to the face, which made jarring contact. The scout squealed in pain.

He kicked viciously, hoping to knock them to the ground. He made glancing contact, but a fist came out of the darkness to strike him in the nose. He felt a cracking, tearing sound and let out a shriek of his own as his eyes watered. He felt, and tasted, blood on his upper lip; his nose was broken once again.

Hands gripped the top of his head and wrenched him to the side. He kept his feet by sheer willpower, his neck screaming. He swung his left arm over the wrists holding his head and pulled them tightly toward him while reaching to cup the right side of their head with his right hand. He yanked their head down and rammed his knee up. The strike made his bones rattle and ache. A sweep of his leg knocked them to the ground.

They landed hard and Donovan kicked them in the head, feeling sick with himself. He had no stomach for violence. The scout lay still, likely unconscious, so Donovan ran to help Annette, toward the sounds of her fight.

Two adversaries were on the ground, but Annette was in trouble. Their count had been off: there had been four Hunters. The two left standing had Annette pressed against a thick tree, held in place by an unseen force. At Donovan's approach, both Hunters turned to face him. He skidded to a stop, kicking up dirt and leaves.

The Hunter closest to him snorted derisively and walked away from his fellow, toward Donovan.

He gestured toward the blood from Donovan's broken nose. "You've come into this fight at a disadvantage, old man, and brought a gift for me."

"Well, grandparents do love doting on children," Donovan replied breathlessly.

He felt the prickle of evaporation as the Hunters sacrificed the blood to fuel his own magic. Donovan reached into a baggy pocket by his knee and pulled out a stone the size of his fist. It was drilled through in several places by very clever stone masons and held a devious surprise.

Donovan closed off his hearing entirely and lobbed the stone as hard as he could. He knew from past experience that, as it flew, the piercing shriek it emanated was enough to warrant the Hunter's flinch. Another pocket at his right hip provided him with a wide-mouthed flask of liquid, which he splashed all over the flinching mage.

As Donovan brought back his hearing, the rock had surely landed by now, he heard the cursing, "—'s teeth was that, you bastard?"

"Oil." Donovan dragged a small sulphur-coated twig across a rough patch sewn onto the front of his trousers and flicked it toward the approaching Hunter, who burst alight.

The Hunter's screaming was loud, but more from shock than pain. The oil had landed mostly on his shirt, but his hair caught, too, and filled the air with the stench. Donovan dropped the new dagger strapped to his wrist into his hand and darted forward to silence the distracted Hunter.

When the burning mage fell, Donovan hurried to Annette's side. She lay on the ground, one leg around the last Hunter's throat.

She held her own ankle to pull her leg tight, while her other leg braced against the thrashing man's chest.

Donovan pierced the Hunter's chest with his knife, and the thrashing stopped.

"Thank you," Annette panted. She released her leg, and rolled to her feet.

He grunted in answer, cleaning his knife on the dead man's shirt. He felt nauseous.

"The scream-stone saved my life, Don." Annette looked down at the man she'd strangled. "His magic failed when he got distracted and it let me get around him."

"We should catch up to Kina."

"It's a shame to lose that rock." Annette looked toward where it had flown.

"I have another, and they're making more at the Order. The scout is still alive. Let's go."

Annette helped him bind the scout's hands and fashion a gag, then wake the woman and get her on her feet.

"We're moving fast, and if you don't come with us, you won't like how we leave you."

The scout looked into Annette's deathly serious eyes and nodded vigorously, joining them at a stumbling jog. Annette went ahead, increasing her sight, hearing, and smell to track down Kina. Donovan ran behind the scout to make sure she didn't try to veer away.

Kina had been moving quickly, but, after a couple of miles of jogging, they caught up. She and Annette embraced, then carried on at a pace to eat the miles.

"Are we going to make it?" Kina asked breathlessly. She was in good shape, but the pace was difficult to maintain on uneven ground.

Donovan looked at the sinking moon and nodded. "Veer east. We'll catch them on the road."

*   *   *

Dawn was cracking the clouds into shards of painted pottery when they emerged from the trees. They'd used the cover of the trees for as long as possible and rested only twice — and briefly at that; all of them felt ragged. A wide road cut through the earth at the bottom of a steep hill, and was already liberally sprinkled with people, farmers and apprentices mostly, bringing goods to market or heading to their various trades. It would get busier as the sun rose properly.

"We probably could have arrived in town," Annette admitted.

Donovan agreed. "Better to be sure. Now we can rest and wait for a bit."

The scout awkwardly lowered herself to the ground with her hands in bindings. Kina perched with her knees drawn to her chest and her arms around them, still flexible enough in her youth to be able to rest her chin on her knees.

Annette sat a few feet behind the scout, carelessly picking bits of grass and pulling them apart before letting the breeze take them. Donovan tried to get comfortable on the ground, and only partially succeeded in ignoring the dew as it soaked into and through his trousers. He kept his eyes on the road, but his thoughts wandered.

He had killed several people now, both as Retriever and spy, and, despite the professional soldiers and various fighters he'd spoken to, it hadn't become any easier. When someone's life was in danger, he rarely hesitated. His mind flew to come up with options and chances, as with the Hunter he'd burned just a few hours before, but he never could stop the guilt from claiming him afterward.

In hopes of escaping his dark mood, he looked at their captive. "Are you a blood mage?"

The woman's eyes went wide and she shook her head vigorously.

"Do you have magic of any kind?"

Again, a shake of the head.

Annette asked, "If I take off your gag, will you shout, scream, or in any way attempt to have yourself rescued?"

She hesitated for a moment and then shrugged.

Annette laughed. "At least she's honest." She loosened the woman's gag, to hang around her neck.

Some coughing, spitting, and tongue smacking later, the captive said, "Sorry about the nose."

Donovan probed it tenderly. "I can't hold it against you, considering." His words sounded thick in his own ears.

"You should get that looked at, if you can't set it yourself."

"I've been waiting for a better moment."

The scout looked at the road. "Where are we going?"

Her question was met with silence.

"All right, no questions ..."

"What's your name?" Donovan asked.

"Holly Cooper."

"Why were you working with the Hunters?" Annette asked.

"Because they were Hunters and I like to keep my blood on the inside?" she answered sarcastically. "I dunno anything about them, though. They found me in town; I offer my tracking to the public in my spare time. I was hired, is all."

Donovan and Annette glanced at each other, trying to convey their thoughts without words.

"Um, if you need to discuss something secret, I could cover my ears?" Holly suggested.

Annette's lip turned up in a smirk. "Would you consent to having a Mentalist look you over? If it's confirmed that you don't know anything, and that you aren't associated with the blood mages, we can let you go."

Holly hesitated. "I dunno ... having someone root about in my memories like a pig among acorns doesn't sound too terrible pleasant ..."

"I have a little more finesse than a pig, actually," Kina answered from where she was sitting.

"*You*?" Holly exclaimed. "You're only a girl!"

Kina turned her head and regarded the scout coolly. "I think you'll find that I can handle myself as well or better than any man you know."

Holly blushed. "I only mean you're practically a child."

"Yes, well, when you're good at your trade, waiting is a fool's choice."

Donovan gave Kina a nod of approval.

"I ..." The scout still wasn't convinced. Her bound hands twisted about in her lap.

"There's the caravan," Annette said, gesturing with her chin.

It consisted of four wagons; three of them roofed in canvas, drawn by two horses each. They moved at a slow, steady pace and would be close enough to meet within a few minutes. The surrounding people either held the reins or walked beside the wagons. Each of them flew green and white pennants on one of the corners; innocent enough ... unless it was what you'd been told to look for by Spymaster Whitman Acres.

"Fine!" the scout said, exasperated. "I don't want to travel days away for questions I can answer here. Just ... don't look too close, yeah? Some things is personal."

Kina rose lithely from her seat to kneel in front of the scout. "Don't fidget."

Hands on either side of Holly's head, Kina closed her eyes and concentrated.

"I hate taking captives," Annette said impatiently. "It complicates everything."

Donovan shrugged. "If she has information, we're better off knowing. Kina's willing to look her over, so we both win."

Kina gasped suddenly and retched. She threw herself backward, which unfortunately sent her into a tumble down the hill, shrieking as she went.

"I did tell you not to look too close."

Holly Cooper stood smoothly and dropped the ropes that had previously bound her hands. She turned to face Donovan and Annette, Now scrambling to their feet. She laughed and made a gesture at Donovan's face. He flew head over heels and landed a short distance away, awkwardly arched over his backpack. He groaned breathlessly, and struggled to sit up. Annette landed similarly, further up the hill.

Donovan struggled to reach his boot knife.

"I don't think so, you bastard."

Holly made a clawed gesture and Donovan felt his numbed and broken nose snap like a fresh break. He howled and tried unsuccessfully to staunch the sudden flood of fresh blood.

Annette threw a hillside rock at Holly, but she deflected it without a glance. Hoping to use the distraction, Annette tried to stand, but that hope was crushed as Holly made another sharp gesture and Annette was dragged toward her, along the ground. Annette growled in pain and frustration, as a new cut on her arm gave the blood mage more power to draw from.

Donovan managed to gain his feet, but was similarly dragged forward, barely managing to keep his grip on his blade as he hit the grass again, bruising his chin.

"Seekers, huh?" the Hunter asked, idly scratching her cheek. "I guess the Order is running low on the useful mages." She turned to Annette, pinned to the ground, and said, "Now, what was it you said to me? Ah. 'You won't like how I leave you'." She smiled a sweet, child-like smile; she had dimples on each cheek.

Donovan attempted again to stand, but he was pinned by the unseen force blood mages could manipulate. His arms and legs wouldn't move, as though weighted with stones. Annette screamed in rage and fury as the small cut on her arm ripped open. A matching wound raggedly appeared on her opposite arm. Annette thrashed and cursed, making the blood mage stronger even as she struggled, while her heart betrayed her with every beat.

The Hunter froze in her tortures, and spun around. Kina lay on the hill, having crawled laboriously back to the top. Her face was a bloody mess, demonic in its expression. Blood dripped from her eyes and nose and ears. One trembling hand reached for the would-be murderer and the blood mage grabbed her own head and groaned as Kina's magic worked against her.

Donovan felt the pressure holding him slacken. He pushed desperately against it, knowing his life, and Annette's, depended on their freedom. Annette struggled to her hands and knees, the wounds on her arms gaping and horrible, bared to the world, but bleeding not at all.

Holly Cooper moaned again. She took small, deliberate steps toward Kina, who still lay prone on the hillside, manipulating her magic. The blood on Kina's face began to evaporate, but she did not lose her concentration. Annette crawled, panting with the effort, as the magic binding her down released ever so slightly as Holly and Kina fought. As soon as she could stand, she reached for Holly Cooper.

The Hunter kicked a heavy, booted heel into Kina's face. The girl was silent as she toppled backward again, slumping and sliding bonelessly down the hill. Donovan roared with fury as he got to his knees. Holly spun to face them and her eyes went wide to see Annette so close; her hands were bare inches from Holly's neck.

The Hunter opened her mouth and hands to wreak more damage, but, before she could utter a word, a broad-tipped arrow ripped through her throat. She choked and reached for it with twitching hands before falling to her knees with a cough. Her eyes sought Donovan's. She blinked in confusion and toppled sideways.

The pressure containing Donovan and Annette disappeared abruptly and both of them fell to the ground in overcompensation, but neither could muster the energy to rise again. A woman sprinted into view a moment later, a bow and two more arrows in hand, with a panicked look on her face.

"Are you all right?" she demanded, her voice shrill.

Donovan gestured to Annette. "Help her first. Her arms — they're —"

Two men topped the hill behind their bow-bending savior. One came to Donovan's side; the other to Annette's. Donovan's new friend held a quiver of arrows, but dropped it when he came close.

"Anything life-threatening?" he asked Donovan.

"No. Please, help them."

While the man did as asked, Donovan staggered to his feet. Two newcomers were binding Annette's arms to staunch the sudden and powerful bleeding. Without the Hunter drawing on the power, blood immediately soaked her clothes, and she was deathly pale.

She still managed a small, tight smile. "You're cute with your face pinched like that."

Donovan returned the smile, albeit flavored with fear. He turned to where he'd last seen Kina, fearing the worst. A man and a woman were looking the girl over, and Donovan joined them to offer any assistance.

The man explained, "We heard the shouting. Mero here is a Mentalist; she'll take care of the girl, best she can. We don't have a Healer, but our surgeon has a good hand for stitching, too."

Donovan nodded mutely.

Everything progressed without him after that. Their rescuers carried Annette and Kina to the caravan on the road and tucked them into the wagons to recover. Kina was alive, breathing, but the Mentalist was nervous and wouldn't leave her side. She kept one of the men nearby to run errands for cool water, various herbs, and food to keep up their strength and help them recover. It took an hour to get moving on the road again. Donovan and Annette sat side-by-side, her stitched and bound arms in slings across her chest. Both of them watched the unmoving Kina, neither of them with a word to say.

13

"**I** AM DEEPLY HURT, and could be tempted to believe that you prefer the company of these highly-sanitized walls to the company of your best friend."

Donovan looked up at Whitman's voice. The bard approached him with the aid of his crutch, looking worn, but rested.

Whitman took a chair. "How is she?"

"Which one?"

He patted Donovan's leg. "I am sorry, Don."

Donovan rubbed at his eyes and straightened his hunched shoulders. "Annette will be Healed in some measure within the next day or so, but they're keeping her locked away until tomorrow to get her energy back. She lost a lot of blood. Kina won't wake, and the Mentalist from the caravan said she was 'locked away'?"

He touched his still-broken nose. It had been reset, but ached deeply, and his eyes were still puffy and bruised. The journey to the Order had taken three days, and then they had all been subjected to a once-over by the gate Mentalist before they were free to rush to the Medical Wing. That was hours ago, but Donovan couldn't convince himself to go anywhere else. He assumed that was what Whitman was here for.

The bard pulled a book out of his satchel and leaned back in his chair to read. At Donovan's irate silence he said lightly, "Or would you rather I persuaded you away to bathe and eat and rest? *I* am well content to otherwise remain here for our mutual friend to recover, however long that might be, but I can assure you that she is currently bathing and eating and resting."

Donovan scrubbed his hands across his cheeks and stared at the back of the chair in front of him, seeing nothing with any clarity.

"When we come back first thing tomorrow morning, they will either let us in to see her, or they will not," Whitman said gently. "Waiting speeds the process on not one Whit."

"How often do you manage to insert your name into sentences?" Donovan asked, rising to his weary feet.

Whitman joined. "Not as often as I would like. I realize that it could potentially lose its charm and prefer my *Whit* to be more amusing than irksome." He winked.

In the dining hall, Whitman urged Donovan to sit while he retrieved their plates. Donovan did so, slumping onto the bench and staring sightlessly at the woodgrain of the table. Not many people were eating at this time of day, several hours after the traditional lunch hours, but the sheer size of the Order could barely be visualized, with close to three hundred people dining even now. Only the massive size of the hall made that number seem so small.

Donovan's eyes focused far away as he played through the fight on the hillside again and again. He thought about Kina. She was far too young to face trauma such as she had.

"Stop that," Whitman ordered as he sat.

A kitchen worker followed behind him with a tray.

Donovan helped himself to bread, several small, steaming, roasted potatoes, a mound of mixed vegetables, and a slice of cold ham.

"You are wondering what you could have changed," Whitman said, serving himself, "and knowing you as I do, I firmly say, 'nothing'."

"You've never said nothing in your life."

Whitman's eyes narrowed and he gestured threateningly with his fork. "Either you are using the double-negative on purpose, or you are being facetious. Either way, I do not appreciate having my own humor used against me."

"Or I'm too tired to know what I'm saying. These vegetables are delicious."

"Cad."

Donovan smiled. "Did Seeker Jaynes finally agree to meet with you while we were gone?"

Whitman stalled from putting a large bite into his mouth and answered, "Yes, he did! Finally! Jaynes actually returned this morning, and I have made demands of his time. Of course, I have been extraordinarily busy with Elliott's orders recently, and have lacked time of my own to schedule for a true discussion." Whitman made a face. "Jaynes seems strangely reticent since his return, but I hope to determine why."

When they finished, Donovan let Whitman escort him to his own room. He saw it now as often as he had Retrieving: returning long enough to sleep, and then rising early for the library and to train young Seekers, or he was away on orders from Whitman and Elliott. Still, his own space was a comfort: Lucas's map above his desk, the shelf of books and keepsakes, his rug and quilt — everything where he left it, and where he wanted it. The place was a reminder that he had control over at least a small portion of his drastically-changed life. How had he arrived here from nearly twenty years as an average, everyday Retriever?

A note on the floor from Ruben filled him in on the boy's latest lessons and daily life, so different from Philipa. Donovan smiled. Ruben was sweet to realize how busy Donovan had suddenly become, but still know this old man wanted to keep track of him. Ruben didn't talk about his family much at all, and more and more Donovan felt as though Ruben was looking to him as a father figure. He was more than happy to take the role.

He set the note on his desk, unlaced and kicked off his boots, and groaned with exhaustion and relief. He wiggled his toes and rolled his ankles. A page had brought his bag and left it at the foot of his bed when he'd arrived. Next to the clean sheets, it looked as grungy as he felt, but he couldn't bring himself to bathe just yet. A full belly and fatigue had clouded his mind, and he had only just managed to keep from falling on his face as soon as he'd seen a place to lay.

Giving in to his body's needs, he fell heavily onto the padded mattress and closed his eyes.

*   *   *

Donovan swam to the surface of consciousness and blearily opened his eyes. He stared at the wall as thoughts tried in vain to make their homes in his mind. A gentle tapping came from the door, and he realized this was probably what had woken him.

He wiped the corner of his mouth and rubbed at the small spot of drool on the bedsheet where he'd rested, then rose heavily to his aching legs and feet. His back had stiffened while he slept and he was only able to limp to the door while his frozen muscles kept his tendons pulled taut.

"Yes?" he asked through a yawn. His voice was rough and harsh to his own ears, and he winced even at the dim light in the hallway.

A page stood patiently. "I've a letter from the Head of the Order for you. I wasn't allowed to leave it."

"No, I expect not." He managed a tired smile and held out his hand. The girl gave him the note. "I was about to leave, sir." The young girl explained.

"I've been traveling; home today."

"Would you like me to stay for an answer?"

"Let me read it," he told her.

Leaning against his doorframe, Donovan blinked several times to clear the sleep from his vision, and then opened the letter.

D,

See me as soon as possible.

Donovan shook his head. "No reply."

The girl gave him a cheeky grin and then sprinted off down the hallway to go about the rest of her duties.

Donovan lit a lamp and winced in the sudden brightness while another yawn threatened to crack his jaw. The lights had been low in the hall, dimmed for nighttime. It must be very late.

He stood for another moment, the fuzz of sleep still slowing his mind. In his closet, he gathered clean trousers, shirt, socks, and underthings under his arm, and turned left from his door.

The bathing room was nearly empty, only a couple of men soaking in the steamy water this time of night. Both of them were in quiet conversation, but the tiling of the room brought the sound of their voices, if not their words, to his ears. Donovan set his clean clothes aside on a wooden bench and stripped, tossing his dirty garments under the same bench.

The water was very warm, and he flinched as he descended into it, but started to relax when he submerged his entire body. The heat burned at his face, and he surfaced to scrub at his hair. It was getting thick, his curls clouding like Hector's, though not nearly as loose, but he preferred to keep it trimmed. His beard stubble was growing thick, too; he hadn't shaved in a week.

Trays of soaps, scrub brushes, and towels were placed conveniently around the pool. Donovan made use of them, scrubbing the grime from the road off of his skin until he felt clean. He washed and rinsed his hair and beard, and took the time to shave off his stubble. He had gone through a beaded phase, like most men he knew, but didn't like the shape it gave his jaw. He was most like himself with clean cheeks.

As his brain fuzz finally subsided, he rose from the pool and toweled dry, dropping the used cloth into a laundry bin. He dressed and took his dirty clothes back to his room, holding the soiled pile away from his now-clean self. How he'd worn them so long, he had no idea. He dropped the clothes on his sheets, seeing that they, too, needed to be cleaned after his long nap, and then sat to lace up his boots. Since the chaos of the attack just outside his bedroom, and his new duties, brought new worries and fears, he'd taken to wearing his boot knife most places, now.

Satisfied with his freshened appearance, he stepped into the hall and locked his door. There was a time he had rarely bothered to do so, but those times had changed.

The walk to the Head of the Order's wing took about ten minutes with his long strides. His time bathing and dressing meant that even fewer people were about in the halls. Two older pages hurried at their tasks and he passed three night owls — one with a stack of books, one with a bowl of late-night snacks, and the other possibly still asleep. They nodded at him as they passed, acknowledgement of another fellow unable or unwilling to conform to the standard sleeping schedule of the rest.

When Donovan entered the waiting chamber, he noticed the absence of the Head's secretary. It was, Donovan reasoned, much too late for him to still be up, after all. He crossed to the office door and knocked. A muffled acknowledgement came from inside and he went through.

Elliott sat in the private reading area of his office, a mezzanine level overlooking the rest.

"Shall I come up?" Donovan asked.

"If it isn't a bother, please," Elliott answered. He made a couple of notes in a journal beside him and bookmarked his place. Donovan climbed the ladder with only minor complaints from his joints, and sat across the small table from his superior.

Elliott seemed grayer these days, but still had a flash of determination in his eyes.

"Resting, were you?"

Donovan nodded.

"Sorry to wake you." He didn't sound very sorry, but Donovan knew that was just his way.

Elliott pondered his thoughts before stating, "Our surgeons and Healers are not sure if Kina will recover."

Donovan acknowledged the words, and gritted his teeth. He wasn't sure what he felt, but the guilt was clear.

Elliott continued, "Mentalists have their own methods for activating their Talent and, as I understand it, a side effect of that is the relatively small risk of becoming trapped in one's own mind.

"We are still, after centuries, learning about what Hunters can do, and this has come up before. Creating wounds, too, is rare, but not unheard of."

Donovan's eyebrows rose in surprise. He'd certainly never heard of it.

"What Kina did, already injured as she was, was outstanding. The skill she showed, and the mindfulness she had even in such dire circumstances, was incredible, and she will be receiving commendations."

Donovan nodded, but didn't know what to say.

"Unfortunately, her position puts us in a bind," Elliott continued.

"The mission," Donovan said. His throat tightened.

"Yes. My contact was able to confirm only the blood mage you identified as having the information I needed, which means they will have to locate another Hunter, or we have to wait for Kina to awaken, *and* hope that she still has the information we need."

"Time, either way."

Elliott nodded. "You see my issue."

"Can the Mentalists not access her memories while she is unconscious?"

"Apparently not." The Head let a frustrated sigh through his nose. "The way it was explained to me was that it is as though she is physically unconscious, but mentally awake, and lost inside her own mind. As though it were a mansion and she wanders the halls, lost in the memories of each room." He spread his hands. "To access her thoughts, they would have to find her first, but the mind is a complicated thing and not easily deciphered. She might even wake, but it is possible she would not be fully present." He rubbed at the side of his nose. "You know how the Mentalists can be; I barely understand any of this myself. The elements are far simpler."

"However," Elliott said, "this is not what I wanted to discuss with you. As soon as my contact finds another Hunter we can use, I'll need someone I can trust."

"I am yours to command." Donovan swallowed hard, knowing the promise he was making would result in more blood on his hands, more risk to the lives of people he cared about, and, not least of all, risk to himself. Still, he had to do *something*.

Elliott smiled, pleased at Donovan's proclamation. "How quickly will you resume your classes?"

"Whitman informed the students that I would resume tomorrow morning."

"Fast. I appreciate that."

"New Seeking doesn't take the toll that the old Seeking did."

"Where are the students, in terms of readiness?"

"The more advanced could be field-ready tomorrow, but they would need someone who understands their gift to guide them on when to use it; they lack experience. My practicum focuses more on how to use our senses, how to control them, and how to keep from becoming overwhelmed."

"And the others?"

"The others are either old Seekers returning to relearn their craft, or children new to their Talent. I've only had them three months — and not a full three months at that. The other instructors I trained are extremely helpful, but seem reluctant to step forward so quickly. Old Seeking was much more straightforward, oddly enough — centuries of training created a solid curriculum, and there is more nuance to New Seeking that we didn't have to account for. Director Jaynes has been helpful, but ... unenthusiastic?"

"I'll have a word with him. What will you teach in tomorrow's class?"

Donovan's mind raced. He should have been more prepared for Elliott's questions; New Seeking was all he usually wanted to talk about. "While I was gone, I had them create a new item for defense or offense against another Talent of their choosing. I expect more defense than anything — Seeking tends to lean in that direction. I will look over those, with discussion, and then pit them against one another in a Capture Castle game on the grounds."

"Very good. Do you lack any resources?"

"No, sir. I have what I need."

"You have my gratitude for shouldering the burden I've given you, Donovan. You've faced incredible hardship in the last year, and I appreciate your work."

"We've all faced hardship, Your Honor," Donovan replied. "A job is only tough until it's finished."

Elliott chuckled. "I'll remember that. Thank you for coming to see me at such a late hour."

They shook hands and Donovan made his way down the steps and out of the spacious office.

There was plenty of light to see by, but more shadows than he was accustomed to, and the hairs on his neck rose as he passed the dark places. He only partially succeeded in attempts to keep memories from taking shape in those shadows.

The path to the Medical Wing was a familiar one. He walked softly, uncomfortable with the echo his boots made on the polished stone floors. Silence guarded its territory fiercely, it seemed.

A pair of guards saw him coming and put up their hands for him to stop. One held a spear, the other a crossbow, though neither was leveled at him.

"What's your business here, sir? It's very late."

"I was summoned to the Head's office and, being awake, wanted to visit my friend," Donovan explained.

"What's your friend's name, please?" the guard with the spear asked. He looked at a thick records book.

"Annette Kraemer."

"Admitted when?"

"This morning. Or yesterday, I believe ..."

The guard scanned through the records and nodded. "Your name?"

"Donovan Rudd."

"Really?"

"Um, yes ..."

"Well done, sir."

"... thank you?"

Crossbow Guard grinned and jerked his head at his impressed fellow. "He's a Seeker, see? Wants to join your class when his rotation allows."

"Ah," Donovan smiled. "When's that?"

"Another month, but I'm hopeful they'll send me for early training when my C.O. hears what you can do," Spear Guard said eagerly.

"It's not just me; it's all Seekers. Just a Talent like any of the others."

"All the same, you discovered it."

"I suppose ..."

Crossbow Guard grinned. "Go on in, sir. You're cleared."

They saluted him, and Donovan nodded uncomfortably as he walked past. This kind of recognition was becoming more common. He wasn't afraid to be the center of attention, but had never sought it out, and it made him feel like he was deceiving everyone.

He nodded at a couple of student nurses working late shifts as he made his way to Annette's room. It wasn't locked, but he knocked gently and poked his head in. Annette was awake, and reading by candlelight. She looked up, smiled, and beckoned him in. Donovan closed the door softly and pulled the room's chair to her bedside.

"How are you?" he asked.

"I feel like a child in swaddling clothes," she answered, raising her arms. Her fingers were bare, but everything else to her elbows was thickly wrapped in soft bandages. "Makes it difficult to feed myself, of course." Her face darkened. "And other things." She let out a long-suffering sigh. "Still, if I'm a good little patient, and follow their orders *to the letter*, they assure me I should be *nearly* back to 'almost-normal' in six weeks."

"So you're planning on three weeks?"

"Two is all I can stand."

Donovan grinned. "I thought you were going to receive a Healer. That's what they said when you were admitted."

"Apparently it's worse on the surface than below, and time will be my ally for proper healing. So they say." She rolled her eyes. "Why are you awake? I would have thought you'd still be unconscious. I've only been roused for the last hour. One can only sleep so much in a day."

"Elliott sent for me. Wanted to talk about Kina, and my classes."

Annette grew serious. "How is she? I know it's bad by the way the surgeons keep telling me she'll be fine."

"Not good," Donovan agreed. "She still hasn't woken, and apparently she's trapped in her mind."

Annette grimaced. "I've heard of that. So our journey was for naught until she wakes. Is he ordering you out again?"

"They have to find another target first, but yes."

"Poor girl." Annette shook her head sadly. "She might not make it at all."

"She'll be fine. She might wake tomorrow."

"What happened to master Pessimist?"

"He got tired."

"I'm glad you came to visit."

"Whitman convinced me away earlier. Else I'd have been here the whole time."

"Yes, well, you smell better now, so I'm grateful to Whitman." She winked.

They sat in companionable silence for a minute.

"Oh, did Whitman's Director of Seeking arrive yet?"

"Yesterday, apparently."

"He's the original author for that paper on Seeking battles, yes?"

"Right. Whitman hasn't had a chance to sit with Jaynes yet, but he thinks they might find a lead to track down who the hell the Smiling Man is. Maybe. And from there ..." Donovan shrugged.

He looked at his clenched hands and tightened them before releasing the tension. He held his chin and put his elbows on his knees.

"I hate him, Annette," he said softly. "If there's such a thing as true Evil, that man embodies it. The world would be a better place without him."

She smiled sympathetically. "Do you think he'll show up here again?"

"So blatantly? Probably not. Hell, what do I know? He might be here already, posing as a guard or nurse or academic. I think he might be an Empath."

Annette raised an eyebrow. "Do you?"

Donovan picked at his trousers. "He's a manipulator. It's as though he just understands people and can play on their fears — things they love, things they hate. He brought Marcus to his side with hardly any effort it seems, and when I've encountered him ..." he looked away. "Thinking about that man makes me feel like I'm going to burst alight at any moment. I just feel like all of this is his fault somehow."

Annette said nothing.

"Anyway," Donovan sat up, leaning into his chair. "Enough about that." He forced a smile.

Annette started to reach out, but stopped, wincing. "You should rest, Don. You have a full day, and you've only been home a few conscious hours."

"I'll check in tomorrow. Or later today, rather."

He put the chair back and let himself out, nodding at the two smiling guards. He wanted to visit Kina, but knew they wouldn't let him into her room. Thoughts of the Smiling Man bounced painful inside Donovan's head. Their first encounter played scene by scene, his words echoing in the silent corridors of the Order as Donovan walked. He didn't know how, but he knew the Smiling Man was behind all of this, and he was determined to stop him. Whatever it took to find him, he'd find a way to help.

*   *   *

Donovan yawned as he locked up his cabinets. The class had been good, and very eventful. The day after his promotion to instructor, he'd sought out the custodial staff assigned to cleaning his room and apologized profusely for the state in which they would often find his classroom. Strongly scented oils, ash, candle wax, used torches, and numerous other things were often left behind, depending on what the students needed to learn that day. They were an eager bunch, for the most part.

Almost everyone had followed through with a will on the homework he'd assigned during his absence — especially young Owen, whose impressive contraption had filled the room with smoke. He hadn't seemed particularly upset when the thing caught fire, either, and it was quickly contained.

"How'd it go?"

Donovan looked toward the doorway. "Ruben!"

The young boy had grown at least three inches, and was wearing his brown hair shorter than he had when they'd arrived at the Order. *Was it only six months ago?* His nervousness was gone, replaced with a cool confidence and thoughtfulness that lent him presence.

He was grinning now, sprawled in a seat at the back of the classroom with one leg up on the desk. A heavy-looking book bag was on the floor beside him.

"I'm surprised you aren't attending my class yourself," Donovan said, sitting on a desk close by.

"I haven't the time," Ruben said regretfully. "But I've been experimenting on my own, and I've made headway. Some of your students are in my year and they give me pointers."

"Classes are going well, then?"

"Yes! But that time I Healed you was a fluke — beginner's luck. I haven't managed a bit of it since, and they're particular about how you go about trying, seeing as I'm not in practicum yet. Don't want to get stuck with someone else's attributes, you know?"

"I don't. But I believe you." Donovan smiled. "In your letter you mentioned staying on as a teacher. Do you think they'd let you?"

Ruben made a face. "Maybe. After I've done some time wandering the countryside and showing everyone what I can do. Fancy parties and the like. I get letters from nobles just about every day, all of them trying to win my favor. Hector helps me go through them, and he and my etiquette instructor help me with polite replies."

Donovan met his eyes squarely. "You don't owe anyone anything. Except yourself."

"And you." Ruben grinned cheekily.

"Not even me," Donovan said seriously. "Or Whitman or Elliott or Hector. Learn for the sake of learning. Become the best because you have the option to do so. Stay true to yourself, no matter who persuades you, and in which direction."

"I know, I know ..."

"Where are you off to next?"

"Seeking." He smirked.

"Oh, I see how it is: abandon my classes to be taught by another."

"I have gotten used to the preferential treatment ..."

"Big word for a stable boy."

He looked dreamy. "Ah, it's nice to be reminded of my roots."

"Those roots are barely six months old!"

"Yes, but I feel like I've grown so much as a person."

"At least half a foot if I'm any judge."

"Shelves aren't as daunting as they used to be."

"Who's teaching your Seeking?"

"I have a lot of tutors, and I can't keep up with their schedules and mine. I can tell you there'll likely be four instructors, though. Director Jaynes used to be in all my sessions, but he's been absent lately — busy. My Seeking sessions go on for a while, since I don't get the sickness afterward, but even I can't stay out of myself forever. The pros and cons of being a magus, I guess."

"A once-in-a-lifetime gift should have its downsides, I suppose, else you ..." Donovan paused, thoughtfully.

Ruben cocked his head curiously and waited, but eventually said, "Don? Everything all right?"

"How ... how many magi have there been in the last hundred years?"

Ruben shook his head, "None. All of the magi's names are in the records of the library, but I'm the only one recorded for about three hundred years ... since the Cataclysm. Some people think that had something to do with there not being any until me. But since so little is known about the event, it's hard to be certain about anything."

"I ... need to find something ..." Donovan stared into nothing and thought about magi. The thought was vague and unformed on the edge of his consciousness, and it took effort to tell the lad, "I'll see you tonight."

"Sure. Let me know what you find out," Ruben said, gathering his bag. "Could be I can help."

"I will, Ben, thank you." He smiled distractedly and watched Ruben leave, waving over his shoulder.

Donovan stared through the doorway for another few minutes trying to keep a hold of the thought he'd had, like holding a bubble in his hands.

*   *   *

"Don! Did you find what you were looking for this afternoon?" Ruben asked loudly. He lounged on Whitman's couch with his shoes kicked off and his trousers rolled up to his knees.

The bard himself lay on the floor with a pillow under his damaged knee and a hot-bag on top of it, his crutch beside him. He propped himself up on an elbow when Donovan entered, a smile warming his features.

"No, I hardly had the time anyway," Donovan answered dejectedly.

"What were you looking for?" Whitman asked, glancing between them.

Donovan plopped down onto the couch after Ruben contained his sprawl and made space. He loosened his boots and said, "I was looking for the names of magi."

"I could have told you those," Whitman said reproachfully. "I know the name of every magi back to the creation of the original Order, for certain, and the legends and myths of those who came before. You are wasting the resource that is my mind, Don. Wasting it."

Donovan smiled, "Yes, I know, I'm sorry. I found their names and read some stories and none of them were what I was looking for."

"Which was?" Whitman pressed.

Donovan rubbed the back of his neck. "I thought the Smiling Man could have been a magus."

A thoughtful silence followed.

Whitman lowered his head back down onto his hands and stared at the ceiling. He was uncharacteristically silent.

Ruben, frowning, said, "He hasn't really shown any magic outside of Seeking, though, has he? When he attacked you in Weston?"

"I'm ... not sure. I told Annette I thought he could be an Empath, as manipulative as he is ..."

"And now you think he's a magus?" Ruben asked.

Donovan rubbed his eyes. "I don't know. But every time he shows up, I realized I was feeling a sort of ... dread? It made me think he could have been manipulating emotions, getting people to follow him, making himself seem more powerful than he was ..." He put out his hands. "So, yes, now I think he might be a magus."

"That could explain how he entered into the Order, if he had some way of confusing the Mentalists, perhaps with their own magic ..." Whitman said slowly.

"You believe me?" Donovan asked, surprised.

"I do not disbelieve you," Whitman answered. "Magi are rare, Don. Finding Ruben was a once-in-a-lifetime chance, after all."

"And it's impossible that there could be two in one lifetime?" he asked exasperatedly.

A knock sounded at the door and surprised them all. Donovan asked, "Are you expecting company?"

"No, but my room is often a place of excitement these days." He made a pleading expression, so Donovan stood to answer.

A tall and goateed man stood before him dressed in high-quality messenger garb, satchel and all, but the patch on his shoulder, where normally was the symbol of the Order, instead showed a different coat of arms.

Donovan had only a moment to glance before the messenger asked, "Are you Master Whitman Acres?"

"I am Whitman," the bard said from the floor.

The messenger leaned in to see him and said haughtily, "Under the auspices of the royal seat, I am privileged to bear urgent news from his Majesty King Braun."

"The king?" they all three asked disjointedly.

"Yes. The king."

"What is it?" Ruben asked.

"It is private, young sir."

"Of course it is. Don, Ben, can you step outside?"

The two of them traded with the messenger, who stepped inside and closed the door after him.

"What do you think it is?" Ruben asked, hopping from foot to foot.

"The king is due to come here, isn't he?" Donovan asked. "I thought not for another month, though. It takes a lot to get a king moved anywhere without upsetting anything."

When the door finally opened again, they rushed hurriedly inside, eager for the news. The messenger didn't give them a second glance, but closed the door again with a *snap*.

"Well?" Ruben asked. "What'd he say?"

Whitman didn't appear to have moved from his spot on the floor. "Your fire magic is wearing off on my hot-bag — mind fixing that for me?"

Ruben rolled his eyes good-naturedly and picked up the bag, concentrated for a few moments, and gently replaced it. He jumped back up to reclaim his spot on the couch with his knees at his chin. Donovan sat patiently on the arm of the couch.

"The king has arrived, apparently," Whitman finally told them.

"What?" Ruben demanded. "Already here? How? Where?"

"He arrived four days ago."

"And no one recognized him!"

"How did he pass the Mentalists?" Donovan mused.

"He did not, merely swore them to secrecy."

"Surely not. Gossip goes around this place faster than a hound on scent," Ruben retorted.

Whitman grinned at the comparison.

"Is he staying in the Head's wing?" Donovan asked.

"*That* is private information, master Rudd! But yes, of course. The queen arrived just now. It was her decision that they should travel in secrecy, and to send a messenger to alert certain important officials. Such as myself, of course." He preened for a moment and then grinned cheekily.

"So we don't get any fanfare and fancy parties?" Ruben asked dejectedly.

Donovan and Whitman howled with laughter.

"Look," the boy shouted over them, "I'm *very* special, and everyone in this place knows me, which means that I would *definitely* get to shake their hands, receive their blessings, and, most importantly, eat at their table. My reputation would increase tenfold, and Whitman could stop nagging me about being a mediocre magus in his story."

"I will never stop nagging you," Whitman assured him. "The handshakes and blessings and food — good priorities, by the way — are certain, but adversity breeds excellence. And since no one can challenge you magically, I have decided to set myself to challenging you in as many other ways as I can manage — namely, the threat of a lousy legend. Trust me: you do not want to be remembered forever as a comedy."

Donovan yawned. "Are you two finished? Who is running the kingdom in the absence of our monarchs?"

"The twin heirs have that honor. They're nearly of age anyway."

"Aw!" Ruben groaned.

"You expected both monarchs *and* their eldest children to come fawn over and flatter you? Truly? The rest of their enormous brood is here."

"It's only a matter of time before everyone knows and the rumors start circulating," Donovan pointed out.

"They have a baggage train following. It will be here in a few days, and they will mark their arrival then with all the fanfare and trumpets and feasting Ruben wants. In the meantime, the king and queen can do whatever it is they want without all the fuss and people marking their every move."

"Very wise of them."

"Ooh, I can't wait to lord this knowledge over my classmates!" Ruben laughed. "I'll make hints that I know something, and then when it's made public, I can nonchalantly point out that I knew it all weeks ago. Ha!"

"You are a fiendish little child, Ruben," Whitman said.

"I'll join you both another night. I have to go plot." He jogged out the door, whistling as he skipped down the hall.

"He's your fault," Donovan said.

"I acknowledge the role I have played in shaping him," Whitman agreed. "Something else — now that Ben is gone, I can say: apparently one of the intentions of their visit is to see if the young princess is a good match for our Ruben."

"You aren't serious."

"I am very serious. They have a royal line to improve, and we are at war. Arrangements can be made for alliances with any external countries as needed, using the rest of their children."

Donovan nodded thoughtfully. "Interesting. And far, far above the concerns of my own station."

Whitman smiled at him, and then said, "Before all the fuss, we were discussing a more interesting topic still. I think you might be onto something. I will see what I can find for you, as the library somehow failed to produce your desired results. You probably did it wrong."

"I appreciate that. I'm off to bed. Looks like our interesting lives are about to get much worse."

Whitman gestured erratically. "When I stop drowning in politics and adventure, I will assume that I have succumbed to death."

Donovan laughed. "Have a good night, Whit."

"You, too, Don."

14

"I'M WITH THE BARD," Annette said thoughtfully. "It's an interesting theory, and a better cliff to jump from than anything else you have." She opened her mouth and Donovan scooped up another forkful of scrambled eggs for her to chew.

Donovan swallowed his own bite of peach. "The more I think about it, the more I convince myself. I'm not even sure if my original thoughts on it were accurate anymore."

She smiled and shook her head at him. "And returns to us our dear master Pessimist. Welcome."

Donovan rolled his eyes. "Yes, yes, thank you."

"What are you going to do today?"

"Whitman wants me to join his discussion with Director Jaynes about Seeking battles, but I don't know that have anything to contribute. I told him to send for me if needed. Ruben has been researching the monarchy to have interesting conversation when the royal family invites him to dine, so he's ... occupied. Class this morning was awful: no one could focus, and Owen nearly set Ani on fire, so I ended early and told everyone that their homework was a solid night's sleep."

"You should go riding," Annette told him.

"Riding?" Donovan repeated, raising an eyebrow.

"Yes, fool, riding. I have to live vicariously through you for now, and your day is boring. Go ride horses and eat under a tree and then return to tell me about it. And *really* pay attention so that I get the full experience, or I'll send you out again. I want scents, sights, sounds, tastes, and sensations!"

Donovan laughed, putting his hands up defensively. "All right, all right! I'll go riding."

"Now?"

"Can I go to my room and change first?"

Annette glared at him and tore a bite out of the bread roll he offered. "Your humor is not appreciated. I don't even have a window, and I'm not going to make a burden of myself by requesting to be taken outside."

"You can request it of me, you know."

"Apparently I'm an escape risk, so I have to be supervised by a member of staff."

Donovan stared at her.

Annette shrugged carelessly. "I've been here before ... and I might have signed myself out a few times before they wanted to release me. It really isn't important."

"Did you go riding?" Donovan asked sarcastically.

Annette grinned. "Shoo. I have another book to start *and* finish today."

Donovan took her empty breakfast plate and laid his cheek on her head companionably. "I'll be back this afternoon to tell you about my ride."

"Thank you," she sighed.

"And you should ask someone to take you outside."

"I know. I will."

He placed the dishes on the breakfast cart, and returned to his room. The halls were crowded at this time of day with the usual children, academics, patrolling guards, and messengers weaving in and out of the throng. The walk took half-again as long as usual, but a surprise was waiting for him when he opened his door: a woman seated on the only stool in his room. An unobtrusive second woman stood by the doorway and she nodded politely at Donovan when they made eye contact.

The seated woman wore her long, honey-blond hair in thick, intricate braids above her shoulders, and in twists and hanging loops that looked very impressive and must have taken hours to put together. At first glance, her clothing seemed as common as Donovan's own, but a healthy dose of suspicion, and a second look, confirmed that it was tailored and of much higher quality. She wore no jewelry, except for a gold and emerald wedding band on her left first finger and a silver chain around her neck that disappeared into her shirt.

Her eyes were the same emerald as her wedding band, and her cheeks were blemish-free except for a scar near the left side of her chin, and another like a small check mark under her right eye. She wielded so much confidence, and presence, that Donovan was surprised that his room wasn't bowing outward to contain it all. He took another step in and closed the door.

Once inside, and private, he dropped to one knee and bowed his head. "Your Majesty."

"Rise, subject, and be at ease," she replied formally.

Donovan stood and waited.

The queen raised a slender eyebrow. "We apologize for surprising you in your own quarters, master Rudd." Her voice was soft and low.

"Not at all, Your Majesty. My schedule is not predictable."

"You are not surprised with the news of our early and unanticipated arrival?"

"No, Your Majesty. I'm close friends with one of the officials you notified."

She raised a slender eyebrow. "Do they tell you many private things?"

"Oh, no, Majesty. I only meant that I assist him on many of his projects, and I work closely with him, and some things he deems necessary to tell me so that it doesn't negatively affect either of us in our work. Forgive me." He wasn't sure why he was apologizing, or speaking so quickly. Or so much. *Nervous of royalty at your age, Donovan?*

She nodded slowly. "We know the secret will escape soon. However, we prefer it to be at the time of our choosing."

"Of course, Majesty." He waited, but she only blinked her emerald eyes at him. "Is ... there something that I can assist you with, Your Majesty?"

"Perhaps. We have not yet decided." She tilted her head and asked, "Were you expected somewhere, master Rudd? You arrived in something of a hurry."

"Nowhere specific, Your Majesty." She raised her eyebrow again. "Ah, I told a friend that I would go riding for her. I was going to change my clothes."

"Is she unable to ride, herself?"

"Yes, Majesty, she's currently in the Healing Ward."

"Nothing serious, we hope?"

"Her arms were injured, but the surgeons say she'll still be able to use them. Not right now, though, while they're healing."

The queen's eyes narrowed. "What is your friend's name?"

"Annette. Kraemer."

"Ah."

She appeared to recognize the name, but said nothing further. Donovan wanted desperately to ask, but doubted she would tell him.

"That would mean that our arrival was shared with you by Whitman Acres, yes?"

"Yes, Your Majesty."

"You surround yourself with interesting people, master Rudd." Unsure of how to answer, he said nothing.

"Will it cause undue stress if we ride with you, master Rudd?"

"What?" he said, surprised, and then corrected himself, "Ah, no Majesty. Though I had no particular plan or direction."

"Good. We shall meet you in the stables in a half hour, then." She stood to her full height, only an inch or two shorter than his own.

Donovan bowed deeply at the waist, and the queen's bodyguard opened the door for her. They swept out, the door closed, and Donovan stood.

He stared at the far wall, his thoughts catching up with events. Then, to himself, he said eloquently, "Wait, what?"

*   *   *

The stables were not busy. Of the three buildings, one was almost entirely empty of horses, which the soldiers used in training. The second was for working horses and those for private use, about half full. A third stable, half the size of the others, held overflow for visitors and those who wanted to ride, but had no mount of their own.

Donovan tracked down a stable-hand and started to explain his need.

"Rudd, yeah?" she asked, "The guard back there said you'd be along — already taken care of, mate. Just go choose any one y'like."

Donovan smiled as the horses whickered at him walking past their stalls. A beautiful mare, about sixteen hands tall, was waiting patiently for the queen's bodyguard to finish saddling her. The only change of outfit Donovan could see was the addition of a sword, hung on her right hip.

"Hello again," the bodyguard said. She didn't look up from tightening the horse's cinch.

"Hello," Donovan answered, swallowing nervously.

The bodyguard put out a hand to shake, and Donovan accepted.

"My name is Kath Ballew, and my job is simple: I protect the queen and I follow her orders without question. I recommend you do the same, and we'll get along just fine."

Donovan nodded. "Fair enough, mistress Ballew. Can I help with the horses?"

"Only your own."

Donovan went to the horse she indicated, a sixteen-hand paint with large red and white splotches all over. She took the bit he fed her to put on the halter, and she stood without a lead while he put on her blanket and saddle. He concentrated on his hands to keep his thoughts away from the last time he'd ridden, but it proved difficult, and his throat felt thick with emotion.

"Master Rudd, we are glad to see you."

Donovan turned and bowed. His clothing change had been the addition of a jacket and taller boots. The queen wore a soft white shirt and dark blue jacket, with close-fitted wool trousers that tucked into calf-high leather boots.

She held his gaze. "You seem in a darker mood now, master Rudd. We hope we are not the cause."

Donovan blinked in surprise. "Of course not, Majesty."

"Not pleased at the prospect of riding, then?"

"No, I — lost my partner six months ago on a trip to Philipa, and I was remembering him."

"Ah. We are sorry for your loss."

"Thank you, Majesty."

"In public, 'my lady' will be acceptable."

"Of course, my lady."

"How did your partner die? Not on horseback, we hope?"

"No, my lady, he was an excellent horseman. We were attacked by Hunters. He killed several of them, but was overwhelmed."

Again, her slender eyebrow rose. "You will have to tell us more of him. He sounds to be an interesting fellow." She turned smoothly and attended to her mount, checking the straps and buckles for herself.

Donovan bowed again and finished saddling his horse. The name on her stall read 'Heart of the Rose', and he smiled, stroking her face. "Ready, Rosie? You're in royal company, you know. Not me, of course, but that lady there is the queen. I know you could tell; she's not a subtle figure, huh?"

The horse grunted at him, bobbing her head and stomping. She leaned into his petting and scratching.

Shortly, they mounted and rode out, stopping only briefly at the gate to explain their intentions to the guard before being let through. Kath rode behind and to the queen's right. Morning was quickly turning to afternoon, and the sun was very bright, making him squint and shield his eyes. A cool breeze blew leaves across the road, busy with those leaving or trying to enter the Order; waiting had become standard, and Donovan was certain that businesses were suffering for it.

He led them off the road to Thairnsdale, and toward a well-worn path that led to a distant tree line. They didn't speak as they rode, but Donovan's mind was anything but silent. His thoughts darted this way and that in a jumbled mess that didn't provide anything useful to him. Why had the queen sought his company? What did she want? Was Kath eyeing him suspiciously, or was he reading too much into her wary glances?

When they reached the shade of the trees, the queen said, "Tell us about your partner; the one who died."

Donovan felt a weight descend onto his shoulders. "His name was Lucas Fain. An incredible Healer, and a very skilled fighter."

"You were pursued by Hunters, you said?"

"Yes, Majesty. Two in town where we found Ruben, the young magus. Lucas killed them both single-handedly, only Borrowing my reflexes. Then another seven, a day down the road. We'd come upon Whitman Acres by then, and he was skilled enough a fighter to help, but the last of them killed Lucas. Though he took the creature with him."

The queen's passive expression didn't change. "He sounds formidable."

Donovan nodded.

"What about Ruben Smith?" she asked. "Do his parents still live?"

Donovan considered the question, "I'm not sure," he finally answered. When she waited expectantly, he continued, "Ruben doesn't speak of them much, but I understand his father was taken to prison for brawling, and his mother sold him to servitude with the hostler in his town. He's made no mention of where his father was imprisoned, or if he'd ever heard from his mother again."

"I see. A difficult family."

"Unfortunately."

"Magic comes mysteriously," she mused, reaching out to touch a tree branch as she passed.

Donovan wrenched Heart of the Rose's head up, away from grazing and nudged her flanks to keep up with the queen.

"I've heard he's a clever child; do you agree?"

"Yes, Majesty. I would agree with that — he's smart and determined."

She eyed him sideways. "What are you holding back about him?"

Donovan smiled bemusedly and shook his head. "He's a fourteen-year-old boy, is all, Majesty. A fourteen-year-old boy who went from minding horses to being revered as the most important magic user of our age — and at the beginning of a war, no less. I imagine that would go to anyone's head, is all."

"Arrogant, then?"

"No, just ... overconfident? He could use some tempering, but that will come with age and experience. Like you said: he is a smart boy."

"I assume you know why I'm asking about him."

"Yes, Majesty."

"My daughter Lauris is only a year older, and because the Order lays such a strong hold on the magus — which I can accept, with no parents to claim him — it would strengthen our alliances here. If he is as charismatic as I'm told, he would make a good prince, and, eventually, possibly, general to our armies when the Lord General Baron Ost retires."

Donovan kept his peace.

"You wonder why I'm telling you all this."

"It does seem wiser to keep your plans private."

"You intrigue me, and I'm curious to learn what you might do with what I've told you."

"I will probably tell Whitman and Annette, in case it helps them in any way."

The queen laughed. "I should remove myself from court more often. You've a very refreshing way of speaking your mind, Donovan Rudd."

"Thank you, Majesty. I've never been skilled at subtlety."

"You've told me of your partner, and you've told me of the boy, but what of yourself?"

Donovan shrugged uncomfortably. "I'm not sure there's much to tell, Majesty."

"As I hear it told, you are a *hero* in the halls of the Order."

Donovan touched his chest absently. "I have a lifetime's experience to share with the younger generations. I also have a tendency to take punches aimed for others."

"Your name crops up in the news we receive more and more frequently. But unlike others, I sense no ambition in you. What is it that you want?"

"Majesty, I want to die of old age."

"The work you do suggests otherwise."

"I'd like to succeed in the work assigned to me, retire comfortably, and then die of old age," he amended with a slight smile.

"Surrounded by children and grandchildren, I've no doubt," she added.

Donovan's face darkened and he looked away. "I'm decades past that, Majesty. Just old age would suit me."

They rode for a few minutes in silence until the queen spoke again.

"No one knows anything about you, despite knowing everything about you. I find it to be more than mildly irksome. I know of your tragic past, I know of your work for the Order, your loss of partner, and discovery of a 'new' magic. I know of the man that brought you to death's door twice now, but, like yourself, we are at a loss as to who he is. However, as I said before, you show no desires, no drive, except to complete whatever is put before you.

"I don't like men like you."

Donovan didn't answer, but his hands tightened on his reins, and he became keenly aware of their solitude, and Kath's quiet presence behind them.

The queen continued, "Men like you cannot be predicted, nor guided on a particular path unless you deem it *worthy* by your own inscrutable standards and code. You gather people to you — in your case, very important people — who stay and defend you out of loyalty and friendship. That is itself more tiresome still, because even they will not — or cannot — give any sense of who you are and what you want."

"I seem to be quite a bother to you," he said softly.

"For now, you're a treat. I imagine, however, that if anything against your liking were to occur, we would find in you a very powerful adversary."

Donovan stared at Rosie's saddle horn, many emotions — namely fear — churning within him.

The queen continued, "My husband believes we should bring you to court; the better to keep an eye on the paths you might take and the alliances you might make, but I worry that the politicking would be too much. You'd either be dead or in control within a year."

"You make me sound like a schemer."

"You are, dear, but through no fault of your own. An enigma that intrigues me, as I said."

After grinding his teeth fitfully, Donovan said, "If you need something to use against me, there are always the people I value."

The queen shook her head, stroking her horse's mane. "Like Whitman, whose information and resources we need like water? Perhaps Ruben, because using him against you could never be detrimental; a magus angry ... Or Annette? She would not tolerate that for very long at all. No, you're in an interesting position, master

Rudd, and I'm more and more entertained to learn that you were not aware. There are courtiers who have danced intricately for decades to be in so strong a position, and even they leave a usable trail behind them."

"Am I going to have a tragic accident on this ride, Your Majesty?"

The queen looked over at him, her green eyes inscrutable. "Should you?"

"I won't work against the crown, Your Majesty. I hold no animosity for my country."

"Mmm," she agreed. "Not yet, anyway. I hope it remains so."

Donovan wanted nothing more than to turn back to the Order, away from all of this twisting conversation, but he knew he would have to endure until he was dismissed.

"Majesty, I feel I've irreparably damaged your perception of me, and so I think that *asking* to be released back to the Order will not harm anything more than I already have."

She smiled, although it didn't reach her emerald eyes. "My company is usually sought only for the position I hold, and the power I wield. As yourself, I'm considered too blunt for politicking, though I have some subtle arts, when I choose to use them. I should say that your reputation is intact; I've spoken my mind to no one but the king. I should add, too, that he thinks very highly of you, and my children see in you the hero you deny yourself to be. In my family, only *I* think of you as a liability."

Donovan didn't answer.

"Chin up, master Rudd. We're all beholden and sworn and promised and *cursed* to someone or something. I hope not to be your enemy."

"Of course not, Majesty."

"But we'll never be friends?"

"However you wish, Majesty."

She sighed theatrically. "Are you a good teacher, master Rudd?"

The change of subject was so sudden that Donovan needed a moment to remember that he was a teacher at all. "Um, yes? My students seem to enjoy class, and we make progress ..."

"My daughter Gloria is a Seeker. I've decided to enroll my children in classes for the duration of our stay. There is no greater value than one's education, after all."

Donovan nodded. "We meet at the breakfast hour so that no one gets sick from having already eaten. I assume she was already training in traditional Seeking?"

"Recently, yes."

"I look forward to having her in class, then."

"Does Ruben Smith take your classes?"

"No, Majesty. He has too many others at present. New Seeking isn't a priority in his schedule."

"Interesting. I expect you wouldn't be willing to tell me his schedule?"

"I don't know it, and it isn't a subject Retrievers share with anyone who asks. I'm sure, though, that Elliott would be more than willing to help the crown with whatever it requires."

She laughed. "Venom suits you. I expect we'll speak again soon."

"Yes, Majesty."

"You may go, master Rudd."

Donovan wheeled his horse's head around, nodding to Kath Ballew as he passed her. The bodyguard moved up to ride beside the queen, and to let him pass. Donovan gave Rosie a nudge with his heels and she jumped into a canter. A gallop was more suited to his dark mood, but the ground wasn't even enough to risk it until they broke out of the trees.

He gave the horse her head when they reached the open ground, and she sprinted excitedly, racing across the grass. Donovan let out a yell, half in excitement and half in fury. Rosie thundered across the field and back to the road, still half-filled with the lines for entry to the Order. She was more interested in running than standing about, so they rode for another half hour, Donovan giving only minor guidance, but otherwise letting his temper cool with the companionship of a very satisfied horse.

When she started to slow, they returned to the road. The line had moved, but wasn't any shorter. He found the gate for residents, and passed the time staring at everyone else, practicing his increase and decrease of senses.

Just as he reached the gate, a sudden scent gave him pause. His heart began to race in his chest, and his stomach dropped, but he didn't know why. It wasn't a strong smell, and he couldn't place it, but he knew it from somewhere. Before he could locate it, he was interrupted by the gate guard.

"Sir." Her tone indicated that there were options other than politeness if he didn't pay attention.

Donovan lowered his senses to almost normal and paid attention. "Yes. I'm sorry."

"Name?"

"Donovan Rudd."

"You live here?"

"Yes."

"Occupation?"

"I'm a teacher."

"What do you teach?"

"Seeking."

The guard's eyes widened. "*That* Donovan, I thought so."

"Um, yes."

"What was your reason for leaving today?" she continued, mood improved.

"Just getting fresh air."

"All right, you can see the Mentalists, then." She motioned to the small guard shack, originally built in case of weather, but now multi-purposed.

A man sat inside, another chair in front of him. Donovan looped Rosie's reins about the hook on the wall and sat inside. The Mentalist gave a weary smile and Donovan told himself to relax.

"Ready?" the Mentalist asked, bored.

Donovan nodded. As far as interrogations went, this one was gentle. The Mentalist was good at his job, and all he was required to do was determine if Donovan had recently lied, or was thinking anything nefarious. A vague pressure built in his mind, but it was over in less than a minute.

"You're finished," the Mentalist said. "Have a good day."

"You as well," Donovan answered. He stood, momentarily dizzy, and collected his horse.

After mounting, he let Rosie lead the way back to her stable and handed her over to the hostler. Donovan then walked back to the Order, hands shoved deeply into his pockets. Without paying attention, he found his feet taking him back to the Medical Wing.

Annette was sitting in the cushioned chair with her head on one arm and her legs over the other, a book propped against her knees and held awkwardly in place with her arm wraps. In her teeth, she held a stick wrapped in cloth for turning pages.

She smiled at Donovan, used the stick to mark her place, and set it aside. "You obviously rode; you smell like horse." Her smile faltered when he didn't return the expression. "What's the matter?" she asked, twisting to sit up in her seat.

"I had company on my ride," he answered. "The queen."

Annette's face puckered into a frown. "I assume you didn't like what she had to tell you?"

"Not especially. She thinks I'm dangerous because I can't be manipulated."

"I'm sorry."

"How do you know one another?"

Annette's expression neutralized and she said started to say, "Well ..."

Donovan closed his eyes and put out his palms. "Please, please, don't lie to me. Just tell me it's a secret and I'll drive myself mad not knowing, but don't lie. I really can't take that right now."

Annette smiled gently. "She's my sister."

Silence, and then: "Huh?"

"We don't talk much. Mostly because she believes I'm boring and I think she's a compassionless snake."

Donovan let out a bark of incredulous laughter.

"Truly, though, she's very intelligent and her heart is in the right place. She is only merciless when she needs to be — which is unfortunately often, in her position."

"But that means you're married into royalty."

"Very astute of you, Donovan. Such quick thinking." Her eyes twinkled. "I am also merciless, but I live the quiet life here at the Order to keep myself from temptation." She looked at her arms. "The very quiet life. Obviously."

Donovan leaned against the wall by the door. "Well, what's it like having the king for a brother-in-law?"

Annette shrugged. "He can be a little pompous at times, but he thinks my cooking is delightful, and we have books in common. Usually I prefer him to her, so family gatherings are nice. Big, and expensive, but nice. And the children are all wonderful, of course."

"I guess you're landed and titled then?"

Annette smiled again. "Lady Kraemer owns and oversees her lands when necessary, but otherwise leaves that work in the hands of more capable people. I prefer to entertain myself by working for the Order."

"Well enough." He sighed heavily. "My ride was not nearly as relaxing as you intended it to be," he told her. "I did get some galloping in, though, before having to wait in the lines to come back." He smiled, and then remembered the smell he'd come across.

He started to try to describe it when they both froze. The emergency bells were sounding. They were loud in the Medical Wing; a set was in the tower directly overhead.

Donovan jumped to help Annette out of her chair.

"I can walk," she snapped nervously. "We have to find out what's happening."

They rushed through the organized chaos in the hall: nurses, surgeons, Healers, guards, and visitors helping to organize those too injured to move on their own.

"We should help!" Donovan said as Annette strode ahead.

"Don, you can't help everyone," she shouted back.

"Murder! There's been a murder!" someone shouted.

Donovan stared at Annette, eyes wide. "Hey!" she called after the shouter, but they had disappeared already.

Donovan decided, "We can find Ruben and Whitman. Come on!"

He started off at a jog and she, groaning in frustration, was forced to follow.

The halls grew more and more chaotic and crowded as people moved quickly from the top floors to the bottom, seeking refuge and information. Several were sobbing, and they heard more snatches of talk about murder, but no one said who it was, or how many, or where. The mood was different from the time the bells sang, however; something had happened.

Annette and Donovan moved with the flow until Donovan took off deeper into the building.

"Hey!" Annette yelled, following suit.

"Whitman's rooms are this way."

"Oslan or Jaynes will help him get out, Donovan! He can move faster on that crutch than you think! We have to get more information!"

"You know he'll try to take all his notebooks with him! People are already leaving, not just waiting to be told. You go. I'll be right behind you!"

Annette snarled at him and put on another burst of speed to catch up. She was grimacing as she ran, and a look of concern marred her usually confident features. Donovan's breath didn't last long and his knees and back ached horribly as he approached Whitman's rooms.

Heavy boots from behind made him look around and pull Annette with him against the wall and out of the way. A dozen soldiers in formation jogged through quickly, despite the heavy steel and chainmail armor they wore. A third of them were armed with spears, a third with crossbows, and the rest with swords.

Their commander yelled, "Get outside! It's not safe!" as he passed.

"What's happened?" Annette yelled back, but received no answer.

"Which way are they going?" Donovan asked as he started his jog again.

The soldiers turned down a hallway the opposite of the direction the two of them were heading.

"The Library," she answered, dread filling them both.

Close to Whitman's room, the halls were empty. A couple of doors were left open; their occupants exited in enough of a hurry not to care. Annette slowed, sweat dotting her brow. Donovan's lungs were on strike, expanding, but seeming to take in no air for him to use. The hallway floor had bloodstains now. Small drips and smears, nothing pooled, but leading directly to Whitman's door.

Annette took a moment to breathe, and then turned the doorknob and pushed the door open. It wasn't locked. She took a step inside, cursed violently, and jumped back out, dodging for cover.

Donovan saw the overturned desk, papers and ink strewn about, but the reason for Annette's dodge was made clear when a chair shattered against the doorframe. He flinched and huddled next to Annette.

Fear rose in his chest and throat like bile. "Did you see anyone?"

"A guard, I think."

"I thought Whitman found all the infiltrators in the guard ..."

"TRUCE!" Annette yelled through the doorway. In lieu of a flag, she waved her white-bandaged arm around the doorframe.

"Annette?" Whitman's voice called.

Donovan and Annette looked at each other for confirmation, and then peered around the doorframe. Whitman and a uniformed guard were inside. The guard had his fists raised aggressively, despite a large bloody spot leaking through his shirt. They both looked the worse for wear, covered in sweat and blood. But, other than the guard's torso, they appeared unharmed.

"You need to leave right now," Whitman ordered Annette. His tone lacked any of his usual joviality.

"Yes, well, I tried," she snapped with a glare in Donovan's direction. "What are you doing here, anyway?"

"Running for my life!"

"Running for your life and we find you holed up in your rooms? What the hell happened?"

"Can we talk about this on the move?" the guardsman interrupted loudly. Probably in his late-twenties, his eyes were wide and wild, his breathing fast. "You want those texts, now is the moment or I'm leaving without you."

"Who's after you?" Donovan asked as Whitman continued shoving documents into a satchel.

Annette paced with frustration.

"A man, a magus," the guard answered with a tremor in his voice. "He showed up in the library when I was on my break. He attacked an old man, ripped him to pieces with blade and magic, and then killed a librarian, I think, who went for him. Blood was everywhere. I attacked, but he threw me away like nothing, and my sword after." He gestured ruefully at his side, glancing often at Whitman to see if he was finished collecting papers. "Then he held fire and said that if we didn't bring him Whitman Acres, we'd all suffer for it."

"Director Jaynes?" Annette asked, face lined with worry.

Donovan looked at Whitman, who was keeping his head low. "Oslan?"

"I'm not sure. But Jaynes is dead." Whitman's voice broke and his eyes squeezed briefly shut, releasing two tears onto his stack of documents.

Annette's expression was broken with grief. "Whitman, I'm so sorry."

He cleared his throat. "Most everyone ran, but Robert found me in the halls and helped me back here. I was getting a text I need; something Jaynes had started writing out for me in his letters. I'm sure the Smiling Man is on his way. We have to leave."

"Why did he kill Jaynes?" Donovan asked.

"Reputation is a madman's best friend?"

"If Don's right, and he's using Empathy, he could trace the emotions of anyone in the area," Annette suggested. "The faster people ran, the less he had to compete with, the easier to track the minds he was really after."

"He's a magus," Robert, the guard, said, shaking his head. "Ripped him apart and didn't even pause. Like *nothing*."

"Where's Ruben?" Donovan demanded of Whitman.

Whitman looked up at them, suddenly furious. "I thought you would have him."

"Hopefully he is smart enough to follow his class outside," Annette said.

"Assuming that wasn't their plan all along!" Donovan swore.

The hall echoed with not-too-distant screams.

"We have to run!" Robert yelled, hauling at Whitman's shirt.

Whitman stumbled before planting his crutch, and moved toward the open door. Donovan looked down the empty hallway to check that their route was clear.

"Come on," he said.

They started to follow, but a figure appeared around the corner, and Donovan recognized him immediately.

"Nope, nope, nope, nope," Donovan said, turning about and pushing them all back into the room. He slammed the door, turned the lock, and started to move the couch, but it was bolted to the floor.

"What the hell will that do?!" Robert demanded, close to tears.

"What good is running?" Donovan countered.

"You've killed us!" Robert shouted at Whitman. "You said he wouldn't follow, that you'd be quick!"

"Stop panicking, you half-witted bastard!" Whitman bellowed.

They heard laughter in the hallway.

"Seeking isn't any help here." Annette paced powerlessly. She rubbed vaguely at her bandaged arms, looking around the room for anything useful.

"Don, fetch the case beneath my bed," Whitman ordered.

Donovan ran to the next room and dropped to look under the large four-poster. The case was blocky, made of hardened brown leather. Donovan grabbed it and brought the thing to Whitman.

"Open it, open it," Whitman snapped.

As Donovan did so, Whitman grabbed out a near-ancient crossbow. The string was slack, and the bolts were dusty, but it would probably shoot; crossbows didn't require much maintenance. The bard also draped a leather bandolier over his shoulder, and hooked it to his belt with a practiced motion. It was already loaded with throwing knives — which looked in much better repair than the crossbow.

"Robert, what do you need?" the Spymaster asked.

"A coffin-maker, you piss-headed fool," Robert snarled, white-faced and red-eyed, tears streaking his ruddy cheeks. Nevertheless, he held himself ready near the door.

Whitman looked the guard in the eye. "I am sorry."

Robert rolled his eyes and shook his head. He turned away and took deep breaths, swinging his sword in small warm-up patterns.

A gentle knock sounded.

"Who is it?" Donovan shouted back, hoping to buy time, and dreading the answer.

"I could tell you, but that would be giving it away," the Smiling Man answered, his voice playful.

Donovan's stomach flipped and he felt his face grow hot.

"It's rude to leave a guest on the doorstep," their adversary continued in a sing-song voice.

"Move," Donovan told Robert, pushing him gently, but firmly, out of the way. He glanced back at Whitman, hoping they had some plan, any plan, and opened the door.

The Smiling Man looked genuinely surprised. His hair was disheveled, and his pointed face was flecked with blood like freckles. His hands and clothes had larger splashes. Donovan noticed his very blue eyes were wide, but they quickly narrowed.

"It's been months, Donovan. You look better than when I last saw you."

"Would you like to come in?" Donovan asked politely.

The Smiling Man hesitated, a wry smile playing about his lips as he glanced inside. "A trap?"

"Could one hold you?" Donovan countered.

The Smiling Man barked out a laugh and strolled inside. As he passed, Donovan increased his sense of smell and confirmed what he'd suspected outside: he knew the man's scent now, for all the good it would do him in the last moments of his life.

Whitman sat perched on the overturned desk, his bandolier of knives visible, and his crutch beside him, but his crossbow was out of sight. Annette stood near the couch. Robert was where Donovan had left him, looking at everyone with confusion, but he wisely kept his tongue.

"Good afternoon," the Smiling Man said, nodding at each of them and then plopping down onto the couch to spread his arms across the back. "Whitman! I'm sorry to see that a Healer was so unwilling, unable to fix your knee. No one in residence?"

"Too much damage for now," the bard answered conversationally. "I remain ever hopeful, however."

"Aw, that's a shame. You should find yourself a magus. I'm positive they'd be more than willing to assist."

"Are you offering?"

The Smiling Man gestured with his hands and sketched a bow with only his head. "I hope it didn't take you *this* long to discover my little secret."

"You are surprisingly difficult to locate in any histories," Whitman shrugged.

"Thank you for finding our scholarly friend — *Jaynes,* he was going by. I've been searching for him for *many* years." He laughed with child-like enjoyment.

Whitman's pleasant expression was fixed, but his jaw tightened. The Smiling Man grinned to see the bard's distress, however subtle. He looked Annette up and down.

"One of yours, Whitman? I hope not. It'd be a shame to kill more of your spies and contacts. You must be running low by now."

Annette winked at him playfully. "I belong to no one but myself."

"Did one of mine do that to you?" he asked, gesturing at her arms.

Robert shifted and the Smiling Man's head snapped around. Robert slammed into the wall behind him with a breathless grunt, eyes wide with terror.

"Don't move," the Smiling Man ordered, with his face in a contorted, barely-human snarl. His expression quickly returned to its amused half-smile, but he did not look back at Annette, instead keeping his attention on Donovan and Whitman.

"Donovan, what shall we do now?" he asked.

Donovan shrugged from the doorway. "You came to us."

"I'll admit, I was hoping for more resistance. I'm always keen on warm-blooded death; the emotions are far more enjoyable that way."

"So you came for murder?" Donovan confirmed.

"Specifically, no, but it is a happy side item. I wasn't expecting to find you all in one place!"

"Then for what did you come?" Annette asked, now seated on the arm of the couch.

The Smiling Man glanced at her and away before answering, "I hope you're not stalling for time; usually that's my play." When no one answered he laughed merrily. "Kidnap, you mindless cretins. Goodness, but I am surrounded by the relentlessly tedious. Are you the best the Order has to offer?" He glanced at Donovan. "No, I know the answer to that. Still, Whitman, I'd have hoped the Spymaster had more to offer in the way of information than *nothing*. You've had *months* to learn of our plans. All of our countermeasures have gone to waste now, due to your ineptitude. I had *much* higher expectations of you."

The Smiling Man stood and stalked toward the bard.

"Ruben," Donovan said softly, terror shuddering down his spine.

The Smiling Man spun to face him. "Someone was paying attention." He clapped slowly. "Well done."

No one spoke, but panic and terror flavored the atmosphere.

"Are our murders to occur before or after this happy event?" Annette asked sweetly.

The Smiling Man flapped his hand. "After, of course. I have people dealing with the bitty-boy. Never underestimate the disposable masses." He grinned wickedly at Robert, who was still pinned uncomfortably to the wall.

"All I have now is to decide *how* to do away with you all." He rubbed his hands together, looking from one to the other.

No one moved. No one spoke.

"Argh!" he cried, flopping onto the couch again. "At least plead or bargain or *something*."

"Having trouble performing?" Annette asked pointedly.

He sneered at her. As he did, her foot sprang from the ground and into the side of his head with enough force to shove it into the plaster of the wall behind. Her balance now compromised, she fell off the couch, hit the ground hard, and rolled away.

The Smiling Man roared and started to stand. He was stopped by Whitman's knives flying in quick succession. One pierced the Smiling Man's right shoulder close to the joint, and made his arm fall limp. The rest he somehow dodged or deflected into the walls and ceiling with magical defense.

Annette, standing again, aimed another kick, but the Smiling Man sent magic to shove her against the opposite wall. She crashed into a heavy cabinet, which collapsed on top of her. Whitman slid off the desk to help, his supply of knives exhausted.

Donovan and Robert were both moving. Robert, freed with the Smiling Man's distraction, swung his blade in a wide arc. It was deflected violently, but he released it to keep his balance, and instead jumped onto the couch to block the Smiling Man's view. Fire blossomed, outlining Robert in the unexpected and harsh light. He screamed, but did not flee. Instead, he landed two sturdy punches into the Smiling Man's smiling face before he was tripped to the ground. He rolled and writhed, clutching at his ruined features, and screaming.

Donovan picked up two discarded knives from the ground and advanced. The Smiling Man had finally gained his feet. His nose and possibly a cheekbone was broken and bleeding from Annette's kick and Robert's strikes. Rage burned in his eyes and mirrored the flames he held.

"This is more like it," he hissed at Donovan. Spittle and blood arched from his mouth. "Don't you just taste those *emotions*?"

In answer, Donovan lunged. The Smiling Man launched his flames, but Donovan wasn't there to receive them. He landed on the ground beside Robert, whose muffled screams and sobs came from behind mangled and blistered hands.

Confused, the Smiling Man looked down, which put the crossbow bolt into his forehead instead of through his eye.

From where he lay on the floor, Whitman grimly cocked the old bow again, and laid another bolt in the channel. The Smiling Man stumbled, staggered sideways, weaving to the door and throwing himself through it. Donovan untangled himself as gently as possible from Robert's agonized clutches and sprang to his feet with a protestation of knees to run after his adversary.

The Smiling Man made it to the end of the corridor and around the corner. Donovan heard shouting. He managed another burst of speed and careened around the corner, only to skid to a halt. A pile of soldiers lay about — several dead; others with their armor smoking from electrocution. The first bled from his skull, a discarded crossbow bolt beside him.

Donovan looked about desperately, but the Smiling Man had disappeared. He roared wordlessly and fell to helping the survivors.

15

"TELL ME WHERE WE STAND."

The mood in Elliot's office was somber. The Head of the Order was tired and irate, and even this short meeting appeared to wear on him.

"He got away," Donovan answered darkly, quietly.

He thought the rage of losing Ruben would wear off when he'd had time to calm down, but he still shook inside, like a caged animal ready to kill its way through a crowd. Annette and Whitman looked at him, but did not disagree.

Whitman answered Elliott without vigor, "Twenty-one dead, seventeen wounded — including the royal princess. And one kidnapped."

"Do we know *anything*?" Elliott asked.

Silence and stillness were his only reply.

He looked at Whitman. "The training grounds you located?"

"Abandoned. They collapsed the town a week ago. Dead in the hundreds; but not the thousands we might have expected. They were leaving in small numbers. We recorded some of it, but missed the patterns. It will not happen again."

Elliott leaned back in his chair.

Annette picked at her bandages, a bitter expression on her face. "They always win. We thought we were ahead, but they always win."

"Not always," Elliott said firmly. "This fight is lost, but we'll win another."

"Against a magus? With our own stolen right out of our grip? An impressive, and short, fight, I've no doubt." Annette took a deep breath and sat up straight. "My apologies. I fall quickly to a dark mind these days."

"As do we all, I think," Elliott said. "Still, we must focus on the positive, the doable. Any suggestions?"

Whitman and Donovan shared a glance before Whitman cleared his throat and answered, "Donovan and I recently discovered that our library has a small number of reference materials pertaining to blood magic — possibly the workings and use thereof. We believe it might be wise to pursue that direction of study to better know our enemy and their capabilities. The Smiling Man is not our only adversary, after all."

Elliott's mustache twitched. "Those books are kept strictly out of the need to collect knowledge, and keep the more dangerous kind from those who would abuse it. I have never allowed a study of them — even to the Librarian outside of what she needs to know to store and record them, and I do not appreciate her informing you of their existence."

Whitman glanced at Donovan again. "Perhaps we could pursue another line of study: magi and their capabilities? We know there is more to magic than our memory contains; Donovan's recent discovery proves that. It would not be unwise to remedy our collective memory, and perhaps regain some of what was lost in the Cataclysm."

"I would feel more comfortable with that line of study," Elliott agreed.

"No," Donovan said.

"I beg your pardon?"

"No," he repeated. His voice shook. "We have to know what the blood mages can do, and how they do it. All anyone knows is that they can use blood against you, even their own, and that their abilities vary." He ticked off on his fingers as he spoke. "I've had forces move me and the things around me, I've had wounds inflicted, a Healer-blood-mage-hybrid drained and killed Lucas, they can move objects many times the size any Displacer can manage, and they appear to have little or no cost as ordinary mages do. No nausea, no headaches. We've seen them use fire and electricity, their senses are keener than normal, and they tire more slowly. Our defense thus far has been 'try to kill them first' or 'run very fast'."

He looked Elliott in the eye. "If we are going to fight an enemy who so drastically out matches us, we must know what they can do, and what limits them. Why blood? Where does the magic come from? Do they have some cost that we are unaware of, and can we exploit it? There has to be *something* in those books, and guarding anyone and everyone from them helps no one."

"The few accounts that we have suggest that blood magic is addictive, Donovan. If I let you pursue this course, it is very likely you would not be the same man on the other side."

"Then that is my burden to bear."

"Not if it results in the death or injury of others outside of yourself." Elliott's eyes darted to Whitman and Annette.

Donovan gestured sharply. "With such eyes on me, how can I go astray? Let us put checks and balances in place. I can keep a journal with the day's moods, my thoughts, my feelings. I will have no secrets. I can regularly meet with an Empath or Mentalist; I'll not perform any tests or experiments outside of another's sight — whatever you want, it would be worth it."

Donovan took a deep breath and tried to appeal to the Head of the Order. "Elliott, we may have a chance at an advantage here! This Order holds the majority of mages in the kingdom. The Healer that killed Lucas showed an obvious advantage. What if we could harness that advantage, even in some small way? Gain an edge? Surely, *surely,* that is worth the *possible* sacrifice of one old man."

Elliott closed his eyes. "You know I have to say yes. Spies were never going to be enough, and we knew that."

"Inaction begs for action," Whitman said softly.

"You're to keep tabs on him, both of you," Elliott said to Whitman and Annette. "And I want that journal," he told Donovan. "I'll have my secretary prepare your writ and deliver it to the Librarian himself, lest my intentions be miscommunicated in any way."

"Sir," Annette spoke up. "What are our plans to rescue Ruben? Surely we have some action to take?" Donovan kept his gaze firmly fixated on Elliott, hungry for the answer.

"Until we know where he is, there's little opportunity or option. We will keep our eyes and ears open, but this madman has evaded notice for an apparent many years, so I've little hope that we'll find Ruben before they want to be found."

"He will not kill him," Whitman said with certainty. "From Donovan's encounters, I would bet anything the Smiling Man wants to keep Ruben alive, to be his mentor. To have a companion of some kind. Or a protégé. We will find him."

"See that you do, then" Elliott said. "And I want to know who that damned madman is, Whitman. I don't care if he was born a common thatcher, I want his name and his story and how he came to be."

A merciless curl twisted Whitman's lip. "I can do that."

Elliott looked back to Annette. "The king and queen are withdrawing to the palace."

"You want me to go with them."

"They want Donovan to go with them, and I want you to go with him." He turned to Donovan and continued. "You've been ordered by King Braun to teach the noble children the New Seeking. Many of their parents are loathe to send them here, especially after our most recent ... events. The queen has demanded an escort to keep you in check. Apparently, she doesn't much like you."

"She doesn't much like me, either," Annette grumbled.

Elliott pointed out, "You can better navigate the court without causing tension between our factions."

Annette crossed her legs gracefully. "Try not to start any wars, Don."

"I'll do my best," he sighed. His body felt weary, but his mind was afire. He knew the others were the same.

"You have your duties," Elliott said. "Be about them."

Together they rose and bowed, leaving his office and meandering through the halls, few words between them, but their thoughts very much aligned.

"Stay in touch, will you?" Whitman asked, swaying heavily into his crutch as he walked. "I would hate to miss anything important. I am still composing my epic, you know."

Donovan shook his head. "I'm sure you'll learn the news before I do, Whit. Especially with Annette's eyes on the scene."

"Whatever do you mean?" she asked, batting her eyes at him.

"Come now, it's been obvious for ages. Whitman's the Spymaster and you're his key spy. It makes sense, having so high a noble in the ranks, able to go to court as you're doing. Elliott knew it; he just said."

Whitman snorted and Annette hugged Donovan around the shoulders. "Clever lad. Only took you an age to deduce."

They stopped at a hallway split. "Keep hope, Don," Whitman told him. "Ruben will be all right."

"We'll find him," Annette promised.

"I know," Donovan said firmly. "I mean to be there when we do. And that day, I'll see to it that the Smiling Man goes by a different name."

*   *   *

Ruben opened his eyes, but saw nothing. He touched his face, startled by the closeness of his questing fingers. The ground beneath him was stone, and he crawled slowly to find a wall, scraping his knuckles on its rough surface. He used it to stand, fear making him tremble unsteadily. The wall led him to a door, wooden, but thick from the sound it made when he gently knocked. Braced with iron bands, even. He took a deep calming breath, closing his eyes for all the difference it made and concentrated, *concentrated.*

After a few moments, a weak fire bloomed in his palm. It shocked his eyes, and he blinked furiously to clear the sudden overflow of water, but his flames were enough to see by ... for all there was to see. A small bucket in the corner. For his waste, he assumed, and nothing else but rough stone.

The door had a hinged opening set into it, just above his head and about the size of both his palms. He realized it would be for speaking without opening the whole door. Then, surely someone was listening for him. He opened his mouth to shout, but stopped, suddenly nervous. He looked down at his handful of fire, merrily burning, and found new determination.

"Hey!" he yelled. The sound bounced back into his own ears and made him wince. He yelled again, "HEY! Let me out of here!"

A scraping sound came from the hatch in the door. Startled, Ruben nearly lost his flame.

The hatch opened and the face he'd been dreading appeared.

The Smiling Man grinned. "Hello, little master."

Terror set Ruben's knees to shaking. "Let me out."

"In due time. Not yet, though." The Smiling Man looked almost apologetic.

"I *will* get out," Ruben said with more confidence than he felt.

"Oh, I have no doubt. You aren't my prisoner, not exactly."

Ruben scoffed in disbelief. "Not your prisoner? You have me in a dark cell!"

"For now, yes. I find that the young mind is more easily opened to new ideas than one set in its ways, you'll agree. Currently, you have nothing but anger and fear and suspicion. When you're ready to listen, we can discuss other options. Until then, you will remain here."

"What do you want from me?" Ruben felt tears prickling in his eyes.

The Smiling Man *tutted*. "Already making the wrong assumptions, little master. I don't want anything *from* you. But I want the world *for* you. Don't make too much fire. Lightning is better light, after all. We'll speak again."

"What? When? No! Let me out!"

The Smiling Man gave him a sad smirk and closed the hatch. Ruben heard a bolt slide home and pounded furiously on the wooden portal, but there was no answer.

He released the fire and it plunged the room back into full darkness, but Ruben concentrated his will and *pushed* the door with all his might, succeeding only in Displacing himself into the back wall. The door was strong.

He sank to the floor and set his jaw in determination. They'd come for him, he knew.

Until then, he'd have to make himself ready.

ABOUT THE AUTHOR

Morgan Chalut (she/they) has been writing since she learned that anyone was allowed to do that; it wasn't illegal or anything! While it didn't slow down her talking, it at least gave her parents and six older siblings (and her poor, poor teachers) a break once in a while. She hopes to continue to discover characters and worlds she can plot and explore and share.

Morgan lives in Dallas, Texas with her delightfully handsome and silly, charming, supportive, and lovely husband, Philip. They have two dogs together: Caramel, who absolutely wants to be your friend, and Sammie, who very definitely does not.

You can find out more about the world and works of Morgan Chalut at *morganchalut.com*.

YOU MIGHT ALSO ENJOY

JUST A BIT OF MAGIC
by Barb Bissonette

Every morning, Jenny Smith stares into her magic mirror, searching for glimpses of two girls. Today, she is joyful with anticipation, knowing that this is the day they will materialize in her village.

GRIMAULKIN
BOOK ONE OF THE "GRIMAULKIN" SERIES
by L. A. Jacob

Treading the straight and narrow is not natural to one who summons demons.

MERMAID STEEL
by Jay Hartlove

The power of love over hate.

SKY CHASE
BOOK ONE OF "THE FLIGHT OF SHIPS" TRILOGY
by Lauren Massuda

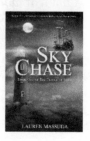

Travel to a vast world of airborne ships and floating islands.

Available from Water Dragon Publishing in
hardcover, trade paperback, and digital editions
waterdragonpublishing.com